THE DELIVERED

KRISTY BERRIDGE

Kristy Berridge: writer, sometimes comedian, peanut butter addict, exercise junkie, woman.

There are many labels I go by, but not one can ever define me. Like all things in life, sometimes I commit 100% and other times I apply varying percentages to the effort and enthusiasm adopted.

To be a writer you must have passion and I have bucket loads, but I am human and sometimes I'd rather go cow-tipping or rob a Seven-Eleven than immerse myself in the written word.

The trick is to find balance. Between my love of keeping fit; outrunning my husband to claim the television remote before being subjected to British drama and my clean-eating lifestyle, washing the plates before eating off of them, I sit down to write with a clear conscience.

Romance and horror are my general persuasions these days, not because my life is lacking, but who doesn't love a bit of blood and guts with a side of lip-locking? I've been drawn to both genres, even combining them more often than not.

The next stage in my journey is as unknown as the next paragraph in my forthcoming novels. It's better to live in the present, celebrate the small victories and of course, apply pen to paper whenever the inspiration may strike; a motto to live by.

— —

Shadow Ink Press
PO Box 80, Yorkeys Knob, Queensland 4870 Australia
Email: admin@shadowinkpress.com.au

First published in Australia 2020 - This edition published 2020
Copyright © Kristy Berridge 2020
Cover design, typesetting: Shadow Ink Press
The right of Kristy Berridge to be identified as the Author of the Work has been asserted in accordance with the Copyright, Designs and Patents Act 1988.

Berridge, Kristy
The Delivered
ISBN: 9780995432727

Also by Kristy Berridge

The Hunted

The Damned

The Aligned

The Condemned

Diary of a Teenage Zombie

100 Days of Happiness

PREFACE

Pungent smelling wisps of semi-opaque steam rose from grates on the city sidewalk, rising high and fading fast. The boy with a blackened face—fingernails caked with dirt and belly empty from days without proper sustenance—lingered over its escape. The warmth was welcome on nights still chilled from the passing winter.

Nervous, he glanced over his shoulder regularly, eerily aware of the long shadows that moved around him as he stood huddled and alone on what had once been a busy, crowded street. The fading bustle had set in long ago; the occupancy of nearby dwellings had dwindled first, followed by vehicles and finally spreading to pedestrian traffic.

At first no one noticed; everyone was too relieved to be saved and protected from seemingly defunct creatures of fiction. As the blood, bombs and death ensued, the safety of the city walls became nothing short of desirable and all had flocked to inhabit its presumed safety. Now, as the boy stood alone and insecure, he wasn't too sure the human race had chosen wisely. The empty pavement, deserted streets and lack of warm-blooded company spoke volumes.

He shuddered and opted to shake off his unease; lingering in the open wasn't wise despite the momentary respite from the cold. He needed to find shelter for the night, edible food and someone to watch his back. The city's internal television broadcasts promised safety, but the inference of *safety* seemed to be lacking. Perhaps the Vampires and the Werewolves were getting inside the walls? Maybe they slowly hunted all that still lingered, finishing what was left of humanity?

The boy sniffed back drippy mucous from a frozen nose and resisted the urge to wipe his camouflage clean. He edged back towards a side ally and merged once more with the darkness that had so far kept him safe.

Around the next corner, a massive screen greeted him; there was one located in every corner of the city. The stoic face of one of the people's saviours was talking; it was another internal broadcast aimed at keeping the rising panic to a minimum. Tonight was no exception. White sub-text traversed the lower screen inciting rumours of sightings outside these very walls, but was quickly followed by flashing pictures of recent kills.

It no longer shocked the boy to see images of the fallen. A strange reassurance had settled upon those who saw them, knowing that with each supernatural that was killed, less were capable of walking the earth. Yet despite the urge to revel in the broadcaster's enthusiasm for the latest entrapments, it was hard to deny the missing; people he had once seen walking these very streets were now gone.

A small crowd—three or four these days—had gathered to observe this latest broadcast and were engrossed as he had once been in the resistance's movements. He was not interested in their thoughts and thus walked with haste and slipped further into the shadows. He then traversed a small chain-link fence until he was high-tailing it down another street, the urge to find shelter almost desperate now.

Although the super cities were extremely large, mostly encompassing what remained of the past, he had grown up here and was more than aware of his surrounds. Perhaps that was why the missing people of his past bothered him so. He had grown up with familiar faces greeting him at every turn. Now when he looked around, the familiar seemed nothing short of a distant memory. Could vampires and werewolves be entirely responsible for what happened behind these walls?

A minute later he stood before another darkened alley. A year ago—possibly less—there may have been people sleeping in cardboard boxes, huddled together for warmth and companionship. Now the alley was abandoned, frequented no longer by those seeking shelter from the night. Why he kept coming here he didn't know. Some habits were hard to break, but instincts did warn him it was unwise to keep returning.

He touched the rusted handle of a door nestled at the end, turning it counter-clockwise and cringing as it squealed in protest upon opening. Beyond, the darkness had washed all colour from the factory floor. Exterior street lamps offered slivers of light through the dirty windows above—shards of clarity in an otherwise desolate location.

He gingerly entered, closing the door behind him. 'Lenny, you here?' He disbanded his native German tongue for French. having lived in this super city since he was a small boy, becoming multi-lingual was the only option for integration. Everyone in Europe had migrated to Paris during and after the war, so most people spoke French to this day.

'Lenny? Answer me.'

The silence lingered like an unwelcome visitor. He'd left Lenny only hours before, sleeping in the corner, clutching a bottle of cheap bourbon to his portly chest. The boy had no inclination to crave something he could ill-afford as a crutch, but Lenny was a few years older and witness to the plunder of his entire family. He'd said it was medicine for his mind.

The boy didn't remember much of his family. He was barely six when the war began. His mother had been mauled by a werewolf on their journey from Berlin to Paris. His sister was shot by friendly fire and his father had fallen victim to the mystery inside these very walls. He barely remembered any of it. He just knew that he was alone, unskilled, uneducated and now seemingly without his friend Lenny.

Unease settled deep into every pore of his dirtied flesh; the shadows grew longer and the silence became a deafening warning he had to heed. As thoughts of danger roared in his ears, an empty bottle clanged against the wall at the other end of the factory, rolling painfully slow across the floor until finally coming to a stop. A whispered profanity followed—an echo to the boy's backwards footsteps.

He located the rusted handle of the door, clasped it between shaking fingers and pulled.

'Where are you going?' a voice said, directly to his right.

The boy jumped, surprised to find that he was shadowed by two men appearing out of nowhere. The door he'd opened was now slammed shut by insistent hands that surpassed his strength.

He dodged their creeping approach by ducking forward and running further into the depths of the factory. His feet disturbed every carton, crate and piece of discarded waste in his path, so it was no surprise that in his fear they'd quickly tracked his movements to appear back at his side.

'I want no trouble,' the boy said, attempting to sidestep them again and failing.

'Neither do we.'

'What do you want?'

'You.'

The boy shook his head, vehement. 'No, I don't do that stuff, but I know some girls on the next block that can fix you right up for a little cash.'

'We're not looking for sex, Boy.'

He tried to creep in another direction, hoping they wouldn't notice. 'Then what do you want? I've got no money.' They were on top of him now, fingers reaching and gripping his shoulders painfully before another escape could be manufactured.

'We need you to come with us.'

'Nah, I don't need to, right? I haven't caused any trouble.'

'No trouble,' the first shadowed man answered, 'but you still need to come with us.'

The boy was about to protest, his mouth opening to emit words, possibly even screams should the hold they had on him continue. Breath had already filled his lungs, but a hand slammed down across his lips, hard and unyielding. He kicked and flailed instead, knowing now that he was in a whole world of trouble.

A door at the other end of the factory opened and they made haste for it, dragging the boy kicking and silently screaming the entire way. An inconspicuous white van was parked in the street beyond, engine running. The panelled doors were thrown back, the inside empty bar another man holding some rope. He stretched it taught in one hand, a vicious leer on his face that robbed the boy of any lingering bravado. Though he kicked and punched with everything he could give, there was only so much he could do against seemingly impenetrable strength.

Thoughts of vampires ran rampant through his mind. He remembered seeing them when he was younger and on the live streams in the super city. It had been over ten years since he'd seen one in the flesh, but he knew what they were capable of.

Now, eyeing these men with a fear that permeated every single inch of his flesh, he wondered if they weren't the creatures everyone had run from so many years before. The super cities

4

proclaimed to be safe—impenetrable to a standard that was never clearly defined—yet how were these vampires behind the city walls? Were they the reason so many were missing? Was there a gap in their saviour's security?

The boy's shrill scream rung loud as he was thrown into the back of the van, doors slamming home on his protests. Inside, the man with rope bound and gagged him, smashing his face against the cold metal floor and wedging a knee against his back. He tried to break free, but every attempt at escape was thwarted. He had no idea what they wanted, but if he managed to get free, where would he run to?

The drive was short. The man who'd bound him had done nothing more than occasionally exert more pressure against his spine or snap his teeth when he'd flinched. The boy could not uncover irrefutable proof that these men were vampires, yet all stolen looks uncovered a hunger inexplicable.

The van doors opened. Men crowded in, yanking him by his feet. The pressure on his back desisted, but more hands meant less viable options for escape. The boy was at loss, confused, scared and unsure what he had done to deserve this treatment. Was he to become another statistic in a world that no longer took notice?

'What are you doing?' His scream was no more than muffled incoherence through the gag. 'Where are you taking me?'

'Be still,' a man with a strange accent answered. 'It will all be over soon.'

A jab on one of his bound arms was followed by a sting of pain. He swivelled, eyes widening as the offending needle was quickly tucked back in a lab coat pocket.

Doctors … The boy thought to himself. *What do doctors want with me?*

'What was that?'

'A sedative.'

As if on cue, the boy's eyes started to droop. 'Why do I need a sedative?' he slurred, reverting back to German.

'What did he say?' The men around him started to mumble, their words lost to an unintelligible garble he could make no sense of.

The boy faded fast, eyes opening and closing, his sense of presence and clarity-of-mind growing more indistinct. He tried

5

lifting his limbs, even wriggling around in his constraints. He had so many questions, all of which he was certain would never be answered.

The next time one of his droopy lids attempted to open, he felt cold and oddly exposed. With no energy to move his head, he relied on touch; cold steel was beneath him, wrists cuffed by warm leather and ankles and torso bound by constraints of unknown origin. The ceiling above was white and lit with too many blinding lights.

'He's waking,' someone murmured.

'He's stronger than the others—resilient. Plug the IV in now and dose him up. He can't wake up again.'

'What are ...' his speech slurred, thick and heavy on a tongue refusing movement. There was activity around his arm, but nothing he could distinctly determine from touch alone. A lady stood above him; her face was eerily blurred by his inability to counteract the effects of the blinding light above. She had black hair—short and a pair of silver-rimmed glasses reflecting his own image.

Drowsiness reclaimed him. The lights above now zoomed past, the woman still keeping pace beside him. She looked down once, touched his arm again and then forgot about him.

The moving steel he laid upon came to an abrupt stop. He tried to roll away, find the solution for escape, but his stubborn limbs were numb to his commands. The people that bustled around him ignored any frail movement he attempted, snapping at locks and touching various dials.

He was suddenly being lifted and then re-shelved on another hard bed. The lights above were now gone and there was steel above him, punctuated by tiny holes.

Where am I?

'He's taking longer than usual to sleep,' the woman muttered.

'It matters not,' the man who'd jabbed him with the needle answered. 'It comforts only them. You and I both know that asleep or awake, we must take what we need.'

'Do you want me start now?'

'Yes, but let's try to keep this one alive for as long as possible this time. We're running out of options.'

Fingers re-touched his arm almost immediately. There were pokes and prods, but no pain identifying abuse. Sleep was almost upon him, but nausea insinuated by fear was yet to abate. These people were obviously not vampires, but they would probably kill him. Safety in a city of impenetrable walls was now nothing more than myth, a story told to the willingly gullible.

The boy always suspected that after the war—and every opportunity thankfully missed to avoid death—that the streets would eventually see his ultimate demise. He just never expected it to be at the hands of a doctor—the same man who'd drugged him—the same man promoting safety for all via live streaming videos.

He supposed gullibility was a coin they all carried in their pockets.

CHAPTER ONE: LANDED

Plummeting to my death—an otherwise horrifying experience to most logical beings—might not have been as bad as first presumed. Sure, I'd screamed, used every piece of foul language in my vocabulary as I'd fallen, but impact had proven mild—almost lacklustre. I'd hit the ground like a tonne of bricks, spewing soil, debris and ejecting yet another string of objectionable profanity, but relief had been swift.

I'd thankfully bypassed the pine trees, avoiding any chance of impalement; it was a torturous experience I didn't want to repeat and a memory from the past I'd rather forget, but now I was face-down in the dirt, anxious and unsure how to proceed. I was miles from Earth—stuck somewhere between heaven and hell—a place known as *Purgatory*.

So why am I in Purgatory? Good question and one difficult to answer without dry-reaching. The obvious and most plausible answer is … I'm dead. I'd either been murdered by the angel that dumped me here or the crazy vampire back on earth out for vengeance. But the irrefutable truth—one that stripped me of all pretence and filled my stomach with dread—I'm in love. I'd been injected with feelings—feelings that had crippled my sensibilities and robbed me of choice; the very reason I was here now.

In the past, I'd avoided the temptations of love by exercising caution when indulging sentimentality, yet now I'd skipped past common sense and virtually sacrificed everything to come to Purgatory. I'd made a deal with the angel Araqiel; it was my death in exchange for one week to find the guy who'd shoved an emotional enema down my throat.

So, who was the bastard who'd made me vulnerable to love and its compelling, all-consuming desire to make rash and ill-conceived, stupid decisions?

The Archangel Michael; otherwise known as Sebastian Marcellus—lead tracker for the Vampires and massive pain in my proverbial ass.

Confused? Don't get me started.

Long story short; Michael fell from heaven some thirteen thousand years ago to be with me. We've lived many, varied lives together; his existence lasting only as long as my own and his identity has always been a secret. Now our past lives had culminated with my newfound knowledge of them and consequently led us into this life where things have grown infinitely more complicated.

In this life I am Elena Manory; I am the daughter of Lucius Valerius, master vampire and spawn of Satan. I'm still technically human until my eighteenth birthday (as is any born vampire created from the coupling of a human woman and male vampire), but I'm also a little different. My birth went wrong. My mother was attacked by a vânător (werewolf) and their blood mingled, interspersing and creating something unique in my DNA. So, I'm not just going to become a vampire, but also a bloody werewolf too. And—thanks to a few blood exchanges along the way with another born vampire named William and an alpha vânător named Roshan—I'd sped the process up. I shape-shift, I self-heal, I drink blood and I have fangs—all of which Sebastian is still surprisingly attracted to despite his Archangel status.

Michael ... um ... Sebastian, chose to become a vampire—unprecedented among our race and I suspect the Angels too. His choice stemmed from knowing he could never be born to a new life on this earth again. Why? His human father—Tiberius—became one of Lucius's vampire thralls two thousand years before my intended birth. Michael/Sebastian's only option was to become one of them, hold true to his soul, but drink the blood of the undead in order to survive.

So, he'd disregarded his heavenly devotion and chosen to become a bloodsucker like me. Can you imagine it? An Archangel posing as a vampire? Well, he'd pulled it off for the last two thousand years, waiting for my re-birth.

What a trooper.

Now here I was in Purgatory, tossed moments ago by Araqiel from the relative safety of the mystical Ley-lines and into the unknown. I couldn't complain. I'd asked for this in exchange for a week with … Michael … um … Sebastian before I had to face judgement. It was a risk, but not seeing Michael or Sebas—

Bloody hell. I'm just gonna call him Sebastian.

Two strong possibilities loomed on my path to ultimate judgement: one; to be sent back to Earth and two; ushered south for the winter. Hell, heaven or the in between of Purgatory was irrelevant. It was all just geography. If Sebastian wasn't there, life would be meaningless for me.

Selfish sentiments aside, I'd left a shitload of mess back on earth I should have tidied up before I died. The Vampires were currently at war with the Vânătors and humans unintentionally involved in a three-century year-old dispute. The borders of Italy had been overrun and Milan was practically in ruins. People were dead in the streets and the army had come to gun everyone down—no exceptions.

The Vânătors had been led by my long-time nemesis— Roshan; he was the last remaining alpha … until I'd killed him and taken on the role of pack leader and ultimate Alpha. I now had the power to end the war and send the Vânătors away, but Sebastian had been assassinated and that completely redirected my attention.

The war would undoubtedly continue in my absence, but I worried. The Vânătors were uncontrollable without my lead. Some would vacate the city and head to the mountains to hide and others would continue to fight the remaining vampires for supremacy over territory. The Humans would be mowed down like cattle, victims of circumstance in a war that was supposed to remain hidden from the unknowing.

And The Protectors? My God they had a lot to answer for. These magically endowed humans supposedly intent on protecting the human race at all cost had been tainted by self-motivation. Once a clan that protected those unable to defend themselves against vampires and werewolves, now digressed from a noble path to place themselves on the scientific most wanted list. From my blood they'd manufactured a serum—a chemical compound endowing super strength, speed—and above all else—immortality.

The Protectors no longer cared for the human race or protecting them from rogue vampires or vânătors. They'd never really cared for me and I suspected they had never cared about upholding the alliance either. Their sentimentality rested solely in

11

their own advancement and the total domination over every species on the planet, but to what end?

Now I was in Purgatory and completely useless to any one cause. My focus had been shot as I now had tunnel vision, seeing only Sebastian's welfare in my sights. I'd left my father and adopted brother Lucas behind to deal with the consequences of the supernatural community's exposure to humans. I felt really, really bad about that, but I'd made my choice. It was a selfish one, but I needed closure—needed to say goodbye to Sebastian.

I rolled slowly onto my knees, marvelling at the crater of dirt around me and the absence of broken bones and bloodied flesh. The earth felt real under my palms, its gritty surface gathering under my fingernails and staining my skin. Pine cones and needles collected around the base of the trees around me, the smell of the woody scent teasing my nostrils. Despite the warm breeze that blew through my hair and the chirping birds that flew overhead, I knew better. Everything here was make-believe, an echo of the world we had once belonged.

I was a little stiff as I climbed to my feet, bruised in places I didn't know I had. Out of habit I waited for my ability to self-heal to kick in, but it never came—odd after sixteen years without Band-Aids and antiseptic.

Araqiel mentioned that pain and pleasure was a state of mind in this place of judgement and that no reaction or physical effect was any more or less intense than your own mind allowed or created. It was still a foreign concept to accept that I was the master of my own emotional and physical manifestations.

I dusted the dress I must have subconsciously created, wishing the flimsy material and inappropriate heel combination was infinitely more suitable; like skinny jeans, my favourite converse sweater and a pair of joggers. Perhaps a wasted thought with no K-Mart around the corner, but marvelled anyway when I was suddenly clad in every item I desired, right down to the nana undies and comfy sports bra I'd tacked on as an afterthought.

I ran my hands over the familiar threads, marvelling at the mystery of instant gratification and wondering if a convertible might suddenly appear on the horizon. When minutes trickled by without a shiny red car appearing, I started to walk, having no idea which direction to head. The surrounding forest appeared quite dense—discernible paths indistinguishable.

12

In the distance the sound of running water could be heard, but navigating its location was somewhat trying. I walked on regardless; the idea of standing idle was positively wasteful of the limited time I had.

'Sebastian?' I shouted, voice echoing around the forest.

There was no answer.

I shouted his name a few more times, hoping it might incite a response, but alas my efforts remained unrewarded. I had been delivered to this place of judgement to be reunited with my Archangel only to discover we were separated by ethereal geography! The trees could go on for miles and I could walk for days, always just missing our chance to be reunited.

That seriously pissed me off.

Ouch!

My hands were lightening quick at protectively cradling my head; a bird swept low, grazed my scalp and now swooped to settle on a nearby branch. I would normally dismiss this brush with nature as accidental, but the bird in question had peculiar gold feathers, a purple beak and eyes as large as any human—green like the forest surrounding us.

It studied me with keen interest, turning its head from side to side to ogle me with those bizarre, almost too large eyes. It was an ugly little thing, like no bird I'd ever seen and I was compelled to stare at its eccentricities. I wondered as it continued to examine me if the fly-by pecking might not have been intentional.

'Why do you keep staring at me you little feathered freak?' I murmured under my breath. 'What have I ever done to you?'

'You died and thus I was forced to leave my comfortable perch in the council chambers and fly here to induct you—very inconvenient.'

'What the—' I spluttered, stumbling back a few steps. Even in a place as strange as this I had not expected the bird to respond to my ramblings.

'Don't act so surprised,' it squawked.

'You're talking …'

'How else am I supposed to communicate with you?'

Jesus. It's still talking.

Did I hit my head on impact?

'Your head is fine,' the bird muttered, seemingly reading my thoughts. 'Is it so strange to believe that talking birds may exist after what you already know exists in your own world?'

Baffled, but also tremendously curious, I took a step forward, slowly creeping closer to the bird, my arm outstretched, fingers ready.

'I know what you're thinking,' the bird said, flapping its wings and hovering until it was on a branch out of my reach. 'And you're not poking me for the sake of satiating curiosity.'

'I wasn't—'

'You were.'

'I—'

'Stand still, shut up and listen.'

Aghast, I stood rooted, looking up at the feathered creature with its creepy human eyes uncertain how and if I should respond. I'd been admonished like a naughty school girl. Was it worth back-chatting the local fauna to salvage my ego?

The bird ruffled its feathers and settled on a higher branch—just out of my reach. Its bulbous head dove under a downy wing to retrieve what looked like a small, folded piece of parchment. It dropped it, but the paper didn't plummet to the ground as expected. Instead, it magically unravelled in front of the bird for better viewing.

'Ahem,' the bird said, clearing its throat. 'Welcome to Purgatory.'

I started to laugh. The absurdity of the situation had finally hit home. I was dead and talking to a bird welcoming me to the waiting room of death while reading from magically floating parchment. I half expected fairies to jump out from the bushes and lip sync death metal or the trees to start break dancing in roller skates. Welcome to Purgatory indeed. The bird made it sound like a bloody vacation.

'Quiet!' It was clearly unamused by my laughter

Familiar though I was with the strange and unusual, I wasn't used to communing with nature and its dialoguing birds. I didn't know whether to take it seriously or throw stale bread at it, so I did what any confused, recently crossed-over girl would do with an irate talking ball of pretty plumage … I apologised.

14

The bird narrowed its lidded eyes, turning its head from side-to-side, undoubtedly measuring the sincerity of my apology. 'Like I was saying … welcome to Purgatory.'

This time I contained any imminent outburst with a personal reality check. Should I really judge the talking bird when I was half-wolf, half-vampire and a dead, sexually confused teenager? I was likely to 'go long' for an old bone, hump your leg for kicks or take out a senior citizen if it meant getting my hands on some blood. I shouldn't point fingers at every unexpected creature I met when I was more messed up and genetically altered than anyone else I knew.

'You may have noticed things run a little differently around here,' the bird continued. 'You cannot die, but you can feel pain and you can feel hunger, but only should you decide to make it so.'

'Right.'

'I'm sensing a lack of understanding in your thoughts. To make it perfectly clear—you're dead. This version of yourself is only your spirit. Your tangible body still exists in the human plane of earth, but here you are—for lack of a better word—the embodiment of what you were.'

'Like a mirror image.'

'If you like the analogy. It is also mind over matter here. If you do not believe you are cold, then you won't be. If you think you are hungry, then you will be. If you see yourself as someone other than what you are not, then you will be.'

'Right, so if I—'

It rolled its eyes. 'Yes, you will see Elvis a lot here.'

'That wasn't what I was—'

'Now for the rules,' it urged, looking back at the manuscript. 'One; you cannot leave so don't even try to escape. Two; you cannot stay any longer than your allotted time unless the council decision is a hung vote. Three; should a hung vote occur you have two choices. One is to be re-born on earth and the other is stay here and make a life for yourself. Four; you will not remember any detail of your time in Purgatory should you choose re-birth. Any questions?'

'Yeah, I—'

'Good. So, according to my records, you have seven days hence to spend in Purgatory in any way that you see fit. When your time is up, you will be transported to the council chambers and presented for judgment. Judgement is final and cannot be changed. Any *other* questions?'

'Yeah, actually, I'm looking for—'

'Good. See you in a week.'

Some induction! The bloody bird was gone before I even had a chance to ask about Sebastian. I was left staring at the vacated tree branch; one large gold feather the only evidence the bird had been there. The parchment was also gone and my questions were unanswered and in abundance.

The sounds of the surrounding forest came rushing back, almost as if the brief interlude had pressed pause on this semblance of existence. I could now hear the chirping birds and the earlier sound of running water increasing as I forged on through underbrush. I could see something through the trees ahead, perhaps the glistening surface of a creek or stream, but it was superfluous according to the bird. I didn't need to drink it nor bathe in it. I guess I just needed geographical goals so I could avoid wandering aimlessly, hoping to stumble upon Sebastian.

Edging closer, I saw rocks and a sand bank; a small, luminous stream bubbled against shiny white granules. Each grain acted like glitter under the direction of the dappled light from above, touched by some unearthly hue. The rocks were wet and undoubtedly slippery, moss gathering in the dampest of regions. Above the rocks, sand merged into grassy banks and finally into the wooded debris currently at my feet.

I kept meandering until my joggers touched the edge of the lapping stream, the rubber soles sinking slowly into the sand. Brilliant flashes from coloured fish swam in the deeper depths— amethyst and orange like the sun. Some had stripes of green; others were spotted with flecks of gold.

Curious, I rested on one knee to touch the surface of the water, surprised to find that what I'd assumed to be free-flowing fluid was actually viscous, sticking to my fingers upon retraction. I found nothing of particular interest when sniffing the fluid, but as I touched it to my lips, it defied expectation; sweet like honey on my tongue. It coated the inside of my mouth and rolled easily down my throat, satisfying and equally as pleasing as the taste of blood.

'I wouldn't drink the water if I was you,' a familiar voice said. 'A couple of mouthfuls and you'll be so drunk you'll face-plant a pine cone and the trees will have their way with you.'

I jumped back to my feet and spun, my face widening into a painful grin. Of all the people to meet in Purgatory, I never expected it to be her. 'Oh my God!' I squealed. 'Kayla!'

Her smile was just as broad as we half-ran, half-stumbled into each other's arms. It had been a lifetime since we'd seen one another. She was my human best friend and the only friend I'd had for a very long time. Despite our obvious differences, we'd found things in common over the years and I'd somehow still kept my supernatural identity a secret.

Thanks to a spate of ongoing, unpreventable circumstances, we'd been separated as friends and communication had been severed. I'd had to uproot my life in Cairns on account of suspicious vânător activity and been sent to headquarters in Bucharest to lodge with the main faction of Protectors.

The lead scientist—Chester—volunteered me in his deplorable science experiment; a shock to the system and a massive disappointment to learn of The Protector's ultimate betrayal and that Lucas had also been flambéed over a Bunsen burner at some point.

I'd long since escaped, met Sebastian and headed to Rome to meet my absent father—Lucius Valerius. I'd soon found trouble again; kidnapped by the Alpha Roshan and suffered three weeks of: *I really don't want to talk about it.* Kayla knew nothing of my supernatural exploits and had thus continued an ordinary, human existence in Cairns. I think I might have envied her that.

She also knew nothing of Lucas and that I'd recently rescued him from another round of The Protector's warped experiments in the Antarctic and discovered yet another conspiracy—my blood, running through *his* veins. Kayla would *die* if she knew that both Lucas and I were freaks.

To sum up: I'd fallen in love, broken hearts, travelled the globe and still found time to bust a few asses in the war between vânătors and vampires, but I'd also lost sight of my friendship with Kayla; only seeing her once in the last six months. I'd also died, so that was a bummer.

'It's so good to see you,' I breathed, relieved at the sight of a welcoming, familiar face.

She hugged me so hard I feared for my spine. 'I'm glad you're here, Elena. This place is …' she choked on a sob and then squeezed me tighter still. 'I'm just so happy to see you.'

I pulled back, alarmed and suddenly sick to my stomach by the thought process weighing in on my emotions. Purgatory was not the ideal reunion and spelled a fate for my oldest friend I couldn't quite comprehend. We were supposed to whip out our bikinis, steal a bottle of tequila and hijack a golf cart to hoon around in until we found a rave to crash—not cry on each other in the land of judgement.

'What is it?'

I shook my head, still attempting the math. 'This is Purgatory.'

'I know.'

'What are you doing here?'

'Biding my time until judgement—just like everyone else.'

I found a tree to support my weight, legs weak with the roiling sickness that still claimed me. My head spun with unsettling tidings. 'No, you can't be.'

Kayla smiled, so calm and yet filled with a sadness so pronounced that it brought tears to my eyes. 'It's okay,' she reassured, patting my shoulder.

'It's not okay. You're … *dead*.'

'Elena, I know.'

'How did it happen?'

She shrugged, casually twirling a piece of long blonde hair around her fingers. 'I was running late for a party, took a corner a little too fast and went over the edge of the range.

'Shit.'

'Don't stress. Everything's fine.'

I sunk to the ground, my head dipping between my knees. 'When did it happen?'

'I don't know. Time works differently here.'

'How could I have not known? I only saw you a few months ago.'

'We haven't exactly talked recently.'

'That's my fault. I'm so sorry, Kayla.'

'What evs,' she said, shrugging once again. 'It all happened in the past and we can't change it. Besides, this place has its benefits.' She pointed out the Gucci shoes and the diamond studs in her ears. 'Purgatory has its perks—expensive ones.'

I studied her face. Despite the all-consuming sadness that seemed to grip her, she seemed relatively okay. Her hair was shiny and healthy, her skin glowed and brown eyes sparkled. She wore an outfit typically suited to her persona—tight and malicious in its constriction of her overly voluptuous figure; any tighter and her boobs would become a necklace, but that was Kayla. 'How long have you been here?'

'About a week. I'm not really sure.'

'What do you mean?'

'I don't know. The bird said he'd come and get me when it's time for judgement.'

I shook my head. 'No, you mentioned something about time being different here?'

Her lips formed the shape of an 'O'. 'Well, sometimes the sun doesn't go down. It'll be dusk for hours and hours with the night stretching on even longer still. Like right now, it feels like it's been late afternoon for at least two days.'

'So, one week here could last for months?'

'Maybe even years … or so it would seem.'

'When did your accident happen?'

She scratched her scalp, searching her memory. 'It was after you came back to Cairns and broke into work with that hot friend of yours. I remember telling you about the party, but you weren't interested in coming.'

At the time, Sebastian and I had been trying to find evidence of Lucas's disappearance. I'd lost my taste for parties, gyrating and underage drinking in lieu of more delicate, adult matters taking precedent.

'A party wasn't something I could surrender time for, Kayla. There was so much happening then.'

'Yeah, yeah—always is in your world.' She rolled her eyes for added effect.

'So, you went to the party?'

She nodded. 'That's when I died.'

'Kayla, that was over a month ago.'

Annoyance dissolved into confusion. 'Really?' She didn't wait for my response before continuing on. 'Wow. What a freak fest. I guess that makes you dead too. Do you know what happened to you?'

'I was stabbed.'

She winced, instinctively touching her chest as if afflicted. 'Brutal. I hope they catch the bastard that did it.'

I didn't have a response as I wasn't exactly sure who to blame for my death anymore. I'd chosen to come here—chosen death to be with Sebastian one last time. I couldn't really continue to blame Araqiel for my shortfalls in reading the fine print. At least now I had a chance to say goodbye to Kayla too.

Kayla kicked a pine cone by her feet and then winced as if pained, quickly assessing her designer shoes for scuff marks. 'Do you want to get out of here?'

'And go where?'

She tugged on my arm, pulling me alongside her. I was still uneasy on my legs, knees threatening to buckle at the mere thought of Kayla's changed circumstance, but there were some facts that settled me. For one; I realised that despite Kayla's faults, she wasn't a big sinner, unless you counted reckless driving, underage drinking and premarital sex. I had faith in her goodness and suspected she was headed for the shiny gates of heaven. And two; she broke for animals. That had to count for something.

She would not see hell on my watch.

'I'm going to take you to my camp.'

'Your camp?'

'Yeah, a couple of other souls and I sort of ran into each other in these woods. We agreed to stick together until judgement.'

'How many are there?'

'Lots. New souls drop in every other day. Today was my day to come looking for whoever had been delivered.'

'You make me sound like *Parcel pick up*.'

She giggled. 'To be fair, most souls are usually confused when they first arrive—the bird doesn't help. I was personally pretty shaken up after the fall. We just try to help newbies get settled and comfortable enough to accept what's happened.'

I started to draw comparisons between Kayla and a Christian outreach program. I barely contained the snort that had gathered momentum. She was hardly the do-gooder type. 'And then what do you do?'

'Some stay, others drift to other realms, but most don't see the point in wandering around until judgement. We usually sit around the fires and talk, dance or have fun remembering our old lives until it's time to move on … well, the younger of us do.'

'And the others?' I said, falling into step beside her.

She smirked 'We can't all be dead teens in Purgatory, no matter how our reckless behaviour in life may support the statistics.'

Kayla hadn't changed a bit and I was strangely reassured by that fact. I was merely devastated that reconnecting with her again meant we were both six feet under.

CHAPTER TWO: DARKNESS

Kayla and I chatted for several hours, feet shuffling slowly through the underbrush as we recounted everything absent from our past friendship. In life I'd never been able to tell Kayla the truth of my existence; I'd been bound by The Protectors and my own fear of rejection. I now spoke freely and without concern regarding my heritage and blood-drinking penchant. There'd never be another opportunity to be honest.

Kayla hung onto every word, listening intently without interjections regarding talk of parties and boy bits. Her disbelief was evident, face screwing up often and sometimes without cause. I told her about the Vânătors, the Vampires and The Protectors. I told her about Lucas and his involvement and everything going on in the background of the world she believed she knew. I even told her about William—the first vampire I'd ever met who'd unlocked a plethora of emotions and latent abilities via his blood. Sebastian also starred in the conversation—the main reason she finally broke her silence.

'Wait,' she interrupted. 'This is someone you're totally hot for?'

'It's a little more complicated than that.'

'I can't believe it. I've listened to you tell me about blood-drinking, your super strength and werewolf war and I suspect you might have hit your head a little too hard on the fall, but falling for a guy? This I can't believe at all.'

I slapped her shoulder hard. She didn't wince or fly half-way across the forest. My super-strength was apparently on hiatus here, along with my fangs and usual burning hunger for all things bloody. 'Come on! We've been talking for hours. I've poured my heart out, told you every little thing I've kept from you over the years and the one thing you choose not to believe is that I'm ...' I cleared my throat, feeling uncharacteristically cheesy and sentimental. '... in love with Sebastian?

She cracked the big one, laughing so hard she needed to clasp her knees for support. 'There. You just said it again!'

I scrubbed a frustrated hand through my hair, pulling at the roots. Why was it so unfathomable that I might have developed feelings? Worse still, why was it more rational to believe I'd shape-shifted and ripped throats out, but not fallen in love?

'Maybe we should just drop it.'

'No way,' she said, still cackling. 'You came all the way to Purgatory just to see this guy again. This is major news!' She took a calming breath. 'You know. I remember a time when you were rubbing up against drunk guys at raves.'

'I think you're getting me confused with you.'

She patted my backside affectionately. 'Where's that chastity belt now?'

'Seriously, Kayla—stop it.'

She sobered, yanking my arm in another direction which also served to hasten our pace. 'Fine, I'll stop teasing, but since we'll be back at the camp in a minute, I want to ask one question.'

'What?'

'Why him?'

I'd asked myself the same question time and time again, but I figured the answer was as complicated as the feelings I'd miraculously developed. So, I shrugged. 'I honestly don't know. He just gets me—always has.'

I neglected to mention Sebastian being the Archangel Michael and that we'd spent approximately thirteen thousand years existing just to cross paths and fall in love. After regaling Kayla with tales of werewolves and vampires; angel and demon mythology would probably incite a heart attack. Without being able to prove my abilities either, she was calling 'bullshit' and sizing me up for a straightjacket.

'So where is he then?'

Another good question—and as I shook my head—earlier frustrations began to creep back in. 'I don't know. I was dumped here with no real idea where to start looking.'

'That bird is useless, isn't he? Well, you've only been here a few hours, cop yourself a break.'

I studied the motionless sun above and sighed. Time had passed—hours even, but according to Kayla and experience thus far, you'd never know exactly how long. It should have easily been dusk by now.

'Maybe he's looking for you too?' Kayla added. 'I know this place seems infinite, but—'

'He doesn't know I'm here.'

'Oh, well that sucks.'

'I should probably start looking for him.'

Kayla released my arm and took hold of my hand, squeezing tight. Her face was suddenly lined with fear and chilling to witness. 'No. You can't leave yet. I know time is deceptive here, but night will eventually come and when it does, it gets really dark.'

'So?'

'Trust me, you need to be near the fire—near the light when that happens.'

I summoned a second sweater for my outfit, purely just for looks. 'If it's the cold—'

'It's not the cold,' she said, all seriousness as she pulled me to a stop. We were now facing each other, her hand still gripping mine and face ashen. 'Do you remember what brought you here?'

'Yes—an angel.'

'An angel that dropped you here in the *daylight*. Think about what drops people here in the darkness.'

The fear that rode her face became a tangible thing, like a suffocating heat that stole even my breath. 'You're talking about demons?'

'Right.'

I shook my head. 'Wait, so you won't believe that vampires, werewolves and magic exist back on earth and that I'm a half-breed with fangs and abilities, but you fully believe in angels and demons?'

'This isn't me being candid, Elena. I wouldn't have believed it if I hadn't seen it for myself.'

I shook free of her crushing fingers and clasped her shoulders tightly instead. 'Listen, we're already dead. Nothing can hurt us here; there is no pain, no pleasure, no hunger and no thirst unless you put faith in it. The bloody bird even reaffirmed it!'

'Tell that to the souls we hear screaming through the night.'

I sighed. 'How long does the night last?'

'Sometimes as long as the day.' She was shaking under my touch, fear riding her unnecessarily. It had been quite some time since I'd been in the company of someone defenceless, weaker and generally unable to keep pace with the supernatural. I was clueless how to ease her tension—a setback of hanging around the immortal for so long.

I wrapped an arm around her quivering shoulders and pulled her into a warm and hopefully comforting embrace. 'Don't worry. I'll stay for a bit if it makes you feel better.'

She squeezed my waist. 'Promise me you won't leave during darkness. Hang around our camp for now and when it's morning again you can search for Sebastian.'

'Okay.'

'Really?'

'Sure, if that's what you want?'

'It is.'

I gave her one final squeeze and then let go. I was determined to set her mind to things less dubious or sinister. 'So where is this camp of yours anyway?'

'Just over the next ridge.'

'It seems like miles away. Given your fear, why would you stray so far from the camp in the late afternoon?'

'It was my turn.' She shrugged and was almost the proud owner of another beaming smile. 'Plus, I had a feeling this time it was going to be you.'

My sideways look was matched with a scoff of obvious disbelief. 'How could you have possibly known?'

Kayla's smile had made a full return—a good sign. 'I heard you.'

'You heard me?'

'Who else do I know that would fall from the sky screaming profanities and still find time to curse an angel with herpes?'

'You heard that?'

She was cackling now. 'The whole damn forest heard that.'

Great.

*   *   *

The camp fell short of my expectations, but didn't disappoint. A girl of the twenty-first century expected nylon tents and deck chairs perched around an open fire while kids munched on marshmallows and men discussed the fish that got away while swigging beer. Purgatory was a world unto its own and absent of the luxuries my memory stimulated—not that anyone couldn't have conjured these items into being.

An open fire did indeed grace the centre of the clearing, but it was assembled with fallen logs, sticks and dried underbrush from the forest. Surrounding the cosy warmth were tiny, rough-hewn huts constructed from tree branches and thatched by coniferous leaves and vines. Behind these huts were smaller fires dispersed at two meter intervals; suspected barriers of light between the campsite and impending darkness.

Dusk had finally fallen, but many hours had passed. Shadows loomed large enough to set the souls in the camp on edge. I'd been introduced to everyone, but knew I'd never remember names—the least of anyone's concern. Every soul present now manned a fire pit, keeping them stoked and burning bright. They huddled on mass, talking, laughing, but always acutely aware of the approaching night.

I had to admit I was deeply curious. I'd met angels, but never encountered a demon. My fear was absent, though I was uncertain if it was Araqiel's earlier speech urging me to dispel notions of fear or pain in the presence of a place not validated by the trappings of life. I'd yet to grow hungry and I was no longer vulnerable to the call of blood, so perhaps his guidance had merit.

Kayla had begged once more that I stay out of the dark. She knew of my stubborn curiosity, but I fully intended to keep that promise as long as I was not trapped in this singular vicinity for days on end. Sebastian was here and I had to find him; time was of the essence.

'Elena?'

'Huh?' I rubbed my watery eyes. I'd been staring at the fire for far too long, mesmerised by the colour and heat.

'Did you hear me?'

One of the new souls on my left was tugging insistently on my sweater. He seemed nice enough, but I couldn't remember his name. 'Sorry?'

'I said, do you want to dance?'

'What for?'

'Fun!' he jumped to his feet and held out his slender hand. I was unconcerned that this might have been an attempt at hitting on me. He wore a 'I love Barbara' T-Shirt, eyeliner, skinny jeans—and believe it or not—a pair of ruby-red slippers.

Protest was not optional as I was yanked to my feet a second later. Kayla laughed, eagerly clapping her hands as I stumbled into his waiting arms. He was quick to pull me close and then snap off in the opposite direction.

'What are you doing?' I shrieked.

'We're doing the tango.'

I stumbled, unusually clumsy on my deft dancing feet, but I was distracted by a task yet completed—finding Sebastian. 'I'd like to stop now please.'

He actually gasped, slapping a wrist to his forehead and claiming distress. 'You can't possibly mean that?'

'Look, um …'

'Adrian.'

'Yeah, Adrian. I've got a lot on my mind at the moment. I think I just want to—'

'Waltz?'

'Ah … no.'

'Jive?'

'Sitting down would be good.'

He scoffed, jerking us in the other direction again. 'Why can't they send souls that actually like to dance?' He didn't appear to need an answer as he dipped me backwards and caught my left leg before I fell, then spun us in the other direction again. If I'd been in the mood to hustle, this introduction to camp side Purgatory would be great.

A lengthy, blood-curdling scream cut any retort building short. Adrian immediately ceased dancing, but refused to let me go. His hands shook upon my waist, his face filled with ribbons of the tension quickly spreading through the rest of the campsite.

'What was that?' I whispered, straining to hear more above the crackle of the surrounding fires and the everyone's panicked chatter.

'You don't want to know.'

I touched a reassuring hand to his trembling frame and patted gently, hoping to ease his fears. A second scream—louder than the first—echoed through the clearing somewhere behind us, silencing any remaining talk from those nearby. 'Was that the Demons then?'

Adrian shook his head, a tuft of his blonde fringe falling in front of his dark, saddened eyes. 'No. That's the souls found wandering alone at night by the Demons.'

'You can't die again. Why be afraid of what technically has no power over you?'

'Fear can consume you and tell you what you are seeing and feeling is real. You could die a thousand times over in the length of one of these nights and still survive to face it again and again.'

'So, you're telling me that the soul we're hearing is being tortured?'

'Has anyone seen Jonas?' someone asked, voice panicked.

'He was by the caves this afternoon, gathering more rocks for the walls,' another uttered.

I looked at Kayla who had conformed to mass opinion and now also wore a mask of fear despite knowing the Demon's powers were limited by the mind's allowance. I left Adrian to be with her. She was shaking, arms wrapped around her upper torso like a security blanket. 'Are you alright?'

'No.'

'Don't be afraid, Kayla. You know you can control the truth of whatever is happening out there.'

Her burning glare made me take a step back. 'Easy for a newcomer to say. I know Jonas. He's suffering now because I left him by the caves to come and find you.'

Clearly this was somehow my fault. 'Where are the caves?'

Her eyes narrowed to slits. 'No.'

'Kayla, just tell me where they are.'

'No,' she said, shaking her head almost violently. 'I know that look in your eyes. You're going to go and look for him.'

'I'll be fine.'

'What did I tell you about the dark!' she shouted.

'I'm not afraid of the dark, Kayla. I haven't been for a very long time.'

'This isn't about the Bogeyman, Elena! You can get your soul murdered again and again out there.' Everyone gathered was watching as she lunged for my hand and squeezed it tightly. She was being irrational and giving into the state of heightened panic being passed around the campfire.

'Adrian, come and sit with Kayla.'

'No!' Kayla screamed again, pulling me closer. 'I won't let you go out there!'

She was starting to make quite a scene. 'Adrian?'

Thankfully, he helped disentangle me from Kayla's insistent hold and bundled her in his lanky arms instead. 'You're crazy for even thinking about it,' he muttered.

'Where are the caves?'

'A couple of miles to the east.'

A gave him a droll look. I must have looked like a girl scout in my past life. I had zero idea which way was east. 'Just point.'

'You shouldn't be doing this,' Kayla sobbed, Adrian's T-shirt now a wet mess. 'They'll get you like they got Jonas.'

I didn't answer; clearly, I had more faith than any singular soul in this camp. The horrified glances of those nearest were enough to confirm that I wasn't being careless, but that everyone else doubted their own inner strength.

I wasn't afraid—couldn't be. I hadn't seen the Demons these people were petrified of, but I'd witnessed enough in life that the trials of Purgatory would remain ineffectual compared to recent exploits. I would choose to believe Araqiel when he'd said everything was a state-of-mind and that pain was just a word.

So, I grabbed a loose branch from the edge of the fire, wrapped the sweater I'd conjured earlier around the end and dipped it back into the fire to use as a torch. Flames licked at the fabric almost immediately, lighting the way. It wouldn't last as long as batteries and a halogen globe, but it was better than stumbling around blind.

Behind, Kayla sobbed. Adrian clung to her, running his fingers through her silky blonde hair and down her back in a reassuring gesture. Everyone else stayed glued to the fires, watching me like hawks, eyes wide and full of fear.

I considered the ramifications of these actions; I was chasing trouble yet again, but how could I huddle around a fire in ignorance and pretend everything was fine when clearly the weak needed a little bit of help?

I turned and walked quickly to the east; the direction Adrian had pointed. Perhaps I was an idiot, wandering into the unknown, unafraid and yet unprepared for what might be lurking in the darkness, but there was nothing left that could surprise me. I no longer found fear in that which I was unaccustomed or unfamiliar—but rather—in the loss of those that I loved more than my own life.

Everything else paled in comparison.

I stepped past the outer ring of the campsite and into the shadows. The forest grew silent, almost as if it listened for my approach. I put one foot in front of the other, concentrating on the broken twigs and what remained of the semi-discernible trail at my feet. Light was scarce, the hastily created torch provided just enough light to see. Getting lost would be idiotic, so focus was a must.

Another scream confirmed my bearings. I disregarded the emotion of hearing the pain-wrought howls and focused solely on the task at hand—not falling on my face. The campsite had become a distant memory; the Demons and their torturous play were now my only guide to finding Jonas—a soul I had never even met.

It was becoming apparent that I really needed a hobby so validation for good deeds wasn't an unshakable priority. There was no rhyme nor reason for me to derail from my own Purgatory-based plans and yet I simply couldn't help coming to the aid of anyone too weak to defend themselves.

I kept walking. My eyes were always cast down to keep track of the trail. It grew more and more difficult to decipher as footprints were scarce, but Jonas's constant screams of pain told me I was still maintaining directional success.

A hideously vicious growl to the right stopped me dead in my tracks. Concentration now broken, I looked up from the path; silver eyes, sharp teeth and serrated claws were illuminated by the torch I clutched tightly.

I took a deep breath and opted to study the creature with clinical detachment. Emotion would not rule me in this place where fear and pain were in the hands of the beholder. It was not unlike a vânător, possibly a hellhound. The only difference—no fur, but skin marred with scabs, cuts and festering wounds covered in leeches and maggots—walking piles of rotting flesh with teeth and a bloody agenda.

As it growled again, several more approached, their fetid breath like steaming wisps of bilious gas wafting from roadside grates. I stood tall and looked at each in turn, unafraid and unmoved by the challenge they presented. In my world I was the alpha. In their world I was whatever I believed I could be, not simply a piece of meat.

I moved forward, matching the approach of one of the hellhounds as it attempted to snap its snout in warning. I lunged forward again, growling like the alpha I am; I was surprised and pleased that my human throat echoed the sentiment with daring conviction. 'Do not growl at me,' I rumbled, inserting authority and certainty in every word or sound uttered.

I can't die again … I can't die again …

The warning growl quickly morphed into something quite feral and since it seemed resolute, I slammed my flaming torch onto the end of its nose. It whimpered and quickly retreated, allowing more room for the others to approach.

They were hesitant, but also eager to rend flesh. So, I growled again to reaffirm my position, but didn't lash out. I needed to ascertain and cement my authority without resorting to violence, simply implant the idea that I was more than capable of it.

'Move.'

They remained still, silvered eyes glistening under the light of the torch and unperturbed by my request. I then used the full range of what I remembered of my alpha inference and snarled enough to put hair on a woman's chest. 'I said move!'

They scampered, whimpering as they dived to get out of my path. Their mangled paws slapped against the thick underbrush as their hides disappeared behind bushes and trees, watching from a distance. The victory was both surprising and satisfying. I had hoped to avoid their decayed teeth and scabby skin brushing with my own. I'd been lucky this time. Not all demons would be canine and as easily swayed by my inner alpha.

I started moving again, the torch held in front to light the way. The forest had grown more silent than comfortable and Jonas's screams were a distant memory. The hellhounds remained at my heels, but no longer interfered, slinking through the shadowed forest instead, watching my every move.

A small part of me wondered if it was my bravado providing safety from the creatures of the night or my origins; I'm not evil, but I *am* the spawn of Satan. Was this helping me to abate the fear of being surrounded by evil despite wholeheartedly gripping onto the notion of hope and change—the part allowing me to bathe in the light?

I swallowed, took a deep, settling breath and trudged over the approaching hill, gripping confidence with both hands and praying that what I saw next wasn't real, but an illusion. How was it conceivable that so much evil could exist in a place labelled for its neutrality? To describe the torture and sodomy these demons performed—not just on themselves—but the souls gathered; I worried for the fragility of the human mind and soul's exposure to so much …

Forgetting myself, I was suddenly bent over and relieving my stomach of its entire contents.

It made no sense to feel ill in this place and yet I'd been exposed to filth beyond any realms of depravity I could comprehend. I had no control over this effect; my body simply knew this was so very wrong to witness.

'Well, well, what do we have here?'

I quickly straightened, wiping my mouth and spitting the remnants of vomit free. A goat-headed demon stood before me; his dark skin was slicked with sweat and ruby-red eyes glowed in the darkness like fire as he assessed me. At his waist hung a leather whip covered in flesh-tearing barbs. Blood dripped like rain onto his hooves where ankle bracelets made from human intestines adorned his flesh.

Jesus.

'He won't help you here, Elena Manory.'

I tore my eyes from the human jewellery, levelling my gaze with his. 'How do you know my name?'

'I know everything about you.' His speech was surprisingly clear for a goat. 'Let me introduce myself. I am Samael.'

33

'I don't care who you are.' It was true, but also my way of dealing with less than desirable situations—arrogance.

He sneered, whiskered mouth virtually puckering. 'You *should* care. I am one of the council members who will be judging you in a week.'

That surprised the hell out of me. 'What?'

'Oh yes. Didn't Araqiel tell you what to expect from this place? Didn't he tell you who owns the darkness here?'

'No.'

'Foolish I would think.' He laughed, the hellhounds around him growling and the winged demons that looked like hairless monkeys positioned in the trees above also brayed like sheep.

'I've come for Jonas and the other souls you have here.'

They all laughed harder. 'You and what army?'

'I don't have an army nor do I need one.'

'Then you are very foolish indeed.'

'I'm just trying to do the right thing.' I sounded a little meek and unintimidating—not my intention at all.

'*Right?*' Samael echoed. 'The darkness knows no right!'

I shook my head, adamant. 'You're wrong. The darkness has no agenda at all … it just is.'

'The darkness breeds contemptuous evil and sin.'

'No,' I reaffirmed, determined to prove a point. 'The darkness *isn't* evil, just the sorry creatures that hide within it because they're too afraid to face the truth of the light.'

Good one. Bait the demon with intestines strung around his ankles.

'Are you calling me a coward?' Samael was perplexed and yet simultaneously annoyed by my backchat.

I lifted my chin, defiant in the face of certain danger. 'I guess I am. What you are doing to these people you wouldn't dare do during the daylight. You risk being seen, being judged and being defeated by those who don't hide in the shadows.'

Samael growled, lowering his head so that his sharp teeth were only inches from my face. 'I wonder if you would be so brave without your torch?'

'I'm not afraid of you.' I was surprised how true that statement was.

'What are you afraid of, Elena?'

'I'll never tell.'

34

Samael had an evil glint in his eye as he smiled maniacally, reached up and extinguished my torch. 'We'll see.'

The light dissolved under his touch and everything grew dark. If there was a moon in this plane it had not yet risen. I could barely see a foot in front of my face, yet I knew they lingered. I could feel Samael's hot, putrid breath on my cheek and his fingers as they gently traced the pattern of my shoulders and headed down my arms. I reminded myself repeatedly that there was nothing he or any other creature could do to hurt me unless I allowed it.

'Are you afraid yet, Elena?'

'No.'

I am in control. Nothing and no one can hurt me. I am immune from pain.

'What if I did this?' Samael's wandering hands paused, moving hurriedly to my chest and ripping a hole in the front of my sweater. His fingers were rough and uncompromising as he pulled at the edges of my bra in an attempt to objectify and expose me to sexual misconduct. I would never allow myself to become a victim again—not after Roshan.

I summoned new garments which quickly covered any exposure and reversed Samael's attempts to grope me. Every time he attempted to tear the material or get to my undergarments, I simply imagined new ones in their place.

'What is this?' he yelled, toying with the new fabric, his advances rebuked by layering.

I held onto my sigh of relief, secretly pleased by the effectiveness of belief.

Samael ripped at my shirt again and again, the hellhounds also attempted to tear shreds in my jeans. I merely kept imagining new items of clothing; his efforts and that of the hounds was hampered by the presence of an unending wardrobe and my ability to recreate what they attempted to steal from me—my dignity.

'We can do this all night,' I said more calmly than sanely plausible, 'but let's not waste our time.'

'Do you think rape is the only way I intend to get inside of you?'

I cringed, the mental images almost crippling. 'You can't hurt me.' I now believed in that mantra, especially in the face of almost certain imminent abuse.

'Can't I?'

'No.' I moved forward, pushing past his groping hands and the reaching claws of the Hellhounds. I ignored every swipe or attempt to brandish my flesh with horrific wounds. There were plenty of moments of doubt and seconds of pain where surprise attacks robbed me of focus, but strength always returned.

I'd almost made it down the hill and closer to the souls, ignoring the shrill taunts and screams of frustrated demons on a mission to disembowel me before my breath caught and I gulped in alarm. Salty blood gathered on my palate, raising fresh terror. With shaking hands, I touched the protruding fist in my chest, foreign fingers slick and warm and gripping what I knew could only be my beating heart.

'I told you I'd get inside of you,' Samael whispered in my ear, his tongue darting out to trace the lobe.

I fell against his chest, winded and caught off guard, but nevertheless mindful not to succumb to the mind's will to incite horror and pain. He held me against him, gleeful over my current predicament. I debated remaining calm when all instincts sought to see me scream in torturous pain. He held my heart in his dirty, sadistic hands and pressed his filthy erection into my back as his dripping tongue ravaged my ear lobe.

Blood gushed like a torrential waterfall from the gaping hole in my chest and landed at my feet with a sickening *thud*. I think what saved me from torment was the complete disbelief in what was happening—my heart in a demon's hand. Every fibre of my being urged me to feel—to scream for mercy. And, as unwanted sensations began to niggle at my self-control, I closed my eyes and imagined the truth of my existence; I was whole, healthy.

My trembling fingers no longer touched Samael's. They explored a chest free of blood and broken bones, smooth and clad in yet another Converse sweater, fresh from the Purgatory drycleaners. Sentiments of pain were mere echoes attempting to touch my lips, but now knowing the strength of self-belief, I wouldn't surrender to a single doubt of my power here again. I had triumphed over urges to relent and was now free to disengage from any unsavoury approaches from the Demons in this realm.

'Where are you going?' Samael chided. 'You will not walk away from me!'

I ignored him, wading through unmentionable depravity, my feet squelching through slick surfaces and tangible human body parts. I was grateful for the darkness and all that I *couldn't* see.

Samael ordered the Hellhounds to ravage every piece of my flesh, tear me open like a Christmas cracker and lick my insides clean, but they knew better. My warning growl once again confirmed my status as pack leader and the hounds remained still, much to Samael's disgust.

'You can't save them all, Elena,' Samael shouted after me as I continued down the hill and towards the souls. 'You can't see in the dark and I will get to them first!'

As if someone from above had heard the Demon's taunt and decided to meet the challenge head on, three moons suddenly peeked above the horizon, bringing enough dappled light to illuminate the forest floor. I could now see clearly. It was a blessing and a curse given the three souls I saw being beaten, brutalised, cut and disembowelled.

A body by my foot was in pieces; she was elderly, somewhere in her late sixties, possibly early seventies. Her insides were her outsides, her skin split open from throat to groin. I resisted the urge to vomit again and instead kicked one of the skinless monkeys that hovered around her face into the scrub to her right.

'No more,' she gurgled. 'Please, have mercy on an old woman.'

'You're safe now,' I murmured, bending down to push away blood-soaked hair from her eyes.

'Who are you?'

'A friend.'

'There are no friends in the darkness,' she spluttered.

'Then save yourself and imagine this was a terrible dream, that none of this was real.'

'Oh, but it is real, Elena,' Samael taunted, running his greasy fingers through my hair. 'It's so very real ...'

'Ignore the voices,' I barked. 'They only have power over you if you let them.'

'I can't!' she choked 'The pain!'

'There's no pain,' I answered calmly, voice soothing. 'This isn't real, just a nightmare gone horribly wrong. I need you to wake up now and be whole again.'

'I can't!'

'Yes, you can. I'm here with you. I won't let anything happen.'

'You can't promise that, Elena …' Samael taunted.

'Are you ready?' I said to the woman, ignoring him. 'Think pleasant thoughts. Imagine yourself healthy and strong.'

'I don't know …'

'Do you see it?'

'See what?' she croaked.

'The lovely dress you're wearing and matching red shoes. And, the scarf you're wearing—it matches your eyes.'

'It does?' She sat up quickly, fingering the silken fabric in delight. 'I haven't worn this dress since I met my husband Clive. He was a pilot you know.'

'Was he?'

'Oh yes, he was so very handsome in his uniform.'

'I bet you'd melt his heart all over again if he saw you in that dress now.'

She shook her head. 'Clive died in the war. He'll never see me again looking like this.'

'I think you'll get to see Clive sooner than you expect.'

'Do you really think so?'

'For sure.'

She looked around, her small smile dimming as she took in the horror around her. 'My—'

'Don't look,' I said, touching her hand. 'Just get up, hold onto me and keep imagining yourself in this amazing dress. Keep thinking about Clive and how nice it will be to see him again. He wouldn't want to see you looking anything but whole and beautiful now, would he?'

She hesitated, eyes growing wider by the second, but I refused to let her go back to the darkness. Samael would have no more victories tonight. 'No, Clive would prefer me like this,' she murmured, still fixated on the horror surrounding us both.

I helped her to her feet, holding her hand tightly and pulling her along to keep up. The Demons followed like a bad smell, flapping overhead, squawking from the tree branches or howling at our feet. Samael also never relented—always circling, always taunting.

The next soul was a man—presumably Jonas. He was a few years older than me and been badly damaged over the course of the night so far. Talk of self-belief did little to persuade him that this horror could be conquered. He'd been tortured for eternity in his mind and thus surrendered to the evil that had raped his flesh.

Me and the elderly lady dragged him kicking and screaming over to the last soul. She was curled in the foetal position with pieces of God only knew what protruding from all over. She was quick for the torture to end, thus eager to believe that my words of belief would end in reformation and safety. Her hasty transformation was what finally convinced Jonas it was safe to do the same.

Still, Samael persisted. His taunts and re-attempts at battery were evil to the core. His demon counterparts spent every other second attempting to strangle, mutilate and maim the barely contained souls I'd managed to free of pain. Some relapsed, but they always came back to themselves aware that pain was now a temporary thought process easily overcome.

The three souls stayed huddled and disturbingly close, gripping me wherever they could find traction and whimpering whenever a demon moved too close. I barked a lot of orders to stay clear and allow us through; the Hellhounds being the most obedient by far. The biggest problem staying safe was that the creatures could smell fear. Irrespective of my bravery, if the others cowered, we labelled ourselves moving targets—pieces of meat in a den of vicious wolves.

'Bravo,' Samael said, clapping his hands. 'You put them back together again.'

'They did it themselves.'

'Do you want to see how easy it will be to pull them apart again?'

'Get out of my way.' I had to remind everyone once again that he was fictitious and anything he said or attempted to do physically was make-believe, easily remedied by bravado.

Samael slammed a hoof against the earth, spraying leaf litter and dirt in multiple directions. 'You think you can order me around in my own realm?'

'Your sick game is over, let us pass.'

'I don't think so. I may not be able to get to you, but I can certainly play with your friends all night.' He circled slowly, coming to a stop next to the older woman who visibly cowered in his presence. 'What do you say, demons? Who would like to crawl through her mouth and eat her from the inside out first?'

I swallowed a mouthful of bile, pushing the souls behind me and using myself as a shield. 'He can't hurt you. None of them can hurt you unless you believe it.'

Samael cackled maniacally, pulled back his hoof and kicked Jonas in the knee cap, popping them from the joints and eliciting a scream.

'It's not real!' I shouted above the sudden din of excitement. 'The pain isn't real!'

The demons swarmed. I wasn't strong enough to help them all. The younger woman was torn from my side, lifted into the trees by the skinless monkeys and impaled to the branches. Jonas was carted away by the hellhounds, teeth ripping at his flesh from every conceivable angle. The older woman practically choked me, wrapping almost every inch of herself around me in fear, but without my usual strength we tumbled to the ground where Samael grabbed her leg and dragged her into the darkness.

Helpless, I scrambled back to my feet, shouting at everyone to remain composed, but my pleas fell on deaf ears, my attempts thwarted by the Demons that swarmed. How could I help with so much opposition?

'Let there be light!'

I turned, a familiar voice tugged at my heart strings as darkness was suddenly swallowed by daylight so warm and bright I was temporarily blinded. Shadows retreated into the trees and the screams of the souls melted into the guttural cries of the burning demons. The ground split like the bursting hemline of the obese and swallowed the creatures and remnants of night deep into the unhallowed pits of Purgatory.

'Michael!' Samael spat. 'How dare you interfere!'

'You have been up to no good in my absence, Samael.'

'You do not know your place!'

Sebastian shook his head, dark hair tickling the tops of his shoulders. 'And you have forgotten yours.'

I took a tentative step in his direction, a smile already lifting my lips. 'Sebastian.'

His eyes found mine. They were no longer the greenish grey I'd grown accustomed to. They were now silver, glistening like

Christmas tinsel that twisted and moved like a thermometer's mercury. He now personified his angelic nature and had become the truest representation of every dream or repressed memory I'd ever had of him. 'Elena …'

'How touching,' Samael teased. 'The two of you finally reunited.'

'Sebastian, I—'

'It's okay,' he murmured. 'We'll talk soon.'

Samael stamped his hoof again, begging attention. Steam escaped his ears like an irritated cartoon character, but we continued to ignore him, lost to our reunion.

I shifted my weight to the other foot, uncharacteristically nervous in Sebastian's presence. 'I'm glad you're here.'

'Do not ignore me!' Samael screamed.

Sebastian clicked his fingers, barely sparing the demon a glance. 'Be gone.'

I flinched, studying the empty spot where Samael had stood. The earth sizzled and cracked; a darkened patch of sulphurous powder now dusted the ground in his absence. Repulsed, my nose twitched at the smell, the rest of me debating how much power an archangel had over the council members. 'Is he gone?'

'For now, but he will return.'

I shook my head. 'I'm glad you're here I had no idea what else I could do to help these people.'

'You did more than most.'

Looking at the weary and whimpering souls did little to alleviate my guilt

Sebastian's tentative step and outstretched hand returned my attention to him. He opened his mouth, quickly closed it again and then said, 'Elena …'

No more words were uttered before his lips pressed together in a tight line and his eyes crinkled; confusion and then just as quickly, anger warred with his emotions. This was normal for us; an initial rush of pleasure at being reunited, then the settling of common sense. To be with one another again was heart stopping, but also a reminder of our past and the steps taken to reach this moment—a million seconds of time wasted on indecision and speculation.

I watched Sebastian intently. My silence was no different than the soundless words he refused to utter or his wandering eyes he no doubt hoped spoke volumes. Speech at this time was lost to us, but the truth was that we *were* finally reunited—a happiness I would not discount.

The solid state of silver in his eyes was new, but the rest of him was the same. A strong chiselled jaw, high cheekbones, sensuous lips and a body I could wash my clothes on. He was everything any woman could ever want—more than I could have ever dreamed. I was relieved he was virtually unchanged here. To have him differ from the Sebastian I'd come to know and love would have been challenging.

Even his current scowl was unchanging, but at least I knew it was concern for me and my presence in Purgatory that had marked it upon his perfect features. What should I have done and what could I say now? Sorry that I loved you enough to die for you?

'Help me, please!'

Spell broken, I turned away, seeking out the voice. It was the woman in the tree; her body still hung limply from the branches. Even with the sun now beating upon her pale skin, she couldn't see past the pain and horror of the night before to make herself whole again. Sebastian had driven the Demons away, forced sunrise and light's intensity to kiss evil goodbye, but it was not enough. These souls still saw themselves as weak, defenceless—human.

I sighed, shimmied up the thick trunk and climbed the gangly branches until I was at her side. She screamed incessantly as I disengaged body parts from tree limbs. None of my reassurances of healthy mind, health body seemed to work. She blamed me for yet another round with Samael's minions—I could hardly argue.

When she'd calmed down long enough to realise the sun was present and the Demons were gone, she pushed me aside, descended the tree and ran to the older woman's side. Surprisingly, *she* did thank me for trying to help when no one else would, as did Jonas.

I didn't need praise. I didn't even need a thank you. As far as I was concerned, it was my job to help those that couldn't help themselves; a fact drummed into me since my upbringing and training with The Protectors.

42

We all progressed slowly back towards camp. I wanted to run off with Sebastian, but the older woman felt more comfortable with me at her side, my hand bundled tightly in her own as she recounted tales of Clive and the war. Jonas enjoyed a one-sided conversation with Sebastian who spent most of his time studying me from the corner of his eye. I reciprocated the eye tag, almost consumed by the desire to finally be alone. There was so much to say and so little time for us. Even in Purgatory, we skirted our own desires.

The younger woman ran ahead as soon as she saw the camp, her bare feet slapping the dried brush and fallen leaves. I'd since learnt her name was Eve. She'd been a preacher's wife. She believed she'd sinned when Samael came for her and Sebastian spent a fair amount of time reassuring her that wasn't the case. My heart warmed to hear his voice and explanations for entry into heaven and hell. Petty crimes were forgiven if you asked for it, but then of course I remembered how many creatures I'd killed.

Not exactly petty crimes …

At least Eve had been settled, though still unabashedly irritated that despite my help, I'd had her inadvertently murdered twice in one night. She'd also concluded that poisoning her husband's parishioners a few weeks ago was in fact accidental and would not see her roast in the southern sauna for all eternity.

I wish I could say the same for me.

CHAPTER THREE: REUNITED

The intense heat from the flames crackled and sizzled, burning my tender skin and consequently drying out my eyes. I'd been staring at the blaze for too long. The burnt orange and crimson hue was almost hypnotic as it danced over roasted logs and dried leaves. I should have moved away, but since I couldn't really be harmed, I remained still.

Barely six feet away, Sebastian and I sat separated by nothing more than our own ridiculous notions of denial whilst trying to string a sentence together and bring cohesion to our thoughts. And, as our eyes met across the crackling flames, it was clear how desperate we both were to be properly reunited and away from any interruptions, but since we'd returned to camp, Kayla had gone postal.

She'd trampled her fears of the dark's passing and had spent most of our return drooling like an idiotic mess over Sebastian, hanging onto his every word and eyeing him as if he'd hung the moon. I couldn't really blame her. He was backed by the God Squad and came with a halo—an attractive package and a walking contradiction.

Sebastian watched me without reprieve through the flames, nodding occasionally in response to Kayla's current tale. I still hadn't figured out a way to explain my appearance in Purgatory or why I'd made such a hasty decision effecting everyone on earth just to see him again. Love was the simplest explanation, but we'd never done anything the easy way and I wasn't sure how to start that now.

Sebastian suddenly stood, eyes as intense as ever. He was coming for me; the whole moment was captured in slow motion as every stride in my direction made my pulse beat like a drum against my flesh. Time sped up again and then he was there, holding his hand out for me to take.

This is your time Elena, stop being a coward!

I took his outstretched hand, letting him pull me to my feet. Our eyes met, our faces only inches apart. Suddenly I knew everything I wanted to say and decided on absolutely nothing at all. I leant forward, inhaled the sweetness of his angelic breath and drew it in deep. We were together again and I couldn't help but marvel at the lengths we would take in spite of common sense or life and death just so we could see each other again.

Sebastian closed any lingering distance between us, his hand now reaching to brush the hair from my face and tuck it behind my ear. The second our lips touched it was as if the fire that had previously warmed us now beat upon our skin and inside our hearts with charring certainty. For thirteen thousand years we had pursued an unending passion and now—even though our time was fleeting—we would never again doubt the destiny in our union— the rightness of these lips combining in raw passion.

People watched and Kayla wolf-whistled like a prepubescent child, but we were lost to their amusement. We had waited longer than anyone could imagine to be together this final time and no one would dissuade us from parting—not even the council members themselves.

'What have you done?' Sebastian whispered against my lips, minutes later. His hands now stroked my back to pull me into the comfort of his embrace.

'I kissed you,' I answered, breath shaky.

'You know that's not what I mean.'

Did I really need to spell it out for him?

Sebastian's eyes narrowed, lips tightening just a fraction. It was enough for me to know he wasn't happy. 'You shouldn't be here, Elena.'

'Neither should you.'

'I have had thousands of years on earth and months to spend with you. It's more than I deserve.'

'Why did you have to go and get yourself killed?'

'That has nothing to do with your appearance in Purgatory.'

I scoffed at his almost chiding tone. 'You died and I had … needed to say goodbye.'

'Goodbye?' he barked, stepping away. 'That's not a good enough reason! I never wanted for you to come here.'

The barb cut deep—deep enough that I was hurt rather than angry. He made it sound as if my presence was a major inconvenience. 'I'm sorry I've disappointed you.'

He recognised the hurt and his eyes widened a fraction. He shook his head, quickly reaching for my hands again. 'You know that's not what I meant, Elena.' He squeezed my fingers, bowed his head and took a deep breath. 'Let's go for a walk. We have a lot to discuss and this audience is too interested in our conversation.'

Our current spectators included Kayla; she watched our exchange with an unhealthy degree of curiosity. I waved her off as she began making kissy faces. You'd think the events of the previous evening would dampen her enthusiasm, but if death itself had not tampered with her carefree attitude, then the torture of lost souls would hardly sober any form of frivolity.

As Sebastian and I left the camp, it became clear that all the souls chose not to linger on previous events. Jonas busied himself tending the outer ring of fires, laughing and joking as if nothing had happened. Eve was bundled in a hut with a couple of children, telling stories with a biblical note—perhaps therapeutic in its own way. Jocelyn—the older woman—sat alone by the fire, a smile on her face while her fingers absently stroked the scarf around her neck. I suspected she was thinking about her husband Clive; a thought I was happy to nurse as we walked on by.

The sun was nestled safely in the sky where Sebastian had left it. Its rays reached far and wide, spreading a fan of dappled light through the canopy of trees and warming the forest floor at our feet. Darkness was absent. Even shadows dared not linger. I wondered how long it would last.

'What are you thinking?' Sebastian asked, perhaps noticing the pensive look on my face.

'I was wondering when the darkness would return.'

'Eventually, but the night will wait its turn while Samael licks his wounds.'

I shot him a sideways look, lips twitching with amusement. 'Being the Archangel has its perks?'

'Sometimes.'

'So, you finally admit you're an angel?'

'Had we not established this?

'You've alluded and I've certainly hinted, but you've never actually said *yes, Elena, I am the archangel Michael.* We agreed to discuss everything after the war, but then—'

'And you agreed not to get hurt or killed, but you lied and hid your true intentions!' He was angry with me again. Typical. I hadn't planned on dying—no one does. Rather than be ecstatic we had a week to explore our crazy relationship, he opted to criticise. Who needs parents with Sebastian around?

'Do you honestly think I planned all this?'

'I think you've made a grave error in judgment. Don't get me wrong, I am beside myself to see you again, but being here does not necessarily mean good things for you.'

I could hardly argue. I was dead. 'I don't regret my decision, but I never said I could avoid any of war's influences—especially death!'

'Of course you'd have an excuse,' he muttered under his breath. 'I should have known you'd get yourself in trouble again.'

'Don't mock me, Sebastian—if that's even what I'm supposed to call you ... *Michael.*'

'You know my name.'

'I have a few names for you right now. Which one should I use first?'

Sebastian sighed, drawing us to a stop. 'Why must we always end up in a fight?'

'It's only a fight because you argue back. Otherwise, it's just me stating facts.'

'Elena ...'

'Don't *Elena* me. My decisions are my own and this time I made the right one whether you agree or not and I don't care if you decide to use your halo like a discus to remove my head because I'll still find a way to get back up and state my damn case!'

He clucked his tongue in contemplation, brushed a hand through his shoulder length hair and then finally looked back at me. The anger in his eyes had melted away and in its place was a touch of humour. 'Use my halo as a discus? Really?'

I shrugged. I was still too mad to enter into playful banter.

'Fine,' he conceded after unsuccessfully half-glaring, half-smiling at me for several charged moments. 'I will no longer argue, but you still shouldn't be here.'

'And you shouldn't have gotten yourself killed. You ruined everything.'

'It was my time, Elena.'

'What a crock of shit. Despite your true identity, we were both supernatural. We were going to live for eternity.'

Sebastian reached out to stroke the side of my face. 'I'm assuming your death was at Julius's hand?' He was deflecting.

'Does it really matter?'

Julius had been one of Lucius's thralls, introduced to vampirism some two thousand years ago. He'd tried to turn his own wife too and coincidentally created a crazed killer. Lucius had taken action. He'd killed Julius's wife and then attempted to kill Julius, unaware that a thrall could not die from conventional methods due to self-healing. It had been early days and the rules of vampirism had not yet been fully realised. Now Julius was a sworn enemy, determined to kill anyone or anything that Lucius personally held dear. That included Sebastian and especially me.

It was irrelevant now who'd slain me. I'd made the choice, wanting to see Sebastian one last time and would not have been dissuaded by anyone. Death was simply the path I had to tread in order to get here.

'I know that Julius killed *you*,' I stated, 'but how did he know that human blood—the blood of an innocent—would kill you?'

Sebastian shrugged, seemingly unconcerned by the logistics of a leak in the angelic community. He'd told me the truth about his only method of existence when pretending to be a vampire, but I hadn't revealed Sebastian's weakness to anyone. 'It doesn't matter anymore. What matters is why you are here. Araqiel promised to watch over you.'

'I chose to die.'

'A reckless decision.' Outrage was making a reappearance in his eyes. 'You do not get any more chances, Elena. Lucius has been your father in every lifetime and in this one he is a vampire with an unending existence. Lucifer made certain that he cannot die or be released from his vampiric soul until he decides otherwise, hence, no more you!'

'Sebastian, you're not telling me anything I don't already know.'

'Then why would you do it?'

'I think you know why.'

He simmered down, shoulders slumping as he sat on the edge of a fallen tree log. Its surface was covered in moss, undoubtedly damp and uncomfortable, but it appeared to be the least of his concerns.

A stubborn lock of dark hair fell in front of his eye as he looked up at me. He didn't attempt to move it, knowing my fingers would skim his cheek and tuck the strand behind his ear. And, as I did so, he pulled me close. His gaze filled with so many conflicting emotions it hurt to look upon him. 'Please don't tell me that you died to be with me.'

'Okay,' I murmured. 'I won't.'

'Elena?'

'You said you didn't want to know, so let's keep it that way.'

'Elena …'

I groaned. 'My reputation will be shot if I keep talking.'

'Elena …'

'Will you stop it?'

'I need to know.'

'Why? So, you can hear me openly admit that I chose death because the thought of being without you was—' My breath was lodged somewhere in the middle of my constricted throat, knees suddenly weak and barely able to support my weight. It was unexpected to feel so much longing for one person, to know that I would literally do anything for them—even die.

'Elena, please finish what you were saying.'

'Do I have to?'

His fingers dug into my hips, a small growl erupting from his throat; not exactly a threat, but a clear indication he was over my stalling. I'd morphed into a walking contradiction. I constantly demanded the truth from him, but was disinclined to reveal the deepest of my secrets. So, I forced myself to finish, glad that his hands held me so tight. I was certain to fall down without the support.

'I … um … well … I …'

'Yes?'

'Sebastian … I … um … I guess what I'm trying to say is, that being without you … it would be …'

'Yes, Elena?'

'Stop interrupting!'

'I'm sorry.' He wasn't. I could tell by the tightness in his jaw that he was biting down on his amusement.

I pointed a shaky finger, attempting to remain stern. 'You're just lucky that living without you is worse than death itself.'

His smile was effervescent. 'Now was that so hard to admit?'

'What?'

'Nothing.' He buried his face against my stomach, hugging me close. I was still frowning; positive the admission was centred more on cracking my shell than admonishing my reasons for coming to Purgatory. 'Never the easy road for us, is it?'

'No challenge, I suppose.'

'With one more challenge ahead, do you think that now—in this place—you can finally admit what we are to each other?' He was peeking up at me now, testing my resolve.

'Can you?' I absently stroked the top of his head. I wasn't trying to pick a fight, but rather, wondering if one week in this place would be enough to explore our love given the fact we were both too stubborn to say it!

'Yes.'

'So out with it.'

He watched me from beneath the long strands of his silky hair. His lips were suddenly moving and words erupted, but they were all in Italian. Nothing I understood.

I shoved him away, annoyed. 'Seriously, Sebastian? You're supposed to be the adult between the two of us. I would have thought my affections were perfectly clear. I just died to be with you again. That says something, don't you think?'

'So, you *do* love me?'

'What are you, a puppy? Of course I do, you idiot.'

The hasty smile on his face was enough to eclipse the brightness of the sun. It even dampened all impulse to be annoyed by his constant deflection. Perhaps now that I'd ripped open my chest, shoved my heart in his hand and more or less said *don't break it*, something had changed within me too.

So, there I stood, arms now folded across my chest while I kicked at a pine cone as I smiled back at the goofy grin on his face. I really was in love. I was good and ruined for any decent form of rationality from my head ever again. I was now ruled by the very thing I'd spent a long time denying I had—a heart.

Shit.

Sebastian jumped to his feet, quickly re-guiding his arms around me, supercilious smile still planted on his features. I knew what was going to happen even before his lips touched mine. We were going to kiss, but this would be different. This kiss would say everything that our words never could. This kiss would be the one that forever bound us.

My fingers sought the soft hair at his nape, eyes locked on the silver depths forever enticing. He found the curve of my spine, moving us so close that no breath could pass between us. Our lips parted with expectation and were just as quickly united, melding together as one and moving with a love so desperate tears sprung to my eyes.

Coherent thought ebbed. All that remained was the tingling of my skin, the warmth that flushed my face and the sensation of his touch. We moved together like we fit; we were two pieces of a puzzle finally reunited. I was home.

Heat flooded parts of me I never knew existed, a fire I was willing to let burn. Sebastian drank from my lips like he'd never sampled anything finer—nibbling, teasing, tasting. When we finally parted, we were both panting like zoo animals, drunk from the elixir of our love and eager for more.

I steadied myself in his arms, knees weak and legs trembling. How could I have ever thought I would be better off alone?

'I've waited a long time for that,' Sebastian murmured, easing us backward until he was sitting on the fallen log again, me perched on his lap.

I half-smiled, half-frowned. 'We've kissed before.'

He shook his head. 'Not like that.'

I agreed so I didn't debate logistics. 'I'm sorry you're here, Sebastian. I forgot all about Julius. I never expected him to immerse himself in our war.'

'I was always coming back to Purgatory. It was just a question of *when*.'

'I was too busy hunting Roshan.'

'Did you kill him?'

I nodded, climbing from his lap to settle myself onto the log beside him. 'Lucas and I hunted him together. I knew Roshan wouldn't immediately run if he detected Lucas's scent. I also knew Lucas would protect me better than everyone else.'

'That's not true.'

I smiled, nudging his shoulder with my own. 'You know what I mean.'

'So, the wolf howling that I heard. Was that you?'

'Yeah, I managed to shape-shift and chase after Roshan. It wasn't a pretty end, but it had to be done. The last alpha had to be destroyed to stop the production of more vânătors.'

'Except the last vânător wasn't destroyed …'

I shot him a wry look. 'She is now.'

Sebastian wrapped an arm around my shoulder and pulled me close. 'I'm sorry that you died, Elena.'

'I'm not.'

'Well you should be.'

'No. Now I have some time to spend with you before judgment.'

'The bird came to you?'

'Yes, though I suppose we only have six days left now that you sped up the night.'

'Do you regret me doing that?' he asked, studying my face for a reaction.

'Of course not,' I responded vehemently. 'I had no idea what happened here at night. I was beginning to think I was in way over my head.'

Sebastian squeezed my shoulder. 'This place is supposed to be neutral. Samael has been taking liberties in my absence.'

'Sebastian, you've been absent for over two thousand years.'

'I know.'

'That's a long time for the souls here to be abused. Don't the other council members have any say?'

'Nakir and Munkar—angelic though they may be—are lesser angels. They lack the fortitude required to stamp down Samael and Mammon's bad habits.'

'And now that you're back?'

'Things will change.'

'For the better?'

Sebastian released my shoulder, arm slumping back to his side. 'I'd like to say so, but Lucifer will ensure they both hound me nonstop. I may not always have the energy to help those that cannot help themselves.'

'What do you mean?'

'Lucifer wants a rematch.'

'Whoa, wait a second,' I said, hands motioning time-out. 'Can he get in here?'

Sebastian shook his head, his whole façade sagging as if the weight of the entire world rested on his shoulders. 'No. It's my choice to re-issue the challenge between us, but until I do, the Demons will harass me and those trying to find peace here until I do.'

'So, the stories I read in Lucius's library about you are true?'

Sebastian's eyes were full of sadness, regret and a hint of something else I couldn't quite place. 'I *am* the Archangel Michael.'

'You've beaten him before. You'll beat him again.'

'It's not that simple, Elena.'

'Why not?'

'Because I chose to fall from grace. I don't have the same powers I was once endowed with.'

'Because of me.'

'Yes and no.'

I felt guilty about something I had no control over, so I stood and began to pace, arms folded in front of my chest, allowing my mind to wander dangerously. 'Why would you give it all up when you already had everything?'

Sebastian stood, collected both my hands in his and made me reluctantly stop. 'I didn't have you.'

I was at a loss. 'Have I really brought you that much happiness? In this life we've known one another only a few months and already so much has happened and gone wrong. Not to mention inadvertently getting you killed!'

'And I'd do it again.'

'But to forsake heaven and its perks for me? You must be crazy.'

He smiled, squeezing my fingers. 'No, not crazy, Elena. I made a choice. I served heaven for many thousands of years. I stopped the Apocalypse and I sent my brother to hell. Our father didn't mind me having a little something for myself.'

'So, this was an approved plan?'

'Once an angel starts to feel, they aren't really much good in their post anymore. To be an angel is to be objective. When I saw you for the first time, I could no longer think clearly about anything else. I had to fall because you changed me.'

'I'm starting to feel really bad about that.'

He laughed now, eyes sparkling with mirth instead of sadness. 'Don't be. I'm not.'

'But now you're stuck in Purgatory!'

'A small price to pay for thirteen thousand years with you.'

I studied his face carefully, eyes narrowing. 'Makes me think I have a lot to prove in the next six days.'

He chuckled again, but didn't answer, kissing the end of my nose instead. He slowly released my hands and glanced around, drawing my attention to the surrounding forest. 'Despite the Demons, it's actually nice here most of the time.'

'You mean when souls aren't being molested?'

His frown was as fleeting as my comment. There was no escaping the reality of this place, but it also wasn't at the forefront of my mind.

'Sebastian, will you be with me when I'm judged?'

'If the council allows an audience.'

I nodded, though I hoped I could count on his support, even if it was just his presence. 'Do you think I'm going to hell?'

'No, of course not.' His expression was neutral—unreadable.

'You sound adamant even though you know what I am.' I waited for him to say something—anything, but as silence ensued, I carried on. 'The bird said I had some options if a hung vote occurs, but Lucius also said I'm spawn of Satan, therefore damned. They may all agree on that.'

Sebastian took the longest time to make comment. So much so, that I grew uncomfortable under the weight of his questioning gaze. 'Elena, there are things that even you don't know about yourself. Just because you are Lucius's daughter—born of the master vampire and tainted by the seed of a vânător—does not mean you deserve an unending existence in hell.'

'I've done a lot of bad things, Sebastian.'

'All of them in self-defence.'

'Not true. Sometimes I enjoyed killing vânători. When I slaughtered Roshan's den in Paris, I don't remember executing it, but I know I woke up satisfied.'

'That's not your fault.'

'Oh yeah? What about when I almost tore out your throat? I wanted to kill you, Sebastian. In my wolf mind, you were against me and everything I stood for.'

'The council will take everything under careful consideration.'

'That's not an answer.'

'Then just trust me when I say that you will not go to hell.'

'How can you possibly know that?' I said, exasperated.

'Because part of you is pure, Elena.'

'Are you referring to my virginity?'

Shock was suddenly etched upon Sebastian's features. 'Um, no, I wasn't.'

'Oh.' I felt like a right git. 'I just thought—'

'It's not about your sexual status; it's about your soul, Elena.'

'Of course it is.'

'But if you'd like to discuss—'

'No.'

He now smirked, averting his eyes from my growing discomfort. 'Another time perhaps.'

We were both silent for several minutes; me locked in the embarrassment of my own mouth's urge to spew forth unnecessary information, him lost to his own thoughts.

'What's it like to be an angel?' I finally asked, breaking the uncomfortable pause.

Quiet contemplation was upon him. 'I'm not sure I can describe it. It's not like any human experience.'

'Okay, then what was it like … falling?'

He shrugged, crossing his arms over his chest. 'It was … exciting. I was diving into the unknown, given a chance to live life as it is done on earth. I'd observed for so many years, always living apart from it, but when I finally reached out and grasped it, it was almost surreal.'

'It must have been hard to choose to become a vampire.'

'It's had its moments.'

'You've had to kill people.' I posed it as a statement rather than a question, knowing the answer to be true. To have lived with my father as a part of his coven for over two thousand years was to be entangled in vampiric affairs.

'Never without cause and never the innocent.'

'Does your father Tiberius know what you are?'

Sebastian shook his head, lips twitching. 'He's always been as curious as everyone else, but never questioned me. I think some part of him knew I had a greater purpose. I was human for more than the eighteen years. A born vampire would have undergone the change by the time I realised that Lucius was your father and that his wife had been murdered with you inside her. If I hadn't have turned, I would have grown old and died, but then it occurred to me that Lucius could impregnate someone anew, giving you another chance at life. But since he'd already made my father a thrall which consequently changed the possibility of my own rebirth, I had no choice but to become like them.'

'So, one day you simply decided that you'll become a vampire?'

'Something like that. It's partly why Lucius has never quite trusted me. He still questions my father about it; how did I turn without the blood of another vampire or if I'd been given it, who was responsible?'

'He probably knows by now.'

A wry look was passed in my direction. 'Well, you did tell just about everyone I know.'

'I don't think anyone believed you were an angel for a second. Even now I still almost choke on the thought of it.'

'Why?' Genuinely curious, he stood, head cocked to the side, eyes questioning.

'You're Sebastian Marcellus, head tracker for the Vampires and burdened with the reputation of a serial bed-hopper.'

'I thought I explained my interludes with other vampires?'

'No one knew that in order to survive you had to drink vampire blood and avoid slurping on the innocent. Thus, everyone just thought you were a big old slut.'

'Elena!'

'What? I'm just saying.'

He turned away, contemplating the scenery again. 'What do you suppose is happening right now?'

57

'What, back on earth?'

'Yes.'

I shrugged. 'Nothing good. When I left, I'd only just killed Roshan and the human army was closing in. Vampires and werewolves were being gunned down. I didn't have a chance to really try and communicate with the packs so they probably went rogue. And as for Lucius and Lucas, they're probably fussing over us.'

'You predict anarchy?'

'How can I not?' Gloominess took up residence in my heart. 'Too many humans now know we exist and Karina and Lucas's magic can't hide what has happened.'

'We both have such poor timing.'

'I agree.'

'Then what are we going to do about it?'

'What can we do? We're both dead. At least I'm confident that Lucas will do everything in his power to bring The Protectors to justice.'

'Do you still believe that The Protectors divided us and pit the Vânătors against us?'

'What does it matter now?' I said, frowning. 'All we can do is hope that humans find acceptance, The Protectors are made to pay for their crimes and that Lucas and my father find some way to wrangle the remaining vânătors.'

'And Julius?'

'He got what he wanted—revenge.'

'So, all that's left is the here and now,' Sebastian murmured, slowing turning and taking my hand in his.

'I guess so.'

'What do you want to do first?'

An open-ended question if ever I'd heard one. 'Surprise me.'

Sebastian smiled, leaning forward until his lips touched mine. 'Remember you said that, Elena.'

'Then you better make it good. Nothing really surprises me anymore.'

'Well then hold on tight. You won't want to miss this.'

CHAPTER FOUR: LAKELANDS

The thought of screaming seemed to come naturally; a true desire to open my throat as wide as it would go and exhaust my lungs of oxygen and my vocal cords of sound. But I was made of tougher stuff, recently thrown off the Ley-Lines by a supposed angel moonlighting as my earthly support. I was almost certain I could handle *this*.

I closed my eyes, my fragile mind under the impression that if you couldn't see, then it wasn't happening—an understandably naive approach considering recent events, but an adopted process here in Purgatory.

I'm not so great with heights, but since I was now wrapped up in the arms of a flying vampire—who thought getting vertical would be a fun new way to spend time together—meant that I had to get my shit together. It was irrelevant that I was solely focused on the probable and almost certain, sudden stop at the bottom claiming my unlife. And—though his seductive voice whispered not-so-innocent suggestions as we flew high above the clouds—I remained unmoved. In fact, I was seriously considering knifing him the moment my feet touched solid ground.

Belated talk of murder aside, the view—when I did manage to sneak a peek—was amazing. Purgatory was a mass of contradictions; many different worlds converged with little effort at all. Snow-capped ridges touched desert sands and forests melded into water-based cities. Weird and wonderful animals caressed the landscape below and birds with weird humanoid faces and spider shaped legs dominated the skies.

I was impressed, if not a little creeped out by the talking wildlife that fluttered past. That aside, flying aimlessly was rather freeing, but being *freaked out* held me firmly by the short and curlies. I mean, I had faith in Sebastian. He was an archangel and trusted soldier of heaven, but he was also a really dead vampire that was upwardly mobile without a set of wings.

Maybe it was wrong to doubt the ex-archangel for lack of feather, but even aircrafts have wings—a fundamental rule of aerodynamics. On earth, the Vampires and vânătors jump and traverse the landscape hundreds of meters at a time or leap buildings in a single bound, but this was a defiance of gravity. I had to assume that either Sebastian had had one hell of a running start or had an invisible jet-pack shoved up his ass.

Stop button?

Someone please push it.

'You're so tense,' Sebastian murmured, wrapping his arms tighter still. I tried not to consider the possibility that his grip needed resolidifying this high above the horizon.

'Well, several kilometres between solid ground and unbreathable airspace will do that to me.'

'Elena you're already dead. You can't die again.'

'Said the dead vampire reincarnation of an archangel to the half-breed telekinetic human vampire who recently *died*. Do you seriously believe that anything's certain anymore?'

He chuckled, kissing the top of my head. 'Where would you like to stop?'

'Now.'

'I said *where*, not *when*.'

'Over water. I'd like options on the landing if you're going to balls it up.'

'Elena ...'

'*Sebastian*,' I mimicked in a sarcastic tone. 'I'm just not comfortable with this. I'd really like it if you just got my ass back down on solid ground.'

'You would make a terrible angel.'

'On account of my justifiable fear of flying without a parachute?'

His chest rumbled under my cheek. 'No.'

'Then what?'

'Your unending need to curse.'

I gave an indignant snort. I had the perfect rebuttal, but he'd never been a fan of my potty-mouth, so I kept it to my colourful self. 'So where are you taking me anyway?'

'My favourite place in Purgatory—the Lakelands.'

'What's so special about the Lakelands?'

'The calming sound of the running water and the view from my window.'

'Window?' I asked, curious. Purgatory appeared built upon a transient population of souls, no one ever staying long enough to set up permanent residence. Although, flying over the Desert Lands proved me wrong with canvas tents pegged into the shifting sands. In the forests where Kayla resided, they'd built makeshift huts and bunkered down by the fires. In the snow I'd seen souls lingering in the jutting caves that marked the cliffs. I supposed it wasn't impossible to think that those that did linger would want a little piece of normalcy.

'So, you've created a place for yourself, a peaceful place where you wait out my next reincarnation with you?'

'Yes.'

'Does that happen a lot?'

'Reincarnation?'

I snorted. 'No. Do the souls often build themselves homes?'

'Some. It's largely dependent on their judgement.'

'Go figure ... a booming property market in Purgatory.'

'Not exactly.'

The roar of the river below grew louder as Sebastian began his descent. I risked a peek; gushing water and jagged rocks were abundant and undoubtedly out to get me. Waves crashed against them almost violently, their gleaming points beckoning for impalement. 'Are we there yet?'

'Nearly.'

'Hurry up and put me down.'

I screamed as Sebastian let go. I rapidly slid down his chest, grappling for his wrist and holding on for dear life as we flew over the water below. 'What are you doing?' I yelled up at him.

'You said to put you down.'

'Not here you fuc—'

The bastard let me go. Now I was certain that Araqiel and Sebastian were related.

Irrationality took over as I hurtled towards the rushing water. I'd faced Samael and had my heart ripped out. I'd killed vânätors and I'd maimed vampires. Hell, I'd gotten up to a lot of serious shit, but memories of the past can be debilitating and for

61

some reason, the memory of being impaled to a tree by a vânător late last year was still as fresh as a newborn baby.

I cracked the surface of the water, my back slapping the swirling membrane under a badly executed landing. Torrential water rushed all around, cold arms stealing an embrace. Surprisingly it didn't hurt, but shocked the hell out of me, stealing breath. The good news was that the rocks remained motionless. No crazy barnacle fingers reached through the water to slice up my limbs. The bad news; the water was sticky like honey, the same as the creek I'd encountered yesterday. It was like trying to swim in glue, impossible and ultimately pointless.

My head went under and the gelatinous water closed in all around me. It poured down my open mouth, sweet and favourable to my tastebuds. I swallowed, wondering if they'd find me in centuries to come, trapped like a mosquito in amber tree sap. Would I ever resurface?

My foot hit the bottom and I quickly used the hardened surface to kick back towards air. I suppose I didn't specifically need the oxygen, hence instead of trying to hold my breath, I'd been sampling the sweet nectar of the river, gulping it down like my life depended on it. A voice in my head kept telling me it was good for my skin and a fantastic accompaniment with cornflakes. Go figure?

Cool air quickly touched the surface of my skin as I finally burst through the surface. The sticky substance rolled off my skin like oil, leaving my face and hair surprisingly clean and dry. Since the rest of me was still immersed, I used my tongue like a paddle; my arms and legs were completely ineffectual.

When that also remained a pointless exercise, I started drinking the water again. I figured eventually I'd drink the last drop, the river would be empty and I'd be able to walk back to shore.

What if I just stayed here? What if I build a little water house and make friends with sea horses and hang star fish from my ears?

'Elena?'

'Hey, Babycakes,' I slurred. 'What are you doing over there?'

Sebastian shook his head, laughing quietly to himself. 'Babycakes? Okay, you must have drunk the water. Why don't you come out now, I want to show you something.'

'Ooh, that sounds promising. Are you going to leave your clothes on?' I started to laugh, rolling awkwardly in the water until I was mostly looking up at the sky. 'Do you think if I fart right now the bubbles will make me float?'

More laughing. 'Okay, okay. Stay where you are. I'm coming to get you. Clearly you're way past helping yourself.'

'Don't forget to wear your shoes on your hands.'

'Why?' Sebastian asked, dubious about a serious response.

'Because you already have socks on your feet.' I tried to tilt my head forward and after much splashing and turning again, I finally saw my own feet just below the surface. 'Wait. I have socks and shoes on my feet too. Wow. My hands think my feet are really greedy right now.'

'*Right.*'

I heard splashing behind me, chunks of water spewing up and landing on top of my face. I sucked it down where it landed close to my lips, revelling in the sweet taste and warm fuzzy feeling in my head.

'Elena, stop drinking the water!'

'Make me ...' I giggled, disappearing under the water so I could drink some more. I farted too. I really wanted to know if the bubbles would make me float.

They didn't.

Sebastian grabbed me roughly by the wrists, dragging me backwards through the water until my face was no longer submerged and the water grew shallow. My head bumped the back of a mossy rock as I was hauled across the sandy river bank and onto the pebbles of the shore. 'Are you okay?'

I gazed up at him, smiling. 'Do you wanna see my boobs?'

What had been concern on Sebastian's face quickly ebbed in lieu of the grin he fought to contain. He attempted to focus instead on lifting me into his arms. Clearly walking was not an option. 'Is that better?'

'I have nice boobs,' I giggled, voice still slurred.

Sebastian smiled. 'I know.'

'Did you know that I have two? One for the left side and one for the right.'

'Really?' Sebastian said, undoubtedly humouring my drunken stupor.

I nodded vigorously. 'Oh yes. Two; one for each hand. Do you think God did that on purpose? I mean he made socks and shoes to keep your feet happy. Do you suppose he made boobs to keep your hands happy?'

'I would think so,' Sebastian chuckled, now moving us towards a small dwelling etched into the side of the rocky cliff face adjacent to the river.

'Are your hands lonely, Babycakes?'

'Very.'

'Okay, then when we get where we're going you can touch my elbows too. I have one left one and one right one. I suspect they get lonely at the back of my arms.' I started to frown, suddenly most upset. 'You know, come to think of it, I never look at them all the way back there. Do you suppose they're pissed off at me for ignoring them?'

'No, Elena.'

'Promise?'

'Promise.'

'Okay then. You can touch them too. No *grabbies* though. I don't think my boobs would like that.'

'Okay, Elena.'

'And can you leave my pants on? I haven't had a chance to—'

I was out like a light half way through that sentence. It was just as well. I was about to give him a run down on my lack of weed-whacking in the nether regions. I really did need to find that censor button of mine.

Oh, and to stay away from the water …

*   *   *

I came to feeling pretty groggy, but otherwise okay. Attempting to sit up meant that I banged my head on a hanging homemade lantern, but the pain was temporary—just like Purgatory. Moving around it, I turned my focus upon my crusted eyelids, rubbing them vigorously and yawning profusely.

As the room slowly came into focus, I realised it was drawing close to dusk again, the night evidently soon upon us. How much time had passed and why the hell had I been sleeping, especially in a place that had no need for it?

The last thing I remembered with any degree of clarity was Sebastian and I flying over Purgatory and his ill-fated decision to drop me into the—

Oh shit, the water ...

I climbed the rest of the way out of the bed, marvelling at the height between the bed and floor and thankful my eyes were now fully adjusted to the dim light. The bed—like the rest of the immediate vicinity—was carved from rock. All aspects of the hardened bed base were softened by animal furs—warm compared to the cool air inside the room. I knew this had to be Sebastian's abode, specifically his bedroom. Though nothing personal adorned the walls or screamed his personal influence, I knew it was his. My fingers skimmed the smooth stone of the marble walls knowing that his hands had touched this place.

'Elena?' I turned as he appeared in the doorway, hands tucked casually in his pockets. 'How are you feeling?'

'Fine.'

'Are you sure?'

'Hey, I'm sorry I drank the water.'

He smiled, a lock of dark hair falling in front of his eye. 'Don't worry about it. You didn't know.'

Ah huh, sure.

'Are the clothes okay?'

'Clothes?'

He gestured to my body. I looked down for the first time since waking, studying the outfit he'd retrofitted me with; a short, white and extremely tight strapless sundress paired with bare feet and messy hair hanging loose around my shoulders. 'Seriously? This is what you see me in?'

'It's what you asked for.'

'Why would I ask to wear a condom?'

Sebastian bit back his laughter. 'I seem to recall you saying something about easy access.'

Mortified, I snapped the top of the dress open to search for a bra. Finding nothing to greet me, I slapped a hand against my butt feeling for a panty line. There was none.

Jesus ...

'Don't worry,' Sebastian said smirking, 'I can assure you the only thing I saw or touched were your elbows.'

'What?'

65

He shook his head. 'Never mind. Why don't I give you a minute to rustle up some new clothes and I'll meet you in the other room.' He was gone before I even had a chance to reply.

A few moments later I wandered into the adjoining room. It took only a second of thoughts to swap out the body bandage for underwear, denim shorts and a cotton t-shirt. Now more suitably dressed, the first thing that greeted me was a massive window; a view of the sandy banks of the river outside and the rushing water as it toppled over slippery rocks and hurried downstream was a welcome sight. Beyond that, cliffs rose above and beyond, creating a sheltered alcove for Sebastian's lower abode.

I ambled over to the window ledge and peered higher above. Cut-out residences in the cliffs above were built on-mass and dull lights flickered inside representing other souls who'd chosen a continued existence in Purgatory. I was a little sad for them. This was it for them, an unlife unending in a place where beauty existed, but horror happily hunted the delivered.

'Do you like it?' Sebastian asked, moving behind me, his breath warm on my neck.

'It is beautiful here, there's no denying that ...'

'But?'

I shook my head to close the conversation. There was no way I wanted to remind him that spending eternity in a place with lost souls and little possibility of change was depressing. Unless— of course—he took on Lucifer again. 'Nothing,' I said, turning my megawatt smile on.

'Are you sure?'

I gestured to the furs spread across the centre of the floor; any other furniture or adornments either recently stolen or never retro-fitted. It was a golden opportunity for a subject change too. 'What were you doing before I woke up?'

'Just laying around, waiting for you.'

'What do you usually do when I'm not here?'

'Pretty much the same thing.'

I snorted, hoping to inject some humour into an otherwise sad little thought. 'Sebastian, you need hobbies.'

He chuckled, nodding his head in agreement. He finally tucked his stray lock of hair behind his ear and motioned to the rugs. 'Shall we?'

'Shall we what?'

'Sit. Talk.'

Sit and talk? An interesting notion.

In truth, we didn't do much talking. I skimmed over the details regarding my search for Lucas and my shape-shifting. He spent time adequately revealing our past lives and his angelic one, knowing they were answers I had sought for a while. But after an hour of watching his lips move, I started to realise that the past wasn't nearly as important as our present. With limited time, I stopped worrying about the space in between and started focusing on the chemistry that always drew us together in *every* life.

So, I Practically launched myself at him. I figured being demure was silly after months of denying what we both truly wanted. After all, we'd spent thousands of years happily wrapped in each other's arms. What's a little death between soul mates?

Sebastian didn't do much protesting. Angel or vampire, he was still male and his lips seemed pretty eager about consoling mine and putting conversation to rest. I swear we rolled all over that rug for hours, our lips pressed together and our hands full of misadventure. I was already starting to remember some of my earlier offerings, embarrassed, but equally pleased that neither of us were lonely anymore.

'Elena?'

'Yeah?' I murmured, rolling around in his arms so I could look up at him.

'I love you.'

I grinned. 'Thanks, Babycakes.'

He laughed, his forehead touching mine a second before he leant further down to nibble on my lower lip. 'Starting to remember some of the finer details of your Purgatory drinking experience, are we?'

'I don't know what you're talking about.'

'Ah huh.'

'You don't believe me?' I said, grin broadening until my cheeks hurt and his teeth became a little more insistent in their pursuit.

'Never.'

'Where's the love?'

'I'm about to show you.'

I slammed my palms against his chest in jest, attempting to push him away without much success. I suppose that by entangling my legs with his I was giving mixed messages. 'Just because you broke out the big guns with the love stuff doesn't mean you're getting laid tonight.'

He bit my lip harder, drawing an excited breath and chuckle from deep within. His silver eyes glowed as he crept up my body, looking proud as punch that he could incite such a response from his teeth alone. 'What else are we going to do until the wee hours of the morning?'

'Play checkers.'

'No.'

'Monopoly?'

He practically whimpered. 'Elena, have mercy, it's been over two thousand years—you're killing me.'

'Oh, that's a good one.'

'Seriously.'

I laughed. 'Sebastian, we have time and I have things I need to consider.'

'You can't get pregnant in Purgatory,' he blurted, the desperation not quite disguised within his voice.

I frowned. 'Thanks for the head's up, but what's the rush?'

'Six days left and two thousand years without.' He pressed himself harder against me to reiterate his point. 'And six days and nights will not be long enough to be with you.'

I felt myself blushing, imagining the possibilities of such a marathon. I'd read about them, just never quite imagined myself naked and horizontal with Sebastian and a number plastered across my back. I shook the image away. 'I don't even know what to say to that.'

'Don't say anything,' he murmured, drawing close once again, his lips resuming earlier trails, his tongue darting out to stroke the skin of my neck. Encouraged by the murmurs of delight I tried to keep to myself, he followed the curve of my neck until he reached the hollow in my throat. 'Just close your eyes, Elena and feel what we've been denied for so very long.'

I swallowed what felt like a golf ball, eyelids fluttering as his mouth dipped lower, his tongue eager in its exploration. I knew I should have been thinking about this, considering the prospect of savouring my virtue for a moment not pressed by urgency, but with

Sebastian I was held captive, drowning in desire and the press of his skin against mine. What the hell was I waiting for anyway? Candles and a ceremony? A sacrificial lamb?

'Fall into me, Elena,' he murmured against my skin, fingers already collecting the material of my shirt and pushing it up higher and higher.

I grabbed his searching hands, lifting my head to look down at him. 'Two thousand years and that's the best *give up your virginity* line you come out with? Sebastian, you really need to—'

A scream halted my words.

Sebastian swore, the first real guttural cussing I'd ever heard him utter. I waited for him to be struck down by lightening or something equally impressive, but perhaps he'd been hanging around me too long and 'shitballs' was acceptable under certain *strained* circumstances. 'You've got to be kidding me.'

I blew out a resigned breath, equally annoyed by the interruption. 'The working day never ends for the almighty, does it?'

Sebastian shot me a stern look. 'This has really ruined my night.'

'Those darned tortured souls,' I muttered sarcastically, smiling to lighten the mood. 'I told you that you weren't getting laid tonight.'

'This is not a funny moment, Elena.'

I snickered anyway, trying to not think too hard about what might be going on in the darkness beyond. 'Come on, help me up so we can go and sort this thing out.'

He pulled me to my feet, but held me close. 'You think I'm letting you confront Samael and his demons again?'

I shoved him back, quickly settling my hands on my hips and giving him the look that the comment deserved. 'Do you think you really have a say?'

He groaned, running a hand through his tousled hair. 'Come on,' he said, taking my hand in his again, 'stubborn to the very end, we'll go and put Samael back in his box, but when we come back—'

'We'll talk.'

'Talk?'

'Yeah, you're going to tell me about this arrangement with Lucifer and his minions so we can organise a better existence for you here. We can't do this every night—you can't do this every night.'

'Agreed.'

'Then we're going to talk about the subject we've both been avoiding.'

His face fell flat. 'And that would be?'

'My judgement.'

'Why?'

'I need to …' *Figure out how to save you.* 'I need to know a couple of things.'

He turned away, jaw clenching. 'This is not what I had planned for tonight.'

'Aw, come on, Sebastian.'

'What?'

He looked so adorably cranky and petulant that I couldn't help the giggle that escaped my lips. I stood on my tip toes so I could kiss the side of his stubborn lips and wrap my arms around his waist. 'Good things come to those that wait.'

Sebastian looked down at his crotch in dismay and then right back at me, eyes pleading.

This time I laughed harder, squeezing him as tight as I could, the love inside me practically bursting through my skin and pouring into his. 'Come on. Let's go and kick that asshole's butt again so that you don't have to spend another night here as the two-thousand-year-old virgin.'

'Are you trying to make me feel better?'

'Yes.'

'It's not working.'

CHAPTER FIVE: EARTH

Lucas rolled over, arm slipping off the edge of the cot and hitting the cold concrete floor below. The rough surface grazed his fingertips, the frigidity slowly rousing him from slumber. His eyes flew open when the texture changed. Warm and wet, he knew his fingers were being appreciated by the vânător that slept at his feet.

He stretched and reached blindly until those sodden fingertips now brushed the matted fur at the vânător's snout, extending further until he was met with the lusciously soft fur of his head and ears. The vânător rumbled his approval, nails clinking against the concrete as he shuffled closer, Lucas's hand now running down his back and massaging his spine.

'Morning, Toby,' Lucas murmured, rolling again until he could see over the edge of the cot.

The vânător barked his reply, moving hurriedly onto his back until Lucas was patting his belly instead.

'I can't believe I'm patting you. In approximately five minutes you'll be human and we'll be having a very *different* conversation over breakfast.'

Toby barked his approval, easing back to his paws to commence the change. He didn't need to be human. He was quite content remaining in wolf form, but it was easier to communicate with the Vampires using vocal cords rather than growls and barks. Not that Lucas was a vampire like the others. In fact, he was something completely different—something more.

Lucas was a Protector, born to two Protector parents— George and Susan Manory. As far as Toby knew, Lucas hadn't seen his parents in over ten years, especially since he'd uncovered the hand they had in his transformation. Once an ordinary Protector— powers based on the magical spells learnt during adolescence— Lucas was now something more. His blood had been synthesised with Elena's when they were children, her bite the catalyst to future change. Now Lucas was immortal, forever eighteen and endowed

71

with telekinesis just as powerful as Elena's and almost as proficient as the master vampire. He still wielded the spells of the Protectors, only now you couldn't see them coming. Lucas was the most powerful Protector in existence—if only that made a difference. The war had changed everything, the world was never going to be the same and the Protectors had seen to that when they aligned with the Vânătors to see the downfall of all vampires.

Toby straightened, the last bone snapping and quickly reforming, making him human once more. Fur dissolved and the pink tinge of human skin manifested, his fangs dissipating as the mouth reformed and lips shaped themselves over neat white teeth. He moved his lips, getting used to the feel of his tongue trying to shape words that were foreign to a wolf. 'S-sorry I licked you,' he said, shaking his head until he finally felt settled.

Lucas slapped the side of his leg, rolling over in the cot again until he was flat on his back. 'I'm getting used to it.'

'It's hard to separate myself from wolf tendencies.'

Lucas smiled. 'You haven't eaten me yet, I'm pretty damn grateful about that.'

Toby pulled a face of disgust. 'I don't eat Protectors.'

'I'm not just a protector, am I?'

'No, but just because some sweetness of vampire has been thrown in, doesn't mean you're going to taste any better.'

'I'm glad to hear it.'

Toby bent down, gathering the clothes he set aside the night before. He slipped them on quickly, knowing that humans and vampires didn't appreciate the werewolf's wry appreciation for the naked form. Clothes seemed excessive when already paired with a skin suit borrowed from the taste of human flesh and blood.

Lucas sighed, throwing an arm over the top of his face. 'I don't think I'm ever going to get used to this.'

'Used to what?' Toby said, buttoning the last of his shirt.

'The world gone to shit, The Protectors running just about every major corporation left on the planet and the Vânătors making nice with the Vampires.'

'We aren't all nice.'

'No, I suppose not.'

Most of the Vânătors had dispersed when the guns came rolling in. Humans hunted the easy targets, focusing on the wolves they'd believed problematic in France not more than a few weeks before the war had broken out. Vampires had compulsion to help pave the way through the societal breakdown. All the wolves had was the ability to shape-shift, probably the only thing that had saved them thus far.

The wolves that fled still fed and pillaged those they came across; survival their only thought, consequences be damned. There were others like Toby that fought for integration, understanding that the world was changing and acceptance from those powerful enough to save them was a necessity. With every alpha now destroyed, the Vânătors were an endangered species, death coming quickly to those that chose not to assimilate.

When Toby had met Sebastian Marcellus and his vampiric brother William Granville just before the war, they had given him the option to hide, to find as many of his kin as he could and distance himself from the pending war. But later, when hope was lost and humans began hunting them to near extinction, Toby had sought out the vampire that had tried to help him. He'd met Lucas instead, the first Protector that had tried to understand him rather than kill him. They'd been friends for over six years now, though Toby was often saddened by the thought that he would never be able to thank the vampire Sebastian for his kindness at the beginning and giving him a chance to live. He'd later discovered he'd been killed during the war, his younger brother William surviving him.

'I'm going to find something to eat. You want anything?'

Lucas didn't move, his arm still draped across his eyes. 'Coffee, but I doubt you'll be able to find me any of that here.'

'I could rustle up a rat?'

Lucas's lips twitched, a wry smile forming. 'How many times do I have to tell you, Toby? I may be a freak, but this freak does not like the taste of blood.'

'Fine. Then I'll cook you up the meat once I've drained a few.'

'Great. Rat for breakfast *again*.'

'Oh, stop complaining,' Marianne teased as she rounded the corner. 'It's not like we don't try to find you something decent to eat around here.'

Lucas shifted his arm, rolling his head to the side until Marianne was clearly within his sights. He had no idea how she did it, but every day that went by she seemed to grow more and more beautiful. He crooked a finger at her. 'Come here.'

'I'll leave you two alone,' Toby said, bowing his head and leaving the room as quickly as possible. He passed the scary blonde vampire, noting how her sapphire eyes tracked his every movement—calculating and always watchful—dubious of the lack of nefarious intentions of others around her lover.

When the dank corner of the passage was clear, Lucas shot forward, grabbing at Marianne's hand and pulled her down onto the cot with him. She squealed with delight, laughing as he rolled them both over until he was positioned above her. 'Morning.'

'I hate that you still have to sleep,' she complained, as she nibbled at the skin of his neck. 'We could have so much more fun.'

'Well, I'm awake now,' he answered with a grin, leaning down and claiming her lips with his own.

Her hands slid down his back, tracing eager patterns across his skin until she reached his hips, her fingers slipping around until she found the zipper on his jeans. 'Do we have time?'

Lucas groaned, feeling her cold fingers slip through the confines of fabric that separated them. 'I don't know, but I'm willing to make some.'

'Who are you kidding?' Caleb laughed from the other passage intersection. 'It'll all be over in a minute. You could do it twice and still have time!'

Lucas and Marianne groaned in unison, Lucas collapsing on top of her and burying his face in her neck. 'Do you ever get the feeling we'll never have any privacy?'

Marianne wrapped her legs around his hips and resumed stroking his back. 'With all the Vampires and some vânători left in Italy now living in these old tunnel systems, I think it's safe to assume that you and I might have to get a little more creative with our free time.'

Lucas started kissing a slow trail from her neck down to the top of her cleavage. 'Free time is so hard to come by.'

'It is,' she panted, gripping his shoulders tightly and pushing him further down.

'I can still hear you!' Caleb shouted.

Lucas grunted, slapping his hand against the edge of the cot.

'Don't you have a spell to make him disappear?'

Lucas grinned as he sat up slowly, looking down at the bulge in his pants. 'I think I'd have trouble concentrating right now.'

Marianne giggled, grabbing at his pants in an effort to pull him back down again. 'Then think of something to give us some privacy.'

'Can't … concentrate,' Lucas reiterated, watching as her long slim legs wrapped themselves around him, her heels digging into his butt in effort to drive him back into her arms.

'Lucas!'

'Shit!' Lucas shouted, punching the edge of the cot again. 'What is with everyone's timing this morning?'

'Lucas!'

'Yeah, I'll be there in a minute!' he yelled back at William.

Marianne was all smiles. 'Just think, it's going to be great sex when we finally get some alone time again.'

'It'll be quick!' Caleb shouted back, somewhere from the corridor beyond.

'Can everyone just shut up?' Lucas pleaded. He climbed off the cot, staring back at the love of his life with absolute regret. It had been over three weeks since he'd buried himself in her arms, felt her naked skin beneath his. He really needed to come up with a solution to this endless disruption to their privacy—and fast.

Lucas sighed heavily, turning his back on Marianne and her perfect skin and seductive lips. He needed to focus on getting rid of his arousal, not encouraging it. As it was, the smell of her essence swam across the surface of his flesh—citrus sorbet—a beckoning sweetness that almost made him turn around and succumb to her wiles.

'What do you suppose William wants now?' she said, sounding equally irritated. It was sweet relief for Lucas to hear that tone in her voice. For the longest time she had been in love with William, even categorically hating Elena for her initial infatuation and his response to her. Things were different now. Marianne was in love with Lucas and William was interested in another.

'I don't know,' Lucas answered. 'Has there been any change with Elena?'

'No,' Marianne murmured. 'I looked in on her myself about an hour ago.'

Lucas fell silent, thinking of his sister's lifeless body in the other room. She had died during the war. Her death and the one who caused it was still a complete mystery. Her body had been saved, transformed by Lucius's bite and blood transference, but her soul was gone. It had been just over ten years and she was still absent. The lights were on, but nobody was home. 'Do you think she'll ever wake up?'

'I don't know,' Marianne said, coming up behind him and wrapping her arms around him. 'I hope so.'

'I thought you hated her.'

'That was before I realised what it meant to fight for the one you really love. I thought I was in love with William, but until I met you, I never knew what it was like to really pray that it was reciprocated. I understand now that she was also just searching for the same thing.'

Lucas patted her hand. 'Do you think she found it, wherever she is?'

'I'd like to think so.'

'I think she's with Sebastian now.'

'What makes you say that?'

Lucas entwined his fingers with hers and pulled her gently behind him. She followed obediently into the next room. Caleb— the Goth vampire that had befriended Elena in the past—sat vigilant on a chair by her side, flipping through a magazine. He looked up as they entered, smiling at them slyly, wiggling his eyebrows with loaded connotation. 'Look,' Lucas said, ignoring Caleb and drawing Marianne closer. 'She's smiling now.'

Marianne gripped the edge of the cot, studying Elena's face. She was so beautiful now. She had always been attractive when she was human, but now, as a vampire, her skin was like cream, her long, dark hair shiny and framing her face like a silken cape. Her eyes—though fixed pointedly at the ceiling and empty of life—glowed as if a light had been switched on behind them. An unusual combination of both green and brown, they swirled together like a kaleidoscope, framed by eyelashes that were long and plentiful.

She *was* smiling. Her lovely pink lips were moist, twisted into the most beautiful and contended smile that Marianne had ever seen, assuring her that wherever she was, Elena was currently happy.

'I miss her smell,' Caleb said, running a hand through his spiked pink and blonde hair. 'She used to smell so edible. Now she smells like Lucius and your pet dog.'

'Don't bring Toby into this,' Lucas chided. 'He's helped unite the Vânătors and the Vampires once more. It wasn't so long ago that the Wolves and the Vampires were companions. It was your blood and arrogance that turned them against us.'

'Okay, pipe down,' Caleb muttered, patting Lucas's shoulder. 'I was just saying that I miss Elena too. She was my friend, you know.'

Lucas nodded. 'I know, I'm sorry.'

'Smiling must be a good sign.'

Caleb nudged Lucas in the ribs with an elbow. 'Well, if she has found Sebastian—wherever they are—I suspect he's doing *everything* in his power to make her smile like *that*.'

'Caleb, you're such a pervert,' Marianne admonished, brandishing him with a filthy look. 'Have you got nothing better to do?'

'Sure. I just choose to watch over her.'

'And I appreciate that,' Lucas interrupted. 'Julius is still out there somewhere.'

'We haven't heard from him since the war,' Marianne said, squeezing his hand. 'It's likely that he's dead.'

Lucas shrugged. 'Maybe, but I appreciate Caleb's vigilance. Every vampire and vânător has access to these tunnels now, some may still have an agenda.'

'The Vânătors will not hurt her,' Toby said from behind them. They all spun around, eyeing his blood-stained lips and skewered rats in his hand. 'Elena is our alpha. She is the last of our leaders. No one will ever hurt her. We will all die to protect her.'

'You never said anything,' Lucas said, stepping forward and taking one of the cooked skewered rats from Toby's outstretched hands.

'You never asked.'

Lucas frowned, taking a bite out of the rat's back. Gross, but choices were slim these days.

'Lucas!'

Lucas closed his eyes, chewed, took a calming breath and then swallowed as he opened his eyes again. 'He's not going to leave me alone, is he?'

Marianne and Caleb grinned, shaking their heads. 'He takes the protection of her very seriously.'

Lucas rolled his eyes. 'You'd think I was the bloody vampire mediator around here. Let me through.' He edged around Toby, patting him on the back and handing him back the half-eaten rat.

'Do you want me to come?'

'No, Toby. This will just be about Karina wanting to go outside again.'

'You'd think after Lucius gave him permission to turn her that he would have settled down knowing that she was virtually unbreakable,' Caleb muttered.

'She's still turned, therefore vulnerable to death,' Marianne answered.

Lucas left them debating William's rationalisations. He often forgot that Karina was a trained Protector like himself. On top of that, she was now a vampire. She was strong, fast and immortal until death claimed her either by silver or sunlight. She could die numerous other ways, bullets, knives, fire, drowning— but so could Lucas. Immortality for them was about living on borrowed time. They both wanted to make the most of it while it lasted.

Lucas passed a couple of vampires in the tunnels on his way to finding William. He knew just about everyone by name now. They'd stopped trying to feed off him a long time ago, realising his powers exceeded their own. He may not have been as strong or as fast, but his reflexes were as sharp as they came, his magical and telekinetic defences hard to beat.

'Lucas!'

'Yeah, yeah, I'm coming.'

'Will you stop bringing him into it?' Karina barked as he rounded the corner. 'It's not fair.'

'Lucas,' William said low and evenly, his face twisted in anger. 'Will you kindly tell Karina that going outside is a very bad idea.'

'Mate, she's been inside for two weeks.'

William's nostrils flared. 'Do I not bring you blood? Am I not enough to keep you entertained?'

'I just want some air!' Karina snarled. She settled her hands on her slim hips, tossing the long mane of jet-black hair over her shoulders. Her green eyes glowed with anger, her usually pouty lips thinned into a vicious line.

Lucas slapped a hand against his forehead, his back hitting the concrete walls a second before he sunk to the ground. 'I can't believe you two have dragged me into another one of your fights. William, you do remember she is a vampire, don't you?'

'I don't care! It's madness outside. You know that, Lucas.'

Karina was one of the Protector children he had grown up with back in Cairns. She'd also been instrumental in getting him captured during an attempted fight when bunking with the Protectors in Antarctica ten years earlier. She'd felt so unbelievably bad that she ended up being the one to also help him escape said capture, consequently surrendering her to the mercy of the Vampires and making her an outcast to all Protector clans.

'She's got cabin fever. She just needs to go out for a bit.'

'So, you're siding with her again?'

'This isn't about sides. Karina's an adult; she has been for a while now. I know you love her, but keeping her caged up is only going to drive her away.'

William's jaw clenched and then released. He studied Karina's wilful pose, his eyes narrowing on the determination set by her mouth alone. 'I don't want you to get hurt.'

Karina softened, her hands dropping to her sides. 'I know that, baby, but I need to get out.'

'Can I come with you?'

She closed the gap between them, vampiric speed putting them instantly in one another's arms. 'I wouldn't want it any other way.'

Lucas evacuated the area once the kissing began. They had the most volatile relationship of anyone he knew, but for some reason it worked. Lucas honestly thought that Elena had given William a hard time during the early years of initial courtship. Karina gave her a run for her money. They fought all the time, but their passion for one another was somehow fuelled by aggression and an endless need to be suffocated by the other's presence. Ironically, William had met his match in Karina. There was no way Elena would ever have been so compromising.

'Lucas,' William shouted after him. 'We'll go topside in about five.'

'Yeah, yeah. Some of us might as well get some action around here,' he mumbled under his breath.

'I heard that!' Karina hurtled at his back.

'Whatever.'

Lucas found Lucius in the main tunnel. There were loiterers everywhere, the noise of so much talking echoing off the barren walls. Wolves that were yet to change stalked among the Vampires, graciously accepting pats where possible. Others who'd already shape-shifted were gearing up for another night out, scavenging for food as the rest of them did.

To put confusion to rest, Lucas had become accustomed to sleeping the day away and waking at dusk. All supernatural entities found the sunlight uncomfortable—the Vânǎtors and any turned vampires deathly allergic. Lucas and Lucius were the only ones immune to the sun's effects—definitely an advantage. Lucius was the devil's creation, not permitted to die at any cost. Lucas was something else entirely, though he'd grown used to serving the night's agenda.

'Morning, Lucas.'

'Morning, Lucius.'

'Any change in Elena?'

Lucas nodded, tucking his hands into his pockets. 'Before I went to bed, I noticed she was smiling.'

Lucius's eyebrow rose marginally. 'Is she now?'

'I don't know what's happening with her soul right now, but it can't be bad.'

'No, it cannot.' He turned, directing orders to those that had begun to overcrowd the main junction. The wolves he sent into the night, ordering them to wait for Toby for direction. The Vampires interested in going topside he made them wait in the adjoining passage for Lucas and the others to join them.

'Are you expecting something to go wrong tonight?'

Lucius turned a dim smile on his face. 'I hope not, Lucas, but times are tough for us. The Protectors hunt us more than ever before and the humans give them whatever they want, seeing them as saviours of their race. Even with all my powers, they are defunct against thousands of Protectors.'

'I bet the humans don't know they're being farmed.'

'If they do, they don't live for long. It's why they live in the super cities. It keeps them separated from us and any influence we might have over media outlets.'

'No,' Lucas said, shaking his head. 'They keep us separated because they want us to starve to death. They know, that even with all of the farming lands, orchards and deserted supermarkets left in the abandoned cities, blood is the only thing that all of you need in order to *survive*.'

'In the end I fear that we might be the only ones to remain, Lucas. I cannot die and you are the only one of us that can live off the land.'

'We'll figure this out eventually, Lucius.'

'When? There are so few of us left. Contact with other cities is almost non-existent. We have no way of knowing how many of us are left and making more vampires is pointless without the blood we need to survive.'

'Then we need to survive until we figure out how to beat the Protectors and that starts by going top side and finding what we can to feed on, yes?'

'Yes.'

Lucas turned, stopped only by Lucius's hand on his shoulder. 'What is it, Lucius?'

'I need to tell you something.'

Lucas turned slowly, suspicious by this change in demeanour. 'What?'

'Thank you.'

'What for?'

'For being the strength that I needed when Elena …' He swallowed. 'You remind me so much of the son I lost so many years ago. I think perhaps he would have been just like you if he'd had his chance to mature.' Lucius turned away. 'I just need a minute. I'll meet you topside soon, you know what to do.'

Lucas nodded, shocked by Lucius's admission. They'd got on just fine since their initial meeting on the day of Elena's death, but there had never been any defining emotions between them. The two of them co-existed; a common purpose to survive, united by Elena's blood. Now Lucius was comparing him to a son he'd lost some two thousand years ago, before he'd become a vampire. Lucas was honoured, but confused. Sentimentality was not Lucius's strong point. Was it an omen for what might happen tonight?

He shook it off. He couldn't let himself doubt his abilities when the world outside was more dangerous than the hundreds of fanged supernatural entities he surrounded himself with daily. The war had ravaged town after town, city after city, turning people against people and everyone against the Vampires and vânätors. What lay beyond was a barren wasteland of everything the world used to be. History marked the two world wars as devastating. It was nothing compared to the wrath of frightened humans wielding weapons of mass destruction in an attempt to kill them all.

Milan had been ground zero, levelled within hours, buildings burning to the ground and centuries of history lost. As vampires and vânätors fled, the humans pursued, annihilating anything in their path to serve self-preservation. Transport had been cut, every special-ops team with acronyms for names was called in. Soon every country was involved and firing missiles at one another without thought or consequence.

Now, what everyone called the super cities was all anyone could call home—anyone human. They were walled prisons fuelled by magic and powered by The Protectors. They were designed to keep the rest of us out, but Lucas knew the truth. They were keeping the Humans in; the pretence of safety the word on everyone's lips.

The serum had finally been perfected. Initially manufactured from Elena's blood, the idea was to empower the Protectors, endowing them with the strength and the immortality of the Vampires. Blood lust supposedly a myth, no one factored in Elena's vânätor half and assumed that a connection to the Vânätors might have been an advantage. With the entire Protector population now infected, they craved blood. A drawback that had been unproven during initial testing.

Lucas couldn't help but pity the Humans. He'd been one long enough to identify with their need to cling to salvation. The Protectors had stepped in as a powerful body of willing support, offering what appeared to be ingenious technology to keep some of the major cities safe. Magic was the backbone of every trapping, but humans were willing to accept it as science if it meant keeping the Supernaturals at a distance. Only Lucas and a few others had witnessed the true transformation of the Protectors. They didn't often leave the cities, but when they did, you knew you were being hunted, marked and then delivered as a sacrifice of triumph to fuel the Human's beliefs.

The world was all kinds of messed up when the Vampires and werewolves were the good guys.

How the tables had turned.

Lucas bobbed his head in acknowledgement to William as he rounded the corner of the junction, Karina gluttonous with satisfaction at his side as she looked longingly at the escape hatch. Most of the Vampires were already gathered, dressed dark to blend in with the shadows, talons and fangs at the ready in case they were ambushed. 'Is everyone ready?' Lucas asked.

'We are.'

'Okay, let's go.' Lucas climbed the steel ladder first, inching slowly to the top. He listened for sounds coming from above, settled only by the sound of the wind.

'I hear nothing to worry about,' William said from behind, knowing that Lucas didn't have the hearing of a vampire and would appreciate the follow up check.

'Thanks.'

'You're welcome.'

Lucas reached the top of the ladder, studying the well-sealed hatch. Only the strength of a vampire or vânător could manually budge it, but with a few spells under his belt, Lucas was just as competent. Unfortunately, if the Protectors ever discovered the visitor tunnels Lucius had once used to greet vampires at his villa, no spell would keep them out for long.

The steel groaned as Lucas used the power of his mind to move the hatch; cool air from above rushed into the underground tunnel systems as a preview of what was to come. The heavy-set garbage bin used to hide the opening was also pushed free via telekinesis, allowing Lucas—and the others—access above ground.

He emerged ever-cautious, searching each direction for signs of hunters. It used to be the Humans that came after them brandishing weapons. Now it was the Protectors, fearful of letting even one drop of human blood end up in vampiric hands.

Lucas climbed the rest of the way out of the tunnel, still watching the night for danger. Everything was quiet in the alley. The rooftops were absent of predators, the streets typically deserted and filled with the decaying leftovers of a once thriving metropolitan city. Rome was now host to nature itself, the burnt offerings of buildings and crumbled homes a breeding ground for animals and plant life.

'I smell deer,' William murmured, emerging from the tunnel and sniffing at the air. 'It's close too.'

'That's good. How many will it feed?'

'One deer will only feed two or three of us fully.'

'Shit.'

William patted Lucas's shoulder and then bent down to help pull Karina out. 'Don't worry, I smell quite a few.'

'I miss Synth blood,' Karina complained. 'The Protectors weren't using their heads when they burnt the place to the ground, were they?'

Lucas touched the blackened building next to him. The old walls of Synth Corp still stood proud, but anything of use inside had been burned beyond recognition long ago. Lucius had tried to recreate what was lost, but he still needed human and animal blood donations in order to synthesize any form of substitute. But without the right filters, machinery, additives and the synthetic plasma compound, recreating it was a bust.

'We'll have some deer soon,' William answered her. 'Can you smell it?'

She nodded, helping the next vampire out of the hole. 'Yeah, it's close.'

'I'm worried the Vânătors are going to smell that too,' William added.

'Toby won't mess things up,' Lucas said. 'He knows what's at stake.'

'I know you like your pet wolves, Lucas, but this is serious. The Vânătors are still attracted to our blood. When food starts to get a little too thin and they are starving, who do you think they are going to feed off?'

Lucas shrugged. 'Let's cross that bridge when we get to it.'

'It's alright for you,' one of the other vamps said, plucking an opened tin of Spam from the garbage bin and pitching it at Lucas. 'You can still find food that won't try to eat you.'

'Can I?' Lucas answered angrily, throwing it back. 'It's been three years since the Protectors started raiding every town they come across, bringing food back to the cities for the Humans. I eat where I can—just like you.'

'You're also most likely to survive.'

'Yet I still climb up here nearly every night helping to hunt food for *you*. Don't make out that this isn't dangerous for me. My body might have stopped aging, but I'm no different to the Vânãtors or the turned vampires. I can still die a human death.'

The vampire had the good grace to look embarrassed. 'I'm sorry, I didn't—'

'Think?' Karina answered. 'I may be a vampire now, but I'm still a Protector like Lucas. You're lucky we both care enough to want to stay and help.'

'Are you expecting a thank you?'

'Enough of this,' Lucas muttered. 'Let's stay on topic and find those deer.'

'Agreed,' a couple of other vampires murmured.

Lucas let William take the lead—the Vampires in toe. Their sense of smell was keener for tracking blood. They moved fast—faster than Lucas's feet could actually move without assistance He often relied on levitation spells to propel him forward above ground. Magic was the only thing that kept his pace even with the fast-moving vampires.

Tonight, they darted backwards and forwards across deserted highways and back alleys, moving between abandoned buildings and crumbling residences. The Vampires operated on instinct alone, following their sense of smell in the hopes it would lead them to satiating their thirst. It was a method that more often than not worked.

Just up ahead, nibbling at grass tufts that grew in the enormous potholes on the side of the street were about four or five deer. They remained oblivious to the predators slowly closing in. William was at the front, emerald eyes eager and focused on the prize. He faltered only for a moment, his nostrils flaring, his eyes now darting back and forth.

Lucas looked around, sensing tension from the other vampires. He could not see far in the darkness, only the deer in the street and the closest buildings. Something was wrong, body language said as much.

His eyes flicked back to the deer, their heads snapping upright, senses on alert. A growl could be heard, guttural and unexpected in the stillness. William cursed, the sound lost among the sudden scampering of claws on pavement and the growls of the Vânãtor hunting party.

The deer attempted to run, caught seconds later by the sharp teeth and uncompromising claws of hungry wolves. Snapping snouts and tearing flesh broke the stillness, the Vampires attempting to charge in and claim portions of their own.

'They're taking the food!' some of them screamed.

'Wait!' Lucas shouted, using telekinesis to slap a protective barrier around Karina and William, the only two vampires still within distance who were attempting to intervene. They rebounded off the particle shield, landing against the ground, stunned and annoyed by the interception.

'What are you doing?' Karina shouted at him.

'Look!' Lucas pointed skyward, sensing the buzz of energy from those he had once called kin. He used the barrier to pull Karina and William back further, hiding them in the shadows and closer to his own hidden position.

Lights from above made him squint, shielding his eyes from the sudden brightness. The Protector's hunting vehicles hovered above the ground, magic the propulsion. They were sleek and shiny, equipped with silver laden weapons—all they would need to bring down any and all members of the undead.

The Vânători—too hungry to be fearful—continued their attack on the deer, renting and tearing, oblivious to the death that came their way. Lucas wanted to help. Toby was not among the wolves, but some of them were his kin, born from the same alpha. The Protectors surrounded them. The Vampires who'd charged in now also caught in the spotlight.

Lucas moved closer to Karina and William. A hunting vehicle was in range, close enough that they could bring it down if they worked together. The other two vehicles concentrated on the feeding members, circling in anticipation. Some of the Vampires knew they were in trouble, jumping or running in the opposite direction before spells could be hurtled to slow their escape. The Vânători fell victim to the Protector's magic, growing still and silent as the Hevannatara curse took effect.

Living statues now scattered the street, immediately gunned down by the weapons strapped to the hoods of the hunting vehicles—precious blood painting the pavement.

Lucas concentrated; the hunting vehicles were circling, spotlights searching for more prey. Street debris was not rare after the war, always something telekinetically at hand to use as a weapon. Lucas didn't need debris. The vehicles themselves were easily manipulated.

He focused on the hulls—shiny and sleek in appearance— he imagined them flimsy like foil. He saw the hood crumpling on one; inch-by-inch metal peeled back towards the cockpit, the driver trapped like a sardine in a can. The screams were brief, the Protector in question using strength and magic to save him. In the end, Lucas was fast, his mind clever and practiced—death was swift.

Some of the Vampires returned, hearing screams of pain they immediately attacked the second vehicle, jumping onto the hull and tearing the cockpit apart. Lucas didn't watch, his attention now diverted to the craft hovering not more than a few feet above their position.

William growled, lips pulled back in anger, fangs ready and talons already slashing at the underside of the vehicle. Karina followed suit, clawing angrily at the metal, watching it peel away like a knife through butter.

The Protector inside was good. Karina was hit with the Light of Mellar and temporarily blinded—useless in her cause. William was better at evasion, ducking and weaving to avoid magical entrapment, but he was distracted by Karina's dilemma, now useless in his pursuit of attack.

Lucas focused on containing the craft, his own magic battled by the Protector inside. They were strong and very good, but no Protector could ever match Lucas's abilities.

The Protector faltered, clawing at her throat as Lucas encased her in a telekinetic bubble, closing the thread of air particles and cutting off oxygen. They ripped off their helmet, a sprawl of honey-coloured hair bouncing around her shoulders. Powder-blue eyes, intense and filled with fear

looked back at him. It had been a long time since he'd seen those eyes. It had been even longer since anyone could break his concentration.

The barrier shattered and air came racing back. She gasped, coughing profusely until she found herself again. Her hands left her throat, pushing back the voluminous hair, her eyes narrowing, recognition present. She didn't move any further. She just sat there, the screams of her dying kin fading into the background. 'Lucas?' she croaked.

Lucas clucked his tongue and buried his hands in his pockets. At first, he thought all speech would evade him in light of this shock, but then something came over him. There was indifference for the woman who hadn't lifted a finger to change his fate or save humanity. 'Hi mum,' he finally said, tone droll. 'It's been a while, hasn't it?'

CHAPTER SIX: INDIFFERENCE

Willliam stopped scratching at the bottom of the hull, staggering backwards until he could take in the view of the Protector he had once thought was both honest and decent—Lucas's mother. He noticed the spill of her blonde hair first followed by the blue eyes bulging with shock and simultaneous relief. She had eyes only for her son who looked back at her in equal bouts of disbelief, despite his indifferent demeanour.

'I can't believe it's you,' she croaked, rubbing her fingers over her throat. 'You don't know how long I've searched for you.'

Lucas snorted his incredulity. 'Please, it's been over ten years. You expect me to believe you've been looking for me?'

William grabbed Karina around the waist as he edged closer to Lucas. She stumbled into his arms, awaiting her vision to return after being afflicted with the Light of Mellar spell. 'Is that Susan?' she whispered to him.

William kissed the side of her cheek chastely, eyes fixed on the floating hunting craft above and The Protector still encased within it. 'It is.'

'Lucas, I assure you,' Susan continued, voice weary and deflated, 'I've been looking for you since you left Antarctica.'

'And before that?' Lucas questioned, folding his arms across his chest. He was angry now. William could see it in the set of his jaw and the rigid tension riding his shoulders. Even the surviving vampires and vânători from the fray kept their distance, well aware of Lucas's powers should he decide to lash out at those around him. He'd been in moods like this before, anger fuelled by Protectors decimating friends and followers of the coven during the war's aftermath. Needless to say, the colosseum no longer existed.

That had been the day Thomas Woodland was killed—
William's best friend, Marianne's brother and Lucas's closest
vampire companion.

'Before that?' Susan echoed in confusion. 'What do you
mean *before that?*'

Lucas scoffed. 'When you, dad and Chester petitioned
Karina to ambush me and send me packing to the science lab! You
know, I could have gotten past the fact that you filled my body
with Elena's blood when we were younger, hoping it might save
my life from her bite, but now, as an adult, I can't forgive or forget
you trying to hold me prisoner and experimenting on me!'

Karina shrunk back further into William's arms. He held
her close, knowing that even after ten years guilt still rode her. She
had betrayed Lucas then, preying on his vulnerabilities and over-
active hormones to keep him prisoner at the IMI. But realising The
Protector's true intent, she had consequently abandoned her father
and disbanded everything she had ever known to make up for the
betrayal. She had repented enough as far as William was concerned.

'Experimenting on you?' Susan said, the same supercilious
look of confusion etched on her features. 'I'm not sure I know
what you're talking about.'

Lucas shook his head, fingers curling into tight fists at his
side. The metal of his mother's craft soon groaned, slowly folding
in on itself, his anger manifesting as the most indescribable torment
possible.

Not quite sure what was happening, she scrambled around
in the cockpit, trying to pry herself loose of the paraphernalia
holding her captive. 'Lucas, help me!' she cried. 'My strength
counts for nothing! What is happening?' She continued to press at
the metal closing in all around her and though her palms left
indentations, the hunting craft still advanced on her personal space,
seemingly insensitive in her pursuit for life.

'How could you not know?' Lucas muttered, turning his
back on her. 'How could you not know that dad and Chester
drugged me and shackled me to a gurney for three weeks straight?'

Karina—vision now restored—reached out and touched
his arm, an attempt to stop him from crushing his own mother
with his mind and regretting it later. 'It was George and Chester
who approached me, Lucas. Susan may not have known their
intentions.'

90

Lucas looked down at the delicate fingers brushing his arm with concern. He wanted to pry them loose and tell everyone to shove it, but in truth, he'd stopped blaming Karina long ago. She'd suffered as much as he had over the years and given up much. The only blame left was reserved for those who were supposed to protect him from harm—his parents.

'Look at me, Lucas,' Susan shouted as she clawed at the twisting metal around her. 'I didn't know! I thought you ran away the day you came to our bunk and we told you about the serum and Elena's blood in your veins. I thought you really had run away and I've been looking for you ever since!'

'Bullshit.'

'It's the truth!'

Karina's grip tightened on his arm, bruising in her grip. 'I think she might be telling the truth, Lucas.'

This time he did shrug her away, twisting back to look at his mother's face for evidence. He expected to see fear, imminent death playing a role in her plea for deliverance, but what he saw was raw emotion. Her eyes shone with bloodied tears not only marking her as a changed being, but a woman overcome by her emotion. She wasn't fearful of death, she searched for acceptance—she searched for forgiveness. Was it an act? Lucas didn't know, but his heart swelled with an emotion he'd long since shelved as possible, accepting that his parents were the past and that wrongs would never be righted, that this life as an outcast and a hunted being was the only future to expect.

Stricken by the prospect of yet another loss, he released the hunting vehicle from his mindful grip, letting it crash to the street with his mother inside. He wasn't sure he believed the sincerity in her eyes, but he wasn't quite willing to kill her yet either.

The remaining vampires and vânători started closing in. They may have lost their appetite for blood after the slaughter, but they never lost their desire to kill the enemy that constantly opposed their existence. But Lucas was already walking away, leaving her fate in the hands of someone else, determined to sort through this unexpected knot around his heart.

'Wait,' Karina shouted, jumping to Susan's defence before the renting and tearing could begin. 'Don't harm her, she may be useful.'

Susan seemed to notice Karina for the first time, eyes narrowing as she took in her altered appearance—in particular—the black talons that now slashed at the cockpit in an effort to free her from the bonds of twisted metal. 'You're a vampire.'

Karina shot her a wry look. 'And now so are you thanks to a little genetic altering courtesy of Elena's blood. Are you proud I've managed to join the club?'

Susan pursed her lips at Karina's sarcastic tone. 'If you were so opposed to what we stood for and what we were hoping to achieve, then why did you become one of them?'

Karina looked back at William, smiling as he moved in beside her and wound an arm around her slender waist. 'Love. I am what I am not because of some dream to conquer the world and live forever. I became a vampire because I couldn't bear the thought of ever living without *him*.'

William leant down and gently kissed her lips, brushing her hair behind her ears as he finally looked back at Susan's surprised face. 'Not all of us fight for domination.'

Susan studied their faces a moment longer, finally shaking her head. 'You do realise your father was devastated that you left the IMI, Karina.'

'It wasn't an easy choice,' she said, leaning back down to slash at the metal again. 'But it was easier than letting Lucas rot in a laboratory.'

Susan flinched. 'I honestly didn't know. If I had … I …'

'I believe you,' Karina murmured, 'but it may take a bit to convince Lucas. It took him years to forgive me for my role in his change.'

'How could I have not known? George told me he left the same day he discovered the serum's intent.' She shook her head. 'After he left our bunk I kept staring at the back of the door, thinking he would come back. After a few hours I went looking for him, sure that he would have changed his mind at the futility of trying to escape, but I couldn't find him.'

'Did you try the labs?' Karina muttered, slashing at the last piece of metal that pinned Susan's legs. She freed herself, carefully extricating herself from the craft, ever watchful of the Vampires and vânători that hissed and growled at her.

'I've never had the need to go into that area of the IMI.'

'Well, clearly you should have and then maybe you would have noticed that Lucas was handcuffed to a gurney, drugged and pumped with bag after bag of Elena's blood.'

Susan stared past Karina's sarcastic expression, focusing on Lucas's retreating back. 'How different is he? I can see he hasn't aged. That's our fault, isn't it?'

'He's still Lucas,' Karina said, stepping into her field of vision, 'but yes, your secrets and lies have changed him. He's harder now—not as forgiving.'

'And his powers?'

William slapped a hand across Karina's mouth before she could speak. 'I think we've answered enough of your questions,' he said, slowly easing his hand away again as Karina nodded her understanding. 'We have some questions of our own.'

'Do you think I'm leaving this city now that I know my son is here?'

William smiled, flashing his canines at her. 'Did you really think we were letting *you* leave this city now that you *do* know that Lucas is here?'

'Touché.'

William stepped forward, edging his way closer to Susan, the surrounding vampires and vânători forming a tight circle of defence should the need arise.

'What are you doing?' she asked, tension now clear in her voice.

'I must ask you, the serum has enabled self-healing, has it not?' he probed, watching as her eyes followed his every movement, tracking him with a speed borrowed and concocted from Elena's blood.

Her eyebrow rose suspiciously. 'Why?'

'Answer the question.'

'Tell me more about my son.'

William shrugged. 'Okay, have it your way, but knowing would have been infinitely better for you.'

'Why?'

'Because this is really going to hurt.'

*   *   *

Susan came to with a start, cursing when she realised her predicament. She was captive. One vampire and two vânătors kept watch and Lucas was nowhere to be seen. Thanks to the serum's properties, her face did not sing with the expected pain that a vampire's fist would usually incur. Her skin was unblemished, but her ego wounded. She was angry with herself for allowing her hunting party to be decimated and not able to circumvent capture. She was even more aggrieved that after ten years of looking for Lucas he did not emanate her sweet relief to be reunited.

She looked around, studying the concrete walls surrounding her. Though moss gathered in the cracks and water dribbled in crumbled sections, she knew it was too thick to break through. Pressing her ear against its rough surface only confirmed the depth in which it was poured, faintly hearing connecting rooms or passages adjacent. It also didn't help that there were three, very angry looking Supernaturals watching her every movement. Eventually she might have been able to sneak past a sleeping vânător, but a vampire? They never slept unless they so desired. She could perhaps take them on in a fight, but three against one? No amount of serum would help her bounce back from that.

'Where is my son?'

The three Supernaturals just looked at her. There wasn't even a twitching of lips to suggest that one of them would answer. How odd it was to see them united, standing side-by-side and tracking her movements. In the past, it had been The Protectors and vampires in alliance, now they were opposed because of the war and the serum. The Protectors had wanted to dominate all species and the war had allowed them the time to do it. But what had they really won in the end? Most of the world's cities were reduced to rubble and they were all slowly fading.

Humans were an endangered species.

'I want to see my son.'

Still they ignored her. What was it going to take?

'Lucas!' she screamed at the top of her lungs. 'Lucas, where are you?' Her voice echoed around the tunnel walls. Any faint noise she had heard before dimmed at the sound of her voice. There was no doubt that she had been heard, though undoubtedly and conveniently ignored. Surely someone—if not Lucas himself—would be here soon. They would eventually tire of her screaming his name, her voice a persistent torment through this dirtied sewer they now called home. But in the end who would they send and would they keep her alive long enough for her to gain Lucas's trust?

She was beginning to doubt it.

CHAPTER SEVEN: AWAKEN

I stumbled through Sebastian's front door in the Lakelands, the soft glow of morning's light streaming through the hand-carved window of the front room, warming the stone at my feet.

I wiggled my toes on its surface, drunk with not the water's narcotic effect, but with the gluttonous pride of victory. We'd spent the night hunting Samael and his demons; this time Sebastian actually allowed me the freedom to kick ass without consequence. I let sixteen years of pent up aggression towards the IMI, my father and every other little thing that had pissed me off, take control of my body and unleash it on the unsuspecting.

Samael didn't know what had hit him. The archangel Michael and his soul mate had been hell-bent on making his night a misery. I think we succeeded. The Demons were back in their sulphurous depths for the day and the souls of Purgatory were free to wander the night without fear. It was a small victory and one I would relish for now; the picture of Samael licking his wounds enlarging the smile on my lips.

'Still gloating,' Sebastian murmured against my ear as he pulled my back against his chest, kicking the door shut behind him.

'We did good,' I mused, leaning into his warm embrace. 'And thanks for not holding me back. I really enjoyed taking my frustrations out on those creepy monkey things.'

'I have frustrations of my own,' he said, kissing the curve of my neck as he walked us over to the hides still covering the middle of the floor. He pulled us down, his arms still cocooning me against his chest, his breath warm and inviting against my skin. I had a feeling I knew where his frustrations were leading, but I had other ideas.

'I'm sure you do,' I breathed, closing my eyes as his hand swept across the bare skin of my legs. 'But you need to tell me how we can stop Samael from pestering you for eternity.'

'Not now.'

'Sebastian, I only have five days left with you. I don't want to leave knowing that this is what your nights will entail forever and ever.'

He sighed, his body going slack behind me. 'I don't think you realise what a buzz-kill you're becoming.'

'I did tell you that I wanted to know everything.'

He was groaning, his hands tightening on my waist as his head slumped forward on my shoulder. 'Elena, I don't know what to tell you. Lucifer is very upset that I've trapped him in hell and he wants a way to get out, hence Samael's persistence.'

'And what can we do to get him off your back?'

'Nothing.'

'Aw, come on.'

'No. I'm serious, Elena. Lucifer is exactly where I want him—trapped. If I go down there now and challenge him to another fight and … Put it this way, vampires and vânători are not the worst thing he could unleash upon the world should he be victorious.'

'So, if you don't challenge him—'

'Then Samael will torment me until I do. It's a catch twenty-two and there's nothing I can do about it. I'd rather endure several lifetimes of Samael's endless grief than an eternity under Lucifer's reign. Do you see my dilemma?'

'I guess so.'

'So, are we done with this conversation now?' he asked, voice light again as he began to pursue earlier exploits, namely *my* neck with *his* lips.

'Not quite.'

'Elena …'

'Can I change anything with my judgement?'

'What?' He stopped the kissing thing again, his embrace stiff and uncertain. His fingers twitched, the skin of my thighs his target. At first, I thought he was diverting topics, but then his breathing stopped for a few moments. Shadows outside lengthened, darkening the room around us. When he finally moved it was to pull away from me, to turn his back and hide his true feelings on the subject behind a mask of neutrality.

'Sebastian,' I said gently, turning around slowly to see him now standing by the window. 'I just want to help.'

'You can't help.'

'Are you sure about that? I have choices, don't I?'

'I don't know what you're talking about.'

I hung my head for a brief second, knowing all too well that tone in his voice—avoidance, denial, lies. 'Fine, play it that way. I know you think you're trying to protect me. I guess in some twisted way you've always thought that keeping the truth from me would help.'

He scoffed, wheeling around to glare at me. 'You make it sound like I had an agenda! Elena, lying to you was never something I aimed to do, but I had to keep the truth of my existence from you to avoid this very situation! And, the one time I began to reveal myself to you, I gave up my chance of rebirth. How does that make me the bad guy?'

'Now I'm pleading ignorance … what?'

'Did you think there wouldn't be consequences for revealing my angelic nature to you?'

'But you didn't, I guessed. Araqiel came to me and I put the pieces together with his cryptic choice of conversation.'

He shook his head almost violently. 'No. Don't you remember, back at the villa before Lucius held the multi-coven gathering? You came to my room after our meditation session in the garden. We talked, we pretended we didn't want to rip each other's clothes off and then I relented. I gave in. I believed in you, in the person you were in this life and trusted—'

'The feathers,' I whispered, cutting his spiel short. 'The blinding white light and the feathers. I saw your wings, didn't I?'

'You saw a glimpse of me before Araqiel interfered. It was his wings you saw. I no longer have wings, remember?'

I pinched the bridge of my nose before rubbing at my temples, wracking my brain trying to remember. 'He knocked me out, didn't he? That's why I can't remember clearly. That's why I woke up in your bed and why I had this dream—'

'Yes.'

'So now—because of me—you're stuck here.'

He took several steps towards me, features softening. 'Elena …'

I held up my hands to stop his approach. 'No. Don't try to make me feel better.'

'I wasn't. It's not your fault. I just wanted you to know that sometimes our choices aren't necessarily the right ones when motivated by pressing emotion. At that time, I could feel your longing to know me. I could taste it as clearly as the desperation I felt to finally reveal myself to you.'

'Why are you telling me this now?'

'You're asking questions about your judgement. I want you to think carefully when the time comes what's best for you, not what's best for everyone else.'

'The bird said if it's a hung jury that I can choose to go back to earth or stay here with you.' I shrugged. 'I guess what I'm trying to say is, given Samael and everything, I'm going to—'

'Don't say it,' Sebastian chided, angry fists balled at his sides. 'Don't you dare say it.'

'But, Sebastian …'

'No. You can't do that to me. You can't put any amount of hope in my thoughts. I have accepted that I have you for the next five days, and I'm going to make the most of every second I have with you, but I will not allow myself to imagine that this can last any longer than we've been allowed.'

'But—'

'No buts.' He started walking towards me, strides purposeful. He stopped in front of me, dropping to his knees, his hands immediately gripping my hips, eyes blazing with uninterpretable emotion. He pulled me down with him.

'Sebastian?'

'Conversation over.'

'No, it's not, we've only just—'

'Elena … for once in your life—just shut the hell up.'

Shocked and clearly geared up for rebuttal my mouth began to move, but he quickly closed the distance between us, pressing his lips against mine before words could escape. Stubbornness urged me to push against him, to tell him that the conversation wasn't over and that I wanted to stay, wanted to help him fight the loneliness of forever. But common sense also conveyed the need to revel in the gift of the present and accept that there were some things that cannot be changed; at least not without blindingly disregarding others' choices. Sebastian and I were together now. Thousands of years always led us to the point where we fall into each other's arms. I had to trust in his belief of the process, understand that even though there were no secrets between us now, circumstances would eventually separate us again. All we had was now to explore the mutual longing we shared, to finally awaken the longstanding and forever unbreakable connection between us and plan for the future later.

We rocked backwards, propelled by the force of his kiss. My back hit the soft furs covering the stone floor, warm and as welcoming as Sebastian's embrace. His arms closed around me protectively as his body settled above mine. His weight was comfortable; natural in a way I had never known. It was almost too easy, instinctual to open myself to him further. I wrapped my legs around him, crossing my ankles behind his back. I pulled him into me, arching myself against his frame, a gentle way to communicate what I felt as mutual eagerness.

We both exhaled noisily, our lips torn apart as Sebastian found my neck, his movements taking him slowly down my body. My fingers found the softness of the furs beneath us, curling around the tufts and bunching hard enough to turn my knuckles white. I needed an anchor as Sebastian continued to delight in every crevice, every patch of burning skin that cried out for his attention.

I wondered if I could lie there forever; thoughts of judgment, demons, angels and the war back on earth nothing but a distant memory as my body attempted to throw a hazy blanket over reality, mottling the edges of logical thought. Could I get lost in the sensations of Sebastian's sensuous touch? Could I let everything else go and just feel what I'd fought so long to deny?

I tried to pursue an answer, but everything coherent was suffocated by a fog of self-indulgent bliss. I was a riot of conflicting sensations, each more confusing and wonderful than the last. Logic had somehow escaped my usually steely grasp. The tips of my fingers tingled and my toes curled, the slightest touch of Sebastian's tongue pushed any doubt further from my calculating mind.

Breath came in uneven gasps, almost as if I'd forgotten how to breathe—a victim trying to swim back to the surface of myself. I was cast adrift in sensations, blushing profusely when I realised how vocal I'd become, but Sebastian merely smiled at his captive audience, satisfied that his efforts drew a positive response. How could I have ever believed that connection was irrelevant, that

I could sail through life and unlife devoid and undeserving of the miracle unfolding inside of me?

My t-shirt inched upwards, higher and higher until futility of its purpose led to it being discarded all together; a useless piece of cloth barring the exploration our bodies seemed to crave. Modesty for the briefest of moments made me hesitate. The urge to cover my exposed undergarments became overwhelming as I wondered if I was everything he had expected—dreamed of after two thousand years of abstinence. Was I too thin? Was I too eager? Was my naivety too obvious?

But as Sebastian gazed down upon me, eyes hooded and filled with heat and irrevocable longing, doubt of his desire ebbed away. To be wanted was one thing, but to witness utter devotion swimming in another's eyes and to hear his breath hitch with need? It was enough evidence to capture my heart and shelve immediate plans of covering the assets of any lingering self-doubt.

And then Sebastian looked upon me for the longest time, speechless. He carefully observed every portion of my exposed flesh, eyes hungry and lips moist—slightly parted to allow for shallow, eager breath. I was equally enamoured, unable to look away as he drew his own shirt overhead, discarding it with haste. Perfection in every sense of the word I could interpret filled my vision; tight abdominals, narrow waist and broad, muscled shoulders.

Studying him in that moment, I knew that God himself had designed Sebastian. He was the seamless formation of all things righteous and male. His silver eyes were aglow, unearthly in their perception of even me. I knew he would find a way to look at me like that forever, despite the obstacles that barred our path. This was only the beginning and yet it felt so treacherously close to the end.

His hands uncharacteristically shook as he reached out, brushing the very tips of his fingers against my ribs, curving them around the shape of my body until he touched the edges of my bra. His look turned questioning, eyes seeking permission, his touch suddenly unsure.

I took a deep breath and met my hands with his, warm and eager we finally locked eyes, certain where this would lead. There would be no more interruptions, no more conversation—no more hesitation. Our hands and hearts were united as we parted the flimsy fabric together, a total immersion of seduction now imminent.

We found each other once more, lips meeting and tongues delighting in the taste of one another. Hands became a blur upon flesh—touching, teasing, tantalising. What had started out slow and deliberate soon became desperate and a desire to sink into the other, swim inside our skins and never come back for air.

I thought we'd be lost for hours to the sensation of one another, locking lips—tasting and teasing. But desperation seemed to grip us both. No longer did we take the time to explore, to run our fingers across skin and sample the different textures between our bodies. Eagerness overcame caution and we rode seduction to a different level that saw all remaining clothes gone. They were now a distant memory and a mere stepping stone to bring us closer together. I yearned for him to see me, to look upon my naked flesh, exposed and vulnerable with nothing but the drug of love touching those flashing silver eyes—total devotion the unspoken words on his lips.

'Elena?' he murmured, 'I need you to know that I—'

I pressed my lips briefly against his, halting his words. I pulled back, running my fingers up and down the length of his spine in reassurance. 'I know what you're going to say and I don't need to hear it. Those words have been shown in every touch and every look you have given me.' I shrugged, giving him a cheeky smile. 'Plus, it's corny. You and I know the real deal and that's all that matters.'

He shook his head, a slow smile spreading across his face. 'You never stop surprising me. From the very first day we met until this moment I always thought—'

I sighed, trying to look bored. 'Are you going to talk all day?'

He pressed himself intimately against me, chuckling when a small moan escaped my lips. 'I wasn't planning on it.'

I arched myself against him in rebuttal, revelling in the responding flicker of his eyelids and the restraint he tried to portray as I wrapped my arms around his neck, reaching up to flick my tongue teasingly across his lobe. 'So shut the hell up and get on with it, Sebastian.' There. Karmic retribution for earlier, except this time I was sure to be satisfied by the outcome of his retort.

He laughed, throwing me back down against the furs, his lips found purchase on my flesh once more. 'Quiet is the last thing we're going to be.'

I pondered the thought, convinced he was wrong until we found our rhythm again, alternating between the stroking of skin and the touch of lips. The desperation built to a crescendo once more and soon he was poised above me, silence now a companion as combined acknowledgment of this moment was understood. Our eyes locked, every inch of Sebastian pressed against me, the warmth of our bodies only a tenth of the desperate need stoking the embers within.

He kissed me one last time and as his lips drew away, his body sunk into mine. I cried out—not from the pain I'd expected from this virtuous union—but pleasure. It rolled through me like warm waves upon the sand, spreading throughout and drawing uneven breath from parted lips. Every movement was joyous, pleasurable; the intensification building like a roaring furnace below, uncontrolled and unexpected.

I wanted to revel in the sensation forever, hang onto this moment of bliss and bury myself inside its comfort. But all I could do was cling to Sebastian, my nails digging into his flesh as the heat finally spilled over, breaking down barriers and expelling any inhibitions that may have lingered. Silence was indeed a forgotten concept, our rhythmic bodies united for the final time, our heads thrown back as words undeterminable through the cries of justified release were uttered.

We didn't move for several heartbeats, each lost in their own world. Eyes were closed and breathing was tormented. I let go, my arms falling to the rug, joints rubbery and skin tingling. Sebastian slumped against me, gathering me in his arms and burying his face against my neck. It was over, but the promise of more to come still rolled through me in a sensuous caress. 'Elena ...' he whispered.

'Yes?' I panted, equally exhausted as he sounded, but extraordinarily ready and rearing for round two.

'That was ...'

'I know,' I said, running my nails up and down his back.

'Do you want to—'

'Hell yes!' I all but shouted as I eagerly rolled with him until I was straddling him, the tortuous yet pleasurable story starting all over again. If there was one thing I could thank Purgatory for—it was unending stamina.

Sebastian and I made love for days. Occasionally we stopped to talk, laughed about the past and even spared a few hours to put Samael back in his box. We never lost sight of what was important in these final days—each other.

But of course, days soon rolled into nights, and though we never strayed from each other's arms for long we knew time was running out. We did make the most of every moment we had, our love blossoming on a level I couldn't even begin to describe. Judgment loomed yet we persisted on ignoring it. We kept the future tucked in the dark recesses of our mind, focusing only on the delights of our flesh and present pleasures.

Tomorrow was apparently a concept that could wait.

*　　　*　　　*

Sebastian sensed Araqiel before words were even uttered. Angelic presence left a smear of pulsing energy upon his skin, a tingling that couldn't be ignored. It was the same for the Demons. His stomach rolled at their sulphurous scent, a beacon for dark presence. In this instance, he would have preferred to see a demon. Time had filtered by too quickly and judgment loomed. The angel didn't need to speak. Sebastian already knew why he was here.

'Brother.'

Sebastian didn't move and saw no need to answer. He sat on the stone window ledge of his Lakelands home, watching Elena as she wandered through the shallows of the water outside. She'd been skipping pebbles over the surface, contemplating her decision. Though she said she'd made up her mind, Sebastian had urged her to take some time and consider the ramifications of setting up permanent residence in Purgatory.

It wasn't that he didn't want her to stay. In fact, he would have given anything to spend eternity wrapped in her arms. After all, she was the reason he fell from grace in the first place. He'd chosen her then and he would choose her now. Nothing had changed. His love and devotion were just as strong as ever. But to be an angel—even a fallen one—meant his conscience warred with him to accept his responsibility and protect the human race. In order to do that, Elena was better off back on earth.

Elena knew this was an option, but she was also fixated on less desirable outcomes. To have the blood of Lucius Valerius running through her veins was to be marked as the spawn of Satan and thus a candidate for hell. Though she tried not to let it show, Sebastian could tell that she thought about the possibility of descending almost daily. What she didn't know was that she'd also been blessed. The angel Uriel had been present at the time of her conception and the powers-that-be somehow knew that existence as everyone knew it would eventually hinge on Elena's life or death.

There was no way that Elena was going to Hell. There was also no way that Elena was going to Heaven. The shiny gates didn't open for anyone with demon blood flowing through their veins. Likewise, the Demons rejected anyone with even an ounce of righteousness lighting their path into the fiery pits of the underworld. This catch twenty-two meant that she could either stay or leave Purgatory. She just didn't know these were her only two options yet.

'Have you told her anything?' Araqiel asked, coming up behind him. He rested his elbows on the sill next to Sebastian, leaning out the window to catch a glimpse of Elena now throwing a boulder into the water in frustration.

'No.'

'I see.'

'No, you don't *see*,' Sebastian muttered. 'How could you? Araqiel you have no idea what it feels like to have emotions.'

'And what does *feeling* have to do with the truth?'

'Everything.'

'I don't follow.'

Sebastian shook his head. 'I can't tell her about her choices. It's not that I want to lie to her, but if we talk about it, she'll know how I feel. She'll be swayed by my deepest desires and I can't have that resting on my conscience.'

'You think she'll choose Purgatory?' Araqiel started to frown, not sure if that idea worked in with his current plans for Elena's destiny.

'She already thinks she's leaving me alone and at the mercy of Samael. She forgets what I am, what I have been for thousands of years before her existence. And although I know that I will be fine in this place, she also knows I will ache for her every minute we are apart.'

'You are right, Michael,' Araqiel said, patting Sebastian on the shoulder. 'I am glad that I do not feel as you do. I cannot afford to be conflicted by my choices.'

Sebastian drew a deep breath, held it and then slowly released. He watched as Elena threw a handful of rocks into the water and then kicked a broken tree branch by her feet. She swore—much to Araqiel's disgust—then slumped down to the ground, pulling her knees up to her chest and staring out over the water. Sebastian desperately wanted to go to her, soothe her and ease his own burdens by making these choices a moot point, but she needed this time to think carefully, to be unswayed by his desperate need to keep her by his side.

'It's time,' Araqiel murmured, patting Sebastian on the shoulder again. 'The council is asking for her.'

'I know.'

'You must tell her now. The only reason you have had this extra time is because it has been … shall we say … difficult to find a moment when you weren't both otherwise … occupied.'

Sebastian started to smile, the image of Elena naked and pressed against him forever burned in his retinas. 'Yes, well, you did say we had a week together. We made sure to make good use of our time.'

'Indeed,' Araqiel said, clearing his throat. 'Now, about judgement. You need to get her there soon. If you don't, Samael and Mammon will come looking for her and you don't want that.'

'Agreed.'

Araqiel stood, nudging Sebastian's shoulder with his own. 'Are you going to be alright?'

'I'd rather not say.'

'I see.'

Sebastian scoffed, throwing his head back and shoving Araqiel away. 'No. You really don't.'

'Then I shall leave you be. Take your time to say your goodbyes, just don't start something that we'll have to come and break up.'

Sebastian waved him off, already leaping off the window sill and heading outside to say goodbye to the love of his life.

CHAPTER EIGHT: JUDGEMENT

'**I** notice we're flying again,' I grumbled, snuggling into Sebastian's embrace. 'Of all the wonders in this place and no one thought to invent some sort of public transportation system? Better yet, one of those *beam me up Scotty* things.'

Sebastian kissed the top of my head, his chest rumbling against my cheek; a sure sign I'd made him laugh. 'Do you honestly believe you'd be happier being molecularly torn apart and re-pieced back together versus flying?'

'I want to offer some sort of snappy retort, but I've got nothing. I'm too busy trying to keep my stomach down.'

'Liar. You can't get sick in Purgatory.'

'Debatable.'

This time he laughed loud enough that I could hear him. 'Well, we're almost there. I'm about to set us down over there.'

'You never did tell me how you can fly without wings.'

'A man has to have some secrets.'

'And you are so good at keeping them,' I mused, wrapping my arms even tighter around his neck.

'Still bitter?'

Only marginally, I answered, 'I'm just a little tense right now.'

'Everything will be fine, Elena.'

I scoffed. 'Everything is so far from fine, Sebastian.'

He squeezed me tight enough it imbued his concern, his lips brushing the top of my brow like delicate petals to ease all anxiety. 'Trust me. Everything is going to work out. You will make the right choices and so will the council. It will be like none of this ever happened.' Sadness marred those last few words—a sadness I yearned to replace with hope. The problem was, I was equally entrenched in the pity-party.

'*Like it never happened*,' I repeated, my voice barely above a whisper. 'I could never forget you, Sebastian. Not now. Not ever.'

The ground gently met with the soles of my feet as Sebastian set us down.

'You may not have a choice,' he answered in an equally hushed tone.

I shook my head, adamant as I drew back from his embrace. 'No, Sebastian, you don't understand.' I thumped my hand against my heart to hammer home my point. 'No matter what they may do to me here today, I will never, ever forget us again.'

He brokered a forced and well-practiced smile. Even in the very depths of his eyes they were absent of faith and dulled by the sentiments of the seemingly unconvinced. He may not have believed that my heart would etch this latest connection and burn it into the very depths of my hidden valley of emotions, but I knew I was different in this life—so very different. I'd dreamed of Sebastian even before our first meeting, knowing those silver eyes would one day look upon me and our love—the endless gravitational pull that always saw us united.

'Pretty to think,' he murmured, seizing me in his steely arms once more. He tilted my chin, kissing my lips with a gentleness that made me ache for more.

I gripped his face tightly between my hands, making sure our eyes would meet as I leveraged our lips apart, not wanting the intent behind my words to be brushed aside as just another idle comment. 'No, not pretty to think. You mark my words, Sebastian. Whatever happens on this day, I will find you again and when I do, I'm going to walk right up to you without pretence or hesitation and do this ...'

My trembling lips found his once more, now sure in their movements and determined as ever to prove that after thirteen thousand years of reincarnations my soul would no longer forget the past. I may have been an emotional pariah before, but Sebastian had achieved the impossible and opened my eyes to the possibility of a future. I refused to forget my trials and tribulations. I usually succeed at everything I attempt based on illogical and rash bouts of determination. And, I knew now as I kissed him one last time, that no entity or power would disintegrate the most powerful lesson of all … love.

We finally separated, reluctance not just a word in the back of our minds. We both knew this was it. Judgment loomed and there was no going back. I took a moment to draw breath and

110

brandish my heart and mind with the memories of his arms around me.

Looking down, I began to study the ground at our feet. Polished stone—so hard and unyielding compared to Sebastian's grip. I could already feel him slipping away, his fingers brushing mine as the separation we'd agonised over now came to fruition.

'It's time.' Such ominous words if ever I'd heard them. 'And you're late.'

I detested the interruption, but glanced to my left, expecting the grating voice of Samael to suddenly manifest into physical being, but he was nowhere near. Regardless, his words slithered across the surface of my flesh, coating me in the putrid breath of the dead. I even refrained from wiping my ear, knowing he hadn't actually touched me, but certain his tongue had traced the edge of my lobe.

'Keeping us waiting is not wise,' Samael taunted. He appeared before me, moving from the direction of a large round table where a red-skinned demon sat immobile and two angelic entities boasted seats on his right.

Samael moved like a gluttonous slug, slow but purposeful to bring me before the council members. I busied my eyes with tracing details. The other council members were extraordinary versions of both good and evil and the perfect distraction from Samael's slippery fingers as they pulled me closer for inspection.

Over the past week I had grown somewhat accustomed to Samael's games. His demonic minions had wreaked endless havoc on the souls of Purgatory. And now I saw yet another version of this incessant game-player, more serious and non-anecdotal. The game and its players were contradictions—horror juxtaposed against beauty and yet a fair and definitive line between good and evil sat to serve judgement upon me. Here at this rounded stone table, I saw a red-skinned beast slicked with sweat, stench ripe and forked tail ready to strike. I saw a goat-headed sadist with a penchant for the macabre, his long dark fingernails picking rotting flesh from between his teeth. And to the right were two angels; men of indeterminable age, skin flawless, hair like silk and eyes flecked with silver. All sat calmly alongside their opposition, comfortable, like balance could only be maintained with equal forces present.

Samael began to circle me now, hooves an inch from my toes and his hot breath fanned the side of my neck, fingers still trailing the skin of my arms and back. Sebastian made motions to interject in the beast's looming presence, but now wasn't the time for a show of moral support. I suspected Samael would not hurt me in front of the halo squad, but Sebastian may have been banished from my judgement and I needed him near.

Thankfully, Araqiel appeared like the mythical being he was, fanned his wings and encased Sebastian within the downy fold. Sebastian of course protested, but Araqiel held him imprisoned. 'Come now, brother. You cannot interfere or you will be punished.'

Samael smirked at Sebastian's grunts of disapproval, but essentially ignored the proceedings and focused on his mission to spark revolt within me. The circling had stopped, though his probing fingers still sort to taunt my failing levels of patience by dipping much lower than my spine insisted was appropriate.

'If you keep heading south, I don't care if you're a member of the council, I'll tip the balance to the other side's favour and end you.'

'Is that so?' Samael rasped, perhaps flawed by my unexpected bravado. He pulled me roughly against his beastly chest, snout grazing the side of my cheek as he traced those persistent fingers up and down my arms now. 'What I wouldn't give to have you bound and gagged after this, to tear your clothes off and expose your vulnerability so that I may—'

'Samael,' one of the angels snapped. 'You will have your chance to question her resolve. You will not, however, continue this charade during the light of day.'

Samael snarled, licked the side of my cheek and then shoved me forward. He followed the unexpected rejection with a swift kick in the backside that sent me sprawling, my hands bracing the stone table upon impact. No one reacted as I steadied myself, pride wounded, but otherwise unharmed.

'Was that necessary?' the other angel asked.

'She is defiant. She must know her place!'

'She is here without protest. What more do you ask of her?' The angel turned to look at me, eyes twinkling with silver. 'My name is Munkar and this is my brother Nakir. I apologise for Samael's behaviour.'

'Do not apologise for me, Angel,' Samael spat, as he lowered himself back into the chair beside his demonic brethren. 'I do as I please.'

Munkar, disinterested in his comments, waved him off and gestured to a chair nearby. 'Please, sit down. We have much to go through before we can make our final decision.'

'We do?' I said, pulling the heavy chair out and sliding into place. I'd assumed they already had my persona pegged, but Sebastian's tight-lipped smile suggested otherwise. Araqiel still had him bound by feathers, but it was a formality now. No one could really stop Sebastian if he wanted out.

'Of course,' Munkar replied. 'Judging the soul is not an easy process and your decisions play a part in the factors which sway our own.'

'Right.'

'So, we will start by questioning you and we expect you to answer honestly. If you do not, the chair that you sit upon will make your judgement more than uncomfortable. Do you understand?'

'What the—' I studied what had been an ordinary chair seconds previous. Threads of crimson smoke now appeared from nowhere, wrapping around my wrists, neck and ankles like gnarled branches of a tree. They bound me rather securely to the chair's stone structure, the red tendrils engraving burning blisters upon my skin. The more I struggled against the imprisonment, the more it seemed to hurt.

I furiously focused on trying to remember that in Purgatory pain was optional—simply a state of mind. Yet the more I tried to convince myself of this fact, the hotter those sheaths seemed to become. 'What the hell are you trying to do to me here?'

'Stop moving,' Munkar offered, though I'd clearly worked that out for myself. 'You cannot dull the pain of the flames here. In this judgement you are not in control of your interpretation of this world. We are your judge, jury and executioner. Do you understand?'

'I understand.' The flaming tendrils ebbed, infinitely less painful than before. Okay, so all I had to do was agree with them, tell them whatever they wanted to hear. I was going to hell anyway, unless by some miracle they let me stay here.

Ahh shit! I'm kidding I'm kidding! I shouted in my head as the flames started up again. *I'll tell the truth! I'll tell the truth!*

I breathed a sigh of relief as the flames dimmed once more, mere smoke and crimson veins encircling my skin like a slithering snake, restraining but not biting … for now.

'You ruin the best part,' the red-skinned demon murmured. 'I do enjoy to watch them struggle and scream. Why must you always warn them, Munkar?'

'Mammon, this is serious. You can get your kicks in hell. This place is neutral and thus not to be misused to exacerbate one influence over another.'

I glanced at Sebastian. His eyes were downcast, lips pressed into a thin line. I noticed the working muscle in his jaw; a tell-tale sign that he was clenching, clearly biting back whatever bitter retort he wanted to expel at the Demons.

The one called Mammon snapped his fingers at me. 'Pay attention.' He looked over my head at Sebastian and Araqiel. 'He should not be present.'

The angel Nakir nodded his blonde head in agreement. 'It is true. Michael, you cannot stand beside her in judgement. You have had your time with her, now you must go.'

'I wish to stay.'

Mammon shook his head. 'No.' He started to smile, leaning across the table in eagerness. 'Unless of course you wish to finally grant a rematch against Lucifer? If you would agree to that, then we will agree to let you stay.'

'No,' I shouted, shaking my head. 'Sebastian, get your butt out of here. I'm not going to have that on my head too.'

'Elena—'

'I said no. Now go before you do something stupid to protect me.'

'Silence!' Mammon roared, slamming his fist upon the table. 'Either you fight or you leave, the choice is yours,' he said, pointing to Michael. He focused his attention back on me. 'As for you …'

I gasped, the smouldering threads encircled my throat more tightly, cutting through my neck like butter. I could smell the stench of burning flesh, knowing I had spoken out of turn, but I refused to let Sebastian unleash Lucifer from his box because I may have been in a little bit of pain.

114

Okay, I was in a truck-load of pain right this second, but the fate of the world was not worth the burn marks on my soul. I'd get over it. I always did.

'I'm leaving,' Sebastian shouted. 'Just stop hurting her, I'm leaving now.'

I turned my head in the vice-like grip, relieved again as the pain started to dissipate. Sebastian and I locked eyes for a second, a thousand words passing between us in the blink of an eye before he was gone. He ran, hurtling himself from the ledge, his wingless body soaring upwards into the sky. The sun from above hid his form until he was nothing on the horizon but a smudge—my soul mate gone forever.

Araqiel made motions to follow suit, but the Angels interjected. 'Stay, brother. Whatever decision is made here today, Elena will need passage.'

Araqiel nodded, folding his arms against his chest, taking a step back. I could barely see him in my peripherals, but it helped knowing he was present. I may not trust the feathery bastard, but he had led me to Sebastian. That counted for something.

'Now that we are alone,' Samael sneered, leaning back in his chair. 'We can begin our questioning.'

I opened my mouth to speak and then closed it again. I really didn't want to be sliced and diced by the threads again. My questions could wait.

Samael sighed loudly. 'What?'

'Well, I guess I just want to know why you have to ask questions. You know what I am, clearly that can only mean one thing.'

'You presume to tell us how to do our job?' Mammon growled.

'No, of course not. It's just ... Well, I'm the master vampire's daughter. Doesn't that automatically buy me a one-way ticket South?'

'Ordinarily that is true,' Nakir intercepted, 'but in your case there are exceptions.'

I could feel myself frowning. 'Exceptions? Is it because I'm also half-vânător?'

'If anything, that just makes you even tastier to our side,' Samael said, rubbing his hands together. His face soured in an instant. 'But unfortunately, you're tainted.'

'Tainted? I don't think I understand.'

'That is why you will shut up and let us ask the questions,' Samael snapped. He was clearly unhappy about something, his snout opening and closing as if he tasted something bitter within his mouth. I resisted the urge to flip him the bird. I was trying to be respectful of this process, but after a week of watching him gut and rape Purgatory victims, I had the urge to stub out a flaming torch on the top of his head like a giant cigarette.

'We are going to gather some background details,' Nakir said slowly, shuffling through some piles of paper in front of him. 'We need to be accurate. So, the first question will be regarding your birth. Please give details of your mother, father and a description of how *vânător* came to be in your blood.'

I took a deep breath. I'd told this story many times before, but apparently, I was missing some details myself otherwise I wouldn't be *tainted*. Perhaps listing off the basics would shake something loose that I'd missed—something the IMI had once again failed to impart. 'My mother's name is Elena—don't know her last name. I guess it never mattered to me since I know she's dead. My father is Lucius Valerius—master vampire and very much alive. Well, as alive as you can be when you're undead.' I snickered at my little joke which amused no one, so I continued, 'Um, I was born in Corsica if the information the IMI gave me was correct, but I was raised in Cairns, Australia—hence the accent.' I was rattling on, but these details seemed menial after everything. How could they not know who and what I was and what had I missed from the past that made me even more genetically cocked up than I was now?

'And the blood?'

'Vânător blood became a part of me while I still in my mother's womb. She was attacked, a vein source opened. She managed to kill it, but its blood must have somehow dispersed through to me. At least that's the theory.'

Nakir smiled, noting the currently non-lethal attachment of the crimson restraints. 'Good. Now, please describe when your body first started changing.'

'Are you referring to puberty?'

Mammon and Samael rolled their eyes.

'No, Elena,' Munkar murmured, hiding a smile. 'We are talking about your changes from human to supernatural. We are trying to establish choice.'

'Hey, I never asked to be what I am.'

'No one is suggesting that. Now, please … continue.'

I took another deep breath. 'Okay, I felt the first signs of my strength after I 'accidentally' ingested alpha vânător blood. It was a mutual exchange, but I was unaware of that at the time.'

'How can that be true,' Samael mocked.

I wrinkled my nose up at him. 'Because he was draining me of blood. I wasn't quite with it.'

'Yet you bit him back!'

'Hardly. He was wounded and the blood dripped into my mouth. I didn't have fangs back then and I wasn't exactly into it or in need of it.'

Samael wanted to argue further, but Nakir waved a hand to shut him up again. 'When did you next sense change? We know that you can shape-shift now and that you feed on blood.'

'Again, not by choice, but I guess I'm glad it all happened. I've been better able to protect the ones I love since my turning first began.'

'Please elaborate,' Munkar pressed politely.

'Well, I drank vampire blood from a friend and he fed from me in return. Since that night I've had fangs and …' I paused, studying their expressions. 'What?'

The council members all leant back in their chairs, awareness flashing across their faces. 'We have seen this moment,' Mammon said. 'Araqiel defended your actions even though it was clear that you knew what you were doing.'

I started to blush, not wanting to think that these members of the council may have had a live-streaming video of William wrapped between my legs, our lips barely parting for air. 'In my defence,' I began, 'William and I—'

'We know.'

'It's not what you think. We cared for each other, but nothing ever—'

'Happened?' Mammon finished. 'He made you a changed being and you practically begged him for it.'

I was frowning deeply. 'We were both caught in the moment. I don't regret him biting me.'

Nakir passed a warning look to his demon counterparts. 'I think what my offsider is trying to say is that perhaps your innocence may have been compromised.'

'Compromised? Are you asking if I'm a virgin?'

Samael cackled, slamming his fist against the table. 'Clearly you are not. Lust for Michael licks your skin like the moon coats the surface of water with light. It can't be hidden from those that look upon it.'

I wanted to fold my arms across my chest in defiance and embarrassment, but the crimson threads still held me captive. 'Then clearly you didn't watch the film to its end. Sebastian and I may have found each other in Purgatory, but in life, no one ever touched me.'

'Is this true?' Mammon pressed.

I looked pointedly down at my captive threads. 'Shouldn't I be burning up by now if I was lying?'

'So, she was a true innocent at the time of her death,' Nakir mused. He looked at Munkar. 'It is just one more thing that cements our opposing decisions of her.'

Samael scoffed. 'Please, do you not remember the other virgins we have running around in hell? Just because her living body was unviolated does not mean that her actions as a lethal killer have not earned her some face-time with Lucifer.'

'Agreed,' Munkar said, nodding his head, 'but it's really beside the point.'

Samael's amusement faded as he threw his head back and roared in anger. 'Then why are we here? Why are we bothering with these questions? In the end it makes no difference. Her actions are irrelevant. Neither one of us can accept her, we can only keep her here— torture her—'

'We must follow procedure, complete the paperwork.'

'I want to stay here,' I whispered.

All eyes found me, words and flying insults had been halted by my admission. I'd never thought they would hear me, never realised how much I wanted to stay with Sebastian until it was uttered. Even in death and everything that opposed us in this place I couldn't bear the thought of never seeing him again.

'Be careful what you wish for, Elena,' Mammon said, stroking the table top with a clawed finger.

'I have done a lot of bad things,' I conceded, looking down at my lap in shame. 'I know what I am and I accept that. You're right, I am tainted. I'm dangerous and I'm not sure what I will become. At least here I stay as I am now.'

Munkar shook his head. 'Yes, Elena. You are tainted, but not in the way that you may think. Never before has there been a soul quite like yours. We argue because we are uncertain where to place you. Heaven cannot accept you. You yourself understand those reasons and I am sorry to say that you will never find peace there.'

I nodded, knowing that the pearly gates would never admit a half-breed like me. I was still astounded that an arch angel had even fallen from grace in the first place to pursue my tainted ass for over thirteen thousand years. 'Yes, I do understand.'

'Then you must also understand that you cannot go to hell either.'

I shook my head, unsure if I had heard correctly. 'Say what?'

Samael was roaring in anger again, his meaty fists beating down on the table top, threatening to mar its perfect surface. 'I am livid that we are having this conversation. She is evil to the core—a virgin yes—but her blood runs thick with Lucifer's. She belongs in hell and yet on a technicality that you all failed to mention until an hour ago we must step aside and let her choose. I know you concocted this entire scheme, angels! And when we get to the bottom of this—'

My head slammed back against the chair, his outburst a complete surprise. Both demons had been relatively contained and now I could see that they were angry—not necessarily with me—but circumstance.

'Samael,' Mammon chided. 'I am no happier about this turn in events than you.' He snarled and snapped his pointed teeth in the Angel's direction to reiterate his point. 'But clearly the revelation of the girl's conception was a mystery even to her. We will contain our temper, finish the assigned paperwork and plot our rebuttal. They planned this a long time ago and I am certain that Araqiel had a hand in it, but we will find a way to restore balance.'

Confused, I looked backwards and forward between the arguing mass. Araqiel merely shrugged, a small smile playing at the edges of his lips. Just what in the hell was going on?

'We did not need to give you these details,' Nakir said, adding insult to injury. 'It is none of your business.'

Mammon snarled again, ejecting saliva from his mouth. It landed in a hiss of acidic fluid in front of the Angel's clasped hands. He moved them away, disgusted by the display of petulance. 'Uriel is one of *us*. Do you relinquish all details of *your* demonic activities to us?' He paused, waiting for an answer. 'I did not think so.'

'It is far too contrived,' Mammon grated through tightly clenched teeth. 'You give us this information only hours before her judgment and now she stands before us and we have so little choice.'

'It is in her hands,' Munkar countered. 'It always has been. Knowing that she possesses angel blood makes little difference.'

'Except her ultimate destination!'

'Whoa, hold the freaking phone,' I interrupted, fairly unconcerned about the possibility of a good tongue-lashing and barbeque Elena on the menu. 'Did you just say I have angel blood?'

Both demons growled at me, the threads constricting around already blistered and sliced appendages.

'Elena, just as the part of you that is evil cannot allow you to enter heaven, the purity within you stops you from descending,' Munkar explained.

I thought I'd be relieved to hear such an outcome. I'd spent many sleepless nights dreaming of endless saunas in the pits of damnation, always praying I had choice, but nevertheless wondering if my father's deal with Lucifer had not condemned all vampiric entities. Now it turns out I was delivered from evil by a philandering angel intent on exhausting all options for me to be allocated in either resting ground. No, I wasn't relieved, I was worried. Not for my soul, but for my heart.

'Don't over think it, Elena.'

I glared at Araqiel. He stood composed as ever, arms resting across the front of his chest, his white suit bunching under the strain. I didn't know if he was reading my thoughts, but the look on his face suggested he'd had a sneak peek. He dropped his arms, straightening his tie and collar, closing the distance between us so he could rest an assured hand upon my shoulder. 'Do not doubt that he loves you. That much you can be certain of.'

I studied his perfectly manicured fingers, feeling warmth radiate from his touch. It didn't seem to make me feel any better. 'How can I not doubt him? How can I be sure it wasn't the part of me that was angel that drew him to me in the first place?'

The council looked at each other in confusion, the Demons suddenly arguing over who should rid the council chamber of the winged interruption. I had eyes only for Araqiel, everything else fading into the background as I searched for the truth in those speckled depths.

Araqiel knelt in front of me, his hand still holding me, anchoring me to his version of the truth. 'This is the first lifetime we have stepped in and changed things between the two of you. We needed to protect your soul for not only Michael, but for a greater purpose. Elena, Michael has always been drawn to your strength, your wit and your charms. The blood that runs through your veins is yours. You—Elena Manory—are the girl Michael wants. It has nothing to do with the angel present at your conception.'

'Are you sure?'

'Enough!'

Araqiel let out a protest as he was thrown backwards, an invisible force knocking him off his feet. He sailed across the stone, moving past the council dais and into a clearing where he finally came to an abrupt stop. His back hit a tree trunk, the gnarled branches moving and contorting until they held him against their rough bark. He struggled, but he could not be freed, his wings crushed uncomfortably behind his back.

'No more interruptions!' Mammon bellowed. 'Judgment must be decided. Night approaches and we have much to do to correct what has been done here. Clearly our votes will be hung in this instance so she must either stay or leave.'

The two angels shared a barely concealed look of satisfaction between them. 'Very well,' Munkar said, nodding his head in agreement. 'Elena, think very carefully about your choice, it cannot be reversed.'

'I have made it.'

Munkar narrowed his eyes at me. 'Are you sure? Are you not curious what is happening back on earth?'

Samael sputtered, shoving the angel in the shoulder. 'What are you doing? You cannot tell her what is happening on earth. She must choose based on what she knows.'

'She knows about the war, she knows that the Vânătors and vampires are being picked off by The Protectors and she knows that eventually the Humans will be farmed like cattle thanks to the serum.' Munkar paused, studying my reaction. 'Nothing to be surprised about unless you start to count the negatives and realise there isn't much hope for mankind or the Supernaturals.'

Samael looked at the angel sideways, suspicion pinching his brow. 'No, I suppose there isn't.'

'Who do you suppose will be left to clean up the mess?'

'It won't be her.'

'Then it will have to be her brother.'

'What?' My neck fell victim to the tightening threads once more, a gasp of pain escaping my surprised lips. 'What has Lucas gotten himself into now?'

Mammon's face flashed with anger. Outwitted, his eyes burned brightly, his tail darted backwards and forwards as if deciding on a target. Judging by the look on his face it was Munkar. 'This person you speak of is fine. Munkar seeks to fulfil his own agenda and he knew this press of conscience would change your mind.'

'I just need to know if Lucas is okay. I can't stay here knowing he could be in danger again.'

Munkar shrugged. 'I shouldn't have said anything.'

'And yet you did,' Mammon spat. 'This council decision is a farce.'

'Please, you must tell me. Is Lucas in danger?'

Samael leaned back against the chair, patting his hand against Mammon's sweaty shoulder. Defeat flowed from the very pores in his skin, the sweet stench of victory reflected in the Angel's smiles. 'It was well-played. This round definitely goes to them, Mammon. Come, let her return to earth. I suspect things will be changing soon anyway.' He climbed to his feet, pulling his demonic counterpart up behind him. 'We rest our case. We are not defeated, but we see your angle and realise we cannot change what has been set in motion this day.' He nodded to Araqiel. 'I will be watching you, angel. You may have succeeded in this small victory today, but if you do what I think you're going to do with that Time Contract, I'll find some way to hunt you down and kill you myself.'

'And it will still be worth it,' Araqiel replied vehemently, finally yanking his wings free of the tree's gnarled confines.

Samael shrugged. 'Do not forget who we work for, angel. He always finds a way to break even the most defiant. Just remember that whatever you change, we'll figure it out and spend eternity hunting you for the error in judgement.'

'I gave you my word. You now have Michael in Purgatory. You cannot convict me on my use of the Time Contract.'

'If it's a direct violation of the rules of interference, we'll do as we please.'

Araqiel was quiet for the longest time, eyes unblinking before he said, 'Then I guess I will have to find someone else to use it for me.'

Samael and Mammon's gaze darted between me and Araqiel. Puzzle pieces were falling into place for some, but for me all I could manage was a blink. My mind racing, I tried to listen, but their words were a mass of confusion, circling my mind like water in a drainpipe. I tried to chase the logic, swim through the ripples and understand everything that had come to pass, but I was too frightened for Lucas, wondering if it was a ruse to send me back to earth or if there was the possibility that time had passed as Kayla had said it could and that now he was in danger. Staying meant an eternity with Sebastian and endless days of basking in each other's affections, but could I risk Lucas on a *what if?*

The answer was no. No matter what my feelings for Sebastian dictated, Lucas was my brother. We were bound by blood, childhood, love and trust. He was everything to me and if there was even a remote chance that something had happened to him …

'Send me back.'

Samael snarled, gripping Mammon tightly by the arm as he lunged forward across the table, his tail shooting out like a dagger. It sliced the empty air in front of me, unyielding of flesh, but it had the desired effect—fear. 'Be careful little vampire,' Samael chastised, drawing Mammon further back. 'We'll be watching you.'

They both turned their backs on us and left, the shadows of the surrounding forest seemingly swallowing them whole. Birds stopped chirping and the sun visibly dimmed, mirroring the discontent in the council chamber. It was going to be a long and torturous night in Purgatory for any wandering souls.

I sent out a silent prayer—not to the powers that be—but to Sebastian, asking him to protect those that couldn't help themselves—and of course—to forgive me for this choice to leave.

Nakir and Munkar, now alone at the stone table sat forward in their chairs. Nakir flicked a hand and the restraints that burned and bound instantly slid away into oblivion. I flexed my hands, staring down at the angry welts and cuts, my fingers automatically reaching up to graze the tortured skin of my neck.

I shook my head. I could worry about that later. 'Send me back.'

'Are you sure?'

'Yes.'

'Do you swear that you were not coerced in any way by any council member?' Nakir readied his pencil and paper in front of him, prepared for that last tick box his apparent paperwork required in order to relinquish responsibility.

I cocked an eyebrow at the both of them, my resentment for the process and its hypocrisy nearing a dangerous level of uncensored blurting. 'Seriously, I have one thing to say to you— you're all assholes. Your idea of right and wrong is seriously skewed and to be honest, I'd probably be better off back on earth with the blood-suckers. Coerced? I never had a choice.'

The Angel's eyes widened, their mouths dropping in surprise.

'Look, I know I shouldn't cuss in front of you, but there you have it,' I tacked on, feeling somewhat guilty because of Araqiel's cough of objection. 'Just send me back to earth so I can be done with all these games. Whether Lucas needs me or not, I'll be there for him and away from all of you.'

'And Michael?' Nakir asked, his lips finally working their way closed.

I dragged in a steadying breath. My stomach was a riot of sickness, my heart alone aching as if a hole had been cut into the very centre of its thumping core. I had to ignore it. I'd survived before, closing the door and throwing away the key as if emotion was an unnecessary accessory. I could do so now to survive. I wouldn't forget, but I wouldn't let his absence cripple me either. 'He's an archangel,' I muttered, flexing my fingers into fists to stop

124

myself from clutching at the throbbing pain in my chest. 'Sebastian will be fine without me. If I know anything at all, I do know that.'

Munkar nodded. 'Then are you ready?'

'I have to be.'

'You do realise that you will not remember your time in Purgatory?'

'The bird told me, but I don't believe it.'

Munkar smiled. 'I'm sorry, but it's true. It is to protect the souls you've met here and to protect future proceedings.'

'Fine, whatever. Believe what you want, but if I can cheat both avenues of death and make it back to earth, I can sure as hell retain my memory.'

He shook his head. 'Goodbye, Elena, and good luck.'

I sighed, unappreciative of the underlying meaning. After everything I'd been through lately, I really wasn't in the mood for more drama when I woke up. 'Am I going to need it?'

'You will have to wait and see.'

Wait and see.

Bloody angels. They were all freaking assholes with an agenda. I was actually looking forward to revisiting the shady nature of the Vampires, bask in the predictable nature of a predator and leave behind the insanity of a place ruled by idiots constantly undermining and meddling in the affairs of others.

Shit. I really needed to find new friends. Only I could hunger for the company of the Damned.

CHAPTER NINE: PROPOSITION

'Seriously, Lucas,' Karina muttered. 'Are you just going to keep ignoring her like this? She's going to drive everyone crazy.'

Lucas took a deep, calming breath, studying his hands which were curled into fists in his lap. The knuckles were white, his nails biting into his palms. He didn't believe he was angry anymore, not after listening to her scream his name for days on end. He was conflicted, trying to stay strong for the group and keep his head clear of emotion.

Lucas cleared his throat; the following deep breath was not nearly enough to calm the angst within. 'That *woman* supports everyone that experimented on me and also had a hand in the Antarctic ambush. As far as I'm concerned, she can stay in there for three weeks and think about what it's like to be left alone and helpless.'

'That *woman* is your mother.'

'Doesn't alter facts.'

Karina screwed her face up at him. 'Okay, so she messed up, but she's your mum and she's been looking for you for ten years. Don't you think that counts for something?'

'No.'

'Lucas ...'

'Don't *Lucas* me. How can I believe anything that comes out of her mouth? She lied to me and she'll lie again. It's what The Protectors do, isn't it? Karina, you and I know from personal experience that the IMI will chew you up and spit you out to serve their own personal needs.'

Karina finally sat down on the cot next to him, nudging his shoulder in comradery rather than standing above him in judgement. 'Look, I know this isn't easy for you, Lucas. I can see this is eating away at you. She's your mum, you feel guilty about locking her up and throwing away the key, but she is here and she might be telling the truth. It's been a week. You should go to her, listen to what she has to say and then make up your mind.' Lucas made motions to interrupt but she shushed him. 'All I can say is that she is your kin. Lucas, if it was my father in these tunnels— regardless of the past—I'd want to talk to him.'

'Yeah, but—'

'Look, if nothing else,' she said, interrupting him yet again, 'you can always find out what she wants. She might be our way into the super cities.'

Lucas stood and then begun to pace, running a hand furiously over the stubble of his shaved head—frustration evident. 'And then what? Supposing mum does lead us to the super cities undetected, what if it's a trap? And if it's not, then what? What is it that you think we can change from the inside? We're still the enemy in human eyes. It doesn't matter that the IMI are farming humans for their blood. They would never believe us.'

'Lucas, that's—'

'No. There's nothing to come from this. Even if we do eventually get into the super cities, bring down the IMI and restore balance, the world is still a shitty place to live.' He kicked the edge of the cot, stubbing the end of his big toe. 'Gah! Why the hell are we bothering anymore?'

Karina shook her head—exasperated, dark hair spilling like a curtain around her shoulders. 'This isn't you, Lucas. You don't have a defeatist attitude. Over the last ten years you've been the one that kept us all positive and alive. I don't want to hear this crap from you now because you're too damned scared to face your mum.'

'What?'

'Don't *what* me, you know I'm right.'

'I'm not afraid to face my mother.'

Karina snorted. 'Yeah? Then why the hell has she been left to rot in the end sewer for over a week? Lucas, someone will kill her soon if she doesn't stop screaming out your name. Hell, I'll kill *you* soon if you don't do something about it!'

'That makes two of us,' Caleb muttered, appearing in the doorway. 'That woman has been moaning and groaning for days. Plus, she doesn't look so good and she smells really bad. The vamps bearing down on her have begged me to take their place.'

'Alright,' Lucas snapped. 'I'll go and see her.'

Karina and Caleb both let out simultaneous sighs of relief. Lucas ignored them both, pushing past Caleb as he left, treading the long path in the underground passages of the sewer tunnels to talk with his mother. He wasn't happy. Not in the slightest, but there were questions he did need answered. His avoidance to-date had not been based on cowardice alone. He'd wanted to see the serum's capabilities, find out how long its effects lasted and if starvation of the familial subject altered anything.

'Lucas, a word please.'

Lucas stopped in his tracks. He backpedalled, fingers grazing the dirtied tunnel walls until he appeared at the opening of Lucius's tunnel exit, approximately a mile out from the old villa of Valle Santa where base of operations used to exist. Now the villa was rubble, but Lucius still hung close by, pulled by the memories of his past and Elena's resting body.

'What is it, Lucius?' he said, finding the master vampire standing alone by Elena's bedside.

'I saw your mother today.'

Lucas took a deep breath, fighting the urge not to rub his eyes in weariness. 'And?'

Lucius turned slowly, his eyes lingering over Elena's body as he moved. So, it was a surprise when Lucas noticed the first smile on Lucius's face in years. It was also a warning sign that his mother had gotten up to her old, persuasive and manipulative tricks during their meeting.

Lucas groaned. Was he the only one that recognised his mother for what she truly was? A liar? 'Ah hell, Lucius. What has she convinced you of?' Lucas quickly backed out of the dingy, dank room and studied all visible sections of the tunnel from this vantage point. 'She is still here, isn't she? I mean, she didn't find some way to con you into escaping?'

Lucius's thick laughter rumbled behind him. It was comforting to hear after so many years of sadness. 'No, Lucas. I cannot be compelled and I do believe that I am old enough to know when I am being played.'

Lucas stopped ogling the passages for an escapee Protector and instead, turned back to focus on the master vampire's smiling face. 'Then why are you grinning like that?'

'I think fate might finally be working in our favour.'

Confusion settled in as Lucas's brow wrinkled. 'What are you talking about? If my mother has said something or promised something to you, I probably wouldn't believe it.'

Lucius shook his head, the smile still etched upon his ageless features. 'Yes, your mother does like to talk, and no, I didn't believe a word that she said until I saw her this afternoon.' He gestured to the chair by Elena's cot. 'Please, sit down. I want to—'

'Just tell me what she said,' Lucas grunted, folding his arms in front of his chest. 'I don't want to sit down. I've been sitting with my thumb up my butt all week thinking about how I can score everyone some blood. I've done enough sitting around. Just tell me what's going on.'

Lucius's nostrils flared just enough to let Lucas know he was being rude. 'Suit yourself.' The smile parted ways with Lucius's face after that, replaced with a more serious and pensive look. 'The Protectors and the IMI as a whole are liars, but your mother—I believe—has been looking for you all these years.'

Lucas started to protest, mouth gaping and arms flailing, but since Lucius gave him that look that often made him consider taking a paring knife to his skin to peel back like a giant rucksack so he could hide inside himself, he shut up. 'Sorry,' he murmured, straightening up and giving the master vampire the respect he deserved. 'I'm just reluctant to believe anything anymore.'

Lucius's gaze softened. 'Lucas, I understand your animosity. I have much ill-feeling towards The Protectors myself, but in this instance, you may be interested to hear what she has to say. I know for a fact that I was surprised; semi-impossible after two thousand years.'

'What exactly did she tell you?'

Lucius folded his arms across his chest, gaze now completely neutral. 'She told me about the super cities and what the IMI are doing to the Humans. She explained the serum and how it works and why she's been taking it for so long. Lucas, the serum isn't all it's cracked up to be.'

'What do you mean?'

'I mean that we might actually have a chance to win this war.'

'How?'

Lucius shook his head, suddenly and unexpectedly uncharacteristically smiling. 'I want to tell you, but it's better that

130

you see for yourself. Just promise me you will be kind to her. I believe she is trying to help you even if her motives are all wrong.' He held his hand up before Lucas could say another word. 'Go to her, see for yourself and then we will talk.' He quickly dismissed him, turning his back on the current conversation, once again distracted by Elena—vampiric sleeping beauty. Was she ever going to wake up?

Lucas watched him and his sister a moment longer. He noticed how Lucius's hand was always hesitant as he reached out to stroke the pale and lifeless fingers of his daughter's hand. His vigil was endless. Lucius never stopped hoping she would one day awaken, but since it had been over ten years since she was killed, Lucas's faith in her return was waning.

Lucas left the passage, spinning on his heels and hurrying down the long, ever-darkening and smelly tunnels to find his mother. There was no mistaking her hoarse voice shouting out his name over and over again. Though it was not exactly loud and irritating to his ears, vampiric hearing would find the incessant babble a reason to kill. Although he was grateful in this instance that his own powers did not extend to listening to her pleas at all hours, her cries instilled a sense of guilt. Not that his mother deserved any better treatment.

He rounded another corner, passing two vânători that shot him the stink-eye. Even in wolf form they snarled, black eyes burning a hole right through him, teeth snapping and aggression level high. He really should have come sooner. The local wildlife were preparing to turn on him for subjecting them to his mother's unending, vocal annoyance.

'Lucas, I know that you're here. I just want—'

'I'm coming. Stop shouting!'

Silence overcame the passages and deep sighs of relief were now all that could be heard from her watchers. Lucas apologised profusely and sent them all on their way for some much needed down-time. There was no questioning of his resolve, just a filtering of relieved vampires exiting the sewer main before they were called back to guard Susan again. She would not try to escape as she would not be capable. Lucas was far too powerful these days. Something she would learn quickly if tempting fate.

It took several thudding heartbeats and staring at the sodden floor before Lucas finally shifted his gaze to his mother. She sat propped against the crumbling, concrete wall in the corner of her tunnel, frail and dirty. Her usual shoulder-length hair was mussed and incredibly greasy, but appearances bothered her not as she broke into a grin, Lucas in her sights. She attempted to claw her way closer, but was instantly blocked with an impenetrable barrier she could not decipher. It was a spell she was not familiar with.

Since becoming of age, Lucas's powers had expanded and now came easily and without thought. Every spell he had ever learnt was as simple as breathing and now telekinesis was somehow instinctual and a part of his repertoire. No longer did he suffer any form of pain from wielding his abilities; he even gave Lucius a run for his money.

Susan touched the shimmery surface of his barrier, poking at the web of particles sewn cleverly by her son's mind—completely impenetrable. She marvelled at its tactile surface; cool to the touch and unyielding despite efforts to collapse it with her own magic. Lucas was infinitely more powerful than she'd realised. 'Lucas …'

He moved closer, inspecting the damage the last week in captivity had inflicted, shocked to see her looking so terrible. 'I'm sorry, I thought starving you—'

'You didn't know,' she said, shushing him. 'And I wanted you to see this. I wanted you to know that I've waited to find you before stopping everything.'

'Stopping everything? Mum, despite this I don't want you dead. I may be pissed at you but please, don't talk like—'

'I know that, sweetheart. It's not what I'm referring to.'

Lucas crept a little bit closer. 'Then what are you talking about?'

'The serum, Lucas.'

'The serum?'

'Yes, I wanted to find you before I stopped taking it.'

'You're talking like taking it wasn't a once off situation. You have to take it regularly to maintain vampirism?' He did the once over on his mother again, absorbing her dishevelled appearance and thinning frame. 'So, the serum is flawed, was never perfected by Chester?'

She nodded ever so slowly as if it pained her to admit any form of truth. 'Thankfully it's not addictive, but in order to remain immortal, the serum must be injected weekly. I've only been doing all this time so that I had the opportunity to find you.'

Lucas hid his disbelief well. 'What happens if you don't take it?'

'We become mortal again; our powers disappear and we go back to life as a Protector.'

'Are you mortal now?'

She nodded again and if possible, more hesitant than before. 'Its effects are wearing off. I can feel conversion upon me. At least I know what to expect, I've tried it several times, but I started aging rapidly and knew I needed to keep taking it to find you.'

Lucas made no effort to respond, still studying the new lines that were now etched on his mother's face.

'At least we've learnt our mistakes through Beryx.'

A random thing to say, Lucas was now intensely curious as to where this conversation was headed. Many moons ago, Beryx had been the test subject for the IMI's trial run of the serum. At that time, Beryx and Lucas had been paired as bunk mates in Antarctica as well as sparring buddies to test their opposing brawn and magic wielding capabilities. In the end, Lucas had claimed victory on account of his developing powers, but he'd never really known what had become of the Romanian test subject.

'What happened to Beryx?'

Susan looked away, gnawing wildly on her bottom lip. 'He died.'

'You mean Chester killed him.'

'Not intentionally. The first trial of the serum had side-effects that we thought we understood. Clearly we didn't.'

Lucas swallowed the lump forming rapidly within his throat. He hadn't known Beryx all that well, but from their brief interaction, he'd seemed like a nice enough guy. He'd clearly been caught up in something way over his pay grade. But why his mother *now* revealed this information was the true mystery. 'Why are you telling me this?'

'Because you are my son and I love and trust you.'

Lucas scoffed, drawing an offended gaze from his mother. 'Then tell me why you spoke to Lucius about the serum. You hate vampires, you always have. Why now are you revealing IMI secrets to their leader?'

Susan sighed as though on the brink of passing out, not surprising given she'd been without food and the serum's effects for over a week. Her head found the wall, rolling at an awkward angle. Even so, she still managed to look down her nose at him. 'I don't like what we—The Protectors—have become.'

'And what is that exactly?'

'Worse than vampires—worse than even the Vânǎtors.'

Lucas arched a brow. 'That's a big statement coming from such a loyal follower of the IMI.'

'It's true,' she said, voice hoarse. 'I never believed when we started the initial trials of the serum that we would become worse than our enemies. Lucas—don't get me wrong—I believed in the war and the fight against the supernatural entities preying on humans, but when we became the predators …'

Lucas crouched down so that his gaze was level with hers. He needed to understand everything and looking into the very depths of her soul was the key. 'You're talking about the super cities and the consequent human farming you've initiated?'

Her powder blue eyes narrowed sharply. 'You know about that?'

'Why else would you lock humans up like Fort Knox? At first, we thought you were protecting them from us, but then we started to find bodies piled up outside your city walls. There were no bite marks. They were just drained of blood. Coincidence? I think not.'

'W-what did you do with the bodies?'

'What do you think?' Lucas spat, anger simmering. 'The blood may have been drained, but the flesh still satisfied the Vânǎtors, leaving the Vampires a little more time to avoid being on the menu.'

'I see.'

'I don't think you do. I've never said life was ideal before the war, but how they are now? No one wins.'

'I know, Lucas. It's why I've been looking for you, praying to God that you were still alive and out here somewhere, willing to help me do what needs to be done.'

Lucas was on the verge of a serious eye roll. 'Do you expect me to believe that? You seemed pretty happy about ploughing down a street full of vampires and vânǎtors earlier this week. Some of those people were my friends.'

'I can't change who I am at heart. I will always despise those creatures, but I despise what The Protectors have become with the serum even more. I'm willing to swallow years of prejudice to put an end to the disease that plagues us all.'

'What are you suggesting?'

'Destroying the serum.'

'Destroying the serum will not stop those in charge from producing more.'

'I want to kill Chester.'

'Whoa!' Lucas chided, climbing back to his feet again. 'You want me to help you disrupt the production of the serum and kill Chester only to unleash a bunch of Protectors and humanity back into society? We've been starving out here for far too long for that to be safe. The Vânători are behaving at present, but without the proper guidance they will slaughter for food.'

'Which is why I want you to help me find a way to kill all the Vampires and vânători too,' she finished.

Lucas shook his head in anger, his hand running backwards and forwards across the top of his scalp in agitation. He was vaguely surprised the guarding vamps who'd scattered for some downtime only hissed at her comments, the sound echoing across the sodden tunnel walls. 'You don't know what you're asking of me.'

'Lucas, I know you've changed and that the IMI has had a massive hand in that, but you are still a Protector. You have to help me do what is right to help humanity.'

'Help humanity?' Lucas shouted at her. 'And what is it that *you've* been feeding on these past ten years, mum?'

Susan closed her eyes, pinching the bridge of her nose. She opened them again, guilt the newest addition to the range of emotions sweeping across her face. 'Yes, I have been feeding on human blood, but it's what my body needed while on the serum. Lucas, I just explained that I needed that to find you.'

'And now?'

'Now I have passed my usual dosing day and the effects are wearing off. My body requires food and water, not blood anymore. Now that we are together again, I don't need to take the serum anymore. We can figure this thing out together and find a way to unite all humans again and kill off the Supernaturals.'

'Are you kidding me?' Lucas shouted again, now pacing backwards and forwards in front of the barrier. He was furious. 'Do you even realise what you're suggesting?'

135

'Of course, it's for the best.'

'And what did you tell Lucius when he came asking these questions?'

'I told him about the serum.'

'But not your end game I'm sure.'

'Of course not, he is the master vampire and the direct source of contamination. He also needs to be killed.'

'Have you even considered me in all of this?'

'You're my only concern.'

'Mum, I am not just a protector anymore. Whatever the IMI did to me when I was a kid with Elena's blood—it's changed me.'

'Do you feed on humans?'

'No, of course not.'

'Then you should have no problem destroying those that do.'

Lucas threw his hands into the air, exasperated. 'And what about what I want?'

She frowned, confused by the conflicting opinion. 'I'm not sure I follow.'

'Marianne!' Lucas shouted, his voice echoing down the tunnels. There would be no doubt that she would have heard him, if not already listening to their conversation, secretly seething and plotting ways to assassinate his mother when he wasn't looking.

'You rang,' she murmured, appearing at Lucas's side and reaching for his hand. Susan pressed her back even more firmly against the wall, taken aback by the vampire's sudden appearance and the dainty fingers that entwined with that of her son's.

'*This* is why I won't help you,' Lucas said, deliberately shoving their interlocked hands in front of his mother's face. 'Do you even remember Marianne?'

Susan peered closer, eyeing the blonde vampire from head-to-toe. 'I do remember you. You came with those vampires to our IMI in Cairns seeking help to find an alpha.'

'And we helped you,' Marianne grated through clenched teeth, 'though now I'm wondering why on earth we should have bothered given what I just heard you say.'

'It's for Elena,' Lucas murmured, kissing the top of his lover's knuckles. 'It's not for them, but for Elena. Don't forget that.'

136

Marianne's features softened as Lucas's lips left a warm trail across the surface of her frozen skin. Anger dissolved as he pulled her close, tucking her head into the crook of his neck and wrapping his arms around her. He may not have been a vampire, but in Lucas's arms she felt safe; more protected and loved than she ever thought possible.

'L-lucas?' Susan stuttered, confusion now a permanent resident in the set of her brows. 'What is this?'

'This is Marianne and we're together. So, you can see how killing her and the rest of my friends might be a problem.'

'You're together?' she repeated. 'I mean, how could you? She's a vampire!'

'Yes, she's a vampire. She's also beautiful, smart, supportive and I'm completely in love with her, but I suppose that means nothing to you?'

'W-wait, go back. You're what?'

'And Elena? What about her? Is she not worth saving? She was family once. You took her in and raised her. Does her life mean nothing or is she still just the convenient test tube for the IMI's experimentation?'

'Elena's alive? I always thought—'

'She's alive,' Lucas snapped. 'She's also the alpha of all existing vânător packs. If you even think of escaping and running back to The Protectors to betray me again, I'll make sure we launch an attack on the super cities that make the war look like fun time at the park.'

'Lucas,' Marianne warned, tugging on his arm.

'No, she needs to know that if she betrays me again, I'll kill her myself!'

'She gets it,' Marianne murmured.

'No, I don't,' Susan said, drawing slowly to her feet. She reached out, planting her hands against the barrier Lucas still had her mentally confined with. There was the brief hum of magic in the air as she gently tested his defences with her own powers, but to no avail. 'I can see why you hate me. I even understand that it's going to take time for you to trust me, but I do have your best interests at heart. I want the IMI's supply of the serum cut so they can mark the error in their ways and restore choice. I want to kill Chester, knowing he is drunk with power; a virtual unstoppable force among our ranks. But most of all, I want you to be safe. I want my Lucas back and be damned those that get in my way.' She eyed Marianne for the final deliverance of her speech, lips curling at the edges in disgust. 'I've seen too much over the last ten years to ever learn to trust their kind. Lucas, let me help you.'

Lucas shook his head, drawing Marianne closer. He soothed fingers over her waist, trailing her spine until her found the silken curls of her hair. He wound them around his fingers, concentrating on her sweet scent and the clarity her presence seemed to bring him. 'I'm sorry, mum. I'm going to keep you here and not because I think we're going to patch up our differences any time soon. I'm keeping you here because I want to help humanity too, but I'll find a way to do it that doesn't involve mass slaughter. I'm going to protect the people I love and that includes the supernaturals that walk these passages.'

Lucas was certain that as the words left his lips, the truth had been spoken. Not more than fifteen minutes before he'd felt dejected and useless, positive no good could ever come from ending the war. Now—listening to the bigoted speech that poured forth from his mother's lips—he knew he believed in something. He believed in protecting the ones he loved above all else.

'But, Lucas,' Susan pleaded, banging her fists against the barrier, 'don't you want to be normal again?'

He laughed, releasing the silken locks of Marianne's hair, grappling for her hand for support. 'Normal, he said derisively. 'What the hell is *normal* anymore? If you figure it out, then please let me know.'

'Lucas, please, we need to talk, I haven't fin—'

'Lucas!' Caleb hollered from somewhere within the passages. His desperation drowned out the sound of his mother's fresh pleas. 'Lucas! Get here now!'

Lucas and Marianne passed a panicked look before they ran in the direction of the vampire's voice. He was unconcerned about leaving his mother. His barrier would hold for a while and there were still watcher's nearby. The Vampires and vânators would be back lickety-split to kill her if she thought about trying to escape. That much he was certain of.

'What's happened,' Lucas shouted as they drew to a clumsy stop before the pink-haired vampire.

Caleb was practically dancing on the spot now, his face a mass of uncontainable smiles. 'You're never going to believe this.'

'What?' Lucas countered, straightening up and sucking in a breath of fresh air.

'Elena's finally awake.'

CHAPTER TEN: AWAKE

The last thing I remembered with any degree of clarity was being brutally stabbed. So, my first instinct was to clutch my chest and run shaking fingers over my flesh in search of a jagged line or a bloodied wound while fighting the overwhelming urge to panic. Except there was nothing. There was no oozing blood, no gaping hole or mind-numbing pain. My skin was chilled, smooth—perfect … and that simply didn't make sense.

I cracked open my eyes, intent on marvelling at this miraculous recovery for myself. Not even a half-breed like me could survive a knife with murderous intent straight to the heart. I mean, I had been stabbed, hadn't I? I remembered the war, the church, Sebastian on the steps poisoned by a blade that—

I bolted upright, seemingly cured of my drowsy and inquisitive state. 'Sebastian!'

'Easy, Elena.'

'Ahhh!' I cried, clutching my ears instead, confused by the cacophony of noise I heard everywhere; numerous voices, scratching, footsteps, moans, the sound of dripping water—it was all overwhelmingly loud.

Someone touched me—tentative at first—but then firmer; their skin was cool against my own. I strained to identify them, but my eyes refused to cooperate. Someone had spewed a kaleidoscope of colour throughout my vision and I was blind with a newfound awareness I couldn't interpret. Unexpected hues were in abundance and the detail of everything my retinas settled on was overly magnified and difficult to decipher. Light formed in mirrored shards and reflected what I thought could have been concrete. It was possible I saw grains of sand, flecks of dust and granite throughout its crumbling façade, but that seemed impossible to identify such detail.

A giant rat was also on the attack from across the corridor. That was until my focus adjusted and it seemingly disappeared within a tiny crack in a wall unfathomably too far away to be plausible. Was I trippin'?

'Elena, take it nice and slow, focus on one thing at a time.'

I was certain I could hear my father's voice; so loud in my head, vibrating through my canals and echoing through the space in between, but he was competing with my thoughts and an abundance of scarily loud versions of white noise.

'Quiet your mind, dull your senses.'

Sebastian …

'I need to get to Sebastian!' I yelled, trying to be heard over the noise within my mind. I had to focus and fast, concentrating on one noise at a time and decipher its origins. I didn't have time for whatever this was. Sebastian needed me and this burning I felt inside, the strange sensations and …

Wait. What the hell is happening to me now?

I must have slid from whatever bed or cushioning I'd been horizontal on not moments before, very much aware that solid concrete now connected with my knees as I fell to the floor. It wasn't as unyielding as I'd imagined it would be, even as I howled with weird kinds of internal pains, the concrete parted like sand beneath me, spraying up little plumes of dust.

Now on all fours, hands clasped me from every direction, attempting to haul me back to my feet, but I could barely move—pain undeniably present. The touch of others only exacerbated the sensations, so I anchored myself to the damp stone and brittle concrete beneath me, searching for solid support and grounding, hoping these worrying symptoms would soon pass.

'What's happening to her?'

Lucas.

I could hear him as clear as a bell. No other noise within my head could dampen his voice from my mind. I noted his apprehension and the tension radiating from his voice. Not just words, but I could sense the emotional soundtrack of his mounting anxiety. It tangibly wrapped around me, smothering me with emotions I couldn't handle on top of this monstrous pain. Why was this happening to me? Why was I hearing all these things? Why could I see everything and yet could focus on nothing?

'She's not used to her new gifts,' I think Lucius answered. 'She's overwhelmed by sights, sounds and touch. It's like being born all over again.'

142

'How can we help her?'

'We can't. She needs to figure this out for herself.'

I managed to contain a pretty descriptive expletive and slumped further towards the cooling surface of the dirtied floor. The stench of mildew was overwhelmingly present in every breath I took, almost cloying as the spores attempted to clot my lungs with their blackened intent.

I decided to close my psychedelic eyes to block visual stimulus and distractions. I also absently slapped away the hands that tried to move me from my damp haven on the floor. I needed darkness and I wanted quiet. I couldn't think straight, see straight and my stomach was suddenly roaring with a need that was practically crippling.

I knew this pain. I knew what it was like to hunger, to feel my body slowly contort my insides, scratch at the walls of sanity and ignite my thirst for blood. This hunger was as sudden as the onslaught of visual and auditory stimulus, not the creeping slyness of vampirism I was used to controlling. This was desperation; my body's way of telling me it would take action without my consent. It was …

I lunged like a lithe jungle cat, surprised by my own quick movements and thought processes. I'd been possessed by a hunger demon, my body now on autopilot as I grabbed the nearest body, my lengthening talons hooking into skin and pulling at their flesh like a helpless fish on a hook. Blood—the sweet saltiness of its stench tainted the mildewy stigma of the surrounding air, cloying my senses and control. My fangs were now primed to finish what my talons had started.

Panic ensued as shouting rented any audible space. Hands grappled with me left and right, but I was stronger than I ever remembered and hungry to boot; my victim was already within my grasp. Faceless, nameless—this catch was merely food. I hungered and I would feed. Consequences be damned.

A milky wrist appeared in front of my face; vision suddenly askew with a delectable morsel of throbbing blue veins filled with liquid satiation. My talons retracted as I released my current prey without too much thought and latched onto the offered prize in my immediate line of sight. Easy food. The even sweeter scent of vampire blood; a rare treat that the vânător within me yearned for.

Canines uncomfortably long, I bit down into flesh, marvelling with a smug grunt as blood oozed into my mouth like warm caramel. Pain ebbed as the sweet relief of my tongue eagerly lapped satisfaction down one pint at a time to soothe the burning pathways within. I sucked and dragged, my lips a rubber seal as I took as much as I could without hesitation.

I was being man-handled once more. Hands came at me from every direction; different sizes, shapes and colours as I struggled to focus on what I was seeing and feeling. Naturally I kicked out, defending my right to feed, digging in deeper with my fangs and sucking harder.

'Elena! Stop, you have to stop!'

What?

'She can't kill him, Lucas. Lucius knows what he's doing and you're lucky he stepped in as she's not going to stop feeding anytime soon.'

Stop?

'Look at him! She's taking too much. Why is she doing this?'

'She's awake,' another voice boomed, oddly familiar. 'She will feed until her body has recouped. It's normal. It's why we are so dangerous after our night of official turning.'

'But Lucius …'

'Lucas, you know Lucius is a true immortal. He cannot be killed, only weakened.'

'Lucas, I'm fine,' Lucius wheezed. 'This is why I have stood vigilant all these years.' A long pause and a gulp. 'I knew eventually she would wake and hunger, craving not just human blood, but vampire blood too.'

'Because she's half vânător.'

'Yes.'

'It makes sense that she would feed from the one person here she could not kill.'

'Come on, Lucas,' another voice said, female this time and annoyingly loud. Why couldn't I turn the volume down? 'Let's get those cuts on your shoulder cleaned up.'

'No, I want to stay with her.'

'Lucas …'

'I'll be okay.'

144

The body attached to the wrist I fed upon now slumped against me, taking us both to the ground like a sack of potatoes. The blood flow had ceased and my fangs detached as my head hit the floor and fractured yet more of the concrete beneath us. I expected to gasp in pain, but once more it was like landing in sand. Pain in every region of my body was now nothing but a distant memory as my bloated stomach thanked me for the sustenance.

I blinked several times, using my lids like washer wipers to clear my vision and find focus. The ceiling above came into view first. Ordinary, I soon realised it was a myriad of layers, colours and textures created from the ingredients that rendered it a solid structure. Every little moss-covered stone, escaped water droplet and rough mortar joint could be distinguished and it was both beautiful and horrifying.

I blinked again, a familiar face now blooming in my vision. His crystal blue eyes were clouded with unshed tears and brimming with a slight saltiness not dissimilar to the waft of a day by the seaside, his raggedy brows drawn together in concern. It took me several minutes to stop analysing every pore, hair follicle and angle on his face before I had a full conceptual view and understanding of his importance. 'Lucas?'

His brow smoothed to silk and relief washed his features like the summertime rains of the tropics. He blew out a breath faintly reminiscent of beans and then broke into a grin. 'Yeah, E, it's me.'

My gaze drifted from the miracle of his face, distracted once more by the intricacies of the ceiling before I turned my head slowly to the right. I noted that the microscopic community of mold and bacteria kissing every surface of the concrete ceiling and floor also blanketed the walls with speckled filth. 'Lucas, where the hell am I?'

He laughed, another tainted breath of relief. 'You're in the underground tunnels under Rome.'

'Why?'

'It's a long story.'

I looked in the other direction, my hair scraping across the floor with every movement; the sound was like dry brush crinkling under a heavy-handed touch. Did I need to condition? What the hell was going on with my senses?

Lucius lay prone on the floor beside me, inelegant in his slumped nature, eyes closed and his arm draped across my chest. I forgot about my apparently lifeless hair and tried to get my acid-tripping vision to settle on his somewhat distorted features. 'Lucius?'

'I don't think he'll be answering anytime soon,' Lucas responded, drawing my attention back to him.

'Did I do that?'

Lucas nodded, his earlier relief to see my coherency disappearing as he did his own assessment of my father's lacklustre form. 'I'm afraid so.'

It was my turn to blow out a breath. It was cold; a tingling sensation on my lips that suddenly felt completely unnecessary. I did it again, sampling the sensation and its usefulness, though instincts told me breath was irrelevant.

Realisation began to finally dawn. I held my hands before my eyes, studying them from every conceivable angle. My nails were short, tidy and generally how I kept them—unmaintained. There was red staining caught just beneath a few of the nails and cuticles—blood presumably, so I concentrated on them, waiting to see if they grew into the long back talons I knew were prevalent to a vampire's arsenal.

'Um, what are you doing?' Lucas asked.

I cringed. 'Shh, not so loud.' I kept studying my hands. My fingernails were already morphing, shaping themselves into black pointed daggers, transforming my hands into something quite terrible and unexpected.

I bolted upright, Lucius's arm flinging into my lap. He roused, rolling over on the floor as if I'd disturbed his sleep. I was too distracted by my hands to pay heed to his unconscious state. 'I'm a vampire.'

Lucas scratched his shoulder, a fresh trickle of blood oozed onto his already stained t-shirt. 'Um, yep.'

I licked my lips. I was relatively sated, but I could still eat again and Lucas didn't smell half bad. He had a faint whiff of something metallic inside of him, but otherwise … 'You're bleeding.'

He looked down at his shirt, rubbing his fingers across the wound again. 'Yeah, you scratched me.'

'Scratched you?' I gave him the look that the comment deserved, pulling his shirt to the side and cringing when I saw that said scratches were in fact puncture marks. 'I did that?'

'Yeah.'

'I'm sorry.'

'You didn't know what you were doing.'

My eyes darted left, now observing Marianne who cautiously approached. She was slowly lowering herself by Lucas's side, face wary. She made each movement slow and deliberate; at least, that's what it looked like—still frames of a camera clicking by one after the other.

I shook my head, rubbing at my eyes for good measure. 'Where's Sebastian?'

I refocused just in time to see Lucas and Marianne pass a look between them; my new eyes clearly identifying angst. 'Why don't you take a few minutes to get used to your new body. It must be confusing.'

'Confusing? Where the hell is Sebastian? I was just with him, the war ...' my face screwed up as I cruised through a million shuttered thoughts of Sebastian's slumped form against a set of church steps. 'Now I'm here and he's not. Seriously, where is he?'

Another long-winded pause. 'He's gone, Elena.'

'Gone? What are you talking about?'

'He vanished.'

'Vanished?' I was aware of my parroting responses, but simply couldn't stop. With all of these over-developed senses, I couldn't think straight. I squinted, searching yet again through confused memories flooding in and out in a chorus of unsynchronised images. I tried picking through them in an effort to sort fact from fiction, but was incapable with the barrage of blank spots.

'Elena? Please say something,' Lucas prompted, voice radiating that sickening vibe of hesitancy.

'Lucas, what are you talking about? I was just with Sebastian. He was stabbed and I think I might have been too.' I pinched the bridge of my nose. 'Except I'm fine now. Lucius must have made me a thrall in order to save me, but that doesn't explain Sebastian.' I looked up again, eyes undoubtedly filled with a hope that was waning. 'Tell me he's okay. If he left us ... fine, but just tell me he's okay.'

'Elena,' Lucas said calmly, placing a reassuring hand on my shoulder. 'A lot has happened. Sebastian didn't just disappear.'

'Then where is he? And don't just say he's gone.'

Lucas appeared exasperated, turning to Marianne for support. She stepped right in, never one to be mindful of my feelings. 'It's been over ten years since the war started, Elena. It might be hard for you to understand, but although your body has been here with us, you were gone—in a comma unable to be reached. A lot of time has passed and everything has changed. What you think only just happened has been in the past for a very long time. As for Sebastian—he died, disappeared on the steps of a church the same time you were stabbed and only minutes before Lucius turned you.'

I swallowed several razor blades as I was bombarded with a very real desire to scream at the top of my lungs in both denial and frustration. 'I died, but Lucius turned me?'

'Yes.'

'And I've been a vampire for ten years, but somehow not able to wake up?'

She shrugged. 'More or less.'

'And you say Sebastian died and that in the end, I did absolutely nothing to help him and that his body simply vanished without a trace?'

'You did everything you could, but then you were taken down by some unseen force. There was a knife protruding from your chest and you were dying. Lucius stepped in and tried to save you. Meanwhile, Sebastian just disappeared. Not one of us knew how or why. We still don't and there's also no logical explanation as to why you never woke after Lucius turned you. It's like you disappeared too.'

'Disappeared,' I whispered, trying to draw connections and failing. I looked into her sapphire eyes, searching for truth and understanding. 'Then tell me where the hell I've been all this time?'

Marianne shrugged. 'That's what I'm saying ... we don't know.'

'Bullshit.'

Marianne rolled her eyes, tossing her willowy mane of blonde hair about her slender shoulders. 'Look, we weren't exactly happy about it either. You kind of left us in a tough position.'

'Marianne!' Lucas chided. 'You promised.'

'What?' she said, all innocence as the well-timed rise of her blonde brows rose heavenward. 'I was there. She dumped her responsibility of driving the Vânǎtors from the city and focused on the affections of her libido, running straight to the angel's side despite the risks. Then she went and got herself killed leaving us with the Vânǎtors and a war we had no hope of winning.'

'And what would you have done if it was me?' Lucas chided, glaring at her. 'Would you have ignored my death?'

'That's not what I—'

'Hang on a second,' I interrupted, 'Since when was the war's outcome placed squarely on my shoulders? Sebastian was—' I stopped, reaching up and gripping my ears tightly as howling rang anew throughout the tunnels. It echoed, reverberating off everything that I touched, racing along my skin and diving deep into my core. 'Jesus, make it stop!'

'It's the Vânǎtors,' Marianne answered. 'They know you're awake.'

'So?'

'So, you're their alpha. Despite your sleepy-time they remember you, smell themselves inside you. They've been as vigilant as we have waiting for you to wake up.'

'They're in the tunnels with us? They're secret tunnels!'

'A lot has changed, Elena.'

I closed my eyes in an effort to dull my senses, allowing me to concentrate on turning the volume down within my throbbing ears. Being a vampire was starting to suck. 'Can't they keep it down?' I opened my eyes ever so slowly, pissed that I had to work on refocusing the retinas again too.

Agh!

Marianne shook her head at me. At least, that's what I thought I could see as butter-blonde curls stirred dust motes the size of matchboxes in the air before me. 'Look, you just need to focus on dulling your senses. I remember what this is like. It's hard for the first few days, but I promise you'll get the hang of it.'

'That's not reassuring. I feel overwhelmed, like I'm drowning in my own senses. I can't even begin to describe what I smell right now.'

'It'll pass,' she said. 'Eventually you'll be able to choose what you see, hear and smell. Just remember, you don't need to breathe, so you can stop inhaling any time you want.'

The noise of the wolves died down, enough for me to unplug my ears. 'Can I have a minute?'

'What?'

'Are you okay?' Lucas asked, leaning in front of Marianne to inspect me like some dial-a-doctor. 'Do you need more blood?'

I shook my head, trying not to pay attention to the puncture marks still oozing on his shoulder. 'No, I think I just need a few minutes alone to digest everything. It's a bit too much, you know?'

'Lucas, come on,' Marianne said, rising and dragging Lucas to his feet behind her. 'Let's give the girl some space.' As she hauled Lucas towards the door, he found some way to yank free before running back to me. He landed on his knees, cringing only slightly as he threw his arms around me. He kissed the top of my head and squeezed as tightly as his body would allow.

'I'm sorry, I know this probably feels over the top to you, but I've missed my little sister all these years. It hasn't been easy ... figuring everything out.'

I hugged him back. I'd grown used to my excessive strength over the last few months so it wasn't hard to avoid crushing him like a bug. I was definitely stronger now, but the same principal applied. 'It feels like I only just saw you, Lucas.'

'It's been over ten years.'

'Yes, you all keep reminding me.'

He released me slowly, patting the side of my cheek with his hand as he edged away. It was calloused now; the hands of a man that worked for a living. Not the Tetris-playing, porn-surfing little nerd I remembered. What else had I missed?

'I'll leave you to it.'

I studied him longer, watching his hands slip away. His tall, slim body was still lean and as muscled as the last time I'd checked. He had not grown his hair back; still shaved short against his head and actually quite becoming with the angular planes of his face and the inquisitive powder blues eyes framed by blonde lashes. A lifetime may have passed, but he still looked exactly the same.

I snapped out, grabbing his hand before he disappeared entirely. Gripping his fingers, I pulled him backwards. He stumbled, but I held him steady, planting my dirtied palms on his shoulders as he resumed his earlier kneeling position. 'Are you sure about this ten-year-thing?'

'Yes.'

'Then why the hell do you still look eighteen?'

He broke into a grin. 'Side effects of your blood and the IMI's tampering.'

'So, you're immortal?'

'I'm no vampire. I can't run fast and I'm not strong, but yes I will live forever if I look after this body and I'm pretty damn good with the telekinetic stuff now.'

'Better than me?'

'Naturally.'

I sighed, suddenly overwhelmed again. Not by sights, sounds and smells, but by my own twisted emotions. So much had happened that I didn't understand. It was like a chunk of my memory had been stolen, leaving me blank and unknowing. I was living in the past and everyone else was in the future. Sebastian was apparently gone and my brother was immortal. 'I need that minute now, please.'

Marianne resumed her earlier grip on Lucas, tugging him back towards the door. She stopped to grab Caleb by the arm too, but he was more reluctant to budge. I hadn't seen him standing there, hidden in the shadows of the passage beyond, but he was watching. His blue eyes seemed to penetrate the darkness; his pink hair a neon glow stick I was unsure how I'd missed.

'Caleb,' I murmured.

'Elena.'

I held my hand out, waving the other two off so that we could be alone. If there was anyone here that could tell me about Sebastian, it would be this vampire—this friend.

He clasped my fingers, pulling me slowly to my feet. He was smiling lightly; just the edges of his lips curling upwards, enough to let me know he was happy to see me. He brushed the brittle hair from the side of my cheek and tucked it behind my ear as Sebastian had once done, then patted me on the shoulder for good measure. 'You smell different now.'

I snorted, the first sign of laughter. 'I'm not tasty anymore, huh?'

'Not in the slightest.' He pointed to my father still lying on the floor. 'I can see you're not too fussy, though.'

151

I punched his arm playfully, marvelling at the rising sensation of normality attained via Caleb's presence. 'You know I didn't mean it.'

'You don't seem too upset.'

My smile waned. 'I'm trying not to think about anything too hard at the moment. I'm just grateful he did what needed to be done to ensure everyone's safety. I'll thank him properly after he sleeps it off.'

Caleb nodded, attention focused back on me as he then held me at arm's length, let go of one of my hands and then spun me on the spot. 'Death becomes you.'

I found those hints of a smile touching my lips again. 'You think?'

'Well, I always thought you were attractive, but now …' He tapped ebony-stained fingernails upon his lips as if in quiet contemplation. 'Now you're stunning. Although I'm not sure the mildew agrees with you.'

'I'm not sure a lot of things agree with me, but thanks.'

He whistled. 'Sebastian would have been blown away.'

We both stopped smiling, frivolity now absent in the reminder of what we had lost. 'So, he's really gone?'

'Yes, Elena.'

I released Caleb's hand and fingered the centre of my chest, flattening my palm against the surface of my smooth flesh, expecting my heart to crumble in its casing. The problem was it no longer beat; my chest was nothing but an empty cavity now, a vessel filled with memories of the past and hopes for a future that would never prevail. I was dead both inside and out, unsure how to move forward without him and unsure if I wanted to.

Caleb caught me as I started to descend once more, wrapping his arms around me and holding me close. 'I thought they might have been mistaken. Sebastian can't be gone, he just can't. He's a god damn angel for Pete's sake!'

'I know.'

'How? How? I would know, wouldn't I? He doesn't feel gone, he feels close, like we only just saw each other.'

'Ten years would feel like yesterday to you.'

'Yesterday sucks.'

His arms tightened, but not uncomfortably so. 'Yes, it does.'

A sob escaped and then another and another before I was suddenly swamped by uncontrollable tears that stained my cheeks with the crimson life I'd robbed from Lucius not moments before. Crying was a form of vulnerability I had always been reluctant to present to the outside world. Yet the more I tried to supress my emotions, the stronger the flow became. And though I didn't need breath or the exacerbated pain of this moment, I found myself gasping for it, desperate to turn back the clock and fix all the wrongs—wash away the past with my tears.

You aren't ready yet. A familiar voice echoed through my head. *Focus, try to remember—never forget what you lost.*

I ignored Araqiel's chatter in my thoughts, irritated that he still lingered in the dark recesses of my mind. Where had he been when I needed him? I never expected miracles, but to let Sebastian die and to accept that his life was worth less than my own?

Unacceptable.

'It's okay, Elena. Let it all out.'

Caleb's voice I *did* listen to. I had nothing to say to Araqiel. I was still too confused, angry and grieving. I'd lost so much—been through so much in such a short space of time. And to remember? Didn't he think that I wanted to? To be able to make sense of the past?

Remember him.

I'm trying!

'Shh,' Caleb murmured, his hand soothing my back. 'Everything will be okay. Eventually it won't hurt so much.'

'How can you know that?' I hiccuped, burying my face closer against his chest, feeling stupid and irritated by my own display of unrelenting weakness.

'He was my friend too.'

'I know.'

Silence ensued. In that tiny concrete basement that smelled of mould and rat's droppings, I clung to my friend—to the link in this strange new life that bore so many ties to the past. I was completely unprepared for change and now prayed silently for acceptance and strength. It was not to a higher entity because they were simply bothersome, but to myself.

For so long I had denied my feelings for Sebastian in an attempt to protect myself from this God-awful sense of loss I now felt, but it was for naught as the guttural sense of love lost and

153

never-to-be-found was overwhelmingly present. I'd let myself go, opened my heart to him and now I was bleeding on the inside—dying all over again.

I don't know how long we stayed like that, clinging to one another. It must have been hours, possibly even days. People had come and gone, my own father had even awakened and tried to break Caleb free of my hold, yet I couldn't face the real world yet without him.

Caleb never complained, never tried to urge me to stem the flow of tears. He simply hung onto my limp body and let me cry a river of blood all over his aging death metal t-shirt.

Nothing would ever be the same again.

As we stood in our private embrace, time ticking over, each lost to their own worrying thoughts, I started to grow eerily calm. I reasoned that change might have been beneficial in order for growth—not just for me—but for the ensuing peace of our multiple races. I pained like I'd never pained before, but I knew the consequences of idleness and transient thoughts muddled with laboured emotion. I could cower in Caleb's embrace forever and feel sorry for myself, spiral into depression and be one with the mouldy surrounds of this basement, but was that truly in my nature?

No.

I finally stepped back from Caleb, wiped my face and squared my shoulders. I expected him to say something—anything—but he just smiled, the corners of his mouth lifting into a grin as he studied the resolute expression on my face. I took him by the hand and his fingers curled around mine, firm and reassuring. 'Let's go.'

'Are we done now?' he asked, following behind me into the passage.

I nodded. 'Yeah, it's time to figure some shit out.'

He laughed, the sound echoing off every wall in the near vicinity. 'Okay then.'

'Nothing else to add?'

'Yeah … Welcome back.'

CHAPTER ELEVEN: CHOICES

Eyes firmly focused, I studied the distance ahead, goal in sight. Blades of grass whispered in the prevailing wind, brushing against my ankles with feather-light caresses; so soft and in juxtaposition to the broken asphalt and glass that littered the rest of the ground like iridescent pebbles. The wind … more tangible than I could have ever imagined since reawakening; every particle and drop of moisture was present against my skin. I was so much more aware of everything around me now—sights, sounds and smells. Everything was stimulating in some way. Everything new and different.

The harsh nature of reality came into focus. The city of Rome was but a forgotten memory; the streets were now the very interpretation of neglect and lack of human interaction. Vines and shrubbery grew wild, clinging to the mortar joints of shop fronts and homes. Abandonment was glaringly obvious as nature's inclination to overtake what man had created now ruling the once bustling streets of this busy metropolitan city. Time had swept through like a destructive tornado, ripping apart the memories I had and whisking away the chance of seeing life spawn once more. All that stood in Rome's place was the husk of what was once deemed civilisation.

'Are you ready?'

I glanced left. William was grinning at me, the playfulness of his emerald eyes always enough to stop my heart—if I'd had one anymore. I grinned back, somewhat amused that we could slide into a friendship after all the complexities our past offered us.

Easily distracted by my new vampiric gifts, I now studied my fingers as they dug into the ground for traction, marvelling as the bitumen parted under my grip like crumbling pastry. I'd been strong for quite some time, but never quite convincingly so. I finally mustered a reply, 'I don't know if *ready* is quite the right answer, but I'm still gonna try and kick your ass.'

155

I looked up again only to see his grin widen; straight white teeth almost luminescent under the microscope of this seemingly uncontrollable vision.

'Nothing's changed. You're still as cocky as ever.'

'Shut your lips, Tic-Tac mouth. I'm being blinded by the glare from your cheesy grin.'

'Still having trouble focusing?' he jested, laughing as if it was all a big joke. Perhaps it was to everyone else. I was a freshie and they hadn't seen one of those in a while. Maybe it was a belly-laugh to see a vampire walk into walls and shout at people three feet away. However, I was *slowly* getting the hang of it.

'Just when I think I have it all figured out, I can suddenly hear things from miles away, feel the wind like sandpaper against my skin or see things in a range of technicolour that I didn't even know existed.'

'Stop beating yourself up about it. Did you know it took Karina three weeks to stop falling down manholes?'

'Really?'

'She couldn't focus properly, kept seeing things further away than they actually were and misjudged a footstep or three.'

'You know I can hear you!' she shouted from the end line, probably for my benefit as I had trouble using all senses simultaneously.

William bit his lip in an effort to contain his outburst while I now let my wandering eyes drift over the makeshift ticket-tape we'd hastily draped across two upturned cars in the distance. Five kilometres was more than enough to test my speed, my agility and my focus; all three of which I was definitely at odds with at present.

The bold words *'police line, do not cross'*, were clear and present. Even from this distance, the yellowed hue of the tape and its dirtied edges could be easily recognised. It was everything else that was a little murky, like a camera lens unable to focus on both foreground and background simultaneously. I was not nearly good enough compared to my vision in vânător form. Why was it hard to be a vampire but so easy to be a wolf?

I refocused my retinas, following the tape line to the first upturned vehicle. Karina stood atop, hands resting upon her slender hips, long dark hair whipping behind her like a midnight cape. She watched me carefully, teeth grating ever so slightly as I suspected she listened to the easy banter between me and William.

The upturned car and Karina dissolved into the background as I zoomed out, the yellow tape now nothing but a streak of colour in the otherwise bleak distance. I made the mistake of looking at William again; nothing but deep pools of emerald green to meet my focus. I felt like I was drowning, caught inside the beauty of his eyes.

'Easy there,' William said, placing a steadying hand on my shoulder. 'Your pupils are too dilated.'

'Tell me about it,' I mumbled, closing my lids for the briefest of moments before opening them again.

'Better?'

'Yeah.' At least I could see again. But once I started to move? What might happen if my fumbling focus could not keep pace with what we all assumed would be the swiftness of my moving vampiric body? In all likeliness, I was going to plough into the side of a building. 'You sure it took Karina three weeks?'

'Three highly amusing weeks.'

'I can still hear you!' she shouted again.

A rumble resonated from William as he bent his head down, hiding yet another one of his dazzling smiles. He echoed my stance instead, digging his fingers into the ground and stretching one leg out behind him like an Olympic athlete ready to clear the chute. 'She's jealous.'

I coughed—uncomfortably so—uncertain whether I wanted to make any comment on conversation that undoubtedly related to either mine and William's past or his and Karina's future. It was still a little too weird for me to actually see them together. It felt only yesterday that William was still pursuing me, eager to pull me from Sebastian's sway and … I supposed it no longer mattered at all. 'I would never do anything to threaten what you both have built with each other in my absence.'

I felt rather than saw William studying the serious expression on my face. I was all for avoiding eye contact now. 'You mean that, don't you?'

'I only ever wanted you to be happy, William. And, I can see with Karina that you are. Jealousy is a waste of everyone's time. I'm no threat.' A part of me really hoped that she still listened as she stood upon the rusting chassis of the upturned car in the distance.

'No, Karina's not threatened by you and me. She knows that's ancient history. She's jealous of how quickly you're adapting to vampirism. You've only been up and about for a few days and already you're working on homogenising your new senses.

'*Winging it* is more like it. I'm only a leg up because your blood moved the schedule forward while I was human. I had some time to get used to some of these changes.'

William no longer answered me and I chanced a look, his eyes were fixed on the distance ahead. At first, I wondered if he might have been angry for mentioning our past while Karina loomed close or even discussing our exchange of blood, but then I realised as his features softened and his pupils dilated that he wasn't the slightest bit interested in what I had to say. He had eyes only for the vampire in the distance, a blurred shadow with wind-whipped hair and the aura of magic.

'Besides,' William croaked, clearing his throat what seemed like several minutes later, 'Karina knows she's the only one for me. The only one I could ever love now.'

Ordinarily I might have rolled my eyes at William's fanciful declarations of love and whimsy, but I stopped myself. He was the type to shout your name from the rooftop and declare his feelings at the drop of a hat and I often cringed by such notions directed my way, but now I fully understood the look in his eyes. Karina was to him what Sebastian had been to me. I supposed our past mistakes were the blessing for his future. I may not have had Sebastian anymore, but at least he had found Karina.

I turned, now cripplingly overwhelmed by the sudden flood of grief that touched my unmoving heart. It was like icy fingers digging through my insides, twisting and turning everything upside down, filling me with a terrible emptiness I had no idea how to fill without … him.

'You miss *him,* don't you?' he whispered.

All I could do was nod and take a deep, shuddering breath.

'We may have had our differences—Sebastian and I—but it was clear how much he loved you by what he was willing to give up to be with you.'

I didn't trust myself to speak.

'Elena, I—'

'Let's not talk about it, okay?'

'Okay.'

158

Well, that had been a little too easy! William never shut up about anything! 'What's your angle?'

He seemed genuinely perplexed by my suspicion and raised a hand in defence, the other still firmly planted in the bitumen. 'No angle, I'm just saying I understand and respect your right to privacy, so I won't probe.'

'Are you trying to distract me by confusing me?' In the distance, Karina slammed her foot on top of the car for the umpteenth time, muttering something about us being crazy spending so much time out in the open.

'Distract you? I would never stoop so low.' He looked outraged even by the mere suggestion which only served to boost my rising amusement.

'Well, that's good. I mean, I've always really liked that about you, William.'

'Liked what?' Doubt and a hefty barrel of suspicion was now squarely locked, loaded and pointed in my direction.

'Your honesty, your integrity ...' I buried my fingers just a few millimetres deeper into the ground, propping up on one foot as I got ready to spring forward with the other.

'Thank you, Elena.'

'Oh, don't thank me, William. I don't possess either of those qualities.'

'What do you mean?'

I lashed out while he was distracted, catching him in the side with my left foot and connecting with ribs. As an older vampire there would be no pain or suffering, just the fleeting moment of guilt that shivered through me as his body crashed through the shop front beside us. Glass was spewed in every direction, the shards only just missing my toughened skin as I launched towards the finish line and towards Karina.

Asphalt parted under each crushing step and I knew I was being too weighty. I needed to change tactics if I were to be nimble and feather-light in my attempts to move forward with unpredictability. The foreground was hazy, but I could hear Karina shouting. It was too much for me to focus on all abilities at once. Instead, I concentrated on speed, leaping over debris as I approached and narrowly avoiding sheet metal strewn haphazardly through the street.

William was fast. I knew he approached without even having to turn my head. The ticket-tape was close, but he was closer. His guttural growl echoed through me and a second later I was under attack, plummeting to my knees as his arms and legs were now wrapped around me like a reptile constricting its prey. Street debris sprayed in every direction, the nearest car victim to our deadly roll.

We hit metal at an impact that would have put a bulldozer out of commission. The cabin cocooned our bodies in a twisted shell, bending, popping and groaning under our weight. More glass shattered and emptied from the windows, raining down upon us like tiny diamonds. The ticket tape was the last to fall, floating down on the wind and coming to rest across the top of our feet. We'd finally come to a stop, arms and legs twisted, massive grins on our faces and not a scratch to be shown for our efforts.

'Who won?' we both shouted, clawing at the other to get out of the way.

Karina jumped from her perch atop the car, boots clicking across the ground as she walked towards us. She tapped those long, slim fingers against her hips, a scowl marking her face. 'Do you even realise how much noise you two just made? I wouldn't be surprised if we were attacked right now because of your stupidity.'

'Yeah, but who won?' I pressed, shoving William in the face as he elbowed me in the stomach.

'Did you even hear me?'

'There's no one out here, Karina. The city is deserted.'

She huffed, clearly unamused. 'The Protectors are everywhere, especially now that Susan is missing. Don't you think that they might start looking for her?'

William disentangled himself from my limbs and helped pull me back to my feet. We dusted off, no longer feeling elated. Karina's words rang true in our ears. 'Lucas said he hasn't felt them near. She's been with us well over a week. If they were looking for her, they would have located the craft by now and quite probably us.'

'Lucas doesn't know everything,' Karina muttered. 'I saw them early this morning before sunrise, they were—'

'You what?' William bellowed, taking a step towards Karina. I had to give her credit, she didn't step back and didn't falter. She merely pressed her lips into a hard line and planted both hands on her hips in further defiance.

'Don't even look at me like that,' she said to him, squaring her shoulders. 'I told Lucas they would come and I was right.'

The sound of knuckles cracking drew my eyes down to the tightly curled fists at William's side. 'You went outside without me?'

'Don't start.'

'Karina—'

'I said, don't start. William, if I want to go outside, I damn well will. You two seem to think it's okay to run relays along the highway in the middle of the night, but it's not okay for me to keep an eye on our enemies.'

'Do you even realise how dangerous it is to be out here alone?' William continued as if he hadn't heard a word she'd said. 'You're the most important thing in my life. I can't risk losing you to—'

Karina rolled her eyes and slapped a hand across his lips. 'Save it. I'm glad I did. If I hadn't, the patrol that swept through here last night would have found the hunting vehicles.'

I felt like an intruder, watching them glare at one another, each arguing their point. I thought about tiptoeing away, letting them continue to verbally assault the other, but something Karina had said caught my attention. 'Wait, are you saying you got rid of them?'

She turned her attention on me, letting her hand drop from William's lips. 'The Vânătors made short work trying to get into the cabin and feed on the occupants of the first two crafts. I merely grabbed what was left, pulled them apart and threw the pieces into an abandoned building close by.'

'And the third craft, the one Susan was in?' William asked. He wasn't any less annoyed with her, but he was curious enough to unclench his fists and listen.

'Well, you'd shredded up the underside a fair bit with your claws and the interior was a little crushed thanks to Lucas's mind-bending tricks, but otherwise it still seemed to be in good condition.' A small smile tugged at the corner of her lips. 'I thought it might be useful. I thought maybe someone would be able to fix it, so I hid it too.'

Doubt brushed my mind for a quarter of a second as I imagined this rake-thin girl I used to study with back at the IMI pick up machinery comparable to the size and weight of a car and put it out of sight like she was just tucking it into her purse for good measure. 'Where did you hide it?'

'In the Synth Corp building.'

'Does it still run?'

She gave me a droll look. 'They're powered by magic, the *Levitartium* spell to be precise. I suspect all the lights on the dash are for the curious humans who wonder how the machinery operates.'

I was obviously missing something. 'Then why do we need to fix it?'

William was already catching on, nodding his head in understanding. 'We need it to look operational aesthetically, so when we use it to gain access into the super cities, no one will suspect anything.'

I'd heard a lot about these super cities since I'd woken up. It was hard to believe that in only ten short years the entire world had gone to shit, common sense dying with it. The cities supposedly housed the last of the human race and small divisions of suped-up Protectors supposedly sustaining life behind the magically enforced walls.

The first few years were described as the craziest. The media—while it still existed—went nuts, recounting the fall of Milan as the devil's work and the end of the world for all mankind. People surrendered to pitch-fork mentality, brandishing weapons on friends and neighbours—anyone who looked suspicious or out of place. Thousands of innocents were killed by mass panic and a lot more simply killed for fun. When humans turned to chemical warfare and sent forth armies, everything was lost. Even some vampires and vânătors fared no better, revelling in the newfound freedom to hunt and feed. Retaliation was already the word on everyone's lips, so making a meal out of it was the planet's idea of a solution.

When the bombs finally stopped falling and the guns stopped smoking, there hadn't been much left. For every one of us that had fallen, a hundred more humans perished. Arrogance became fear and then there was no one left to fight, nothing left to etch out an existence. Money had become a useless commodity, farmlands ravaged by nuclear bombs and radiation exposure. Public transportation was disbanded, classed as moving buffets for those of us that lingered in the shadows and fed on blood. Heavy

162

artillery had sprayed holes through public and private domains, rupturing the last vestiges of normalcy. The hidden were soon hunted and water supplies irreparably polluted by the dead or the debris of the living.

Fear escalated and entire cities were levelled. The IMI used any media coverage left to fill the survivors with hope, to guide them to these supposed sanctuaries designed to farm their blood. They were impenetrable to any supernatural entity, growing in popularity with every year that passed. People would migrate across countries, risking life and limb to cling to some vestige of hope in these places built upon despair.

I'd since learned that there were six super cities; Paris was the closest to us. The second was rumoured to be in Moscow, the third in Beijing, the fourth in Sydney, the fifth was in Cairo and the sixth was in Buenos Aires. I never would have believed that there were enough Protectors to spread around, but there you have it.

'Elena?'

I shook my head. 'What?'

'You're staring into space,' William said, touching me on the shoulder as if I needed grounding.

'I was thinking about the super cities.'

'Do you want to see the hunting vehicle?'

'What?' I obviously wasn't drawing the connection.

'Come on,' Karina said, tugging me by the hand. 'Lucas will want to see it too. He's been brain-storming ways to get into the cities for years. This just might be what we need.'

'And what will we do when we get in there?' I asked, not sure if anyone had actually thought about what lay beyond the magical walls.

Karina choked, slapping a hand against her chest. I was already reaching out to her when I realised she was laughing, turning to face me in astonishment. 'Since when do you question the irrational?'

I frowned. 'The Protectors are supposedly as strong, fast and as blood-thirsty as we've been portrayed. Even if we try, we'd only be able to smuggle one or two people inside that will undoubtedly get caught and slaughtered for the effort. Tell me. Why hasn't Lucius just slapped his hand against the ground and caused a mass earthquake or hurled debris at the wall or—I don't know—bent the buildings in half with his mind?'

163

'Elena, you know better than anyone that no supernatural can defend against a Protector's magic despite some of our limitations. Lucius may be able to do all those things—and believe me—we've actually tried a few of them, but the fact remains no one is getting into one of those cities unless we're *let* inside.'

'I scratched the top of my forehead, aware that it was just a reflex and not a necessity. 'What did Susan say? Lucas said she wants to kill Chester. There must be a way inside.'

'Do you really want to let her loose?'

I shrugged. 'She's human now. It's not like she can outrun us.'

'This is true, but she's still a Protector and still with full use of her magic.'

'Which I'm sure between you and Lucas she can be prevented from using ...'

'Not necessarily.'

'What about compulsion?'

Karina and William passed a look between them. 'It's never worked before,' William murmured. 'They know what it is that we are capable of.'

'That's because you've never been able to get close enough. Lucas could make Susan watch, make her listen to you, William.'

'To what end?'

Karina was now nodding vigorously. 'She could get all of us into the city. Like a Trojan horse we could all enter under the guise of being her prisoners. From inside we could take out the major players and Susan would help and she wouldn't question earlier loyalties.'

'It's an idea,' I agreed, 'but that's still only one city. There would be five others on alert, aware of what we might be able to achieve with the Paris hub. We won't be able to play the same trick twice.'

'That's true.'

'Not unless we convince her to bring in more players from other super cities,' William continued. 'We compel them and launch a global interception.'

'Another war? Is that really what we need right now?' I asked.

'No. We just need enough time to take out the heads of house, destroy the production of the serum—wherever that may be—and alert the public to the IMI's intentions.'

I was feeling less than enthused by this plan. 'And then what? It's not like humans are going to fall to their knees and thank us.'

'Elena, they don't know they are being farmed for blood. If we can tell them then maybe—'

'Maybe what? They'll be relieved? I don't know, William. I just don't know. It seems that everything is hopeless. If we manage to actually pull this crazy idea off and let the Humans free, they'll just be running from the rest of us.'

'I don't understand.'

I touched him gently on the shoulder. 'I've always admired you for your restraint of human blood, but I cannot say that the rest of us are as strong. I've only been awake for a few days, but I know you are all thirsty. Hell, I can feel my wolves' hunger breathing down my neck. Their thirst is my thirst and even I don't know how restrained I can be.'

'We should talk to Lucas and Lucius, see what they think about this plan.'

'You do that,' I said, patting him on the shoulder again and turning away. I was not convinced that starting another war and letting the Humans loose into a starving society was a plan that would work without a lot of fatalities.

'Where are you going?'

'For a walk.'

'Not alone you're not.'

I threw him a droll look over my shoulder but kept on walking. 'William, you've never been able to pull that crap with me in the past. What makes you think I'm going to start listening to you now?'

'Just let her go,' Karina chided, catching William by the hand and pulling him back.

'But, Elena, it's dangerous and Julius was never found.'

Julius. There was a name I'd sooner rather forget. That psychopathic vampire had been out for my blood since unearthing my ties to Lucius. Revenge was a constant companion for him and I still wasn't sure if he hadn't already sought it in my human death. 'I'll be fine.'

'At least tell us where you are going?'

I searched the horizon, trying to make sense of the highways of rubble and desolate paths of the past. I shrugged, only one word instantly coming to mind, only one word that could ease the apprehension I felt. 'Home.'

*   *   *

I had expected William to follow me. At the very least, I expected him to run back to the tunnels and tell someone I was being an idiot for wandering the streets alone. It was nice that he still cared—that he worried about my safety, because I was almost scarily certain that I no longer did. I had lost something I could never get back and now my life was of very little consequence to me. Sebastian was a constant torment in my thoughts and the changed world I'd re-entered meant that I also now had no idea where I fit in. My friends had moved on; even Lucas had changed beyond rational thought. I'd left behind a dorky older sibling and come back to a man that mattered; a man more powerful and capable than I could ever be.

I felt lost in this strange new world despite having my father by my side; a man I still barely knew. I had Lucas—and of course—the few friends that had not died during the war, but I no longer had my heart. How long could I function without it? How long before the emptiness inside swallowed me whole?

I kept moving … slow even by a vampire's standards. I didn't watch the skies or search the horizon for danger as perhaps I should have. My eyes were downcast, watching as my bare feet crunched over grass, glass, metal and bitumen. What I left behind in my wake was nothing more than dust. Not a single ounce of penetrable danger made a mark on my flesh. I felt an unhealthy dose of invincibility—untouchable even by those that saw me harm. Did I even really care if they could? Would it matter if Julius found me now, walking the streets of Rome, alone and seemingly vulnerable?

No. To die would be a release, even if I did wind up in hell thanks to my vampiric blood, but there was still the off chance that I could see *him*.

I shuddered, gripping my arms tightly as I convulsed. It was not the cold. I no longer felt such trivial things. Some unseen force rippled across my skin. It fluttered my eyes and flashed colour through my vision. At first, I thought my newfound electrics were going crazy again, but then I saw him. I saw *us*.

I brushed my hand through his long, dark hair and Sebastian smiled up at me. His eyes flashed silver, a reminder of his angelic nature. His hands were already reaching for me. I had been distracted by the spell of his gaze. We toppled to the ground, his lips finding mine. We …

I shook my head, rubbing my eyes and seeing nothing but the debris of a ruined city around me. I looked again, searching for Sebastian. I could still feel the silk of his hair between my fingers and the feel of his lips on mine. In the air I could smell freshly sawn pine and the scent of spring rain and warm leather tickling my senses—so tangible—I felt I could reach out and touch him, a memory so vivid, yet so difficult to place.

Sharp nails pierced the flesh of my palm. The stinging reminder of reality only brought back the present and wiped such intimate thoughts from my mind. It had been nothing more than a passing thought or perhaps a dream, yet what I had seen in my mind for those few seconds had felt real. Maybe wishful thinking on my part, my flesh somehow remembered being in Sebastian's arms. My whole body burned with the awareness of his touch, I just couldn't remember when, why or how.

You're going to drive yourself crazy. I told myself. *You have to stop thinking about what could have been. You have to move on with your life.*

I can't …

You don't have a choice.

I took a deep, unnecessary breath, allowing the air to fill my lungs. I sampled how long I could hold it, turning my thoughts to anything but him. By now I'd crossed into the old township of Valle Santa before it became clear that I could hold the air indefinitely. Unfortunately, it was also clear that thoughts of Sebastian would never leave me either. I was doomed to be a pathetic love-sick idiot, incapable of moving on, stuck in the past and without hope for the future.

I spied the Villa in the distance and ran towards it, welcomed by the sight of a place I'd recently perceived as home. I'd loved Cairns—even missed my life in Australia and the simplicity it had brought—but there was something about Rome, something so familiar and welcoming it was scary.

I stood still and in awe of the old timber front doors not more than a few seconds later, marvelling at their existence after such time and tragedy. One of the doors may have hung by a single hinge and drooped towards the ground like melted wax, but they held resolute in unison. The knotted oak was battered and bruised, the metal rusting and crying for oil, but I was home.

I strolled past the fountain of rubble that lined the cobblestone driveway and pushed through the creaky doors. They protested and groaned, but the single-hinged door gave way and crashed into the wall beyond. In the courtyard, half of the building had crumbled, left for dead and scattered across the unkempt property. The old swimming pool was now filled with sludge and indeterminable waste. The downstairs rooms had been looted, the gardens taking over and crawling through the villa like unwanted guests.

The door to the music room was gone along with a sizeable chunk of the wall. The painted wall mural was covered in mud and various stains that my nose told me was blood. The piano Sebastian had so often played was in pieces, the ivory keys resting across the terracotta in fragments of unforgotten memories of the past.

I turned in disgust from the room and leapt to the second story, bypassing what was left of the stone stairs. My room and the left-hand side of the house were completely gone, but one door at the end of the hall still remained. I bolted for it, blowing through the fragile timber like a tornado, shattering the last vestiges of this haven in a blur of splintering rain.

I stopped, my eyes squeezed shut, hands curled into fists at my side. What did I expect to see? What was it that I wanted to see?

I opened my eyes slowly, dropping to my knees as the room came into focus. Blood slithered down my cheeks in an unwanted caress. I couldn't believe that the room was virtually untouched. The French doors had been blown away and half of the back wall was missing, but the shelves were still lined with his musical instruments, his bed with its assortment of black rugs and sheets still stood proud in the centre of the room. Vines crept across the walls and moss clung to the cracked mortar and spread across the exposed terracotta floor, but the bed remained untouched.

I slowly crawled towards it, drawn by the faint smell that still clung to the sheets. Mould, damp and age jockeyed for supremacy—but in the end—the Archangel had left his mark in this space.

Dust mites welcomed me as my palm slapped against the mattress, dancing through the air like a pungent fog. I gripped the sheets tightly, hauling myself up onto the bed, dampness enveloping my body as I slowly spread out. I inhaled deeply, revelling in the smell of his skin and the memories of happier times.

Rolling onto my back, I gazed at the ceiling, closing my eyes for the briefest of moments so I could remember a time when I had woken up in Sebastian's bed—a time when everything felt unhurried. A time when I'd believed I had eternity to connect and make peace with our unusual emotional ties.

I shuddered for the second time tonight, gripping the sheets tightly at my side and bunching them within my tightly coiled fists. Vivid images flashed past my closed lids; flesh upon flesh and the smell of his skin upon mine, everything I was trying so hard to ignore. The pain of his loss was just too much.

I gasped, encompassed by the longing gaze of his silver eyes upon me. Impossibly tangible I was already reaching up, touching the smooth planes of his face with my fingertips, watching as those eyes closed with our connection. He came for me, his lips eager for my own. The touch was unforgettable, the softness of them leaving me breathless and wanting.

I looked down, confused, enamoured by the barrel of sensation flooding through me, both familiar and welcoming. We were both naked now, entangled in each other's arms, delighting in the pleasures of our flesh. We were two people moving as one, my body arching against his as we united in every way possible. Pleasure tore a path right through me, my fingers leaving the balled sheets at my side to grip the firm flesh of Sebastian's back. We moved to a rhythm of unending need, every part of me crying out for truth and resplendent release.

I held him against me with everything I had, watching as the colours of our union started to fade and this tangible memory promised to be nothing more than a whisper of torment across my skin. I ached and desired, knowing that Sebastian and I had been so much more. Deep inside of me I knew that his death on the church steps had not been the end for us. I remembered the feel of his skin, the touch of his lips and the promise in his words.

I clung to the last vestiges of his image, feeling him slip through my fingers slowly, my nails now finding purchase on nothing but air.

I floated back to reality, my insides aching with need and my mind a mass of confusing thoughts. Sitting up slowly, I ran my hands up and down the length of my body, so certain he had just been here, possessing me, reminding me of what had been. I didn't want to believe that I had conjured this dream of him based on a whim of loneliness. It had all felt so real, once again so familiar.

The drying blood on my cheeks cracked and flaked away as a frown marked my brow. Something wasn't right, but I was damned if I could figure it out. Persistence pressed my mind for answers. I had so much to consider in this new and strange life, yet I was still undeterminably held back by the past, lingering on Sebastian's absence and his ever-present memory in my thoughts.

Why?

Because you're starting to remember what should not be possible … *You!!!!*

With lightning efficiency my head flicked back and forth in search of an entity in the otherwise empty room. In times past I had grown used to hearing the angel Araqiel inside my head, even thought I'd been crazy for a while, but now that Sebastian was gone, I no longer expected his presence in my mind or life and almost rejoiced at its reappearance.

'Araqiel?' I whispered his name tentatively at first, unsure if I had heard him in my thoughts or simply conjured him from old habits.

'Yes, Elena.'

He was suddenly perched on the mattress beside me. His long blonde hair was loose today, spilling across his shoulders like a silken curtain. His blue eyes sparkled with the silver flecks of his angelic origins, his skin as luminescent and blemish free as I remembered. He still wore the white suit, though he no longer hid his wings from me. They were open behind him, the soft feathers so clean and oddly out of place amongst the dankness of the abandoned room.

'You're in my head again.'

He smiled, stretching his legs out to recline. He rested his head on his hand, rolling onto his side to face me. 'I'm always with you, Elena.'

'Why?'

'Because you are important.'

'Important? I highly doubt that.'

'Yet here I am.'

'Invading my thoughts and crowding my personal space. What do you want, Araqiel?'

'I am merely here because now more than ever you need someone on your side.'

I snorted, actually annoyed by the comment. 'Then where were you when I needed you ten years ago?'

'I was with you.'

'Then why is Sebastian dead? Why did he leave and I stayed behind?'

'Are you so sure that you didn't leave?'

I knew my face spoke of murder. As much as I was secretly pleased to see him, I'd never liked the shadow games he played. 'I don't want to play twenty questions with you right now.'

'You're mourning him.'

'Of course I am! Ten years has passed in the blink of an eye, but to me he only died a few days ago.'

'And what do you think you were doing for ten years?'

'I don't know,' I muttered. 'Everyone keeps saying I was in some sort of coma.'

'And do you believe that?'

'I don't know what to believe.'

He tapped the bedcovers, drawing my attention to his perfectly manicured fingers. 'What do you remember?'

'I can't say.'

He now tapped the underside of my chin, drawing my eyes up to meet with his once more. 'Think carefully.'

I tried to turn away, but he held my chin tight. Mortification tried to creep clever threads of pulsing veins across my face, but my vampiric genes would have none of it. I could no longer blush, no longer feel warmth spread across my flesh. Regardless of deceased bodily functions, the feeling did not abate. 'Some things I just don't feel comfortable talking about.'

171

His eyes measured the sincerity in my own, seeing deeper inside me than any other entity could. 'I am surprised that you remember any interaction at all.'

Pushing my embarrassment to the side I said, 'Are you saying that what I just saw, what I just felt was not just—'

'Loneliness?'

I nodded. There was no point in pretending he hadn't seen what I'd conjured as I lay in Sebastian's old bedsheets.

'What do you think?'

'I think I shouldn't know Sebastian's body that well. I think I shouldn't know anything I just visualised.'

Araqiel's lips twitched, wry amusement slowly seeping into the seriousness of his gaze. 'Perhaps not a coma after all ...'

'Then where the hell was I, Araqiel?'

Lips now pursed at my uttered profanity. He'd never been particularly fond of my potty-mouth. 'It matters not.'

'It matters to me.'

'But the knowledge changes nothing. You are still here and Michael is still there.'

'Purgatory ...' The word whispered across my tongue with a certainty that scared me. Though I was still filled with a mountain of doubt, I knew with blinding clarity that Sebastian lingered in the in between. I was stuck on Earth and he was bound by Purgatory, waiting for his next opportunity to be with me. The only problem was, I was never going to be reborn again. I was a vampire, bound by my father's blood and the inevitable descent into hell upon my true death. It was just another certainty that Sebastian and I would never be reunited.

'That's not exactly true,' Araqiel murmured, clearly reading my thoughts.

'What's not true, that he's in Purgatory or our thousands of years together are at an end?'

'The latter.'

I stiffened, refusing to let any vestige of hope refuel my unmoving heart. The crater in my chest was already gaping and fresh. No amount of time would ever heal its ragged edges. I was not about to believe that there was a solution to mend the damage that had already been inflicted.

'I have been acting on your behalf,' Araqiel continued. 'Much has come to pass since you and I first crossed paths.'

'What have you done?' I murmured, curious, angry—and yet as always with him—confused. What would an angel do in my stead? What problems could he have heaped upon me now?

'I have advocated for your right to choose at every turn. I believe, Elena, that your decisions up until this point have been selfless and beneficial to those around you.'

My eyes narrowed as I listened closely. I was waiting for the punch line, the '*but*' that was sure to spell my demise.

'Michael's fall to earth was no coincidence. He chose you. Of every being on this earth he saw something in you that was impossible to ignore—impossible to resist. He chose you then and I choose you now. I finally see what he understood all those years ago; the strength, the love and the conviction to always make the right choice despite your own desires.' He sat up slowly, his gaze never breaking mine. 'I used to think that humans were weak, driven by greed, lust and power. To some extent they are or the world would not be as it is now. And yet here you are, choosing to wake again in a time that needs you more than ever.'

'I didn't choose anything.'

'Didn't you?'

I blew out an impatient breath. 'Araqiel, what's your point?'

'My point is that once every few thousand years there is someone like you; someone who can change the fate of those around them.'

'I don't believe in fate.'

'But it believes in you, Elena. So much so that Michael was willing to die for your choice—for your right to change the past, present and future.'

'I don't understand.'

'You will.' He placed his hand inside his coat pocket, shuffling around until he found what he was looking for. Extracting his hand slowly, I noted a small piece of parchment and a feathered quill. He held them tightly, seemingly afraid that I might snatch them from his grasp.

'What are they for?'

His fingers unfurled slowly, cautiously. 'This, Elena, is the Time Contract and the Quill of Destiny.'

I studied the rather ordinary items, unease washing over me as he brought them closer for my inspection. I swallowed the

173

self-induced lump in my throat, fighting back a wave of self-doubt that would have taken me to my knees if I'd been standing. I sensed change in the air, a decision coming my way more weighted than the grief in my heart—a decision that for some reason would alter nothing and yet change everything. Where did this clarity come from? Why did I know that my choices in these moments— in this life—would somehow echo through the sands of time and change absolutely nothing at all?

I was standing on the precipice of forgotten memories of the past. I was looking into the mirror and not seeing a reflection of myself but a life parallel, one I had no control over and one I had no hope of altering.

'What do they do?' I asked quietly, trepidation a companion wisely walking beside me.

Araqiel smiled, though for the first time since our meeting I sensed his own fear for the power held within his palm. 'They change everything, Elena.'

I shrunk back, feeling smaller and more insignificant by the second. I was also tempted, seduced by the possibilities of righting some wrongs—a dangerous line of thinking from someone crippled by loss. 'Some things can't be changed.'

'Are you so sure?'

'I know nothing can be changed without consequence.'

'And what if I told you it could?'

'I'd tell you to leave right now before temptation overtakes me.'

His smile widened, his eyes sparkling with some undefinable emotion. He closed his fingers around the parchment and quill and placed them back inside his coat pocket. 'Good, Elena, very good.'

He vanished after that, the ruffle of his feathers still stirring the stale air in tangible clouds that brought movement to the lifeless strands of my hair. I didn't move for the longest time, contemplating the vacated place beside me and pregnant thoughts not entirely absent of selfish need. I had come so close to dancing on that line of unchangeable motion, giving into temptation and altering past events. Would I have the strength if he came to me again? In the end was I not still human enough to show weakness?

I suppose I would find out soon enough.

CHAPTER TWELVE: COMPELLING

'Elena, where have you been?'

I studied the seriousness of my father's expression, watching as his eyes narrowed the longer I refused to answer. I had nothing to say, wasn't sure I owed anyone explanations anymore.

He softened, hesitantly reaching out and brushing the skin of my cheek. His rough fingers came away with dried blood, evidence I had been crying earlier. He rubbed it between his fingers, conspicuously sniffing the air and drawing his own conclusions. 'Are you alright, Elena?'

'I can't really say and I don't especially want to talk about it.'

'I can't read you now that you are a vampire. Your thoughts and memories are blocked from me.'

I wrinkled my nose. 'That's a good thing, Lucius.'

He shook his head. 'No, it's not. I had no idea how to find you. William told me you had left on your own despite protests. It's too dangerous to be outside alone.'

'I needed to go home.'

'To the villa?'

'Yes.'

A hesitant smile touched his lips. 'It is nice to hear that you finally feel like my home is your home.'

'I always knew, Lucius. It just takes time for me to trust people.'

He nodded, knowing for the better part of our time reunited, I'd been wary of even his touch. I had warmed to the villa and its surrounds, instinctively knowing that my past self was meant to be born to the life, but understanding I had blood ties to a father I had never known took a little more convincing. 'I'm glad you are back now. We have been waiting for you.'

'You have?' I started as a vânător sidled up beside me, nudging the side of my hip with his muzzle. Ordinarily I might have retaliated in violence, my mind still warped by early Protector training, but instead my instincts took over and I automatically reached to graze the soft fur of his head and neck.

The vânător nuzzled closer, wagging his tail in contentment as my fingers slid across his skin, rubbing backwards and forwards in sheer contentment. A part of me felt comforted by the nearness, calmed by his presence.

'We are planning on opening negotiations with Susan.'

I scoffed, looking up from the vânător at my side. 'You mean you're planning on trying to compel her? Don't tell me that you believe the Trojan horse theory will actually work?'

'Lucas feels confident for the first time in a long time. He likes what William and Karina have come up with, apparently thanks to an idea suggested by you.'

'Yeah, but I don't know if it's a good idea.'

'We are running out of options,' Lucius answered flatly. 'Even with all my power, I cannot compete with the shields they've encompassed the cities in. I don't know if this is new magic or old, I can only manipulate that which I can see.'

'And between Lucas and Karina they haven't been able to disable the spell?'

He shrugged. 'They say that there are multiple uses of the spell enforced by different Protectors. They can weaken the defence but not pull them down entirely.'

I gave the vânător a final pat and then folded my arms across my chest. 'Why did I bother waking up?'

Lucius frowned, turning us both to the side with an arm now wrapped around my shoulder. We walked slowly, those lingering in the passage we inhabited cleared a path for us as we moved. 'That's not something I can imagine you saying, Elena.'

It was my turn to shrug. 'It just feels like no matter how hard we all try to prevent the worst, it happens anyway. Sometimes I wonder why we bother at all.'

'What are you saying?'

'I wish I could go back to Cairns and back to the life I used to know before I met William. The first moment I laid eyes on him, the supernatural world started closing in on me. Now Sebastian is dead, the world has gone to shit and I somehow ended up as the alpha of the Vânǎtors.'

'Elena …'

I held up my hands to disrupt the influx of disappointment I heard seeping into his voice. 'I don't mean that I'm not happy that I met you or discovered a world I actually fit into. I guess I just feel listless, unable to stop the proverbial ball of shit from rolling down the hill and steam rolling us all.'

'Language …'

'Don't you wonder what the point of all this is? Don't you think about what would happen if you changed it all?' Clearly, I had gone back to considering the possibilities of the Time Contract's purpose and what could be achieved by using it.

Lucius squeezed my shoulder gently. 'I've told you this before. You asked me once if I had the power to change anything, what would I change. Do you remember what I said to you?'

I nodded. 'You said nothing.'

'Yes, because if I changed the past then I wouldn't have the future. I wouldn't have you.'

'But you could have me. If your wife Selena hadn't died, I would have been born before you were a vampire, before any of this nasty shi … stuff started happening.'

We crossed through an intersecting tunnel, changed direction and began heading for Susan's holding area.

'Perhaps we would be happy again,' he said after a moment's contemplation. 'But I suspect that changing one aspect of the past would only set a whole new unforeseeable amount of events tumbling forth.' He shook his head, glancing at me sideways. 'Why are you thinking about such things, anyway? You cannot change the past, Elena, so you must make do with the present.'

'Well the present sucks,' I muttered under my breath, shrugging free of his encircled arm and darting into the next corridor before him. Lucas, Karina, William, Marianne, Caleb and the vânǎtor known as Toby were already there. I didn't look back, didn't want to see the look on my father's judgemental face.

Toby laid eyes upon me first, breaking from the group to greet me. He was in human form and half-naked as per usual; something I was sure I'd never get used to. He dropped to his knees beside me, virtually grovelling as he grabbed my hand and sniffed at my skin, rubbing it backwards and forwards across his cheek.

Without knowing why, I kneeled beside him, running my other hand through his soft brown hair, kneading, massaging. He emitted soft sounds of delight, curling his arms around my waist and pulling me closer. Ordinarily I would have been repelled by thought of touching them, but the vânător within me had changed when I had turned. I hadn't shape-shifted often to iron out the details, but it was clear I was more in tune with my unleashed animalistic nature.

'Um, Elena?' Lucas murmured. 'You need to stop petting all the wolves.'

'Why?' I asked, unsure of the request. The wolf within longed for their touch—needed to feel the pack close by at all times. And right now, my wolf was enjoying Toby's blatant affections.

'Because you're the only female in the pack *and* the alpha.'

'Ahh huh …'

'And because at present, the urge to mate with you is apparently particularly strong.'

'The urge to um … what?' I jumped back from Toby, mortified to see him more than just a little excited to be touching me. 'Jesus Christ, I thought they were all just happy to see me!'

'They are,' Caleb said with a snicker. 'Can't you tell?'

Toby tried moving closer to me again, but I scuttled backwards, climbing the walls like a spider to stay clear of his grip.

'Oh, would you look at that?' William murmured. 'Well done, Elena. I hadn't thought about teaching you how to climb walls yet.'

'Seems she has some motivation,' Marianne added with a smirk.

'Elena?'

Looking down from the ceiling I spotted Susan. She was sitting with her back to the passage wall, her face and body slightly distorted by the barrier Lucas had erected to keep her caged. I had yet to look upon her since waking. I hadn't been sure how I felt about seeing her again and now here I was, hanging from the ceiling getting my vamp on in front of the very person who'd raised me to despise what I was going to one day become.

I let go, righting myself before my feet hit the ground. I gave Toby one last lingering look as he grovelled backwards, disappearing around the passage entrance before I focused back on Susan. She'd lost weight, aged and was dirty, but she'd otherwise remained unchanged.

'Elena, you're—'

'A vampire.'

'Actually, I was going to say beautiful.'

My head jerked backwards in surprise. 'That's the last thing I expected you to say.'

'You were a beautiful girl. It only makes sense that you are even more beautiful in your unlife.'

I felt uncomfortable having this conversation with her and it had nothing to do with my looks. It was more to do with her choice of inane topic. We had not seen each other in months. Betrayal was no longer just a word, but a consistently repeated action on her behalf and now she chose to comment on my appearance as if there was no bad blood between us? She showed no remorse for what she had done to me and mine and was even less apologetic for what she had done to Lucas. How could she even speak to me without remembering all the lies she had told?

So, I didn't bother answering. I had nothing particularly nice to say.

She sat forward, bringing her face closer to the barrier. 'I always wondered what happened to you, Elena.'

I fought tooth and nail to not roll my eyes. It was an ill-concocted lie spewed forth from a well-practiced mouth. 'You know what happened to me,' I hissed through tightly clenched teeth. 'You sent me to the IMI in Bucharest to be experimented on and eventually killed. I was just lucky I could escape.'

'I never—'

My raised hand served to silence her. 'Wait. Just stop there. Let's not pretend that you ever really cared about me.'

'But, Elena, I did care.'

'No, Susan. You took me into your family knowing I would one day be used as a weapon. You didn't see me as a person, just a commodity. Though I have to admit you did fool me there for a while. But I'll bet that you never counted on me figuring it out and I suspect that you never counted on Lucas overcoming the mountains of deceit you heaped upon him either.'

179

She nodded. 'You're right. I'm not going to lie. I did take in a baby that I chose to care for under the guise of future benefit to the IMI, but I did care for you and prayed that things might have been different for you.' Her hands balled into fists at her sides. 'But as you grew—as you changed—I knew you would never have a normal life. I knew that none of us would have a normal life. I did care, Elena, but I can't change the fact that everything would have been different without you. If you weren't around, I would have my Lucas and my husband without the interference of your blood.'

'George?' I looked briefly to Lucas for answers. He merely shrugged, also without knowledge of his father's status. 'What happened?'

Lucas was no ordinary Protector thanks to a hefty dose of my blood; a bite and fluid transference from me during our youth had become the catalyst for his change now. But George? How could I be blamed for whatever he had become involved with above and beyond the effects of the serum that he had opted to weaponize himself with?

Susan's sooty face measurably dimmed. 'Power happened to George. He's now in charge of the Sydney super city, drunk with the adoration of his peers and incapable of seeing what we as Protectors have become.'

'I would have thought you'd be happy.'

'Happy to see that George has lost all touch with the very foundations of what we stand for? No, I am not happy.'

'Lucas mentioned you have regrets. He also mentioned that you'd like to see my family and friends dead too. Isn't *that* the very foundation of what you stand for; kill all supernatural entities?'

She shot Lucas a very unfriendly look. It was crazy to think she had an ally in a place filled with those she wished dead or dismembered. 'I don't like what you represent, Elena. You know I have never liked vampires or werewolves. I have never hidden that fact. I still believe in what The Protectors stand for; peace for the human race and protection from all supernatural elements.'

'And now you are one of us.' It felt really good to rub her nose in that fact.

'No, I only became what I did to find Lucas.'

I crept closer to the barrier, finally sitting cross-legged right in front of her. 'Is that what you have to tell yourself to feel better about feeding on humans?'

'Are you calling me a liar?'

'I'm calling you a lot of things I'm too polite to say out loud.'

She scoffed. 'Then you have changed more than I realise.'

'And you ruined everything.'

'Excuse me?'

I hadn't meant to make this personal, but I couldn't seem to stop the words from spewing forth. 'I trusted you, Susan. I trusted everything you ever said to me and you blew it. I'm not condemning you for being a bad parent or a liar to both me and Lucas, despite evidence. I'm condemning you now for being a bad human being—a mighty big hypocritical one.'

'I am most certainly not—'

'Just shush it.'

'Elena!'

Ignoring her I continued. 'Susan, the world was never perfect. God knows that what I am and what I represent is not to be celebrated, but it doesn't give you the right to judge. Your judgment and preceding actions are what has robbed every one of us of hope. You and your IMI buddies in conjunction with a lot of stupid decisions have stolen the chance to make things right again.'

She frowned—first annoyed by my assertive manner—then seemingly confused by my very pointed accusation. 'Elena, you don't understand anything. Without the serum, without certain changes … The Vampires—'

'No, you don't understand! My father Lucius was changing things. He had created Synth Corp, opened neutral bars and was trying to help vampires overcome the very cravings you condemn us for. You stole parts of me to create a serum to enhance the very evil you've been fighting against and instead of using it to create vaccines and cures for diseases, you used it to win control. Via your hunt for godliness, I have become the alpha to all packs. There was an opportunity for me to control the Vânători, stop repopulation and prevent them from ever feeding on human beings again. Co-existence was possible.'

'Coexistence?' She practically spat her disdain.

'Instead you've turned humans into frightened cattle with weapons of mass destruction that have since destroyed any semblance of civilisation just so you could rise higher and look down your nose at us. You know, Susan, your skin is no different than mine.'

Her narrowed blue eyes attempted to bore holes right through the centre of my skull. 'You're comparing us?' Contempt painted her face with a hasty blush of fuchsia now.

'There's nothing to compare, we're freaking identical! You say that your goals are nobler than that of anyone linked to the supernatural community and yet if you look in the mirror now, there's no denying the reflection staring back at you.' I shook my head, realising my mistake. 'No, wait. I take that back. You and I could never be the same. You're a step beyond, more deplorable than my lowest act imaginable.'

'Elena, how can you say that?'

'How?' I stabbed a finger directly at her, leaning close enough that my nose practically brushed the barrier between us. 'Because you *chose* to become what I am.'

A collective intake of breath echoed behind me. I had perhaps—in some way—insulted a good deal many of those gathered around me, but it didn't make what I'd said any less true. We shouldn't ever apologise for what we are unless the choices that we consciously make are what carve the path of ill-fated decision making. If it renders the barrier between wrong and right fairly combustible—you're to blame. I hadn't chosen this life. I was born to it. What the hell was The Protector's excuse? To claim they were nobler and that their purpose was 'just' was nothing more than a way to calm the niggling doubt of whatever burning conscience may still reside within their scientifically-altered flesh.

'Oh my God, you are somewhat right,' she whispered. The remnants of the harsh lines upon her face faded quickly into some indistinguishable form of agreeable prankster. 'All this time I have sat back and judged and not really seen how finer line I walked.'

I blinked in the hope that clarity would come, unsure how to respond. I hadn't expected her to actually take stock and see that her choice to become what she discriminated against was illogical and counterproductive. Honestly, I only expected to receive another mouthful of nonsensical bullshit.

'You're not honestly going to fall for this crap, are you?' Caleb asked, leaning down to whisper in my ear.

I appraised Susan with clinical detachment, waiting for some sort of physical tell to indicate that she was indeed lying. There was nothing. Not even a skip in her heartbeat or acceleration of her pulse. That didn't mean much being a trained Protector. If she was lying—putting on a show—then I would be none-the-wiser to her antics. Perhaps this was a new tactic, one I wasn't accustomed to or trained to overcome.

'I don't believe her,' Lucas flatly stated, no hint of uncertainty in his words. 'To have a sudden realisation that your motives were all backwards? Yeah, I don't think so.'

'Lucas.' She now pleaded directly to him, pressing her hands firmly against the shimmering wall of magical obstruction. 'I have wronged you and yours, I see that now.'

Lucas was no push over and shaking his head as a twisted smile of benevolence ensnared his lips was seemingly automatic. He eyed his mother—not with optimism—but disdain as he addressed my father instead, clearly over any more untrusting dialogue. 'Lucius, I'm going to drop the barrier and restrain her with it. Since you're the oldest and more powerful, I think it should be you that does it.'

Susan's eyes quickly narrowed into suspicious slits as she started backing away into the corner once again. 'Lucas,' she mouthed, breath barely escaping her chapped lips, 'what are you going to do with me?'

Ignoring her he said, 'Everyone ready?' We all moved perceptibly closer, analysing and attempting to anticipate signs of flickering magic within the palms of her hands or on the edges of her quivering lips. Either she was too distracted by the looming vampires or scared enough about her undecided fate that surrendering to the foetal position was as defensive as her pose dictated.

'One, two …' Lucas didn't wait for three. He dropped the shield, and with my help, we wrapped another impenetrable telekinetic blanket around her.

Arms glued to her sides and palms pressed against her slender thighs, Caleb moved around behind her to pull her back into a sitting position and essentially hold her head still enough that Lucius could level his gaze with hers. She attempted to thrash about as any scared captive would, but quickly realised the futility of such manoeuvres as the overwhelming scent of vampiric compulsion flooded the dark, dank holding cell.

Susan struggled marginally, attempting in vain to close her eyes and senses to the strength of my father's essence as it searched for a foothold within her subconscious. She started screaming as Caleb roughly separated her lids and yanked them open. The whites of her eyes showed; hollow and as empty as her heart. The struggle and vocal performance lasted only as long as those whites held court and her irises appeared, locking with Lucius's and cinching the compulsion's task. I'd never heard of a Protector being compelled, but then I'd never been privy to any information that the IMI didn't wish me to know and it appeared her vulnerability existed as surely as any human.

She went completely limp—the fight over. Those powder blue eyes I'd grown up with admonishing me now locked willingly with the master vampire. She stared into the kaleidoscope of colour and didn't move a muscle.

It's working …

'Let her head go, Caleb.'

'Are you sure?'

Lucius nodded, but kept his eyes firmly focused on the woman in front of him. 'Can you hear me, Susan?'

'Yes.'

'Are you comfortable?'

'No.'

Lucius allowed himself a mere second to smile in response to her answer. 'I want you to listen very carefully to what I have to say and to answer my questions. Can you do that for me?'

'Yes.'

'Why did you come to this part of Rome?'

'I was looking for Lucas.'

Lucas scoffed, clearly disbelieving of the compulsion's ability to exert the truth. Marianne wrapped an arm around his waist and gave him a reassuring squeeze.

'If you were looking for Lucas why did you bring other Protectors with you on the guise of a hunt?'

'No one knows I'm looking for Lucas. I have to keep up appearances.'

'But your husband—George—he must know your intentions. Does he not wonder why you no longer hail from the Sydney super city?'

'He doesn't interfere. We were over long ago.'

'Is there any way to get into the super cities?'

'No.'

'Will you take us?'

'No.'

'Apologies, it was my phrasing. You *will* take us to the Parisian super city.'

'Of course.'

'Ask her about access to the others,' William interrupted. 'We can't just storm them one at a time. This has to be a precision attack. If one falls, they will *all* be wary of our intentions and be on full alert.'

'That will never work,' Lucas said, returning the warm embrace of his vampiric partner. 'There is no way we could launch a global attack, no way we could possibly obtain access to every super city simultaneously. I know what you're saying, William, but we have to work with what we have.'

'But it won't make any difference,' he argued.

'But it will if we can get in, bring down the IMI branch within and convince the humans of what has been happening right under their noses.'

'Supposing they don't take up arms and gun us all down for our efforts.'

'I'm not saying it's going to be easy, but if we can convince enough people, possibly even disrupt the flow of the serum long enough to show The Protectors the error in their ways then maybe—'

'You're dreaming,' I interrupted, scepticism apparent. 'You're all crazy if you think this is going to work, but Lucas is right in some respects. If you're going to go ahead with this crazy plan, then you need to concentrate on what you can control—the IMI that Susan is currently connected with.'

William's hard stare was paired with thinned lips and a clenched jaw. I understood perfectly what he had hoped to achieve, but I also knew from past experience that biting off more than you can actually chew is the quickest way to choke.

He slammed his hand against the toughened stone of the dirtied passage walls, shaking the foundations and raining a small storm of debris upon us all. Angry, he stormed out of the room, Karina only a few steps behind him. She arranged an apologetic look upon her dainty features as she hurriedly chased after her hot-headed boyfriend, but I was neither concerned nor appeased. I could see this attack ending only in disaster, surprised that my usually perceptive father had not yet seen the trouble I could already predict was coming.

'Karina said something about there being a hunting vehicle left over from Susan's recent attack on these parts,' Lucius murmured, still maintaining eye contact with The Protector. 'Where is it?'

I sighed, completely resigned, knowing they were going to proceed despite the stifling doubt that choked the air around us. 'She said she hid it in the Synth Corp building.'

'Susan,' he commanded, drawing her attention again. 'How many people fit inside a hunting vehicle?'

'One, two at the most.'

He was thoughtful for a moment. 'You're going to make room for Lucas. You're going to take him back to the Parisian super city.'

'What?' Lucas shouted in outrage.

Lucius held up a hand to silence him. 'Do you understand, Susan?'

'Yes.'

'If anyone asks, he will be your prisoner.'

'Prisoner ... yes.'

'Once you are inside the super city you will help Lucas to disable the spells that protect the walls from our entry. You will let us all in and lead us to the clan leader of this division.'

'Yes.'

'Then you will show us the stockpile and any formulations of the serum that may be on hand, the scientists involved and all those capable of recreating it. Then you will help us to destroy it and them.'

'No.'

Lucius's eyebrows narrowed only fractionally. 'No? Why not?'

'The serum is not stored in Paris.'

'Then where is it.'

'The Antarctic,' Lucas murmured. The vacant expression he now wore was a clear indicator that he had rapidly descended into thoughts littered with the exploits of the past better left buried.

'Yes,' Susan answered.

My forehead copped a minor beating as I slapped a hand against the porcelain skin, exasperated. 'We were just there. We could have blown the place up! We could have stopped this months ago.'

'Years ago,' Lucas corrected. 'But we never really thought about it. We were just trying to get my ass out of there.'

'Shit!' I shouted rather dramatically and unnecessarily. 'How could I have been so stupid?'

'Language,' Lucius reminded me in his usually stern tone.

I glared at him. 'Seriously, you're pulling me up on my potty-mouth now?' I swore again, defiance and agitation riding me hard. I looked up helplessly, searching the heavens for some semblance of clarity. 'Why the hell do you have so much faith in me, Araqiel? Clearly it's completely unfounded.'

I felt rather than saw everyone's narrowed eyes upon me. And—when I looked back at Lucius—it was no surprise to see his mouth puckered in displeasure. He had warned me a long time ago not to associate with angels, but the reasons in this moment were irrelevant in comparison to the past's mistakes. I'd made so many errors in judgement that it mattered not if Team Halo were playing me like a fiddle. Every one of my choices had been—and probably still were—riddled with gaping holes. Clearly, I should not be present now or even a part of a group that was once again making decisions for others. I freaking sucked at it.

I stood, spinning on my heels and making haste towards the exit. I stopped short, my nose mere centimetres from a hastily erected telekinetic barrier—courtesy of my brother. I slammed my fists against the surface, angry he was using my own blood tricks against me. 'Let me out of here.'

'Where are you going?' he and Lucius demanded simultaneously, neither one too pleased by my attempted retreat, behaviour or probable tantrum.

'Anywhere but here.'

'What's going on with you, Elena?' Lucas asked, confusion now marring his face. 'You're not acting like your usual self.'

'Maybe that's because my usual self is a liability.'

'Tell me you don't blame yourself for the serum, E?'

'I blame myself for a lot of things.' I slammed my palm against the barrier again. 'Just let me out of here. I don't want to be psychoanalysed.'

'Then tell me at least what's wrong?'

'I just don't want to be liable for any more decisions, okay? I'll back you in whatever fight you decide to start or finish, but I can't be the instigator. I don't make good choices.'

'Elena …'

'Just let me out, Lucas!' I was not above tossing him a filthy look for holding me as captive as his conniving mother.

I was instantly released and on the move within milliseconds, hastily making my way into the connecting passage and seeking freedom as fast as my legs would carry me. Turns out—that as a vampire—that was extremely fast. Before I knew it, I was running down Rome's desolate highways again and on a mission to find comfort wherever I could. My feet burned sizeable chunks in the asphalt I connected with, bitumen spewing into the air as I propelled onwards towards the villa once more and straight back into Sebastian's room.

I flung myself down on his mattress, gripping the dusty sheets between my fingers. I didn't cry and I didn't move. I laid perfectly still, staring up at the ceiling, blank both inside and out. I didn't breathe. I didn't twitch. For all intents and purposes, I was dead—cut off from everything by choice.

'Well, well, well.' A familiar voice echoed from the far corner of the room. 'I thought I had picked up remnants of your scent earlier. Looks like I was right.'

Slowly, I tilted my head to the right. It took a moment for my new crazy eyes to stop focusing on the glistening edges of broken glass that still clung to the beading of the battered French doors. A shadow loomed—as dark and mysterious as the voice I'd hoped never to hear again.

'Julius.'

He clapped his hands as if applauding my memory. 'Well, isn't this unexpected? I'm pretty sure I killed you.'

'You did.'

He strayed from the blackened corner, a slither of moonlight illuminating the menacing smile that stretched his supple lips taught. His fangs were exposed and talons growing perceptibly longer and sharper by the second. His eyes never left mine as he shook his head, coming to rest on the edge of the bed beside me, barely disturbing the covers as he sat. 'Then we have ourselves a problem.'

CHAPTER THIRTEEN: TESTED

Sebastian sat motionless on the sill of his Purgatory home. He'd been like this for days; caught in a trance of self-indulgence, his heart heavy with loss. He'd heard the cries for help on the wind, knowing Samael was back to his old tricks. For some reason, he was unable to move or care. His sole focus had been Elena. Her face consumed his thoughts. As did the whispering of her proclamations of love and lust lingering as he envisaged the feel of her body against his own. All-consuming memories and a desire for a non-existent future tormented his very being.

'Michael,' Araqiel murmured, coming upon him from behind. 'It's not healthy for you to wallow this way.' The angel settled his wings against his back, crossing his arms in front of his chest. He'd expected Michael to turn around and acknowledge his entrance, but lately Michael didn't acknowledge anyone.

Sebastian snorted. 'Wallow? Is that what you call the end of everything that ever mattered to me?'

Araqiel resisted the urge to roll his eyes. Did *feeling* human really mean that all sensible thought was erased from the mind once sexual companionship was abolished? Was it truly the end of the world when one lost the Ying to their Yang?

'I don't even have to look at you to know what is going through your mind, Araqiel. You could never understand what I'm feeling right now.'

'Of this I am quite sure.'

Sebastian patted the window sill beside him, not bothering to turn. 'Have a seat.'

'Why?'

'Because I'm sure this is not just a social visit. You're either going to continue to downplay my loss or you've come seeking advice. Either way, sit or stand. Do you have something to say to me or not?'

Araqiel didn't settle beside his eldest brother. He had no need of it. Instead, he moved through the open front door and leant against its carved entry so he could better see the Archangel's face. A terrible wave of sadness greeted him, an emotion so powerful and all-consuming that it had twisted the usually serene features of Michael's face into something barely recognisable.

Sebastian shuddered, knowing that the judgmental eyes now upon him surveyed his current state in a capacity unqualified. 'Stop it.'

Despite the cloying sensation of Michael's righteous might fading as quickly the setting sun of Purgatory, Araqiel brokered to defend himself. 'There's no judgment, Michael. I may not understand why you decided to give up everything, but I do believe I finally see why you chose *her*.'

Ears ringing with the slightest inclination of Elena, Sebastian turned, catching the watchful gaze of an angel that studied him in earnest. 'What did you say?'

'I understand Elena as your choice. She is multi-faceted and surprisingly selfless.'

Sebastian knew all of this already. He certainly didn't need a re-education in his greatest loves' winning personality traits. But of course, to have the angel disturbing his peace yet again could only mean that the subject matter played part in future tidings—otherwise known as—Araqiel seeking Elena to fulfil some weird self-substantiating prophecy or personal agenda.

Sebastian would remain cautious in his emotional and verbal responses. Araqiel had no real concept of love, only the fingers to grasp the concept surreptitiously and what could be accomplished in the name of it.

'You couldn't possibly comprehend my choice, Araqiel, but I recognise now that you might understand or even revere Elena's strength because it may somehow benefit you.'

Araqiel scoffed as though he completely disagreed, not with the sentiment of her traits, but by way of argument to deflect light from his scheming ways. 'I do not think you have this all figured out yet, Michael. But in the interim, can I not complement you on your choice?'

The silken flesh around Sebastian's eyes tightened as he tried to avoid his narrowed expression. 'I think that it is becoming alarmingly obvious that my choices have nothing to do with what you personally seek.'

'I seek nothing. I am but a humble servant of—'

'Oh please,' Sebastian interceded. 'Do you think I don't know that you've had eyes on Elena since birth? I may not have been able to find her until recently, but I suspect you've known where she was and what she means to me for quite some time.'

'And naturally I made sure she was led to you.'

'Led to me? You mean you let her get intimate with my brother first.'

'I did not expect William to fall in love with her.'

Teeth clenched; Sebastian's fingers bunched by his sides until the knuckles cracked like an autumn branch in the afternoon sun. Simply thinking about Elena wrapped in his brother's arms, kissing his lips and running her fingers through his hair made him want to smite something ... or someone.

'Michael, irrespective of who found her first, you know how this works. Only every few thousand years we find someone capable of inciting change. I believe wholeheartedly that Elena is that person and I must pursue that belief regardless of your personal feelings.'

'Yes, she is bound by the blood of angels and demons, but that doesn't mean she understands what she is capable of. It also doesn't mean that there isn't another one out there like her.'

'She may not understand her true potential, but she understands perfectly what is right within her grasp.'

Sebastian drew a deep breath, trying to calm his now excessively furrowed brows and clenched fists. Was it possible that Araqiel was reaching further than his wing span allowed? Was he seeking more than was possible to give, more than what Sebastian had already given up for him to change the face of vampirism?

He shuddered. 'Araqiel, I suspect this pursuit you seek is beyond her; beyond anyone you will find in this time. If you are thinking of changing Lucifer himself then there is too much history to contend with. I would have said a few thousand years ago that it was possible, but not now and not in a time where the distant past has so little bearing on the present.'

'I showed her the Time Contract.'

'You what?' All resolve crumbled as Sebastian gripped the stone sill beneath him for support. Without anchoring he was sure he would have fallen. To show Elena the Time Contract was to turn possibilities on their heads and alter everything that had ever been. His history with her could be wiped away in a millisecond. The very thought of the action made his stomach roll with sickness. 'Tell me this isn't true? I knew you were bargaining my life for the Time Contract and I even understood knowing that your motives were to alter the interference of vampirism, but to involve Elena?'

'I cannot make a choice to go back that far.'

'Araqiel, you can't. It's too much. I have supported you, brother. I have even given up my life to go back to Purgatory so that you may change Lucifer's ultimate interference in the human realm, but this I cannot abide by. This is more than you can expect anyone to deal with, especially Elena.'

'I needed to know if she was worthy.'

'So, you are testing her? You cannot leave well enough alone?'

'I thought you wanted this?'

'To change some aspects of the past, yes, but I'm looking at you now and I can see that you are eager for more than any of us are willing to give.'

'Do you want out of this place, or not?'

Sebastian held his breath, uncertainty rippling through him. His knuckles were white with tension, his shoulders knotted by stiff posture. There were so many things he wanted to change, but he knew better than anyone that tearing the fabric of time and sewing it haphazardly back together would only incite future weakness.

'Of course I do, but I'm not so unrealistic to think that change will follow anything short of selfish desires. You have chosen Elena, but she always chooses me.'

'Perhaps not this time. Perhaps she will go back further if I explain—'

'What did she do?'

'Excuse me?

'What did Elena do when you showed her the Time Contract?'

Confusion dissipating, Araqiel gave him the barest of smiles. 'She told me to put the Time Contract away, that some things in the past cannot be changed for the better.'

'She wasn't tempted?'

194

'Tempted?' Araqiel eyed the Archangel critically. 'Of course she was tempted. She dreams of you even in the waking hours. She sees things she should not remember and she knows that to have the Time Contract is to undo the past.'

'But she didn't take the opportunity?'

'No.'

Sebastian slumped under the weight of momentary relief—fleeting though it was—angst quickly licked at his appendages and heart once more. 'Do you remember our conversation on the rooftop in Milan?'

The change in topic jarred Araqiel to recall the details. 'Yes, Michael.'

'You told me to make the most of my time with Elena, to protect her as long as I could until my part in the Time Contract's exchange was carried out.'

'Yes. I'm not sure what your point is.'

'You used me. I accepted that my death would mean Elena's protection and that your claim on the Time Contract from Lucifer's hands would mean the alteration of Lucius's past mistakes. Instead what you have done is seen me trapped in a plane where I can do nothing to stop you now. I believed your motives, I believed you when you said you had Elena's best interests at heart, but what I suspect you truly have are *your* best interests at heart.'

Araqiel vehemently shook his head. 'No, brother. I did say to you that the Time Contract would change everything, but I never told you the capacity in which it would. I will protect Elena because she is the key—the only one with the blood capable to change everything, but I make no apologies. You knew that I was bound, that I could not discuss the details until you were no longer earthbound. Now you hold me in contempt for wanting to change all wars, famine and the wrongs of a past that should have never been?'

'She'll never do it, Araqiel. She may eventually use the Time Contract, but she'll never dive back as far as you mean for her to.'

'How could you possibly know that?'

'She simply doesn't understand. The world that she knows now is the only thing she can manipulate. Perhaps the echoes of her memories may stir something more, but anything before the beginning of time is a concept she couldn't possibly decipher. She won't do it. I'm telling you now; she won't change what I started and she could ruin everything simply by attempting it.'

'She is strong. She will understand what it means to go back ...'

'You're reaching. Please, I know now what it is that you seek, but for me it is not a mistake of the past. I know that you have difficulty understanding this, but falling was a choice I would make again and again.'

'I know that it was sanctioned and—'

'No, you don't know,' Sebastian interrupted, angry that he had to break it down for a being with ineffectual relations of human emotion. 'Elena changed everything for me. I don't want to go back. I don't want to be an emotionless soldier of observation. I have no regrets regarding my choice.'

'But what about Lucifer? If you could go back—keep him in check—the world would be a very different place.'

'Lucifer will always make the same choices. He hungers no different than I, but pursues a dark path. Even if I went back, scrubbed Elena from my memory and my life, he would still eventually choose to fall. He has always been different, strong-willed and entitled.'

'You can't possibly believe that if we didn't all start again Lucifer would make all the same choices?'

'Of course I do. You may be able to alter the past, but you cannot change who we fundamentally are.' Sebastian leaned closer towards his brother, hoping his words were marked with understanding. 'You cannot stop yourself from being cast out either. As sure as you are of this decision now, you will once again be conflicted by the choice between good and evil. It doesn't make you bad, Araqiel, it just makes you—'

'Human?'

Sebastian flung his head back and laughed; the first sign of mirth in weeks. 'You could never be human, but in a matter of speaking I believe you could adopt the principal with a little more compassion and practice.'

Araqiel—looking perplexed perhaps for the first time in history's count—shied from Sebastian's watchful gaze and patronising demeanour. 'So, you will not help me to succeed?'

Sebastian softened, though forever watchful of the forgiving nature that could creep upon his unsuspecting heart. 'I can't help you, brother. Purgatory binds me in more ways than one, but even if I could, I don't think that I would help you change that which I truly believe should remain undisturbed.' Before Araqiel could protest he continued. 'See, since I have fallen, I have grown selfish. I want Elena to choose me. Despite what may or may not be altered, the only thing I long for now is her. Consequences of an indeterminable future mean little to me.'

'Interestingly enough though, she did not choose to stay here with you.'

Sebastian knew all too well the undertone of the angel's pointed statement and regret flushed his features. It was only dissolved by the bitter trappings of guilt. Turning his emotionally rippled face so the angel could not surmise further helped little. 'I know what you are inferring regarding Elena's choice, but I also know that she made the right decision.'

'Do you?'

'Of course. It's why you want her, is it not?' Bitterness seeped into his very tone like strong black coffee left unattended over heat. 'She always makes the right decision even if it means she will be unhappy—even if it means we both will be.'

Araqiel unfolded his arms, his face now passive and untouched by any form of responding emotion. 'I shouldn't have come. I thought we wanted the same thing. I did not realise that you had become so blinded by earthly desires.'

'Do not mistake my feelings for stupidity, Araqiel. Where I may be blinded, you have become misguided. I thought that you sort to protect Elena and deliver her to me, but you were protecting what her blood represents. You have treated everyone like your pawn in a game I fear you have little or no control over. I beg you, just let this go. Let Elena decide what is right.'

'I will, brother,' Araqiel said, slowly unfurling his wings. 'I'm just going to give her a little push.'

Sebastian lunged, fingers grasping at the rapidly ascending angel, but Araqiel was swift with his feathered members, soaring higher and faster than Sebastian could counter. He could have given further chase, attempted to shake some sense into the holier-than-thou being, but what good would it have done? The angel was mostly immune to emotional responses and would not hear reason. So why so concerned to alter Michael's fall from grace and Lucifer's uprising?

197

The steps that Araqiel had taken thus far defied most logic and to turn over every cornerstone of detail with measured understanding wrought more confusion. Even William—Sebastian's vampiric brother—had been recruited by Araqiel to protect Elena and help reunite them. But why were such measures taken—if in the end—she would be given the choice to leave everything she'd ever known or loved behind in favour of Araqiel's ultimate agenda? Why give her the Time Contract knowing she could choose to be with him again and not change the distant past as perhaps Araqiel hoped?

The angel was gambling.

Sebastian rubbed his smooth chin, contemplating every conceivable angle. Ideas roared through his head, but none making more sense than the last. Surely bringing her closer to her family and allowing her to spend time with him in Purgatory and watching as their love blossomed once again would dampen the angel's efforts? Why would Elena turn the clock further back than her many lifetimes allowed? Was it possible that she would not choose him if she thought correcting everything in the past would steal away vampirism, the war and the pain and suffering of her brother?

Sebastian swore, a rarity to be sure as some semblance of clarity crept forth in the far reaches of his colourful mind. A blinding light illuminated a thought rather left in the darkened corner of the denial box, but it was time to unearth the concept thus ignored. Araqiel was determined to reverse Lucifer's bad behaviour and the creation of Hell for good and—in order to accomplish that goal—he would need to amplify Elena's guilt.

How?

The grimy angel would rack and display all of her past decisions—the good, bad and ugly—and then amplify her insecurities. He would make her feel as if she were incapable of deciding anyone's fate without severe consequences. He would coax her, champion her decision to opt out of existence all together and ultimately sacrifice everything that had ever been in order to appease Araqiel's version of ultimate righteousness. He would make her believe that to go back even further than her mind could allow would save everyone.

Weakness overcame Sebastian and he dropped to his knees, helpless. Damp earth greeted him as his palms splayed across the sodden soil, breath caught in a throat constricted by a painful spasm of realisation. There was nothing he could do, no way to stop Araqiel or his misguided plans. The lines between good, evil and self-indulgence had been blurred beyond recognition and he suddenly saw that his choice to fall may have infinitely ruined everything.

Would Lucifer still have chosen to break away?

Reality dictated that Sebastian would uncover these truths in painful due course. He was relegated to Purgatory and the trappings of his decisions, but with the Time Contract out in the open ... anything was possible.

Elena could change everything ...

CHAPTER FOURTEEN: VENGEANCE

In a single heartbeat, you can manifest anything from elation right through to the bone-chilling caress of fear. You can make choices; action them and dismiss them just as easily. And—in that single heartbeat—you can take breath, feel life within your limbs and blood rush through your veins. But what do you do when that ticking warmth within your chest no longer exists to guide decisions and action your body?

Suppose for just a moment that you were me; born into a world of fictitious nightmares and born to become a member of the undead and eventually roast in the bonfires of hell. Without the beating of a warm heart and associated conscience, what would you honestly do in my position?

As per usual, I didn't stop to contemplate the outcomes. I merely stared my vampiric demon right in the face and shrugged. Being undead translated to a lack of fear—except of course—for absolute finality, which I no longer particularly cared about either. Unliving in the present without Sebastian was a torture all-encompassing. I imagined meeting Lucifer and suffering a true death wouldn't compare to how I'd felt every second of every day since Sebastian had died.

I no longer felt terrified of what I perhaps should—and thus—now shrugged at the psychotic vampire spewing threats of carnage in my face. Facing him again seemed as harmless as knitting a sweater with grandma. Adrenaline would have once flooded my veins and arteries, but I was now void of the idiosyncrasies of human decision-making. I was immortal—not immune from death—but more powerful and less fragile than the last time Julius and I had danced.

I kept my eyes on the prize and moved slowly backwards until I was propped against Sebastian's old, musty pillows. Appearing unhurried and looking mildly bored was my current plan as I folded my steady hands calmly within my lap. His eyes searched mine, riddled with the pain of the past and brimming with the revenge he'd fought so desperately to seek. I wondered if he sought to disembowel me after unapologetically plotting and planning my ultimate demise for so very long. It was all on account of my father's actions from the past; he'd killed Julius's beloved wife.

Paper-thin skin surrounding pools of icy blue tightened as he continued to drink in my lacklustre response. Perhaps he believed that by clawing at the disintegrating bed sheets with his sharpened talons or staring me down with the menacing depths of his ancient eyes would press on my sanity. Maybe he truly believed I would soon curl into a ball and beg for my life after I'd avoided our interludes in the past. But, all that remained in the face of this newest encounter was the certainty that my existence meant little to the falling sands of time. If he were to strike me now and I died the true death, it would change little, if anything at all.

'You are not afraid of me,' Julius finally murmured, voice quiet yet inquisitive, eyes still watchful in their assessment of my unmoving form and general lack of distress.

'What's to be afraid of?'

'The fact that I'm going to kill you.'

'You're not very good at it though, are you?'

Catching his tongue between his teeth before an angry retort could slip past pursed lips, he considered an answer not fraught with seething rage and welling frustration. I applauded the control. 'I have never failed in my aspirations to kill or plan a kill in the past and I truly believed my record was unblemished until this moment where you take exception.' His voice was even and relatively steady despite his puckered lips of displeasure.

'I'm sorry I ruined your plans.'

The truth of that statement was a genuine admission that shocked both of us in different ways. While his eyes narrowed into thin slits, I was surprised by the confession of my semi-suicidal thoughts.

'I think you might mean that.' It wasn't really a question, more of a boggling statement of fact.

I nodded, my eyes never leaving his. 'I think me being in this life has caused more harm than good.'

Julius didn't say anything for what felt like several minutes. 'Do you expect me to feel sorry for you and recant my promise to avenge my wife?'

'No. It's becoming more and more obvious that everyone has an agenda. Everyone has some sort of goal they're trying to obtain regardless of how it affects others around them.'

'Now you're calling me selfish.'

'We're all selfish. At one point or another we all want what we can't have, sometimes what we shouldn't.' I motioned all around us. 'Now look at us, look at what we've *all* become.'

'You're pretty little speech will not stop me from avenging the death of my wife. I will kill you and I will enjoy it.'

'I know you will. At least … I know you'll try.'

Looking slightly perplexed again he said, 'Then why aren't you running?'

'We're both vampire thralls. We both have the same limitations, strength, speed and stamina. The difference is I'm also telekinetic. If I don't want you to touch me—you won't.'

Julius arched back, the barest hint of smile twisting his previously soured lips. He seemed simultaneously amused and befuddled. 'But you *can* die.'

'So can you.'

The teasing smile vanished. Nostrils flared and the clench of his jaw reignited his imbuing frustration. It was as thick as the dirt that marked the cotton sheets between us. 'Why *are* you still alive? I saw the angel kill you, saw the blade find your beating heart!'

'I did wonder if it was you or Araqiel that stabbed me.' Not that the information changed a thing.

'Lucius saved you, didn't he?'

I couldn't help a proprietary eye roll. 'I'm a thrall now, so yeah, you know how it works.'

Julius's outrage was palpable. 'That wasn't part of the deal!' His bottom lip trembled, saliva coating its surface, almost dripping with the hunger of his ire.

I should have been more concerned, but I no longer cared if that rage claimed me as a victim. I appeared crippled by Sebastian's passing. I felt detached and undeserving to continue an existence where my ability to make good decisions had been compromised.

Wait a second.

'What did you just say about a *deal*?'

'You think you're the only one with connections?'

I'd never considered anyone's status within my life useless or beneficial. Except Araqiel. I considered him a giant pain in the rear end and now my killer; hardly an advantageous connection. 'Did you make a deal with Araqiel to have me killed rather than doing it yourself?'

'Demonic dealings are inevitably beyond your comprehension,' he said, waving me off. 'The point is that you should not have been reborn to this life.'

Patronising to be sure. 'I suppose not.' I pressed back against the pillows, turning my head so I could look out beyond the French doors. 'Yet here I am.'

Julius slipped closer, a move that may have been indistinguishable in months past—but now as a vampire—was just as obvious as sitting on my lap. He tsk tsked me. 'You are so careless for someone inches from death.'

'Careless,' I murmured, feigning disinterest. 'Now that depends on who you think might be inches from death.'

He laughed, a genuinely happy sound that would have ordinarily made my skin crawl. 'Well, that would be you. Except this time, I will make sure that you don't come back.'

'Hmm,' I murmured. 'It sounds pleasant enough, but it's never really true in my case.' I thought about the thousands of years I'd been reincarnated with Sebastian. 'I just seem to keep coming back—like dandruff.'

'Not this time.'

If only I could …

'You know I can't just lay here and let you kill me.' I sighed again, long and full of weariness. I was tired of fighting, tired of so much more than I could explain, but even my stilled heart new I couldn't relent to this fiend. 'Unfortunately, there are people that depend on me—people who have protected me for a really long time in the hopes I would come back.'

'Not this time.' He crept closer still, his taloned fingers making popping sounds as they punctuated the mattress. His face drew near; long pointed fangs were unsheathed with the promise of torture. He certainly looked the part.

'Are you sure you don't want to think this through?'

Though only a few feet from my face he laughed, his chilled breath tickling my skin. 'It's all I ever think about.'

'Then I feel sorry for you.'

'Sorry for me?' He moved another perceptible inch in my direction, not especially interested in what I had to say. He was merely playing the game, biding his time until the moment felt right.

'Yes. You'll never, ever find any peace.'

'I don't need peace. I need my vengeance.'

'I'd still reconsider, if for no other reason than to save your pointless life.'

My words amused him further. 'And why is that?'

'Because I will kill you, Julius.'

He sampled the air, drawing in a breath deep enough to boast yet another cackle of delight. 'There's no one near enough to help you. No one close enough to hear you scream.'

'Hmm, you're right,' I agreed. 'But you forgot one thing.'

'And what is that?' he murmured, so close now that his eyes melded into a puddle of liquid cobalt.

'There's no one close enough to hear you scream either.'

'So, you *are* going to try to kill me. I rather thought you had given up.'

'I guess so.'

For a split second we merely looked at each other; not moving and listening to the wind outside stir the leaves within the overgrown trees. Everything else grew still; the feel of his breath on my face and the singular droplet of saliva racing to meet the end of his pointed fangs.

As a vampire, my skills were still underdeveloped. I knew this because his eyes were blurred, but the saliva in his mouth was in full technicolour focus. I'd have a tough time seeing him coming and going. Whipping out my vânător arsenal was a smarter line of defence despite being untested since my turning.

I thought by now he would have made his move. I imagined the blue, unfocused puddle filled with an immeasurable depth of hate clouding my vision, my neck under surrender and the sweet burst of peace and pleasure from the rupture of his canines in my flesh, but instead we were suddenly moving in battle defence.

In that split second, I summoned the alternate darkness within, filling my veins with rage and bitterness so immeasurable that the beast inside hungered. Clutching at self-control, I refused to let my vânător nature take full supremacy, but also allowed it the freedom to hunt.

The heartbeat passed and another began, Julius was virtually on top of me, but my limbs continued to twist and contort with change. Black fur sprouted through my pores, fingers and toes re-shaped themselves into deadly claws. Fangs of differing shapes and sizes filled a muzzle purpose-built to tear flesh and break bones. My spine simultaneously cracked, bowing and lengthening into something hulking and beastly. My eyes sharpened and a howl of intent erupted, so potent with malice through a snout whiskered and dripping with the saliva of deep hunger. Julius gave pause.

Transformed, I bounded off the bed, Julius hissing at the empty spot on the mattress. The enticing scent of fear tickled my nostrils and I licked the end of my nose to relish how quickly I had reversed the odds in my favour. Ordinarily a vampire would be faster and stronger than a vânător, but I was a combination of both and decidedly better practiced at being a vânător than I was a vampire.

Julius now leapt from the mattress, claws finding purchase in the plaster work of the walls behind the bed. He crawled higher and higher until he was upon the ceiling looking down. Though he held no pulse and his eyes did not betray his inner turmoil, I could still smell the unease.

He hissed again, micro droplets of saliva raining down, each perfectly formed and crystal clear as they shattered upon impact with the floor. I pondered Julius's thoughts and movements, wondering if he measured mine, his eyes now blacker than midnight, his vampiric form swelling into actuality. He appeared to be studying me; his head moved left then right, his lips pulled back tightly into a snarl, further revealing his fangs.

It was unclear if I could climb walls as a wolf and chase after him. I suspected I wasn't as nimble with my paws and a tad heavier than the ceiling plaster would allow. I could—however—jump very high and ridiculously far, so clinging to the roof had little bearing on whether I could capture him within my jaws. I was also telekinetic; an unfair advantage when I could pin him down with merely a thought.

My wolf considered that manoeuvre cowardly. It was adamant that we would roll in this vampire's carnage and bathe in its blood, luxuriating in the sweet stench of his death after a fair victory. I found no issue with such a resolve; a desire to finally rid myself of yet another enemy hell-bent on marking me for death. We would face each other as equals and see which one of us was the victor.

So, it was decided.

Julius moved fractionally to the left and I pounced. My claws scrambled for purchase on the dusty terracotta floor seconds before I was sailing up, jaws open and ready to take first bite. There would be blood, undoubtedly some of it mine as this fray unfolded.

My powerful jaws slammed home with an echoing *thud*. Julius was gone, his arms and legs a blur as he darted backwards and forwards across the ceiling. My skull connected with an overhead beam, disrupting plaster and shaking the dusty and decrepit chandelier by its barely retained foundations.

I plummeted. Not far and nothing damaging. I landed lithely less than a second later, springing forth after Julius for a second time. He was impressively fast and particularly nimble, nothing I hadn't anticipated. The wolf within enjoyed the challenge, unwilling to relent until this vampire's jugular was crushed between my powerful jaws.

We both flew around the room like debris in a tornado, tearing apart walls, cracking the floors and disrupting Sebastian's mementos from whatever home they had once had. A plethora of memories was now ripped from their resting place and torn apart in a war zone of two vicious supernatural entities determined to exercise their right to supremacy. And while Julius hissed and snarled and I barked and howled, Sebastian's many and varied musical instruments became the alternative soundtrack to our deadly game of cat and mouse.

I now had Julius cornered by the door. He'd backed into the armoire and that sweet stench of indecision with a liberal coating of fear touched his being. Black eyes darted like pinballs as he weighed and measured his odds of escape, but his Houdini ability to escape anyone's grasp saw him disappear yet again.

I bounded into the corridor in search of him, focused and driven by scent. He was quick, but I was relentless, catching his shoulder between hungry teeth, twisting and taking him down to the ground. We rolled frantically, our bodies briefly finding air before we ripped through the last vestiges of the wrought iron balustrade. The fret-work was punishing and we howled in unison, Julius conscientious in wasting no opportunity to slash at my hind legs. We tumbled down the stone stairs in a barrage of arms, legs and paws.

I attempted to recapture his injured shoulder, rebuttal to the crippling pain in my back legs as he repeatedly tore at my limbs with jagged nails. I took some pleasure in his tormented release, tasting the sweetness of his blood pour across my tongue—a promise of death. But all was lost as a structural column at the foot of the stairs disrupted our tumbling forms; I dislocated my hip on impact and we were momentarily separated. Julius then took his opportunity and swiped my muzzle and right cheek, claws digging deep and tearing through flesh and sinew.

My face ruptured with agony, but he took a surprising reprieve and scuttled backwards, perhaps tormented more than I realised by the gaping wound around his shoulder. A singular tooth was lodged in what was left of the exposed tendons and ball-and-socket joint.

We glared at each other, breathing rapid and harsh as we counted the seconds until our bodies healed and we were ready for round two. I tried not to think about my mangled face as blood dripped steadily onto the floor or the tooth that attempted regeneration. My hip popped back into place with an audible *crunch*; a split second of pain followed by instantaneous relief.

A new problem presented; the metaphysical cord of consciousness between psychopathic wolf and reasoning vampire had begun a tug-of-war. The wolf inside was inherently dark and wanted to torture Julius until all that was left was an offering for the Tooth Fairy. Thankfully, some semblance of sensibilities remained and I won the final pull for consciousness, pain no longer clouded my judgement and neither did the wolf's desire for justice.

Julius moved and so did I, claws slashing and ripping at the terracotta to find grip. A moment of private panic ensued and a memory so fresh and ridiculously out of context distracted me. I thought of Marcus, one of Lucius's original thralls and long-time patron of the arts and avid protector of the courtyard floor. Irreplaceable, handmade tiles tore apart beneath my paws as I skidded to a stop. I hailed a memory of Marcus, his lips moving with a string of profanities reserved especially for those desecrating his interior stylings.

A pang of sadness and regret rippled through me. It was a distant memory from the past, but it was also a reminder of the current reality.

Marcus was no longer with us. Another story for another day and yet another casualty of this war.

I suffered a vicious blow to the back of the head. Stars circled my retinas as unexpected debris was flung by a vampire with total focus on the deadly venture at hand. I—however—consulted past memories of Marcus and vintage flooring while Julius clobbered my ass with an old deck chair.

Slightly encumbered by the brief flare of pain behind my eyes, Julius wasted no opportunity. A bucket-full of craziness sparkled within his obsidian retinas and I barely ducked as deadlier arsenal was swung in my direction. Talons pursued and came within millimetres of tearing through the very windows to my soul.

Weight shifted to my hind legs; the plan was to sink my front paws deep within his chilled, pale flesh. His response time was epic and I moved a millisecond too late, only catching the cusp of his ribs, tearing a hole through his shirt and drawing minimal blood.

Still, the mesmerising colour and scent leaked in a singular ruby droplet and was one that I hungered for deeply. Julius was more than aware of this and leapt backwards until he was perched on the crumbling edge of the old central fountain. A weird kind of *come-hither* expression possessed his face before he leapt again without warning, clambering back to the second floor.

The wolf within felt chastised and hankered for pursuit. Julius's lithe form hung suspended in mid-air as time slowed, gravity now nothing but a myth in the face of the speed in which our responses were executed. I'd measured the distance, tasted imminent victory and launched from the ground, shattering the remaining tiles beneath my paws. Air was a momentary companion before I collided with Julius. We crashed through the walls of the corridor upstairs like a herd of elephants on the move in Africa, bursting through the other side of the building and tumbling to the garden below.

Dazed, we stumbled until equilibrium returned. Julius swiped at my flank and I threw him through another wall in rebuttal. More debris showered upon us as we rolled into what used to be the library. Chalky powder now layered my sable fur like a coat and I used it like camouflage, darting in and around the falling ceiling plaster without pattern or calculated motive.

As he turned to dodge a collapsing ceiling beam, I deposited my unsheathed claws deep into his spinal column, the weight of me sending him to his knees. Jaws stretched wide and fangs at the helm, I then went deep, closing powerful bone and stretched muscle around the back of his exposed neck; the skin parted as easily as a hot knife through butter.

He screamed, hands flailing and lethal talons attempting to find a hold anywhere within his grasp, but I was safe. My jaws around his neck—and paws against his back—kept him down and harmless. Still, it was obvious that he would never give up—never stop trying to kill me, even to his own detriment.

'Do it!' he demanded, not scared but livid. 'Do what no one else has ever been able to do!'

He taunted in a way that made me hesitate. The seeping misery in his voice poisoned his angry words with a shocking degree of clarity. Bravado aside, perhaps what he actually hungered for now was the release from the debilitating remnants of the past. I had only but to close my jaws in finality, drink his blood and then sever his head from his neck—and Julius after two thousand years of existence—would be dead.

So why couldn't I do it?

Did I suddenly feel some sort of mercy for a man that had hunted and murdered innocent people for centuries?

'I know you can understand me,' he continued. 'What are you waiting for?'

What *was* I waiting for? If anyone had need of death it was Julius. So why was reluctance holding my jaw still? Why could I not close my fangs those last few inches and end the life of an immortal that had personally planned to rip me apart?

I believed it was some semblance of compassion; a dangerous notion given I was now being swayed by my own demons. Or perhaps it was the kinship of an all-consuming pain resulting from an unending existence devoid of your one true love. Julius was indeed the burnt-out shell of a man beneath my paws, begging through the mask of ire to end the hardship of a life he'd never really understood. He'd claimed to want vengeance, but what he really wanted was …

He went slack, his flailing arms flopping to the ground like lead weights. A trick? I watched in amazement as he retracted his talons by choice, his fingers slowly morphing into weapon-less, ordinary hands. He attempted to turn his head to the side, my teeth tearing through more flesh and the skin parting almost too easily as his jugular came into contact with my tongue.

I detached my fangs enough that I could inspect his angle and shake off cravings for his blood. I wasn't entirely convinced by this show of surrender, so my paws remained familiar with his vertebrae. I could re-engage at any time, but for now I was held captive by the return of Julius's human eyes and the way they burned into mine.

He moved slowly, brushing scattered strands of his hair from his face so I could observe his transformation from vampirism. Was I convinced this was already over? No. He was giving up way too soon.

'Please,' he now whispered. 'Let me roll onto my back and face my death like a true soldier.'

Was this some misplaced urge to restore honour and gain my respect? I knew at some point in his youth and human life he'd been a legionnaire for the Roman armies, serving under my father during the numerous battles Rome pursued, but this? Did he expect me to believe he wouldn't try something to prolong his unlife?

I buried my taloned paws deeper. Bone crunched and blood oozed. I was almost annoyed this precious resource was being wasted while I debated the intentions of a psychopath. Surely the answer was obvious … kill him?

'I do not wish to die a coward, with my back turned. I want to see my death coming.'

I had no answer to give. I was a werewolf without a mouth in which to speak, but even if I could, I was certain it would not be to let him get the upper hand on me, swivel within my grasp and gouge my eyes out.

'I'm done,' he continued to urge. 'It is obvious that the longer we fight I am at a disadvantage; in only one of your forms and without using your full potential, you have me beat.'

My full potential?

An idea bloomed as dawn's brush of light kissed the edge of the horizon. If death was truly what Julius sought after such a quick and relatively uneventful fray, then he would have to prove that urge by taking measures upon himself. I'd done enough killing—seen enough carnage and although the wolf within was bitterly disappointed, it understood emotional self-preservation. Blood no longer washed clean from my hands and to add another stain upon them could invariably damage me.

A deep breath and then I closed my eyes, perhaps praying I was about to do the right thing. Letting go was easy, trusting the outcome was not. And although he didn't move a muscle as my weight shifted above him, I wrapped telekinetic energy around his form regardless.

I then concentrated on my form and the reformation from wolf to human. I wanted to be able to communicate Julius's ability to choose, an opportunity that had been robbed from me so many times in the past. And as I thought about broaching the subject of his imminent death, I began to feel the familiar pull of my body in metamorphosis. Legs lengthened, stretched and then retracted. Hair dissolved and my face contorted almost painfully. With the blood of my father pulsing through my veins, I no longer needed to sleep off this form—but rather—change at will.

When I re-opened my eyes, Julius was staring at me. I stood as naked as the day I was born, the vânător shift having shredded any vestige of clothing. I did not feel ashamed of what I was and what I had become and refused to apologise for the mixed-natured woman that now stood before this bewildered vampire.

Ever so slowly, I knelt down beside Julius, observing his wide eyes roam the course of my body. I had no idea what thoughts ran rampant or even if they leant themselves towards an inappropriate process. I merely hoped he'd grab this opportunity of choice with both hands and take the route of honour and courage—a reflection of the man I suspected he'd once been.

Caution still lit the whites of Julius's saucer-sized eyes. And though he inspected my body with the interest of any man with a naked woman before him, he appeared more intent on trying to rationalize my motives, touching the shield around him, fingers grazing the shimmery surface in search of vulnerability. 'I underestimated you.'

I shook my head. 'No, you underestimated yourself and what you could have been capable of.'

'I know my limitations.'

'I'm not talking about your abilities as a vampire and how you might have beaten me. I'm talking about what you could have done differently. You could have had a good life, you know. You could have met someone else, fallen in love and been happy.'

'The words of a naive child,' he muttered, now running his fingers through his hair. 'Do you even know what it is to truly love another, to give yourself body and soul and never look back?'

I nodded, completely assured that I knew that feeling intrinsically. 'I do. But I also know that life goes on when the unexpected happens.' He attempted to interrupt, but I held a hand up to quieten him. 'I'm not saying it doesn't hurt. It feels like your entire chest is empty; it's a hole that can never be filled, but you do have choices. You can wallow and plot your revenge—forever held back by your bitterness—or you can move on, knowing that one day soon you'll be smiling again.'

'Move on,' he shook his head at me, contemptuous glare back insitu. 'There's no moving on.'

I shrugged, wondering if in some respects I didn't agree given my current state of misery. 'Perhaps not, but you owe it to yourself to try.'

'No.'

A flash of bitter agony teamed with a very confused version of understanding mingled with thoughts of opening my heart ever so slightly to this psychopathic vampire. I knew I'd uttered the voice of reason and redemption and the words made perfect sense, but to some extent, Julius's point was also valid in his summation that I'd never truly be happy without Sebastian.

I conceded his point. 'Okay, I get it.'

His lips twitched, fingers testing the barrier of my defence again. 'So, what now? The reality as it stands is that I may not ever be able to beat you given your powers, but I promise that I'll never stop trying to kill you until I'm satisfied.'

'You said you wanted to face death on your own terms.'

'Well, since I suspect you will not release me to fight another day, then facing the true death on my terms *is* what I want.'

'You're right, I can't just let you go.'

'So be it. What is it that you propose?'

I tilted my head towards the jagged opening we'd rammed through the wall. Outside the overgrown garden was still relatively dark, but sunrise was fast approaching. Dusty pink waves brushed the sky, the first hint that darkness was once again retreating to allow the light to prosper.

Julius followed my gaze. For a moment his face went blank and then he took a perceptible breath in, exhaled noisily and then started the slow climb to his feet. 'Not how I expected my unlife to end.'

'Then you understand?'

'I am to burn alive under the eyes of the sun … yes.' He brandished me with a dismissive sneer. 'How I wish I could take you down with me.'

I clambered back to my feet, a snappy retort poised on the end of my tongue, however it was superglued from emission as he moved towards death. My telekinetic barrier still encompassed him for my safety, but gave him the freedom to move towards the hole in the wall that would soon be filled with the sunrise of his demise.

He glanced back over his shoulder, thoughts qualifying his face with curiosity. 'I don't suppose—'

'I won't remove the barrier and give you the opportunity to run.'

'Do you think I'm a coward?'

I folded my arms across the front of my breasts, resolute. 'Does it really matter what I think?'

His gaze fell away. Acceptance now painted his features. He stepped through a few more feet of rubble until he found the garden. Blades of grass whispered between his toes, capturing his attention only momentarily before he settled on searching the skies. Danger did not loom at present, but dawn approached and the sun's rays would soon touch the pasty pallor of his skin and burn him to a cinder.

I hung back in the shadows of the library, no longer immune to the sun as I had once been as a human. Yes, I could withstand it for a while, but eventually I would be encased in flames and join Julius in the true death that awaited him.

'Was it worth it?' I asked him, curious that years of savagery, retaliation and bitterness would come to such an unsatisfying end.

'Was what worth it?' he murmured, still studying the rapidly approaching light. It touched the horizon now, spilling across the landscape and beyond like melted ice-cream dribbling down a child's chin.

'The years of chasing vengeance that never truly came.'

'Of course it was.'

The light now kissed his skin in a feather-light caress. Full strength rays still built in momentum, but it was enough that Julius already appeared pink and uncomfortable. He heeded it no attention, his face still tilted towards redemption.

'How could it be worth it? You're about to die and Lucius and I are still alive.'

Welts and blisters broke out across his skin, hair smoking under the heat of the dawning sun. 'That may be true, but at least I'll have a chance.'

'A chance at what?'

He turned to eye me fully. A smile cracked the corners of his chapped lips, skin weeping from the effort. 'To see my wife again.'

And with that, his whole body caught fire. The urge to look away was compelling, but I forced myself to watch his ultimate demise—forced myself to keep eye contact as long as he held my gaze. When he threw his head back and screamed—the sounds terrifying and punctuated by fear—I massaged the knot of indecision twisting my unbeating heart. Despite what must have been horrific pain, Julius stood resolute. He roared his turmoil until his throat closed over, smoke whispering from every orifice and choking any lingering response. His knees buckled and he finally fell, skin flaking away like dried foliage, seesawing to the ground, captured by the wind.

It escalated quickly and ended just as fast. His lip-less mouth opened one final time, charred and bony protrusions once known as fingers searching for help. He then exploded in a bilious cloud of ash, quickly carried by the morning breeze through the billowing trees of an unruly yard we had all once called home.

I stood rooted in shock, shielded by the shadows of the house, staring at the scolded earth where Julius had been. I thought I'd feel relieved that another enemy was dead, but I didn't. The constant ebb and flow of sadness still consumed my heart, now filled with words that would undoubtedly haunt.

I'd schooled Julius about making better choices; live life or die from misery. In the end, he'd chosen to exit with his despair in the hopes of being reunited with his wife. Neither of us had mentioned that Lucifer knew no mercy and would never allow that to happen. Julius had a one-way ticket to the Southern sauna where I would soon join him if I didn't pull my head out of my ass and accept what had come to pass in my own life.

It was a discouraging thought, but nevertheless true that Sebastian would be disappointed if he saw me now. My priorities were twisted and seeded with self-absorbed emotional loss. He'd fallen from Heaven to be with me, sacrificed grace and an eternity of happiness to ensure I had one. What a giant slap in the face I offered, mocking his memory and narrowly escaping dancing with death … yet again.

My legs folded and I slumped against the solid wall behind me, the plaster cracking on impact, roof dust tickling my brow. How much longer was I going to be selfish? I had a family and friends that I loved, people willing to help and wanting to see me achieve happiness again. It would be a long road and a destination perhaps never reached, but I sure as hell had to try for their sakes.

If nothing else, I *needed* to do it for him and all he had sacrificed for me.

I simply *had* to do it for myself.

CHAPTER FIFTEEN: DOGGED

I returned to the tunnels a little over an hour after sun up. I hadn't meant to linger, dawdle or worry my friends and father, but the sun—even in the early hours—was unyielding in its attempts to capture me in its fiery hold.

To be fair, time had escaped within the bubble of conflict I'd come to surpass. I'd remained immobile for an immeasurable stretch, huddled against the wall of my father's library, staring bleary-eyed at the cinders of Julius's remains. I'd contemplated, procrastinated—and of course—culminated by attempting to leave with a clear head and a solid decision to ditch the past and look to the future.

Intentions were the foundations of best laid plans, but reality doesn't always measure up. I still considered myself weak. I had contemplated the use of the Time Contract to ease the burdens of the past and change the shit I'd waded into in the present.

I had to stop doing that.

Tinkering with the past did not ensure a future without conflict.

While in the library, I'd begun to reminisce. My fingers had flown over the dusted and mildew-ridden shelves, seeking the one book that had fascinated me on first glance some ten years earlier. The content had never captured my interest, nor the pages filled with documentation on both angels and demons. I'd been enamoured by the cover, drawn by the graphic illustration of the arch angel Michael leaning over Lucifer, victory within his grasp.

Michael—also known as Sebastian—was now dead, possibly holed up in Purgatory and wishing he'd never fallen in love with someone who wasn't so freaking complicated. Sebastian's penchant for disastrous brunettes had been his ultimate demise and the reason I had to reassess my selfish nature now.

Anyway, I'd found the book under a pile of rubble. Preservation had been lost as the damp pages clumped and the cover-art I'd so desperately sought was both scratched and torn in the corners. I'd pressed it to my chest regardless, reassured that Sebastian was still near in some way. I'd then headed home, using the tunnel system under Rome to avoid the sun.

What had once been a heavy dumpster filled with indeterminable waste now blocked my way inside our current tunnels. The dumpster sat lonely and without purpose in the corner of the alley behind the dilapidated building once housing my father's blood production company known as Synth Corp. It took only a second with my strength to push it aside and slither into the darkness below. I was eager for a new set of clothes and an end to this night that had passed.

'Elena!'

I froze. I was ill-prepared to be met in this unfaltering state of nakedness. I had attempted to be quiet re-entering the motley crew of tunnel-dwellers, but apparently even my brother sat in vigilance, preparing a lecture for my eventual return.

I did the only thing I could do under the circumstances and bent the book's spine I carried in half, pressing my groin against one side and attempting to hide what I could of my boobs behind the rest. It was by no means a solid plan, but it was all I had.

'Elena?' A long pause was followed closely by shuffling in the dark. 'Elena is that you?'

I thought about ignoring him and pretending I wasn't there. He didn't have vampiric sight and was eyeballing all directions in search of me. He should have been grateful his vision was impaired in this moment and yet despite my current state of undress, I couldn't ignore his perceptiveness.

'Elena, if you don't answer, I'll take you down with magic.'

I scoffed—too loudly. That was all the revelation Lucas needed that I was present. A match was struck and mottled light lifted the veil of darkness. The look of abject horror on my brother's face spoke volumes.

'Elena? Why the hell are you naked?'

I cringed, debating an almost comical answer and deciding against it. Humour was my form of deflection and he'd see right through it.

He politely looked away or perhaps he had to in order to control his upchuck reflexes. 'Answer me.'

'It's complicated.'

'It always is with you.' His sigh was filled with resignation as he ran a hand across the top of his shaved head over and over again. 'FYI, that book is *not* nearly big enough.'

'I'm aware.'

'So, I repeat, *why* are you naked? And for that matter, where the hell have you been? We've all been worried about you.' *Again* was the unsaid word hanging in the air between us. Judging by the determined set of his jaw and the exhaustion bruising the delicate skin of his eyes, he'd had enough of my antics for one night. 'Clearly you've been up to no good.'

'Hmm, not exactly.'

His match extinguished and he quickly lit another. I was met with an eyebrow already arched and on high alert. 'Elena, seriously. We have a lot on our plate right now. We've been trying to hash out a plan to sneak into the super city and you've been doing what exactly?'

'Um, I've—'

The intake of breath to my right drew both our attention. William was standing at the end of the corridor, his mouth gaping at my current state of undress. Karina followed out from the adjoining passage a second later. 'What the—' She slammed a hand across William's roaming eyes and started dragging him backwards. 'Really, Elena?'

'Sorry,' I grumbled. 'It's not like I planned this.'

'You never do,' she mumbled, finally punching William in the shoulder to get him to move his stubborn feet. He stumbled like a drunk after a bar fight; not exactly normal for super-serious, super-controlled and super-uptight William. He could be forgiven for loss of composure under the circumstances.

'What's happening? I smell Elena.' Caleb was the next one to round the passage, he was eyeballing Karina and William strangely until he became completely aware for the reason of retreat. 'In trouble again, Elena?' he laughed, unsurprised by my appearance or everyone's reaction to it.

I so very badly wanted to roll my eyes, but resisted on account that any form of dismissive or sarcastic behaviour would not award me understanding or even underwear. I did—however—warn him with a pointed finger to keep his distance. Caleb being Caleb simply ignored me.

I focused back on Lucas. 'I'm sorry I took off. I shouldn't have without at least saying something, it's just that I'm not in the right head space.' I nibbled my lower lip, mulling that statement over. 'Okay, so I *wasn't* in the right frame of mind, but I'm pretty sure I'll be okay from this point forward.'

'Well, I'm personally all for this new version of *Elena's headspace* if it means she's going to walk around naked everywhere.' Caleb was now closer than I liked and generally making a mockery of the whole situation—not that I expected any different from him.

'I'm not going to make this into a habit.'

'Shame.'

'You're not helping, Caleb,' Lucas muttered. 'Clearly something's happened,' he said gesturing helplessly to my naked body.

'Honestly, I'm fine. I don't want to worry anyone. I just need some clothes and possibly a very large hole to crawl into for a few days.'

'Start digging,' Caleb mocked, giving me yet another amused once over.

'What's happened?' Tiberius, Decimus and Maximus now joined Caleb and Lucas in the passage like the group session for AA had started and everyone had to be there. 'We heard Elena. Lucius is very worried.'

'So is my modesty,' I muttered, teeth clenched. Jeesh. I'd barely seen the thralls since waking due to their various scouting missions and now here they were, clucking like mother hens at the most inopportune moment.

I sighed and clutched the book tighter against me. I was practically bent in half now attempting to maintain modesty. I honestly wondered if it wouldn't have been better to convert back to vânător to equip myself with fur and avoid all conversation.

'What the …' Maximums stopped, apparently at a loss for words.

'Please don't tell Lucius about this,' I grumbled, wishing I could melt into a crack in the wall or the grimy puddle upon the floor.

'Tell me about what?'

I said a very, very bad word and then proceeded to die all over again as my father joined the party. He was momentarily distracted by Karina and William's petty arguing behind him, but was quickly pulled back to the current situation as he observed the throng of spectators and Caleb grinning wildly at my rising level of discomfort.

'Great,' I mumbled facetiously. 'We're all here now. Let's take pictures to remember this momentous occasion.'

'What am I missing?' Marianne countered, roaring around the corner and coming to a stop by Lucas's side. She gave me the once over and then burst out laughing. 'I'd almost forgotten how interesting things can be with her around.' She jabbed a thumb in my direction, still cackling as she asked Lucas, 'That's not one of those magazines you like to read, is it?'

Jesus ...

'Can someone please get me some clothes?' I whispered, mortified beyond comprehension. I backed up into the corner, aware that Caleb's head was practically detached from his shoulders as he angled to allow for a better view of my ass. Thankfully, Maximus slapped the supercilious grin off his face and ordered him to find me some clothes *stat*.

'What's going on, Elena?' Lucius bellowed, clearly annoyed by my latest antics. He gestured for everyone else to take their leave. For *that* I would be eternally grateful.

'Lucius, I'm really sorry that I just upped and left again. I was frustrated by my lack of control, circumstances ... everything ... it's no excuse.'

'We'll get to that in a minute I—'

'Why are your clothes missing?' Lucas interrupted.

I narrowed my eyes at Marianne when she smirked, but she was lightning fast to cover the ever-widening lips before sound escaped. 'I shape-shifted.'

'You turned vânător?' Lucius repeated for confirmation. A combination of distracted and irritable, he re-motioned with a *click* of his fingers for all those still lingering to depart. I didn't think anyone—except for Caleb—was trying to perve on me, merely curious to my whereabouts or even amused by my latest escapade.

I shivered, an old human habit as the tunnel's bitingly cold blockwork bit against my naked flesh. I still clutched the book and wore an unsteady grimace as I waited for Caleb to stop gawking and leave

'Elena!' Lucius pressed.

'I wanted to see what it would be like now that I've turned.'

'And?'

'And can we discuss this after I'm dressed?'

Maximus slapped Caleb again, a reminder of his earlier mission to source me clothes. He begrudgingly left, sneaking cheeky looks over his shoulder as he sauntered off down the passage. Apparently, he was in no hurry at all.

Asshole.

'She's lying,' Lucas piped in, drawing my attention.

'What?' I squeaked. I was shocked by the lack of gumption my vocal cords seemed to have.

He nodded, seemingly onto something. The next match had blown out and while Lucas hurriedly re-lit another, I debated another getaway then deemed the act pointless in lieu of current company. 'I can tell when she's fibbing. There's more to this.'

'Lucas …'

'No, seriously, E. What the hell? You've always been a pain in the ass but—'

'I smell Julius!' Decimus suddenly shouted, alarming everyone in the corridor to battle advancement.

Eww. I must have had some of his ashes in my hair or something.

Still clutching the book gingerly, I yelled over the commotion, 'Stop, it's not what you think. Julius isn't here.'

So much for my clothes. Caleb's painfully slow retreat had halted and even William and Karina had returned at the mention of imminent danger. Marianne had shoved Lucas against the wall acting like a shield and the thralls came rushing back within seconds.

I should never have left.

Too much paperwork.

Lucius didn't relax at my admission and neither did the rest of the vamps who were already trying out their fangs and sampling the air with deep inhalations. 'I can smell him too,' they somewhat all murmured in one way or another.

I sighed. I was going to be in so much shit now. Seriously. Why did anyone bother trying to revive me? 'Put your fangs away, guys. He's definitely not here. In fact, he's not going to be anywhere anymore,' I said, mumbling the last part under my breath. Unfortunately, my father heard me.

'Elena,' Lucius rumbled, clenching his teeth. 'Explain ...'

Bugger. He was pissed and I hadn't even said anything yet. *Here goes ...*

'You can smell Julius because we kind of had an impromptu meeting.'

Everyone looked over my shoulder again as if he might suddenly appear right behind me and yell 'surprise!'.

Lucius's nostrils were flaring like an overworked racehorse and Lucas was trying to manoeuvre around Marianne as if I might somehow need protecting. All I really needed in that moment ... were pants.

'Did you lead him back here? Are you running? Did he—'

'He knew we were all hiding in the tunnel system, guys, he wasn't an idiot, but no, none of the above. I'm perfectly fine, I swear it.'

They continually surveyed the tunnel entrance, perplexed. I thought *someone* might have noticed that I'd referenced Julius in the past tense, but no. They remained on high alert and yet utterly confused. Had they not considered the possibility that I may have actually defeated the Great and Powerful OZ?

More blank stares.

'Oh for God's sake, he's dead!'

'Dead?' a few echoed.

I nodded, convinced that my words and actions of the affirmation would help the information seep through. 'Yes ... dead.'

Bewilderment was the common theme on everyone's face. So perplexed were these vampires—even my brother—that I had no choice but to stand there naked and recount the story from the beginning. A myriad of reactions played out during the course of the retelling—none of them particularly surprising. Most displayed disbelief and finally ended in awe. Lucius and Lucas remained passive aggressive, concerned only for my welfare and not to propagate my ego.

'So ... Julius just walked out into the sun?' Decimus asked. He clearly didn't believe it was that simple.

'Look, I don't think that was his original plan.' I answered, 'But I guess in the end he got to go out on his own terms.'

Decimus snorted his disbelief. Couldn't say I blamed him. Julius had been a force to be reckoned with for centuries and I was a newly turned vampire with a fluctuating skillset at best.

'I can't believe Julius is dead,' Tiberius uttered, voice barely a coherent whisper.

'Are you sure,' Lucius asked, face still speculative and twisted with a myriad of angry emotions. His fingers twitched at his side, undoubtedly itching to shake my wilful shoulders.

'He was one crispy critter.'

'That's horrible,' Karina voiced, displeasure at my current state of undress still a pressing concern. It hadn't stopped her and William from creeping back closer to participate in the conversation though. 'How can you be so callous? A man just died.'

I bowed my head and took a calming breath. 'Perhaps you are right in some regards and I should have more respect for a man that once fought alongside my father as an equal, but, Karina, he was also a total psycho who's been trying to kill me for years! So, forgive me if I take a little delight in his passing.'

'Just stop talking, Elena,' Lucas said offhandedly, passing the thirteenth burning match to Marianne to hold as he slowly unbuttoned his shirt. I presumed he was going to give it to me, not join me in the naked pity party. I was more than a little annoyed that it had taken someone this long to think of it, including me.

'What's with the book?' Caleb asked, turning his head so he could better see the cover and title. At least, that's how he made it look until he winked lecherously at me.

I wasn't sure I could explain the sentiment behind retrieving this treasure from the past, so I didn't. 'Shouldn't I have some bloody clothes by now, Caleb?'

My father's rather noisy exhale drew my petulant gaze his way. 'Elena, you'll find no answers nor comfort between those pages.'

'On the contrary, I'm quite comforted by the fact that I am currently hiding between these pages. Now can I please get some clothes?'

Lucas shrugged out of his shirt and finally handed it to me. 'Put this on.'

I snatched it—albeit gratefully—and then just looked at it as if it were some foreign object never before seen. It was definitely big enough thanks to the shirt tails to protect my modesty, but there was still a serious issue ahead. How was I supposed to put it on while still clutching the book gingerly to my naked body? 'Can you please all turn around?'

Everyone obliged, though I expected nothing less. I hastily dropped the book and was halfway through slipping my second arm into a sleeve when Caleb was back to ogling me. I quickly pulled the two pieces of the shirt together, shaking my head as I fingered the buttons closed. 'Caleb! Boundaries!'

'You never said anything about not completing a full rotation. You just said *turn around.*'

Groans wrought the passage and Maximus went for a third slap to the back of the impertinent vampire's head. Caleb seemed less concerned about the admonishment and more annoyed that he had to once again artfully rearrange the pink spikes that made up his punk-style hair.

In the meantime, with explanations wrapped up and what I deemed suitably detailed, I snatched my book from the floor and made a beeline for the relative privacy of Lucas's room. Being that he was the only individual that required sleep—besides the Vânătors—I also used this space to rest and keep a few changes of clothes.

'Elena, we are not done with this conversation,' my father bellowed. As usual he felt disciplinary action was necessary to drive some semblance of common sense within me. He would have been right ordinarily, but a lot had changed since I'd woken. In fact, a lot had happened in the last few hours that left me less in need of the parental guidance I may have needed in the past. Even Lucas saw fit to follow me, hot on my heels and possibly as unwilling as Lucius to let the matter drop.

I gave pause. 'Julius is dead and I'm alive. I promise you that there really isn't any more to say.'

It was then that I realised my father fretted over matters far deeper than Julius's life status as he looked pointedly at the book still within my grasp. 'To linger on the possibility of him coming back—'

Rooted by unmoving feet, I understood his trepidation and foreboding concern immediately. I also knew the logistics between life and death and that Sebastian was never coming back to me. 'I just feel comforted by it.'

'Elena …'

'Please, Lucius, there are just some things I can't explain to you and Sebastian and I …' Words failed me. Despite his horrendous past and the sorrow that filled his own heart, how could I communicate my darkest fears and sadness without breaking down yet again? So, I re-commenced the short trek to Lucas's dank space at the end of the tunnel. Karina scowled at me as I passed, William's lips twitching in the corners. Lucas of course was following me, Marianne trailing him.

'Elena!'

I knew I should not have ignored the booming call of my father's insistence, but ours had been a tumultuous relationship with shaky bonds not fully formed. Many years of absence had instilled a sense of self-preservation and lack of need on my part to seek his assurances and guidance. To let him dictate or question my decisions at this point after so much forced growing up and experiences felt … awkward.

'Elena! We have much to discuss!'

'I'll get her up to speed,' Lucas muttered behind me. He was no less impressed by my early morning venture than Lucius had been, but he was also my brother and a little more versed in my behavioural patterns. I let him follow.

'I'm sorry about running out earlier,' I reiterated, tentatively brushing the furry coats of a few vânǎtors we passed along the way. Their smell and presence was a sense of comfort well-needed in that moment.

'I know you're grieving,' Lucas answered, drawing up beside me, 'but we need your help now more than ever.'

'I know.'

He grabbed my arm just above the elbow and pulled me to a stop. 'No, you don't. We've co-existed with the Vânǎtors out of necessity, but our control has been tentative at best. Now that food is scarce and we have to spread our hunting zones farther than ever before, we run the risk of running short. We run the risk of—'

'Becoming the next meal?'

'Yes.'

I nodded thoughtfully. 'So that's where I come in.'

'You're their alpha.'

'Who's apparently not allowed to shape-shift,' I muttered under my breath.

'Not true,' he countered. 'Lucius is just … Look, we're all a little blown away how blasé you seem to be after the events of the past night.'

'Blasé? Seriously, Lucas, I couldn't have been less blasé about it. I wasn't expecting Julius to show up, but I was proactive in saving my own life as any one of us would have been.' I began walking again until I found his room, immediately digging through an old crate containing some old clothes not yet dispatched by time or mould. I wanted underpants more than anything.

'Yes, but—'

'We fought, Lucas. It was always going to come to that with the two of us alive and Julius's unending hatred of Lucius unable to be corked. Honestly—and please don't be hurt or mad—but I wasn't scared to face him in that moment because I didn't think I had anything more to lose.' I quickly snapped a pair of underwear and shorts into place and crossed the room within seconds to wrap my arms around him. 'But then I remembered I still had you.'

Lucas resisted the hug, standing relatively stiff for what felt like an eternity before his muscled arms finally closed across my back and squeezed tight. 'I can't lose you, E. The world already sucks, has done for a while now.'

Marianne—who I'd forgotten had shadowed us—now slipped out of the room quietly, nodding her head in appreciation as she propped a piece of splintered timber across the opening for some physical representation of privacy.

'I'm here. I'm not going anywhere.'

'Please don't run off again. I know you think you're infallible. I know you've always thought you can handle anything, but like I said, the world has changed.'

'Now it has one less crazy supernatural with teeth out there trying to kill me.'

The rumble emanating from his chest suggested he was amused, however brief. 'Plenty more out there, E. Case in point—The Protectors.'

I slid away from his grip with a sigh, throwing a shirt I found on the edge of the bed at him in the process. He slipped it over his head and then sunk into the blanketed folds of the rickety bedding. He patted the empty space beside him.

I hesitated a second, uncertain rest was the answer before I fell onto the dust-infused mattress beside him. 'So, I suppose you're going to tell me what the plan is?'

'You saw most of it.'

'Susan still comatose?'

He snorted. 'Lucius is better at compulsion than you think. She may have been a 'yes' woman during the initial suggestion process, but now she's animated—excited about helping us.'

'That doesn't seem right somehow.'

Lucas didn't appear perturbed. 'I'm not going to argue with the process if it helps us to bring down a super city.'

I frowned, still uncertain of its merits. 'That seems irresponsible.'

He chuckled in response, but I could tell no humour filled the expulsion of sound. He now leant his back against the wall and pulled his feet up onto the edge of the cot, arms dangling over the ridges of his knee caps. 'I can't believe you're lecturing me about irresponsibility.'

I rolled my eyes. 'We need to be careful, Lucas. Susan has her own agenda and it has nothing to do with helping any vampire.'

'You don't think I know that? Marianne was right beside me when she more or less said that all vampires should be put to death,'

'And yet you trust her now?'

He shook his head. 'No. But I do trust your father.'

I sighed in deep resignation. Uncertain that some mind-bending tricks were a clear-cut plan for invading an entire city worth of magically altered beings. 'Fine. When does this grand master plan actually come to fruition?'

'Tomorrow night.'

'What the hell, Lucas? Tomorrow night? Are you freaking kidding?'

'No time like the present, E.' He patted my shoulder. 'And mum has already organised reinforcements.'

It was the second time that day I'd uttered a guttural, explicit word. Except now, I almost certainly followed it up with several others. 'Lucas … Reinforcements? What exactly have you allowed her to do?'

'Relax, it's all part of the plan.'

228

'A plan I'm still painfully unaware of. As far as I knew, the *plan* was for her to get you inside, find Chester—or whoever may be in charge in there these days—kill them and then let the rest of us in!'

'How is she going to explain capturing *me*? She's been missing for over a week. They'll know she hasn't dosed up with the serum recently and thus would be vulnerable. When they see me again, they'll know I'm not entirely human. I haven't aged, Elena.'

'A problem yes, but—'

'She's going to pretend she's found me, but opted not to approach given her withdrawal from the serum's dosage and my apparent supernatural mutation. The reinforcements will come in and '*capture*' me,' he said, using his fingers to make inverted commas, 'then you'll all track us back to the super city and wait for my signal.'

Deep welts now ploughed through the porcelain skin of my brow. 'I don't like it, Lucas. You'll be outnumbered.'

'But not exactly vulnerable. You know I've got skills, E.'

'Skills, yes, but—'

'Stop it. It's already done.'

Like arguing helped any situation. 'And what about the serum? Susan admitted that they're still brewing potions of the stuff in the Antarctic. Even if you succeed with this plan to bring down the Parisian super city, it won't stop anything.'

'We'll take that down next. They'll be expecting us to attack the other cities in succession, not disturb the production of their precious serum.'

My eyebrows now formed a singular unit, my frown so severe I was practically squinting. 'That's a bit of a leap and a massive assumption on our part. What we really need is an army with a coordinated attack. Not a Roman tunnel filled with a few hundred fanged discards from society.

'The world has gone to shit, Elena. Our numbers are dwindling. We're doing the best we can with the information and able bodies we have.'

'We're going to be slaughtered.'

'Sacrifice is inevitable when faced with the imminent prospect of extinction. We're doing what we have to do in order to survive. And we *have* to do something soon or we'll starve to death or—like I said earlier—the Vânători will eat every last one of us.'

229

I didn't doubt the scenario, but I also didn't believe it was that dire. 'I'll move the Vânători to the mountains if necessary. There'll still be plenty of wildlife to hunt. I don't believe things will ever get that desperate.'

Lucas's look was riddled with admonishment. 'I keep forgetting that you weren't here to see the nuclear bombs being dropped.'

'Nuclear weapons?'

'They may not have adversely affected us, but wildlife and future generations of the human race *have* and *are* going to suffer. Do you remember reading about Hiroshima when we were younger? Chernobyl? The human race was fuelled by intent this time round. They intended to wipe us all out and in trying to do so, created barren wastelands across the globe.'

'I didn't realise.'

His face softened, fingers twitching over the edges of his knees. 'Sometimes I'm not even certain that I'm safe. I have your blood and apparently I'm immortal since I don't age, but I have no idea what radiation poisoning will to do to me long term.'

He was making my point for me. 'Precisely the reason I think we need to think on this plan a little bit longer. You're not infallible!'

'We need to act now, Elena. We may not get another chance.'

'Said the dumbass who yelled at me not more than five minutes ago for making a decision not too dissimilar about protecting my own skin!'

He attempted to smooth my frown lines away before tapping the bottom of my chin endearingly. 'At least I'll have you with me. I won't be fighting my enemies *alone*.'

His meaning understood, I slapped his hand away, annoyed that he was comparing our two ventures. 'I already told you, I didn't know Julius was going to be at the villa!'

'Knock, knock?'

I can't say I was surprised by Toby tapping on the timber partition. I'd heard him coming. Hell, I'd smelt him attempting to reach me the minute I'd re-entered the tunnels. But Lucas whirled, heart beat jumping into fourth gear. You'd think he'd be used to this sort of thing by now.

I had hoped that Toby would keep his distance for a while. I didn't like the tangible connection being alpha created between me and every member of the pack—especially him. He had advanced to beta status in my absence and lately, he smelt like home. I didn't like it at all.

'Come in, Toby,' Lucas answered, oblivious to my discomfort.

Toby pushed the timber aside, propping it back against the opening where Marianne had nabbed it. 'Hey, Lucas.' He bobbed his head in greeting and then lowered himself onto the floor in front of me. He laid his head in my lap, waiting for some kind of recognition.

I blinked a few times in surprise, my hands held way up high so as not to encourage any further movement. Toby laid perfectly still, hands on the cot beside my legs, one lone eye swivelling to look up at me.

'I think he's submitting,' Lucas whispered.

'He can hear you.'

'Then do something.'

'Do what? Becoming an alpha did not come with a set of instructions!'

'Just pat him or something. He likes it when I do it in the mornings.'

'Lucas, I don't want to encourage anything.'

Toby sighed, burying himself further into my lap. What was I supposed to do, give him a Scooby snack and send him on his way?

'Elena, you need to start leading them. They've been lost for so long. It's only thanks to Toby that they haven't already begun making a meal of us.'

I sighed and ran my fingers through his hair begrudgingly. That is, until the smoothness of his locks seemed to make me feel all kinds of better too and I became a bit more vigorous with my exploration of his scalp. 'Thank you, Toby,' I murmured.

'You're not angry with me anymore?'

'I was never angry with you, just freaked out.'

'I was stating my intentions.'

'Intentions?' I echoed.

'You are the alpha and the only female the pack has ever seen.'

'Oh … *oh.*'

Lucas shot me an encouraging look.

'Toby,' I said, trying not to jerk away from the fingers that now grazed my thighs. 'I can fully appreciate your advances and the reasons why you may think it's a good idea, but I have to tell you now that it's never going to happen.'

He rolled his head in my lap until his chin was balanced on the edge of my shin.

'Um … We won't be … Um … Mating.'

His eyes narrowed and he pulled back. 'Is my coat not shiny enough? Have I not scent-marked your area to your liking?'

'Is that what that is?' I said, sniffing not so delicately at the air.

Lucas bumped my shoulder and frowned at me. Clearly, I wasn't doing this right. Then again, it's not like I'd ever had the opportunity to politely turn down a horny dog before. When the ex-alpha Roshan had advanced on me in the past, we'd drawn blood and kicked and screamed at each other until one of us wound up dead. You can guess which one of us that was.

I tentatively clasped Toby's cheeks, wondering how the hell you explain such delicate matters … um … delicately. 'Look, If I really was a werewolf, I'm sure I'd pick you.'

His frown deepened. Clearly I was doing a poor job of explaining why he couldn't get a leg over me. 'You *are* a werewolf.'

I shook my head, not sure how I could make him understand. 'I know I smell like one, but …' I didn't bother to finish. In the end my argument made no sense. I was as much a vânător as I was a vampire. The difference between us was that I was raised human. If I'd grown up in a pack, perhaps I'd feel differently about the concept.

'Elena?'

'Never mind.' I leant forward and kissed Toby chastely on the lips. 'Just give me some time to figure everything out, okay? I'm new to being alpha and unsure of … well … everything.' I shrugged. 'I just don't think mating or choosing a mate will ever be a priority for me.'

Toby nodded enthusiastically. He had a renewed sense of vigour after a bout of rejection that actually made me more nervous than before. 'That's okay. You're not on heat yet. I understand. I was trying to get in before the others laid claim.'

'Not on heat?' I sputtered, pushing the mutt away from me. I shot a panicked look at my brother who was a little more than amused by the proceedings. 'Is that even possible?'

'We'll find out next full moon,' Toby answered, climbing to his feet. He attempted to kiss me again, but I dodged those canine lips like the apocalypse itself rested upon the soft, pale flesh. 'I'll let the others know you're currently not interested.'

I nodded numbly, too afraid to speak. Lucas barely bid him farewell as one hand covered his gaping gob to trap eruptions of delight, the other braced his vibrating chest. He relented as Toby's footsteps receded. His laughter drowned out all other sounds, including the alarm bells ringing in my head.

'Well,' Lucas coughed, slinging an arm around my shoulder. 'At least you know they'll do anything for you. That's got to help when our plans fall into place tomorrow night.'

'It's not funny, Lucas.'

'Yet here I am—laughing.'

'You said to make nice,' I chastised, slapping him across the chest hard enough to make him wince. 'I did not want to be *dogged* for the rest of my life!' My unintentional canine pun only seemed to make him laugh harder.

'Don't worry. We might be dead by tomorrow night and you'll never have to see the full moon anyway.'

'We'd better be otherwise I'll kill you myself if I'm still being *hounded*.'

He collapsed against the wall, roaring with laughter as yet another pun spurred him on.

'Oh, Lucas,' I muttered. 'Just please shut the hell up.'

He barked at me and then buried his face into the mattress to mute yet another onslaught of supposed hilarity.

What a dumbass.

CHAPTER SIXTEEN: SURRENDER

Lucas's eyes involuntarily rolled back, his body slamming against the crumbling brick wall barely standing behind him. A split second of pain rolled through the tormented muscles of his spine as loose mortar found its mark, but then Marianne's lips seized his once more and all was forgotten to the pleasure of her kiss.

She wrapped her legs tighter around his hips, enthused by this last opportunity to be unified before his submission to the IMI. They both moved with purpose, aware that time was slipping through their fingers as quickly as the threads of their clothes.

Darkness from the approaching night was closing in. The rendezvous was set. They had all but minutes before hunting vehicles flooded the area and Susan came to claim her son and deliver him from supposed evil.

And with the threat of separation looming and the knowledge that their tryst would soon be interrupted, their movements sped up. Fumbling, they greedily grabbed at each other, stroking and caressing, a need so pressing they both wondered if they could ever truly be fulfilled. To be separated now after ten years of hardship was a consideration neither wanted to address. All there was in this moment was each other and the desperate desire to hold onto the only tangible dose of happiness they had found since the war began.

Each other.

Lucas dug his fingers into the taut thighs that harnessed him. Her skin was smooth and cold to the touch, unyielding but never a deterrent. He could never get enough of her; a notion he now fully realised as their bodies finally became one.

A small gasp escaped her parted lips, Lucas tightening his grip and groaning his response. There was nothing gentle or unhurried about this union. They moved with the ferociousness of time escaping, racing the clock to both sexual release and the inevitable parting. A ragged breath and a lingering moan became the mark to their end; their flesh joined but spent—the last vestiges of intimacy fading as reality roared around them in a tingle of approaching magic.

Lucas kissed her lips a final time, lowering Marianne slowly back to the ground. Her arms wrapped around him, her face turned away so as not to show the blood that welled in her eyes. He touched her chin, tilting her face back towards him. 'Don't cry. I don't want to go seeing you like this. I'm going to be okay.'

'You can't possibly know that,' she sobbed, swiping at her cheeks with shaking fingers. 'You're about to be surrounded by the enemy.'

'Which I can protect myself from.' He leant down, grabbing her discarded pants and handing them to her. While he was at it, he pulled up his own half-mast jeans and re-buttoned the fly. He then cupped her face gingerly, kissing her lightly on the lips. 'It'll be fine, Marianne.'

She rolled her eyes, pushing him back so she could quickly re-dress. 'I didn't want our last time to be like this.'

'It won't be our last time.' He started to frown as if seriously contemplating the idea. 'At least I hope not. We haven't even tried that one where you put your legs over your head yet.'

That brought a small smile to the corners of her lips, undoubtedly his intent. 'You know what I mean.' She straightened up, tucking her shirt into the waist band of her newly fastened pants. She ruffled her blonde curls and fixed serious eyes upon him. 'Be careful, Lucas. I've lost Thomas to this war. I can't lose you too.'

He grabbed her by the hips, settling her against him again. 'You won't.'

'Don't let your guard down either. No matter what, keep an eye on your mother, I'm not sure …' she sighed, letting the rest of her words fade. 'It doesn't matter. Just promise me that you'll stay vigilant.'

'I will.'

'Promise?'

'I promise.' He kissed her to close the debate and then took his time to make sure she understood just how careful he would be so he could return to her.

'Lucas?'

A groan of displeasure whispered past both of their lips as they quickly pulled apart at the sound of Susan's approaching voice. She rounded the corner a moment later, Elena and William in toe, watching the Protector's every move like hawks.

'Are we interrupting something?' It was a loaded question if Lucas had ever heard one. Elena's narrowed eyes insinuated a thousand reasons for Lucas to uncharacteristically squirm under the scrutiny. In particular, she studied Marianne's bloodied cheeks and dishevelled clothes, undoubtedly drawing the correct conclusion regarding their recent activities.

Lucas shook his head, not only to dispel lingering thoughts of his and Marianne's tryst, but to end any qualifying remarks that may have further entered the conversation. 'No, you're not interrupting anything, we're finished.'

'Finished what?' Elena murmured, though she sounded as if she didn't actually expect or need an answer. Some not-so-subtle intakes of breath led to a myriad of conclusions regarding what Lucas and Marianne had been engaged in. Her subsequent grimace and rapid eye movement suggested just how uncomfortable she'd become inhaling her brother's post-sex pheromones.

William—ever the gentleman—kept his eyes and mind on the task at hand. 'I can hear the Protectors coming. They'll be here any minute.'

Lucas rubbed his hands over the goose-pimpled flesh of his upper arms. 'I can *feel* them coming. It's been a while since I've felt magic this concentrated. They must be sending a few of them.'

Susan attempted to provide some small measure of comfort and wrapped one bony arm around Lucas's shoulder, purposely separating him and Marianne. She was currently brainwashed and pliable with her thought process, but clearly never going to be a fan of the vampire in love with her son. 'You need to get into position.'

Lucas agreed. 'I know and so do you.' He gave her a slight shove in the direction she should be heading to not only break the brief contact between them, but remind his mother that nothing would ever come between him and Marianne.

Shouldn't compulsion have robbed her of personal sentiment? Or was it only obvious to him that Susan had stepped between them as a physical act of separation?

Face blank and unfazed, Susan trudged towards the front of the old and battered Synth Corp building. By all appearance it seemed she was neither bothered by his brush off or the authority in his command. Perhaps he was merely nervous, afraid that if Lucius's compulsion wasn't as strong as everyone believed then he would be in a lot of trouble very, very soon.

'I'll follow and keep an eye on her from a distance,' William said, keeping pace to fall into line behind Susan. 'Elena, you bring up the rear and then take position in the adjacent building. If anything goes amiss, I want you back down in the tunnels to alert Lucius.'

For once—much to Lucas's amazement—Elena had no argument. She must have been serious when she'd said she didn't want to be part of the decision-making process. She'd been damaged by past mistakes and was now unwilling to take calculated risks based on her own assessment. Lucas wished he could reassure her, remind her that the present was not her fault. If anyone was to blame, it was the powers 'above' that kept interfering in human affairs.

Marianne grabbed Elena by the wrist before a step could even be taken. 'I'm coming with you. I want to make sure Lucas is okay.'

Lucas held his breath, wondering how this close contact would bode for Elena who now studied the hand that held her hostage. They'd never particularly liked each other and yet curiosity now lit the depths of her hazel eyes.

She looked up suddenly, a rather strange and aberrant smile touching her lips. 'I'd like that. I actually can't think of anyone else who would want to protect him as much as I do.' They shared a silent and transitory moment of mutual understanding before Marianne turned back to kiss Lucas one final time. Elena—of course—averted her eyes, shifting her weight from foot-to-foot, the unmistakeable jacket of discomfort now worn tight across her shoulders.

Marianne wrenched herself free of this last romantic luxury and promptly spun on her heels, marching in the opposite direction before anyone could see the fresh wave of tears cascading down her cheeks. Elena was in hot pursuit, stopped only by Lucas's calloused hand on her shoulder. 'Elena …'

She stopped at his touch but failed to turn and avoided his probing gaze. 'I can't say goodbye to you, Lucas. I've said it too many times and won't do it again.'

'Look at me.'

She shook her head, dark waves of sable hair spilling across her shoulders like a silken cape. 'I can't.'

'Then listen to me.'

She stiffened, but didn't reply.

'If something happens—'

'Nothing's going to happen,' she snapped. 'We've been shit on for far too long. I think it's fair to say that someone should be on our side this time.'

'Regardless,' he continued, ignoring her angry tirade. 'Make sure Marianne's safe. I know she can look after herself, but if I know the two of you are together ...'

She sniffed. 'I still don't really like her.'

Lucas bit back a smile. 'I know, but just promise me that if everything does go to shit again, you'll take care of everyone.'

'Nothing's going to happen.'

'E ...'

She broke free and waved a dismissive hand over her shoulder. 'Laters, Dumbass. I'll see you when we're kicking ass in the super city.'

Lucas had to smile at that. It had never been a particularly nice pet name and certainly didn't reflect his level of intelligence, but it did help to calm his rising nerves, perhaps the reason she'd said it. 'You know, you really are a dickhead,' he shouted in response.

'We all have to be good at something,' she yelled back before she disappeared around the corner.

*   *   *

The hunting party had arrived. The thrum of magic overhead that weaved and contorted air particles into intrinsic patterns and sensations upon the skin was an awareness that only Lucas was capable of. He was in position, curled onto his side with a couple of cardboard boxes covering his form. Dirt sullied his clothes and skin; the impression he was unkempt and lingering on the fringe of society an act he was playing well.

He pretended to sleep; arms wrapped around himself in comfort. He hoped they would believe in the hoax, but Lucas also knew that The Protectors were cautious by nature and not so easily fooled. Before he'd left the facility in Antarctica, they'd become somewhat aware of what he might be capable of. They'd trialled his growing abilities against the Protector guinea pig, Beryx; physicality and the practical application of magic. They'd believed then that his unusual magical powers were a result of his blood transfusion as a child with Elena. They never knew that he'd developed telekinesis—the ability to shift objects with his mind. This was now the ace card he'd leave up his sleeve until necessary. But there was one small problem; he hadn't aged in ten years and never would again.

What would they consider him? Miracle or abomination?

A discarded glass bottle—or something of the sort—clattered noisily across the chapped vestiges of the sidewalk. It was immediately chased with a whispered curse and turns of peer admonishment as Lucas had to think fast about whether or not he should respond. After all, anyone still living outside the super cities would surely always be on guard?

He shifted under the boxes, sitting up quickly and playing along. He pretended to search the darkness, looking for intruders. He knew exactly who hunted him, but he needed to show them that he was wary and unsure.

Ahead he could see Susan. She stood stiffly by the open doorway of the Synth Corp factory; eyes probably fixated on him as the rising moon lit her from behind. He continued to scan the room making sure his eyes passed quickly and without pause over his approaching would-be captors. It was dark enough that they would think he couldn't see them, but he didn't want to raise suspicions so continued to act the fool.

Silence ensued. He waited a painful minute longer and then settled back down on his side, preparing for the inevitable snatch and grab. He expected it to come swiftly, but he knew they would be cautious despite their enhanced skills. Footsteps did draw close, the unsure shuffle of those treading upon unknown terrain. Lucas could only imagine hands outstretched and fingers eager to finally pull him back into the fold to exploit whatever strength or weaknesses they could unlock within him. How had he ever trusted them?

They were right on top of him now; six Protectors including his mother, closing in and … Something hit the floor near his head. It was small, like a bottle top and discarded without caution. He sat bolt upright, knowing they would have expected him to hear the careless mistake.

'Now,' was the shouted command.

Lucas—despite knowing his captors and techniques—missed the moment the needle pierced his skin and buried deep. Unknown fluid circulated quickly and without bias through his throbbing, adrenaline-fuelled veins. Eyes wide and lips parted in surprise, he attempted a struggle only to fail under the weight of his defiant limbs. He'd assumed they would confront him, use his mother as bait or possibly attack and subdue. He never expected to be drugged … again.

'No,' he moaned, slapping uselessly at his closest assailant. He searched the crowd of unfamiliar men with blurred vision, looking for his mother, but she was hidden by the warped smiles of satisfaction around him.

Lucas attempted to sample his own magic, calling upon abilities he'd sworn not to use until the most opportune time. Sparks danced from his fingers like party crackers and a barrel may have fallen over across the factory floor. He was fading and nothing useful could be weaponised. How could he have left himself this vulnerable?

'That was almost too easy,' one of them grumbled, pulling his limp body upright.

'I thought for sure he'd seen us when he woke up,' another one added.

'He's probably weak and half-starved,' a new voice piped in.

'He doesn't look like it,' the first one replied. 'He's dirty, but his colouring is good and he has muscle tone. Look at those arms.'

Lucas was sluggish, appendages so heavy he could barely lift them, yet he still attempted to swat away his current captor. 'Lemme g-go …'

As if nothing had been uttered, the second attacker spoke, 'Susan, did you say he's been raiding old supermarket shelves for whatever he can find, eating rats when all else fails?'

'That's disgusting,' another fading voice answered. 'Why didn't you call it in when you found him?'

'Because he's my son,' Susan answered coolly, though the response seemed shaky and uncertain in Lucas's drug-addled mind. 'I wanted to observe if he exhibited new abilities. I was right. You can see he hasn't aged. Elena's blood had more of an effect than we originally believed.'

'Clearly,' the first one responded. 'We need to get him back to the city so Chester can have a good look at him.'

'N-n-n-o Ches-s-s-er,' Lucas slurred, making a last-ditch attempt to summon any form of magical assistance and failing.

'I don't like your methods, but you did good, Susan,' another begrudgingly congratulated her. 'Chester will be pleased.'

In the bilious fog of Lucas's rapidly deteriorating mind he thought he saw that man molest his mother's lips with his own.

'Are you okay?'

'I'm fine.' She pushed him away as if scolded, perhaps worried her son—even in his belligerent state—might judge her actions.

Unequivocally annoyed by Susan's rejection, that same man sneered, holding a small vial of ambiguous liquid, shaking the contents to draw her attention back. 'Take it. You smell human again.'

Susan snatched the vial and the syringe that followed before turning her back to him. Lucas had no idea if she'd injected the liquid he now presumed to be the serum. He was also clueless as to whether the vampiric compulsion would keep her focused. He just knew he was in a shitload of trouble and thankful that Elena and the others kept watch. It was strange to think that he was going to need saving again for the first time in over ten years.

CHAPTER SEVENTEEN: RESTRAINT

I slapped my hand across Marianne's mouth, dragging her against my chest despite her best efforts to break free and fire off vocal protests. Her talons lengthened—black and dangerous—they were a promise of what was to come if I didn't relent.

'Stop fighting,' I breathed in her ear, relieved we were now on an equal playing field.

She held up her talons, eyes filled with a fury unbridled. I had no doubt she would attempt to take me down if she thought it might help Lucas escape. 'Let me go,' she mumbled against my restraining fingers.

I squeezed tighter, pulling us below the ledge of the rooftop we were perched upon. I couldn't risk The Protectors seeing us too. It was bad enough that we were within scenting distance, but to leave Lucas unguarded in case they *had* tried to kill him would have killed *me*, let alone the Protectors. 'I won't let you go until you promise not to go after him.'

She thrashed about like a toddler throwing a tantrum, ramming her elbow repeatedly into the soft tissue of my stomach. I was going to kill her if she didn't elbow a whole through my midsection first.

'He's in trouble!'

'I know he is!' I hissed, endeavouring to keep my voice down. 'But they won't kill him with Susan around.'

She mumbled some form of disagreement, but I didn't catch it. My hand was now fastened way too tightly around her mouth. She pushed her talons to considerable limits.

'We're going to get Lucius *first* and then we're going to follow them and *then* get him back like William said. I know you love Lucas,' I added begrudgingly, 'but there's six of them and only three of us. I'm good, but not that good and I'm pretty sure you and William won't be able to help me hold them off forever. We have to play this smart, Marianne.'

Her response was to stab my abdomen with a blackened claw.

I gasped, barely reigning in the profanity my body yearned to emit in defence of pain. There was—however—a completely audible one that followed as Marianne's distraction led to her slipping from my grasp before I could protest.

While Marianne dashed across rooftops disrupting tiles and making enough noise to wake the dead and make me cringe, I climbed to my feet, ignoring the fading pain as self-healing kicked in.

I moved with calculated purpose, the scenery blowing by in a vampiric blur. My footsteps were assured, light and relatively noiseless. The problem was that Marianne made no such concession as she raced towards her death. I wouldn't have bothered if Lucas hadn't made me promise to look after her.

Blinded by fear and bloody love, Marianne sunk through an unsteady patch of slate, arms flailing as the iron roof below collapsed, dropping her into a darkened warehouse.

Dust plumed like an Indian smoke signal as bricks crumbled and the debris of the past was stirred. Inside, she waded through what I imagined to be old furniture and discarded trash.

I quickly leapt to street level, running as fast as I could to intersect her exit through a broken doorway. She could have jumped, moved through the collapsed roof, but I suspected she'd taken pause, realised how careless her movements were and just how much noise she was making.

Her fingers slid around the timber and I took my chance, kicking it backwards into her face. She grunted, more noise as she went backwards into the closest throw-away pile behind her.

I grabbed her hair before she could run in either direction. 'Are you trying to kill us all?' I hissed, curling tufts of blonde hair between my fingers. To say I was filthy angry was an understatement. While this was happening, my eyes were not on Lucas.

'Let go of me!' She tried to claw me again, but I snapped her wrist, let go of her hair and then spun her around, dislocating her arm behind her back. Her cry of pain was legitimate. Though we were evenly matched in strength, I'd been trained by some of the best martial arts instructors the IMI had to offer. I was also bleeding and predictably annoyed about my abdomen and the prospect of drawing further attention to ourselves.

'You're being a freaking idiot and not thinking about Lucas at all!'

'I'm trying to help him!'

'By getting yourself and the rest of us killed?' I tightened my grip and she grunted again, trying in vain to wiggle free. 'Do you think seeing Lucas drugged again by those people makes me happy? Do you think I want any of this? I was against this plan, remember?'

'Then help me stop them.'

'That's the plan, idiot, but first we need to get reinforcements.'

'No. This was a mistake. I never should have let him out of my sight.'

I couldn't help the sardonic chuckle that escaped my lips. 'He's a Manory. Do you really think he would have asked your permission?'

She growled, turning her head to show me the dawning darkness within her eyes. I knew then that she was beyond being talked down from the proverbial ledge. 'Are you going to let me go, or not?'

'Not. I don't think you understand the gravity of the situation here.'

'I understand just fine.' She swung at me, contorting so she could swipe at my face with her other taloned hand. I couldn't believe the level of desperation. But then again, I had to ask myself, what if it had been Sebastian?

I ducked, relinquishing my grip long enough to sweep her off her feet with a hooked heel behind the calves. She went down like a tonne of bricks, head mutilating a dilapidated book shelf behind her. Before she could fight back, I threw a solid right hook straight to the side of her temple, following up with an uppercut to the jaw. 'Sorry,' I mumbled, watching her lids shutter and then finally close as her body slumped in silent defeat.

I kicked her legs, checking for resistance. She was out cold. I had no idea how long it would last given she could self-heal, but I wasn't going to waste the silence or the opportunity to get her safely back to the tunnels.

William was close. I could smell him; sandalwood and exotic spices rode what little wind tickled my senses. What had once made my hormones do crazy little back flips, now reassured me there was someone who would always love me enough to protect me and mine. I supposed that also meant that Marianne was now a part of the whole 'mine' sentiment too.

Damn it.

I found him in an old butcher shop, arms crossed over his chest in a way that made his biceps bulge and his whole presence seem more foreboding. I rather used to appreciate that view—and sometimes even now—had to check myself from touching flesh that had once sort to possess me. Given the deep scowl that marked his features as he watched me approach with Marianne draped across my shoulder, I figured he couldn't care less what I thought of his physique in this moment. 'What happened?'

'Marianne went ape shit.'

Clearly irritable, William took a fistful of her hair and yanked her head back to inspect for damage. 'You knocked her out.' It wasn't a question, just a statement of fact.

'She wouldn't shut up.'

'I heard a crash a few minutes ago. I'm assuming that was her?' He released her hair so that her head bobbed back against my spine. Annoying blonde ragdoll.

'She wasn't thinking clearly and took off after Lucas. Do you think they heard?'

'I don't know, but we have to tell your father. We didn't expect Lucas to be drugged.'

'Where's Lucas now? I didn't get a chance to see because of … *this*.' I finished the sentence by pointing to her backside.

'They're loading him into the back of Susan's hunting vehicle.'

'Any suspicions raised?'

William seemed adamant as he shook his head, securing those ropey arms in front of his chest again. 'They did ask Susan why she didn't call in the initial attack the day we captured her. She said she saw Lucas running from the fray that killed the rest of her group and broke away, wanting to investigate. She said she hid the hunting vehicle in a nearby factory and pursued him on foot, waiting to see if he was as unique as you are and if he was still salvageable as a Protector.'

246

'And they believed her?'

He shrugged. 'I guess so, though it's not exactly out of the realms of possibility. She did transfer from the Sydney super city and away from her own husband to find her son.'

I snorted. 'I don't think she was too worried about George. Did you see that kiss she shared with that other guy?'

William's eyes narrowed. 'Not our problem.' He flicked his head towards the alley in the distance behind Synth Corp. 'Let's just focus on executing this plan. You can drill Susan about her sex life later if we're successful.'

I shuddered at the thought, but was then thankfully distracted by Marianne starting to stir. 'Should I hit her again?'

He didn't hide his amusement well. 'Let's just get her back to the tunnels. The fact that you seem to enjoy the prospect of hurting her worries me.'

'I wouldn't say *enjoy* ...' I murmured, adjusting the blonde so I could hasten my step to keep pace with William.

'What would you call it then? Jealousy?'

'Jealous? That doesn't even make sense.'

'I mean are you jealous of *their* ... intimacy.'

I scoffed, appalled. 'Eww ... He's my big brother, William. That might have been a *thing* three centuries ago when you were born, but it's kind of frowned upon now, you know?'

He looked less than amused. 'You know that's not what I meant—'

'It's always been me and him against the world,' I blurted, needing to say my peace. 'And now apparently Marianne's along for the ride.'

'A lot has happened while you were asleep, Elena.'

'I can see that more than anyone, William. When I died, Thomas, Nicholas and Eric were still with us. Bloody hell, even Marcus was being an uptight turd, but at least we were all alive and everything mostly made sense. Now some of our friends are dead, I'm a half-breed thrall and my brother is having sex with the girl who once wanted to scratch my eyes out for dating *you*.'

'Oh, so now you're calling what we had *dating*? I thought you always used to say it was just a bit of fun?'

'Don't split hairs.'

'What's going on?' Marianne asked groggily, smacking me on the backside. At least the nails were retracted.

'Damn, she's awake again. Hang on.'

'What are you going to—' William's question stopped short as I held firm to Marianne's legs, raced for the nearest building, turned at the corner and slammed her head into a pile of brickwork and steel.

The *thud* was a little louder than anticipated and half the corner of the building was destroyed thanks to her thick skull, but desired effect was met. 'Okay, crisis averted.'

'She is not going to be okay with this when she comes-to.'

'I know, but she's a liability with her mouth open.'

William's look of outrage seemed tentative at best. There were bigger fish to fry than Marianne's braincells now that we'd arrived back at the tunnel entrance. The Protectors were closer than ever now. We could hear the hum of their magic and the hunting vehicles undoubtedly being prepped and readied. We needed to make sure that we were too.

I knew—looking down into the manhole—that carrying Marianne on my shoulder wasn't a possibility; we'd never fit. So, I dropped her into the darkness below first. There was a loud *thump* followed by the admonishing slap of William's hand across my arm. 'Stop that.'

'She'll heal.' I felt William's disapproving glare on my back as I descended into the tunnel below. Accidentally landing on her hand, I absently apologised even though at present she didn't especially notice or care.

Footsteps preceded our arrival, Caleb skidding to a halt a few seconds later, peering briefly at Marianne's crumpled form with curious eyes. 'How's Lucas?'

'He's been drugged again. We need to scramble before they get too far away.'

'Lucius already has everyone assembled, we've been waiting for your signal.'

William's hand brushed mine as he passed. I felt a familiar warmth spread post touch, but ignored it. Erasing the past and what had been was a goal unachievable with so much history between us.

Unless you have the Time Contract … Araqiel whispered through my mind.

Shut up.

The entire population of our clan seemed to simultaneously pour around all corners of the tunnel exit in the form of liquid fur and jutting teeth. Eager bodies were everywhere, most of them my vânătors.

'Is everyone ready?'

There were whispered agreements and soft howls from some of the humanised wolves who forgot they had vocal cords.

'Stick close, but remain unseen. We're going to follow the hunting vehicles but not attack,' I reiterated for the Vânători. The Vampires were a little more civilised and fuelled by a degree of common sense 'Any questions?'

My father managed to push his way through the crowd. 'I'm glad to see you are safe. How's Lucas?'

'The Protectors have him as planned, but he's been drugged. We won't be getting in the same way we hoped.'

'Susan's compulsion should hold and she'll follow through.'

I nodded having nothing more to add since he seemed so certain.

'I'll lead the Vampires,' my father continued, finally reaching my side. He took my hand and reassured me with a gentle squeeze of my fingers. 'Are you able to lead the Vânători?'

'We will follow her to our death if that's what it takes,' Toby interjected, cheered on by the pressing eagerness of his wolf brethren.

If a vampire could blush, I would have been. 'Thank you, Toby.'

'I'm going to hug you now,' Lucius warned, turning me to face him. He grabbed my shoulders, effectively holding me captive. 'I know you haven't always been comfortable with the briskness of our connection, but the last time we confronted our enemies … you died.'

'Not on purpose.'

'Nevertheless.' He pulled me close, wrapping his arms around me so my face was buried against his battle-scarred chest. His wedding ring still dangled from the gold chain he constantly wore around his neck and dug almost painfully into my cheek. It was a constant reminder of all he had gained and lost over two thousand years of existence—me now included. 'Be careful,' he reiterated. 'Keep your wits about you.'

'I will.'

We separated, his hands lingering on my shoulders. It was obvious he wanted to say more, possibly even ask me to stay behind. But he knew better than anyone that if Lucas was in trouble, I would not leave him flounder. 'Stay with her, Caleb,' he ordered, keeping eye contact with me. 'If she looks like she's in trouble, get her out of there.' Clearly no arguments were permitted.

'I will,' Caleb agreed, though deep down he knew he'd have a losing battle on his hands if he tried to stop me from helping Lucas.

'Right.' Lucius patted my cheek endearingly and ended contact. He stepped over Marianne's body and ascended to street level. Roughly two hundred vampires followed. Some I knew rather well; others were merely familiar having passed by them in the tunnels this past week. Most of them I'd never see again.

William found Karina in the crowd. I watched as they embraced, then argued over Karina's part in all this and then finally ended the futility in a passionate kiss. As they started to leave, Marianne awakened. She was understandably confused and righteously furious with me, but did prioritise Lucas over pursuing a vile word war or a bout of fisty-cuffs.

That left me, standing in a tunnel system under Rome with a pack of wolves at my disposal. Strangely, I wanted to laugh so hard that my skin began to itch and my toes tapped uncontrollably. Since I'd discovered what I was and what the IMI had in store for me, I'd spent the majority of my time avoiding the Vânătors. Now here I was, surrounded and in charge of all remaining packs. Roshan would roll over in his grave if he'd had one.

'Elena?' Toby prompted. 'You *can* do this.'

'I know.'

He was suddenly right there in front of me, covering my epileptic toes with his to calm me. In my book it was unexpected and I growled without thought, his head bowing to submission. I felt bad, but wasn't up-to-date on all doggie customs quite yet. At least the urge to laugh had evaporated. 'Just tell us what you want us to do.'

I eyeballed the sea of naked flesh and fur in front of me, wondering if I wasn't the punch line in some weird kind of porn flick. There were Franks and Beans everywhere and I wasn't referring to breakfast. Where should I look? Would my abused retinas ever recover?

I coughed to clear the uncomfortable bug in my throat. 'As I said before, stay close, wait for the signal. Most all, if I'm not attacking or eating bystanders, then you shouldn't be either.'

Some of their faces dropped. 'So, no feeding off the dead?' one of them timidly asked.

I was about to emphatically state *no*, and then reconsidered. 'Don't kill and eat anyone who isn't directly attacking you. There will be innocent people in the city, if they're running, let them.'

'What about the dead?'

I sighed, flabbergasted and a little unhinged. 'Fine. You can eat the dead. Just don't forget what you're there to do. If any one of our men dies tonight because you were stopping for a snack, I'll kill you and then eat you myself. Got it?'

There were nods all round.

'Right, now those that aren't already, please shape-shift. You'll be better able to defend yourself and others if you're back in wolf form.'

'Are you sure?' Toby asked me.

I chanced another uncomfortable look below his hips and nodded vigorously. 'Most definitely.'

*   *   *

It took a few hours to run from Rome to Paris, but we easily kept pace with the Hunting Vehicles in the distance. I'd always known vampires and vânători moved quick, but to actually experience the wind in my hair and the terrain shift under my feet like an endless conveyor belt was epic. The other thrill to our inherent speed? Our united front. Once enemies, the various entities of the supernatural realm were now allying in the fight against true injustice.

I'm not saying that vânători and vampires are saints and should be praised for taking a stand. In fact, it's almost certain we'd be scorned for considering the label applied to us. But, the actions of The Protectors—apparent human right's advocates—was a disgrace and they needed to be stopped by someone. It just happened to be us. Power was a sickness that could eventually claim us all and the Protectors had fallen victim, becoming the very beings they sought to destroy. It was ironic that justice was now in the hands of the original blood drinkers.

On the outskirts of Paris, we regrouped. Being undead, no one needed to recuperate after the extensive run, but we needed to consider our next move. So, using the innate ability to observe from great distances, we assessed the formidable walls of the city. They were not constructed of brick or steel as one might think— but rather—magic; an impenetrable shield powerful and strong enough to stop us in our tracks.

The greenish hue that glowed from afar reminded me of childhood stories—namely the Emerald City of Oz. Like a radioactive smoulder upon the horizon, curiosities arose, but it was by no means beautiful or whimsical. The city itself had been commandeered for the IMI's purposes; the magical barrier a means to keep the rest of us clear. I suspected they'd selected this quadrant of Paris as it had been least affected by war crimes and ostensibly at a safe distance from where Lucas outlined earlier nuclear fallouts.

But despite the seemingly hostile remains of land and cityscape, I could see that my father had been here before. It was not from the knowing look in his eye—but rather—the wasteland surrounding the magical barrier. His telekinetic touch was the signature of futile resistance. He had uprooted whole buildings, highways, cars—anything he could use as a weapon. It had made little difference. The piled debris—now reclaimed by nature itself—stood testament to the ineffectual attempts at dismantling The IMI's spells.

There was also the ground underfoot. It was cracked, broken and cavernous in some instances where he'd attempted a quake or shift in the landscape. The vestiges of a fragmented, bitumen carpark from a popular fast-food chain poked its busted neon sign from a hollow chasm below. What might have been a child's playground was also now buried under sodden earth with cars sporting ruptured tires and burnt out shells that would never run again.

But that was the problem with magic. There was always some spell in the IMI repertoire that would keep the city standing despite all attempts to submerge or supersede it. In this instance, I suspected it was protected by the cloaking spell *Revatarus* and the levitation spell *Levitartium,* both of which I'd seen performed many times before. Just never with the backing of this level of power enforced by multiple spell casters.

I shuddered at the thought of even entering the Emerald City; too many enemies and no ruby red slippers.

I signalled for the wolves' creeping advance to cease. In the distance, The Hunting Vehicles were welcomed by the city's green glow and the wolves' reaction was to growl and bark—not exactly stealthy.

They grumbled and attempted to follow as I moved ahead of the pack to see what the Vampires were deciding in terms of advancement. Caleb was as good as his word, slipping into my shadow as per my father's instructions to protect me. Perhaps the look on my face urged the vânători to remain still despite the vampire that followed me.

'What's the plan?' I asked, slipping through a gap Tiberius and William had left.

Lucius glanced over my shoulder, nodded at Caleb and perhaps to ensure the Vânători stayed put during my absence. They were good. They hadn't moved a muscle. 'We wait for Lucas's signal.'

'We can't wait for a signal!' Marianne all but shouted. 'If we wait, Lucas will die!'

Lucius never said a word, but his rapid eye movement incited an instantaneous response from another vampire who forcibly slapped an unyielding hand across her open lips and imprisoned her against his chest. 'Do not shout,' Lucius answered with relative calm. 'I do not wish Lucas harm, but I must consider everyone.'

She mumbled her resolve under the vampire's fingers, muffled and unintelligible.

'You will stop this, Marianne,' Lucius continued. 'I understand that you fear for him, but you are not alone in this.'

I'd moved only a step before William grabbed my wrist and shook his head. 'She doesn't need another concussion.'

I rolled my eyes. 'All evidence points to the contrary.'

Lucius ignored our whispering. 'Now, I am willing to let you go if you can maintain silence, but if you run off or you start opposing my authority, I will silence you indefinitely.'

The surprising venom behind his words led to a knee-jerk reaction on my part. My whole body snapped to attention, senses on alert and lips curled in distaste while William's fingers tightened perceptibly around my wrist. I wasn't even aware that I'd taken another step forward. 'Lucius …' I murmured, barely able to conceive of him killing in the name of a little noise pollution, 'she's just scared.'

He then faced me, jaw clenched, mandible twitching. His erratic eyes of topaz and green narrowed with each passing second, darkening with the cloud of vampirism. Everyone grew uncomfortable, including me under the weight of that penetrative glare. I'd challenged his authority publicly; a no-no to be sure.

I shook William loose—much easier now we were both vampiric—and took another step forward. The tension was palpable as everyone kept watch, glancing between me and my father, entirely uncertain what would come to pass. Despite my foolish pride, I had to end this for the sake of resolving the true importance of today's agenda. 'I'm sorry.' A big concession on my part. 'I didn't mean to question you. I was just going to offer you my services.'

His eyes were completely black now, a sure sign of anger and frustration. 'What are you talking about, Elena?'

I moved until I stood beside Marianne, claiming her hand and squeezing her fingers in what I hoped reflected reassurance. I didn't dare look back at her scowling face to surmise her thoughts or distract my father from his. I was about to stick my neck out for her—penance enough. 'I'll take full responsibility for Marianne. She can run with me, Caleb and the Vânătors. I'll make sure she keeps quiet and follows the plan.'

All eyes jumped back and forth between my father and I— a tennis match inevitably stuck in deuce. 'Fine,' he conceded after a thoughtful minute, 'but it's on your head if she blows it.'

'What is the signal anyway?' William asked.

A grateful smile followed my exhalation of relief.

Lucius pointed to the super city. 'When the green haze dissipates and when you can clearly see the streets and buildings … that is when we must approach.'

William nodded. 'How many days are we prepared to wait for this to occur?'

Marianne stiffened. I too felt urgency beating upon my back, but unlike her clouded judgement, I knew that rushing this gig was only going to get Lucas killed faster.

'We will wait no longer than the few hours before dawn. We cannot afford to be out in the open like this. Those of you that are turned—and of course the Vânâtors—cannot tolerate the sun light. It would be a death sentence to linger.'

'It's after nine now. It took us well over three hours to get here,' a new voice added.

Lucius searched the large crowd gathered for the speaker, but no one stepped forward. 'We will leave at five if the compulsion over The Protector proves unsuccessful.'

Marianne attempted to struggle in defiant response, but I squeezed her fingers to the point of pain, nails digging into her flesh. The vampire keeping her quiet gave me a very pointed look as he struggled to keep her under control.

'We will—however—only go as far as the outer provinces,' Lucius continued. 'We'll find shelter during the daylight and return each night until we see our opening.'

Marianne relaxed and so did I. For a second, I thought my father planned to leave Lucas for dead. That would have been unacceptable.

'I want everyone posted in various areas around the city,' he continued, oblivious to my hesitation. 'In a group of this magnitude we are too easily spotted. Spread out, but stay close enough to see one another. When four o'clock comes around, I want everyone back here ready to leave.' He stopped talking, turned and walked off. Clearly that signified the end of the pow-wow as everyone already began to split into groups. The Wolves still stood resolute, waiting expectantly and yet patiently for my command.

Weird.

'You can let go of her now,' I said to the vampire still silencing Marianne.

He released her hesitantly, waiting a few moments as if she may spontaneously combust. 'Is she safe?'

I raised an eyebrow at her, still holding tightly onto her hand in case she tried to bail on me again. 'Are you?'

She nodded mutely, eyes darting back and forth with conspiratorial intent between the city and Lucius's turned back.

'Don't even think about it,' I said, tugging her away from the group and towards the Vânâtors. 'I put my ass on the line for you.'

'And you think I owe you?' she growled. 'You knocked me unconscious … twice.'

'And you freaking stabbed me, so we're even.'

'Let go of my hand.'

'Why? So, you can try and be a hero again?' I shook my head at her. 'I think I liked you better when you were in love with William.'

She yanked me to a stop. 'Don't you dare presume to understand what Lucas and I have. My affections for William were nothing in comparison to what I feel—'

'For Lucas? Empty words.'

'I beg your pardon?' She finally snatched her hand free. 'What did you just say to me?'

I sighed, pinching the bridge of my nose. It was going to be a really long night. 'Do you even love my brother?'

'How can you even say—'

'Just answer the question.'

'With everything that I am.'

'Well, if that's true, listen to Lucius, follow the plan and prove it.'

'What if it was Sebastian?' she pressed, knowing she grated a raw nerve. 'If it was his life on the line and if you could …' her voice unexpectedly faded as if all fight had left her body.

'I love Sebastian,' I finally managed to emit on a shaky breath. '*Loved* Sebastian,' I corrected. 'But sometimes love makes you do stupid things.'

She scoffed. 'I honestly thought you'd understand.'

'Marianne, Lucas is everything to me. He is my blood—my family. I would give up my life for his. There is nothing in this world that would stop me from being there when he needs me. So, go and shove this stupid, negative shit up your ass, because clearly *you're* the one who doesn't understand.'

Caleb chuckled, inappropriate as always with his interruptions and clearly taking his shadowing duties seriously. 'Wow. If only you could tape this conversation, play it back to your earlier self when you were getting us all into deep shit at the Bucharest headquarters.'

'What?' I spluttered, confused by the swift change in topic. I also didn't want to be called out on past mistakes when I was trying to currently make a point with Marianne.

'Do you remember?' he continued, oblivious to my discomfort. 'It was before Roshan took you back to his den, when you deemed breaking into the IMI would be a solid plan.'

'What about it?'

'Well, self-sacrifice was your go-to then, have *you* learned nothing from *that* stupid mistake?'

I turned angry eyes on him. 'You may want to start running.'

'Just saying it's easy to preach after the fact.'

I signalled for two of the closest wolves to sic him. All three took off in the opposite direction, Caleb muttering something about dirty tactics as he disappeared behind an abandoned building.

'Elena, to be fair,' Marianne continued as if Caleb hadn't rudely interrupted with proof I was a total hypocrite, 'you can't expect me to do nothing.'

'It's frustrating, I know. But it is a necessity.'

'I disagree.'

'I promise we'll get Lucas back. It may seem convoluted and a waste of time to simply sit back and watch, but you also have to give him a bit more credit too. He's not exactly helpless.'

'He's not infallible.'

'None of us are.' Had I not sprouted something eerily similar to Lucas only the day before?

'Elena …' She appeared to be calming down, thinking and communicating rationally now. 'He may be immortal, but he's not like you and me. He can die as easily as the Vânătors or the turned vampires.'

'They won't kill him, at least not anytime soon,' I tacked on, more for my own comfort than hers. 'Lucas is way more valuable to them alive.'

At least I think he is …

'I suppose so,' she conceded. I heard placation in her tone and this worried me. Her fingers twitched with irritability and she persisted in casting sly glances towards the city. Would she ever give up?

I had to shake off the doubt and focus on the wolf pack that watched and waited expectantly. Marianne was a pressing concern, but I had to trust that she finally grasped the magnitude of the situation. Still, I approached four of the closest members of my pack, ran my fingers through their fur in greeting and said,

'Watch her. If she makes a move ahead of schedule, do what you have to do to detain her, but don't kill her.'

Marianne muttered some archaic version of a profanity as my fanged babysitters bowed their heads in understanding and began to circle. Like hawks identifying prey, they moved with purpose and constriction; close enough to strike and far enough away to retain independence. The returning scowl was now set upon her features like the permanence of rain after a massive thunderstorm. Lucas's safety was more important than hurt feelings.

'Let's spread out,' I said, addressing the remaining pack. 'Lucius wants us to take positions close, but still far enough away to prevent detection. Wait for my signal if we're going to attack. If nothing occurs, be back in this location by 4am.'

The Vânätors must have understood as they promptly broke off into smaller groups and sprinted away in various directions. There were a lot of initial barks and growls—nothing especially loud—but enough to draw the gaze of curious vampiric onlookers and my father's annoyed grimace.

'And what about me?' Marianne moaned, wading cautiously through the furry flesh now swimming around her calves. 'What am I supposed to do?'

'Wait it out with the rest of us.'

She said something I suspected irrelevant and thus I stopped listening. My own thoughts pulled me under a spell of indecision as I weighed the gravity of the situation before us. Was it wrong to wish that I'd killed Chester when I'd had the chance in Bucharest? Would ending his life in the past have changed the direction in which the IMI had turned the present?

I didn't have answers. I had a million questions and plenty of theories.

I often wondered if I'd never met William, if I'd never snuck out and attended the rave back in Cairns, would I have ever discovered who I was? Would I have fallen in love with Sebastian and contributed to the production of the serum? Could I have stopped everything if I'd swallowed my stupid pride, pushed false bravery to the side and did the smart thing rather than what I tended to perceive as right?

I supposed I could live a thousand years and never really know the answer to any of those questions. Yet somehow—despite my choices and sometimes lack thereof—all evidence pointed to my involvement as the key. I was the daughter of the master vampire and coincidentally born into the hands of Protectors. I was the soul mate of the archangel Michael and key ingredient for the IMI's immortal trappings. Was it just me who thought that needlessly excessive for one insignificant blip in humanity's Richter scale?

Everyone around me believed in fate instead of the happenstance of connective circumstances. I'd always brushed it aside as bullshit, but suddenly there were too many coincidences. What if fate was real? What if this life—this surely exaggerated tale—was merely a stepping stone to true intent? What if all of *this* was merely the preface, the calm before the storm? What if the Time Contract was truly the answer to everything? What then?

'Elena, you're not listening to me,' Marianne complained.

I nodded. 'Yeah, I know.' I left her, marching in the opposite direction and away from prying eyes. It was time to get some answers, if for no other reason than to satisfy curiosity and understand the true weight of how deep a consequence could run.

CHAPTER EIGHTEEN: ANSWERS

'Araqiel?' I whispered, feeling rather ridiculous as I stood surveying the landscape in the hopes he'd just pop up through a crack in the blistered capillaries of broken earth. 'I need to talk to you.' I needed to do a lot of things; measure up for a straight-jacket being one of them, but at that moment, finding the angel seemed more pressing than listening to Marianne bitch about Lucas's demise. I struggled with the thought of it, never mind hearing it over and over again as if it would change circumstances.

When it became obvious that my call yielded no result, I sat upon the hood of a dented rust-bucket of a car. It groaned a little under my weight, but not enough to draw attention. I'd drifted to the fringe of the city, away from Caleb's watchful eye and Marianne's constant protests. I needed to organise and reassess my scattered memories and errant musings of the past, present and perhaps the future.

I ran my fingertips across the charred remains of metal between my legs. At first, rust and blackened soot marked my skin, staining the porcelain flesh, but then flecks of the old green paint could soon be seen; a testament to a life before its death. It was yet another reminder of all that had come to pass, a stain that would take years to erase but would never truly be forgotten.

'Araqiel?' I searched the skies, peering into the darkness for the flap of his snow-white feathers upon the wind. Perhaps it was a move best suited to my five-year-old self, wishing upon stars and fairy dust and all things make-believe, but some of that childhood fiction was real.

'You rang?'

I jumped, not an easy task to scare a vampire. Despite recent difficulty adapting to my vampiric senses, I still heard, saw and smelt everything whether I wanted to or not. It was unnerving to be caught off guard.

His usual white suit was at odds with our surroundings. In a world where dry cleaning was no longer an option, I figured him stupid for wearing it. I supposed that if he didn't care about marring its perfection, then perhaps I should stop dwelling on it too.

His long, blonde hair was tied back with a leather toggle at his neck, wings neatly folded and tucked against his back. His hands were clasped in front of him, elbows perched on the edge of his knees as his shiny white shoes gripped the edge of the bumper. As casual and unconcerned as he may have appeared, he looked at me expectantly.

'You came.' Truth be told, I hadn't expected him to. I'd always thought our connection was a one-way party line; him yelling out confusing thoughts in my head and only appearing long enough to throw riddles at me. 'I've got questions.'

'Ahh,' was all he said.

'You sound like you were expecting this.'

Blue and silver-flecked eyes surveyed my features. 'Well, I did not expect you to turn your nose up at the possibilities of the Time Contract forever.'

'I never said I did or didn't want to use it. I said it was dangerous to contemplate changing the past.'

'And now?'

'I still agree, but I just need you to clarify a few things.'

'Such as?'

I took a deep breath that I really didn't need. Some of my human habits were a little hard to break. 'Well, for one, I need some clarity on whether or not it's me.'

His eyes narrowed ever so slightly. 'What do you mean?'

'I want to know if I'm the problem, the cause and effect of everything to-date.'

If I'd said that to anyone else, they probably would have snorted and told me to pull my head out of my ass, but this was not a matter of conceit. I truly believed that I was the cause—or at least—the key ingredient to the downfall of this life. Granted, I couldn't be held accountable for the actions of others, but I could hold the blood that ran through my veins responsible for a whole host of terrible crap that had come to pass.

'It is not solely you, Elena.'

'But my existence has solidified so many wrongs—the serum, Sebastian's fall from grace, vampirism ...'

'Wait, go back,' he said, flicking a long slender finger at me. I frowned. 'The serum?'

'No. With or without your blood that was always a possibility in the quest for the Institute of Magical Intervention's power.'

'So, you're saying they would have manufactured that regardless?'

'The quest for more power has always been something they sought with or without your blood. The Protectors came to be from the strength of their resolve, turning from humanity and pursuing a course laden with witchcraft and old magic. Do you think they would ever stop searching for the footing that lets them surpass a vampire?'

'Then you're referring to Vampirism as the other degeneration of humanity?'

He flicked his fingers impatiently again. 'Yes, yes. Drinking blood. Not exactly saintly behaviour, but, no. Go before that.'

I didn't want to say it. I'd thrown the possibility out there, knowing I was the arch angel's weakness, but I never truly wanted to believe that by loving Sebastian time and time again we had led everyone on a path far more obscure than the drawings on an etch-o-sketch. 'So, you *are* actually talking about Sebastian and his fall from grace?'

'Yes.'

I jabbed a reluctant finger against my chest. 'All these problems that I'd assumed sprung from my blood are actually because of Sebastian's choice to fall?'

'What do you think?'

I huffed, running my fingers through my hair, wondering if clarity would come the longer I took to decide upon an answer. 'It doesn't make sense.'

'It doesn't?'

'Well, no.'

'And why is that?' He pulled the carefully folded hands in his lap across his chest, the fabric of his suit straining against his biceps. His eyes remained narrowed and constantly scrutinising. I had no idea if it was because my answer bothered him or because he was curious by it.

'I've lived many life times before this one, haven't I?'

'You know this to be true already.'

'But from what Sebastian explained, all of them bore little to no effect on the world as we once knew it.'

Araqiel started to look a little uncomfortable, tightening his arms against his chest to the point where I expected thread to unravel and pop. 'That is not exactly true.'

'Was I supposed to cure cancer or start a revolution if Sebastian was absent?'

'Well, no.'

'Then I don't understand. As far as I can tell, my past lives have raised no issue, but being born into this life and having Lucius become a vampire and change the fate of so many lives is where everything went wrong.' I tapped the hood of the car and then motioned around me. 'We live in a war zone. Look at this place. It's like this because of the Vampires, because of the Vânătors and because of The Protectors. Yeah, the Humans may have dropped bombs and sprayed everything in sight with lead—but the point is—the motion began with our making.'

'I do not debate your thinking.'

My dawning frown was a slow-burning reaction to the massive 'but' in his words. 'Then why do you look like you don't agree?'

'Oh, but I do. Lucius's decision to commit suicide over the murder of his pregnant wife and child has had its ramifications. You know better than anyone that because of this ill-fated choice, his soul is now damned; as are the souls of all the Immortals. Lucifer has never played a better hand. Well, except if you count the Ice age.'

'What?'

He shook his head. 'Never mind. My point is that *yes*, you are correct in thinking that the blood in your veins is the tainted blood that flows through all of the damned. If it were not there, then perhaps a few of the present's failings may have been avoided. But, do you honestly believe that Lucifer would not find some other way to chalk up the score card in his favour?'

'This isn't a game. My life and the people I love don't think this is funny.'

He suddenly laughed, throwing his head back until the column of his throat was exposed, bobbing in invitation of a flogging as he continued to ridicule my concerns. 'Do you honestly believe that? Do you think that anything that happens on this plane is actually within your control?'

'I … I don't honestly know.' And I didn't. I knew very little at all in that moment and was suffocated by the truth of it.

'Well it's not,' he said, head snapping back to glare at me. Levity was now a distant memory upon the perfect planes of his face. 'Since the beginning of time this place has been the playground for the fallen—for the angels like me still trying to earn a free pass back into heaven. It's the hunting ground for demons, the place where people like you exist to torment the maker's creation—humans.'

'Then what is the point of anything if we're to be nothing but puppets in the hands of bored and corrupted entities like you!' I was immediately riled to anger, livid that my existence—everyone I cared about—were nothing more than pawns in a chess game between darkness and light.

'The point is to win,' Araqiel responded, calmer than before, perhaps tempering my rise in wrath.

'To win? And how exactly do you get to win?'

'By using the Time Contract.'

'Then use it!' I hissed. 'Why the hell do you keep appearing to me like I'm the God damn hand that holds the pen?'

'You called me, remember?'

'I called you to answer my questions, not be coerced into playing the hand you've been dealt!'

He frowned so deeply his eyebrows became one. Perhaps he didn't like the words *God* and *damn* manifesting within the same sentence. At that moment, I didn't give a shit about his sensibilities or my use of foul language. 'I *am* answering your questions.'

I shook my head, growing more and more frustrated. 'You're involving me in the petty disputes between heaven and hell. I thought the Time Contract was supposed to change wrongs into rights.'

'No. It makes the present recede and the past indeterminable. Despite your blasphemy and you're intent to stay clear of responsibility, you are the only hand that can wield the pen. You are the one who can change everything.'

'But why?'

'Because you're the only one in the human realm at present that has the blood of both darkness and light within you.'

'What are you talking about? I'm damned, remember?'

'Damned, yes, but not eternally punishable.'

'What … Oh … Ahhhhh—'

I massaged my temples as a flood of confusing images decided to pour over the dam of repressed memories I'd been holding back from conscious thought. Puddles of colour began to accumulate, shaping and moulding themselves into seemingly impossible concepts within my mind.

I saw Sebastian. His body was one with mine, our lips pressed together as we made love over and over again. I had no idea why I'd chosen this moment to fill my thoughts with an image I could barely comprehend, let alone set me on a new and surprising path of violence and bloodshed that left me reeling.

The pleasant tingle of satisfaction from Sebastian's lovemaking fiercely subsided. Those puddles morphed and twisted, the colours sickly and blinding as I began to see other things I was certain I didn't *want* to remember. A red creature with skin slicked with sweat taunted my thoughts. There was also blood—my blood and the blood of others and God only knew what else spread across a barren field. I saw a naked man with the head of a goat, his red eyes watching me, his entire demeanour a taunting promise of pain and humiliation.

I gasped, drawing another unnecessary breath but somehow needing it. I felt overwhelmed, suppressed and confused. What had happened in those ten years of sleep? How could I have felt so much love and passion and yet also experience so much misery and defeat? And if all of that had truly happened, then why had no one seen me arise earlier from my coma? Was it merely a figment of my imagination; horrible nightmares chased by the promise of Sebastian's skin against mine?

'You're remembering,' Araqiel murmured, his hand absently stroking my hair.

I pushed him away. He was the last person I wanted comfort from. I needed answers, not more of this undecipherable show-and-tell without subtitles and an angel getting 'handsy'. 'Please tell me what's going on! I know you know what I just saw and what happened to me after I died.'

266

He took an uneasy breath, perhaps resigned that I would never let this matter drop without suitable explanation. 'You're fighting what should be impossible to recall. It's even more of a reason why you *are* the one I need.' He folded his offending hand back in his lap, face as impassive as ever.

The tide of mixed memories slowly ebbed. Like water upon the sand, they rushed back and forth and then just as suddenly became distant thoughts. 'What have you done to me?'

'I have done nothing. You are merely remembering what you have coined as your 'coma' years.'

'So, it's not all just a dream?'

'Not even close.'

'So, if what I saw is the truth …' I shook my head. 'Where was I if my body was still technically here?'

'Where is Michael?'

'Purgatory.'

He blinked at me, words irrelevant. I knew the answer. Lucius had once told me that death was merely the first step in crossing over. Despite our souls being damned, we first went to Purgatory to await the judgment that always favoured the fiery pits of hell. I guess having already made the journey, he knew that better than anyone. But how had I made it back? Shouldn't I—as a vampire half-breed—be cooking on a barbeque pit in the South?

'But if I …' What *was* clear was that I was slowly putting the pieces together. The puzzle was just upside down and back the front. 'But … I'm …' It was coming, just not in a hurry. 'I'm a genetic fruit salad.'

'Yes, you are a creature of both darkness and light.'

'And what exactly is that? You have failed—yet again—to move past riddles and innuendo.' It was hard not to miss the venom in my voice as I rubbed my temples, eyeing him sideways.

'Elena, you already know what constitutes as darkness. How can you not fathom what would riddle your blood with light?'

'It can't be possible.'

Could it?

'Yes.'

I sat for a full minute in stunned silence, my mind set to warp speed as I considered his words extremely carefully. Surely not? There was no way I could be … 'An angel?'

267

He laughed as if I'd hit him with the pun of the day, perhaps I had. I was damn certain that there wasn't a single person I knew—dead or alive—that would call or consider me an *angel*. 'No, but there is enough of Uriel running through your blood that you can never be classified entirely as an entity of the damned.'

'Shut the front door.'

'I beg your pardon?'

'How the hell can I be part angel?' Araqiel hissed at what I assumed was my use of inappropriate language again, but continued regardless. 'This is crazy. I'm already a vampire, a wolf and telekinetic. What the Frigg am I going to do with wings?!'

'You don't have wings.'

'You're missing the point. How the hell did this happen?'

'I am going to leave if you continue to cuss.'

'I'll pull *your* wings out if you even consider it.'

He sighed, a new kind of weariness etched upon his features. 'The angel Uriel possessed your mother during your conception.'

'For the purpose of …'

'Allowing light to bloom where darkness would have grown. Without her input you would be damned and thus, useless to the cause.'

'You mean unable to play your stupid games?'

'No, Elena. Unable to save the world from the burden of evil.'

'And this is something you think I can achieve?'

He nodded, face solemn. 'I truly believe it—with the Time Contract.'

I slid sideways off the hood of the car and began to pace, agitation shuffling my feet back and forth across the cracked earth. Remaining still was impossible. My mind raced, full of riotous thoughts from a life I could barely remember and now over-crowded with this new knowledge that I could carefully wipe it all clean and start again. But to what end? Where did I draw the line?

'Elena, talk to me.'

'I'm not sure what to say.'

'Always the truth.'

I paused my incessant pacing, hands on hips as I turned to acknowledge him. 'Well, the truth is that I feel like I've been used and abused.'

'I've always been here to help you, Elena—help you prepare for the future ahead.'

'I'm not sure that's the truth at all.' In the distance I heard movement, the sound of the pack starting to fuss. Something had happened and I was running out of time.

Araqiel appeared oblivious. 'Every journey, upset and triumph was an experience you needed to endure in order to appreciate what truly mattered when all else seemed bleak. I needed you to find William, Michael and your family so that you would know unselfish love.'

'But why?'

'So, you would understand and know how use the Time Contract and the Quill of Destiny to rewrite history in light's image.' He paused, moving off the top of the bonnet to find my side. He placed his hands on my shoulders, sensing distraction as the Wolves in the distance drew my gaze.

He then touched soft, but firm fingers to my chin, angling my face back to look at his bottomless eyes of blue and silver; eyes that crawled with the knowledge of the universe and mysteries of the unknown. It was almost too much. Like studying the abyss and seeing everything and nothing all at once; a story book without words yet the promise of an ending.

'Elena.' My name caressed his lips in a whisper. 'You can go back to the very beginning before Michael fought with Lucifer, before everything. You can separate the very thought of evil from darkness. You can make everything right.'

'You're talking about wiping out my existence entirely?'

'It's an unselfish love that serves the best needs of the human race.'

'But Sebastian and I—'

'Will never be.'

For the first time in my life I was speechless.

'Think about putting your own emotions aside. Remember the love that you and Michael have shared and the truest form of joy and happiness he gave up to pursue that love. How you might feel in this moment now that he is gone is nothing compared to the loss he felt when he fell from a life of perfection and utter bliss.' He squeezed my shoulders again as if trying to knead his point into muscle and sinew. 'We all feel the loss even now. If you were to turn back time, Elena and give everyone—including Lucifer—a chance to make things right, don't you think that would be wise?'

I was shocked by the alarmingly low volume of my response. It was like all the air had been sucked from my lungs and what was left was the vestiges of a wheeze. 'How can life be better without an existence?'

'You would be ending all pain, all suffering—all weakness.'

'But that would also mean ending the parts that make us human; pain, suffering and weakness teach us humility—and when recognised—make us strong enough to overcome adversity. To end all life would be to end every lesson—anything that ever mattered.'

'Please promise that you will think about it, Elena. Do not make a rash decision before considering all facets and parties concerned.'

'I am trying to consider everyone,' I mumbled. 'In fact, that's all I think about.'

His grip upon me tightened, fingers searching out the bony cavities of my décolletage and pressing to bruise. 'You might think in this moment that you are considering everyone, but if yet another tragedy occurred involving someone you love or care for, do you honestly believe that you could overcome that suffering, pain and debilitating weakness that would follow and choose the noblest path?'

I attempted to extricate myself from his claw-like grasp, edging backwards until his angelic digits caught my hands and held them captive instead. I shuddered at both the intensity of his penetrative glare and the harshness in which he continued to imprison me. He was almost too intense in his delivery to not be wary or untrusting of his ultimate motive. 'Araqiel, I didn't use the Time Contract to save Sebastian. What makes you think I'll use it needlessly if I didn't use it for love?'

'I wasn't talking about using it to save Michael.'

My lips parted to question him further when an ear-piercing howl rented the air; the promise of retribution. The bone-chilling call rippled right through me. It was the signal we'd been waiting for. Lucas had infiltrated the super city.

'I've gotta go.'

'Just promise me you'll think about what I've said.'

I finally yanked free of his grasp, quickly turning my back on the angel and all he'd divulged. His shaky version of the truth had outlined images of a future I couldn't comprehend. I'd never known a past without human existence and never known a world without Sebastian in it. I would deliberate as asked, but understanding what was right for me, my family and humanity? That I was uncertain. Was starting the story from scratch really the best plan considering the detail that had already been inked in time, mistakes and mastery? That I was also uncertain.

In the distance, the greenish hue of The Protector's magic had bled from the walls of the city. Only a few hours had passed and yet a miracle had been performed. We were to have our chance at infiltration and retribution and also ensure Lucas was safe while kicking Protector ass.

It was shaping up to be quite an eventful night.

CHAPTER NINETEEN: INFILTRATION

Lucas held his hand out. More fingers than he remembered blurred his vision, but since the effects of the drug still coursed through his system, he didn't panic at the twenty-odd digits waving like wildflowers in the wind. He had woken up, could move his hands and wasn't strapped to a gurney. All positives as far as he was concerned.

He tilted his head forward. Nothing encumbered that movement—another win. As he tipped further afield, his shoulders rounded, followed by the forward movement of his curving spine, then waist. Before he knew it, he was slumped over himself, staring at dirtied concrete and the legs of the metal chair he was apparently sitting on.

He fingered the ground; icy and unyielding it jolted him from self-serving thoughts of physical achievement. He was virtually folded in half. He had no idea he was even that flexible!

Focus Lucas ...

He had to find his mother and set the plan in motion before someone *inside* realised there were hundreds of them *outside*, waiting to break down the barriers.

'Ahh, the prodigal son returns.'

Lucas twisted his head to the left. Shiny black dress shoes peeked from the bottom of clean-pressed, linen pants. They sat mere inches from his own, the shoelaces so distorted by his blurred vision that they looked like hairy caterpillars or creepy under-trimmed moustaches. He studied them carefully, willing himself to chase away errant musings in exchange for seeing anything above the bushy brows of the loafers.

Even as Lucas found the energy to slowly pull himself upright within the chair, he knew who the voice belonged to. He knew that when the milky haze cleared and clarity returned, Chester—head of the science division for the IMI—would be standing right in front of him. Killing him would be a delight after the crimes he'd committed against both him and Elena, but common sense warred within. He had to pace his urges. He needed to get himself right before contemplating murder.

'Your poor mother has been through the ringer all these years trying to find you,' Chester continued, moving away to stand behind a lab table and computer close enough to still be within reach. He tapped away at the keys, silent for several seconds before speaking again. 'I must say, I'm surprised that she found you at all.'

Lucas tried working his lips, but everything felt numb and sticky within his mouth.

'A lot has happened since you stole away ten years ago, Lucas. It's a shame you didn't stick around to be a part of the revolution.' More tapping on the keyboard. 'But I can see a lot has happened with you too. Or should I say a lack thereof?'

Chester chuckled quietly to himself when Lucas failed to answer, still chewing through the molasses of stolen speech within his mouth. 'You haven't aged a bit and without the serum no less.'

He started to clap, the movement so abrupt and unexpected that Lucas actually jumped, adrenaline surging through his system, helping to weaken his drowsy state. 'Bravo, Lucas. I mean, really. You have achieved what I've been working so hard to replicate for over twenty-seven years now; immortality without the side effects.'

Chester left his work bench, coming back to stand in front of him again. He touched fingers to Lucas's chin, pushing his head backwards and shining a pen light in his eyes. Cringing, Lucas tried to look away, but was caught in the ironclad grip of simulated vampirism. His fingers were biting and uncompromising and Lucas had no strength to resist.

'I see that drugs still have an effect on you,' Chester murmured, the quiet musings of a distracted man. 'Clearly a higher metabolic rate is not a result of your evolution. Nor do you have the extra chromosome vampires seem to generate.'

Lucas hadn't asked for or wanted answers, but as a man of science, Chester would seek conclusions with or without his permission. Judging by the gauze and rough spread of tape in the crook of Lucas's elbow, blood had already been withdrawn and studied without his consent.

'As far as I can tell, this blood test renders no change from bloods drawn back in the Antarctic.' Chester scratched at his chin, rubbing the insignificant patch of blonde stubble that lingered post serum ingestion. Lucas also realised that the scientist no longer wore his trademark tortoise-shell glasses. With vampiric vision, they'd just have been a useless accessory anyway.

'Now, it is my understanding that early changes within your body had much to do with Elena and the bite she bestowed upon you in your infancy, but this? How has immortality played its part and why are your magical powers far more advanced than any other Protector? Why can you do things that no one else even has the spell repertoire capable of pulling off?'

Lucas shrugged. There were too many questions fired at him to search through his addled mind for an answer. Some sort of smart-ass remark had manifested, but was swallowed by the glue of both indecision and drug haze.

Chester—unfazed by Lucas's lack of vocals—studied him for several, uncomfortable minutes in contemplative silence. 'This has to link back to Elena. After all, her blood is the key. But that doesn't necessarily explain your increase in magic. This is something I haven't been able to manipulate within the serum itself.'

Chester tapped his chin thoughtfully, brows furrowing. During this time, Lucas concentrated on funnelling any surging adrenaline towards his fingers and toes. He wiggled them constantly, trying to circulate action back to his slackened limbs.

'Chester,' Susan breathed from the doorway. 'Here you are.' Her breathlessness would indicate exertion, but when her lifeless eyes found Lucas, he realised that her unfocused, cold and distant appraisal was the compulsion holding strong.

'Susan?' Chester answered, gruff with surprise. 'What are you doing in here?'

'You have my son. I'm going to be wherever he is from now on.'

'That's not necessary. You know I mean him no harm.'
What a bunch of bullshit.

Emotionless and almost too quickly she said, 'Of course. You only want to help him. So do I.'

'Well there's nothing you can do right now. Why don't you go and fetch Anica? I need a scientist right now, not an overprotective mother.'

'Anica won't be coming.'

Chester's eyes narrowed so far that there was serious danger of them being lost to his already furrowed brows. He released Lucas's chin. Whispers of magical light erupted, building slowly within the palm of his hand, flickering with intent to harm. Something was wrong and he meant to get to the bottom of it.

Lucas could now move his feet and arms. He didn't think he was quite ready to stand, but there was no hurry while this exchange unfolded.

Chester straightened, full attention now directed towards the woman standing in the doorway. 'What's wrong, Susan? You do not seem like yourself.'

'There are going to be some changes around here.'

'Such as?' More blue light licked the ends of Chester's fingers. It was not missed by Susan despite the hollow effect compulsion had upon her eyes.

'There will be no more experiments. My son is not a play toy for you to poke and prod. You have the serum that should be enough.'

'The serum is imperfect as well you know, Susan.'

'And even *that* you won't have for much longer,' Lucas answered, climbing unsteadily to his feet. He drew both their attention, giving them plenty of time to position themselves better for attack. Chester had edged his way behind a work bench and Susan stood half behind a partition blocking an unoccupied cot in the corner of the room. Lucas was currently vulnerable in this path of expected crossfire, but he couldn't walk away yet without stumbling.

'What are you talking about?' Chester chided, perhaps distracted by the unexpected turn in events.

'Come out from behind the desk,' Lucas prompted. 'You can't hide from me back there.'

'I don't understand what is happening. Susan, I feel like you are about to betray me.'

'You lied to me about Lucas, Chester. You said he was sick. You said that you were taking care of him. But what you were really doing was reinfecting his body again and again with Elena's blood. I didn't mind that you were saving his life when he was younger, but what you did in Antarctica pushed more boundaries than what I will allow.'

Understanding dawned upon Chester's perplexed features. 'So, George finally admitted his role in this? Is that why you have been in Paris all these years, hiding from the man who chose to better his son and better the cause?'

'I was searching for Lucas!'

'In Paris? Please, do not mistake me for a fool. You last saw Lucas in the Antarctic where—'

'Where he escaped on the freight plane only minutes after security personnel recorded sightings of vampires on the surveillance cameras. You didn't think I wouldn't have concluded Elena's involvement? You don't think I wouldn't have researched the possibilities of her whereabouts and thus Lucas's destination?'

'Well, of course …'

'Then you have your answer. Lucas has always been my number one priority and when you interfered beyond your rights as a friend and a doctor, you lost my respect. Not to mention the countless others you have since mowed over in your quest for power.'

'Stephanie was a traitor. She filled your son's head with lies!'

'Stephanie is dead?' Lucas whispered. A memory of the American haematologist flashed to the forefront of his mind. She had done her upmost to empower him with the information needed to escape the IMI's unrelenting hold and even understand some of his past.

'As is her daughter, Lila,' Susan answered. 'Chester deemed her too young and too weak to be enlisted in the ranks of the IMI.'

'Wait a second,' Lucas muttered in disgust. 'You let a girl with leukaemia die because you were worried she wouldn't be a good enough soldier? And then what? You killed her mother because she protested?'

'I killed Stephanie because she helped you escape!' Chester argued, voice rising dramatically. 'And I'd do it again, just like that bimbo of a nurse who let you look into your own medical files and then helped smuggle you out of the facility!'

Lucas cracked his knuckles, anger barely in check. 'You killed Alba too?'

'She was only human.'

Wobbly legs or not, Lucas lunged, throwing every ounce of power he could into directing a telekinetic battering ram at Chester.

He was immediately flung backwards, slamming with a sickening *thud* into the pristine, white wall behind him. While Chester sucked in a much-needed breath, gasping at air with his shocked open fish-lips, Lucas caught himself on the edge of the counter to steady his unstable limbs.

Crumbling plaster rained upon Chester's immobile feet. His arms and legs flailed, but Lucas cast the net of his mind firmly around his enemy's body. Lucas attempted to support his own bodyweight and thus made his way slowly to Chester's telekinetically confined form, gripping every piece of furniture along the way to ensure he remained upright; the ultimate goal was to wrap his fingers around the scientist's traitorous throat.

Chester—ever observant and hypothesising—said, 'What magic is this?' He appeared undaunted by the grip Lucas now had on his jugular, seemingly more interested in the magic yet to be understood. 'Do you really think you can kill me? You're barely strong enough to tickle my flesh with your fingers.'

'Who said I was going to use my hands?'

'Lucas stop!' Susan screamed. It was a little too late. Lucas had already upended a stainless-steel desk with his mind which was now hurtling across the room. Susan stupidly stepped in front of it, taking the brunt of the hit. She and the desk folded and fell to the ground, the crash of the equipment all that could be heard over Lucas's pounding heart.

'Mum,' Lucas shouted, dropping to the ground beside her. 'What are you doing?'

'We need him.'

'Why?'

'To help bring down the barrier spell.'

Chester roared with laughter, his vocal cords bobbing up and down in his throat as he hung plastered to the wall like a butterfly tacked by an entomologist. His arms were spread beside him, his legs tangled by the awkward angle in which he'd been pinned. 'I'm not going to help you do anything.'

'Then I'll kill you.'

He laughed harder; a mockery Lucas found difficult to ignore. He summoned every sharp pointed object in the room to rise. It took effort, somewhat arduous given the still relatively foggy conditions in the upstairs domain of his brain. But given the alternative to let this man run free, he would bust a vein if he thought he could exact some justice before it was too late.

'Lucas stop!' Despite being slammed by a desk, Susan struggled to her feet quicker than thought. Something had to have cracked or fractured given the amount of pain radiating from her ribs. She could worry about that later. For now, she had to protect the one man she wanted to kill herself; a friend since childhood and a man she had once trusted.

Chester's ongoing levity was infuriating. Despite the incidental weapons moving into position, he remained unconcerned. Pencils, paper weights and computers pulverising his flesh and bones over and over again did little to stay his cocky certainty. The Protectors were strong now and difficult to wound, but they were not impervious to death. They were not true immortals.

Susan's screams of protest were surely loud enough to attract extra unwanted visitors. Lucas thought of silencing her, but was honestly too encapsulated with burning ire to surrender to reason. Despite her urges, the instruments of torment landed upon their mark. Bones cracked and bruising exploded from heftier wounds inconceivably made by the tiniest of objects. Blood now erupted from the result of the ongoing battery.

Lucas was smug in his offerings of pain. Chester no longer laughed—and in fact—begged for mercy and forgiveness for his sins. He'd never understood what Lucas was capable of and certainly had never foreseen this inescapable attack in which the serum could not counteract the effects.

A computer workstation blasted straight through the wall next to Chester's head, tearing plaster from its hold and forcing studwork into the room beyond. Glass smashed and a cry of pain followed, drawing Lucas's attention elsewhere. Chester remained pinned despite pathetic attempts to grovel his way to freedom. Susan clawed at Lucas's ankles, still begging him to stop this attack.

But Lucas was now distracted, studying the newly formed opening in the wall, eyes narrowed as a sight unexpected sent him reeling. Susan caught him in her arms, wincing as he collapsed against her chest. She had lied about her reasons for taking the serum and now that Lucas knew, she held him tighter still.

He attempted to push her away, not wanting to resort to the same violence he'd bestowed upon his enemy still hooked to the wall like a discarded old jacket. 'Let me go.'

'No. You should never have seen what's in that room.'

'You knew about this?'

'Lucas, you know how I feel about them. I'm not ashamed to string up a monster and punish them for their crimes.'

He struggled in her arms, knowing that in order for this semblance of strength to be present, she must have dosed up on the serum once again. 'Let me go, mum, or I will attack you too!'

She released him so quickly that Lucas wondered if he'd somehow burnt her. He fell forward, landing hard on his knees. Pain was fleeting as he struggled to regain composure, legs shaky and muscles weary. He no longer cared that Chester whimpered against the laboratory wall or his mother pecked at his ankles with uncertain fingers; an attempt to perhaps help and hinder. Did the compulsion Lucius embedded in her subconscious war within her? Had she let him go because the master vampire's sway was stronger than her own urges to stop him?

'What are you going to do?' she whispered, voice hoarse and filled with renewed fear.

'I'm going to let him out.'

'No! You can't do that,' she pleaded. 'He's been starved and tortured for ten years. He will attack you!'

Lucas didn't care about what *may* happen. He only cared about saving whomever he could from the fate that had once ridden his own shoulders—fate he could never have over-shadowed without the help of friends both alive and dead. So, slapping his mother's distracting hands away, he concentrated on bending the offending plaster blocking entry to the next room, cracking it and discarding it until the hole in the wall was big enough to climb through.

'Lucas, please, he will try to feed from you!'

'They don't like Protector Blood.'

'Would you eat anything if you were half-starved?'

Point taken.

'I'll be careful.'

Lucas surrendered a cursory glance at the unexpectedly silent Chester. A quick assessment of his wounds suggested that such an abrupt end to his whimpering and begging might have implied fatality, but no. The mad scientist sat curiously still, lacerations weeping and in obvious need of attention, but no longer pressing on his concern. His maniacal face was almost gleeful; the pull at the edges of his bloodied, thin lips suggested a half-smile.

Lucas failed to understand his amusement and had little patience or time to de-mystify the situation. He left him pinned in a puddle of his own bodily fluids, eyes ever-watchful and curious in their exploration of Lucas's movements.

Refocusing, Lucas crawled through the hole he'd created into the room beyond. 'Marcus?' Lucas prompted, approaching slowly and ever-cautiously. 'It's me, Lucas. Can you hear me?'

Marcus was chained like the criminal or wild animal The Protectors supposed him to be; both wrists shackled in silver and ankles bound similarly. His body was stretched taught, almost as though they intended to separate his limbs from their torso, certainly giving him no leeway to test his strength in any given direction. The odour of burnt flesh hung ripe in the air, the silver shackles melting what little skin endeavoured to cling to bone. He'd been strung up like a Christmas turkey, his body frail, half-naked and practically begging for death.

'Marcus, it's Lucas. Do you remember me?'

'How do you know this creature?' Susan muttered, crawling through the hole in the wall behind him.

'I met him after Elena helped me escape the IMI in the Antarctic. After the war started and Elena was killed, I became part of the family. Marcus is one of Lucius's thralls who took me in and accepted me.'

'Lucius's what?'

Lucas ignored her inquisitive ramblings in lieu of critical assessment. He circled Marcus slowly and with the upmost caution. His mother was right about one thing. Marcus was starved and a clear and present danger to anyone the vampire thrall came into contact with. His vacant expression was somewhat worrying, never mind the long brown hair that clung in matted locks around his hollowed face. His skin was translucent, veins throbbed with the urgency of sustenance and hygiene was all but a forgotten luxury. To look upon Marcus now was to see a shadow of civility, a ghost of his former self.

'What happened to you?' Lucas mused, though he did not expect an answer from the chained vestiges of the demon strung before him. 'We thought you'd left. If we'd known you were in trouble, we would have searched for you.'

'Better …' Marcus hissed between cracked lips.

Lucas edged closer to better hear the rasping reply only to jump three feet back again as Marcus snapped forward in his restraints, teeth exposed and eager for blood. Susan quickly threaded her arms around his waist, dragging Lucas backwards, a spell in hand and ready to take aim at the starving vampire.

'No,' Lucas shouted, blocking her attempts to harm. 'He's not himself.'

'I will not let this creature hurt you!' She was exasperated, eyes darting backwards and forwards between the two of them. 'Let's leave him here, Lucas. This vile demon is beyond saving and we have to bring down the barrier soon if we are to execute this plan.'

'I know what we have to do,' Lucas argued, shoving her away from him for what felt like the umpteenth time that night. Had she always been this clingy with him? 'I'm not leaving Marcus here like this. Regardless of the plan, I will help him escape this place.'

'He'll kill us both.'

'No. He just needs blood and common sense will return.'

'It'll be *our* blood if you continue with this foolish idea!' Susan all but stamped her foot, hands balled into angry fists at her sides, blue light playing across the skin of her knuckles.

An idea bloomed that brought a wicked smile to flourish upon his lips. 'I didn't say *our* blood.'

As if his very name had been plucked from the *Harry Potter* sorting hat, Chester began to thrash violently against the wall in the other room. He screamed for help in a half-enraged, half-terrified voice that would not go unheard. Chester knew now that death was inevitable and certainly not as merciful as the pummelling of office furniture might have been. He was right in his petrification. Despite the serum, Chester was not infallible, especially against the tortured vampire he'd kept under lock and key for so many years.

'Do not free him,' Susan snapped, her last-ditch attempts at halting the madness falling on deaf ears. Lucas had already decided. Her response was a resigned grunt, but she was right at her son's back if he needed her, reassuring though doubtful to be of any real help if the starved vampire went rogue.

This was the hard part. Lucas now had to split and yet consolidate his energy. On one hand he needed to keep Chester contained—and on the other—needed to break open Marcus's restraints. There was no way he'd physically get close enough to do it. He wasn't a moron, despite Elena's nicknames to the contrary.

'Ready?'

'I can't believe you're going to set this creature free.'

'I can't believe you're still insulting him before I destroy the restraints. Do you have a death wish?'

Another incensed exhalation of negativity burst past her lips. There was no need to pair words with the enraged look upon her features, but she spoke anyway, venom pouring forth. 'Do what you must, Lucas. I'm compelled to finish what I started by bringing you here, but this is not part of that plan and it's ridiculously stupid and irresponsible—'

Lucas rolled his eyes. 'Mum, shut up.'

'Not safe ...' Marcus croaked, voice barely above a whisper. He was so quiet that while Lucas and Susan argued, they missed it.

'Lucas, if you do this ...'

The warning was filed away, but hardly heeded. Lucas prioritized Marcus's freedom and worked on the manipulation of the silver that bound his old friend. Though a suitable distance was maintained, they both took another perceptible step backwards as the wrist restraints broke free and Marcus slumped, upper body folding in half as his ankles remained agonisingly stretched.

Weakness was mere perception. A half-staved vampire would find the strength needed. And, despite not having used his upper body for a great many years, Marcus was amazingly dexterous as he pressed up onto the tips of his blackened fingers, watching Lucas and Susan from under the veil of stringy hair crowding his midnight eyes.

He snarled, teeth bared and ready to rend flesh. His fingernails shaped quickly into lengthened talons, Chester's screams from the other room were the only thing that distracted the vampire long enough to break eye contact from the current available blood sources.

Ankle restraints now relinquished, Lucas dropped Chester's telekinetic hold and threw all available energy into creating impenetrable protection for him and his mother. Marcus fought with temptation and attempted to win dominion over his urges by turning slowly towards the hole in the wall, his back now to Susan and Lucas.

Chester had since realised his renewed freedom and tried running across the debris-strewn lab to the door, but the hungry predator robbed him of liberty. Marcus was upon him in seconds, pouncing like the caged jungle cat he'd been, teeth barred and urgent for blood.

Talons raked Chester's flesh, spilling blood and eliciting an agonising scream silenced all too swiftly by the spittle-slicked fangs that proceeded to tear through Chester's jugular.

Stomach rolling, Lucas watched as Marcus drank from the fountain of bubbling life, slurping and suckling while blood sprayed in a decidedly artful way across the white walls of the laboratory. Marcus never ceased to admire his handiwork. Instead, he wreathed slick lips over the still warm and pumping essence, drinking greedily, his arms rigidly clasping Chester's broken form and draining him of any life that remained.

Morbidly curious, both Susan and Lucas crept towards the hole in the wall, watching the horror begin to transform the derelict and gaunt appearance of the vampire. His matted locks slowly gained colour and highlights, converting to silken waves that dusted his once bony shoulders. Translucent skin now glowed with renewed vitality, veins pulsed and muscle and sinew reshaped over a frame that was imbued with growing strength.

When he finally gasped completion and looked upon his spectators, his soulless black eyes seemed to sparkle with the mirth of his undertaking. Liquid life-force dribbled down his chin while his tongue laved the length of his now silken lips, fingers simultaneously wiping the excess blood from sight. And while a pink stain lingered as a reminder of his recent feed, Chester's body was unceremoniously dumped on the floor, open eyes still permeated with his final moments of fear.

'It is safe,' Marcus croaked. His vocal cords attempted to work around the sudden influx of moisture with little success. He sagged, hands splayed upon the sterile floor for support. He was visibly shaking, muscles twitching in response to the blood that now sought to repair damage within.

'It's a trap,' Susan whispered. 'You should never have let it free, Lucas. It's a monster. Look what it did to Chester.'

Lucas scoffed. 'And he deserved every minute of sufferance.'

'It is dangerous! Does it look fully fed to you?'

'Stop calling Marcus an '*it*.'

'She fears me,' Marcus answered, gathering enough strength to pull himself to his feet. 'She fears what I know and what I might tell you.'

Susan sneered in response. 'And it's deranged.'

Lucas wasn't one hundred percent certain, but released the barrier around him and his mother regardless. He had to have faith as he certainly didn't believe Marcus to be deranged—just hungry.

Susan shackled his wrist within her steely grasp. Her eyes darted incessantly back and forth between her son and the vampire she truly believed would either tear them both apart or forever fracture the tentative relationship she was trying to re-build with her stubborn and foolhardy son. 'I love you, Lucas,' she whispered. 'I love you more than anything or anyone on this earth. I will stop at nothing to always try to protect you.'

'Let me go, mum.'

'I need you to trust me.'

'Trust you? What are you talking about?' Lucas considered that she might have been up to her old tricks, using emotion to sway results in her favour or just downright crazy. This time, Lucas had no idea what her plan beyond compulsion was or if she was even truthful in her appeal to his better nature. Did he need to trust her? What was about to happen? Was she about to betray him … again?

Marcus ignored them both. He spent time sampling his heightened senses instead, closing his eyes to dampen visual distraction. His ears twitched and nostrils flared. Scents and sounds brushed past the fine hairs that barred entry to the passages of his vampiric form. He listened as if the wind itself could speak and tasted the air for the bitter tang of magical interference. His eyes sprung open, retinas focusing directly on Lucas. 'It's happening.'

'What's happening?' Lucas tried yanking his wrist free. 'Mum, seriously, let me go now.'

'I have to protect you from what is coming.'

His fingers set to work on prying his mother free, but Lucas's narrowed eyes had found Marcus. They regarded one another with eerie stillness, Lucas's confusion mounting and fairly palpable.

'They often forgot I was chained in that room,' Marcus started, eyes still locked with Lucas's and unwilling to offer release. 'They forgot that I could hear every single word spoken.'

Lucas—irritated beyond belief—finally slapped his mother's hands hard enough that she opted to let him go. He needed to hear what Marcus was saying—needed to know what The Protectors may have planned. He couldn't care less that his mother argued her issue with the vampire or sprouted yet more phrases of affection in order to stop him from listening to Marcus. He also didn't care if he was wandering towards trouble as he climbed back through the hole in the wall; Susan glued to him like a shadow.

'She accuses me of trapping you,' Marcus continued, 'but she knows the truth.'

'What truth?' Lucas half-pivoted so he could address them both. 'What's Marcus talking about? What have you done to him?'

'I've told you. It's deranged. Years of being starved has made it insane.'

'You need to get out of here, Lucas.'

Lucas felt as if he'd entered a ping pong tournament. His head swivelled back and forth between the two opponents as he attempted to decipher the winner. Fired accusations now trampled the common sense in his mind and stirred suspicion. Had covertly sneaking into the IMI super city been a well-orchestrated opportunity by the Vampire? Or, the careful planning of someone far more cunning? 'Mum?'

The steady press of magic—the kind that left a tingle upon the skin—began to evaporate as if a vacuum had been created or rain had washed them clean of its touch. Goose-pimples became tangible upon flesh and Lucas was now unsure if it was the release of power or dread that weaved its way between the bones of his spine.

'The barrier is down,' Lucas breathed, knowing the truth of that statement. Shouldn't he have been relieved rather than worried about this fortunate twist in fate?

'Yes,' Susan answered. She now stood off to the side, out of reach and vacant of her earlier emotional pleas.

'I thought you said we needed Chester.'

'She wanted to kill him herself,' Marcus mused, taking small steps to close the distance between himself and Lucas. He reached out, clasped Lucas's arm and basically dragged the protesting youngster behind him and away from his own mother. 'Then once she'd killed him, she would kill the rest of us.'

Susan crept forward, enough that she was met by Marcus's guttural growl. It did not incite fear—but rather—an echoed response of impending violence that only served to exacerbate Lucas's confusion. Who exactly posed the greater threat in this scenario? The vampire who'd carved breakfast from the dead scientist on the floor or his mother that now danced circles around the pair of them?

'Mum, what's going on?'

'I just wanted my son back,' she beckoned.

'And you wanted a way to wipe out as many of the Vampires and vânātors he'd befriended over the years.' Marcus continued to shield Lucas behind his body.

'What?' Lucas was thoroughly confused as he attempted to outmanoeuvre Marcus to confront Susan.

'You don't know what you're saying, *Vampire*.'

'Don't I?' Marcus countered, hand lashing out to push Lucas further behind him.

Why was Marcus defending him in such a manner? Why was this tug of war taking place? Should he fear his mother? Had her compulsion worn off?

'I don't understand what's going on at all.'

'She's known where you were for a while, Lucas. She's been planning this for months. I've heard the whispers and plotting when they thought they were all alone.'

'Stop talking you piece of blood-sucking filth! I've worked hard on this plan and do not want my son influenced by you or your kind!'

'Mum, what have you done?'

'Don't look at me like that, Lucas. I am protecting you! As it is you are coupled with one of these creatures and it makes my skin crawl. How could you let the dead touch you, touch your mind?'

'This can't possibly be about me and Marianne ...'

'This is about eradication, our plan from the very beginning!' Susan was exasperated, face flushed and blue eyes lit with furious fire. 'Chester had many things right, but failed to mention that his plans included subjugating my baby to a life of the damned. He's tainted you—changed you. Not all of it for the better, either!'

All heads spun towards the exit as an alarm rang loudly from the hallway beyond. People could be heard running in all directions, apparently oblivious to the showdown in the laboratory.

'You're too late to stop it now,' Susan said, sneering at Marcus and the hand that protectively kept Lucas at bay. 'It's only a matter of time before I get to him. You can't watch your back for long in here, Vampire.'

'Marcus, what's she talking about? What am I missing?' Lucas made a last-ditch effort to escape the vampire's protective stance and failing. He knew he'd be freed by the use of his own magic, but with this unexpected change in events and allies unfolding, he was not willing to risk anyone's life or limbs.

'You've been played, Lucas. Your mother has been planning this long enough that if you have brought others with you tonight—as she suspected you would—we're all going to have a serious fight on our hands.'

'Planning what?'

'To finish what we started three hundred years ago. To do what should have been done instead of signing the treaty.'

'Oh shit,' Lucas whispered. 'Mum, you can't … The compulsion.'

She threw back her head and laughed, throat bobbing up and down with glee. 'Compulsion? Did you really think that would work on us?'

'But I thought—'

'You thought what I wanted you to think. I needed to protect you and get you back here and away from the Vampires.'

Accusations and seemingly unfathomable explanations were halted as a scream so piercing rung through the corridors beyond. It cut deep; a sound like that only came from someone inches from death. They all knew the difference between fear and finality.

Lucas's mouth gaped. Words slithered across his tongue like glue, emitted only in the form of an incomprehensible whisper. He had no idea how to respond or even if it was worth trying to convince her in the merit of life. She had decided to condemn everyone despite his love or connection to them. The Protectors had not advanced, but digressed to baser instincts and would sooner see blood than adopt tolerance.

More screams rented the air, chased by the hiss of vampires and the growl of the Vânǎtors. Lucas no longer had the energy to communicate logic, let alone untangle the twisted web of thinking his mother had spun. She would never understand him. She would never accept Elena and she would ultimately try to kill Marianne. There was only one thing left to be done.

'Where are you going, Lucas?' Susan called as he dodged Marcus's grip with a tiny bout of magic. He bolted straight for the door, ignoring Marcus's renewed protests and his mother's advances.

Lucas paused, gripping the sterile door frame between his fingers and praying for strength; not the physical kind, but emotional. The lines between what was right and wrong were more blurred than *Mr. Magoo's* vision and he had no idea if walking the line was in fact the right path. He only knew he had to be there for both Elena and Marianne. Nothing else especially mattered now that hope was a notion based in fiction.

'Lucas!'

'I'm going to go and fight,' he replied despondently.

'With them?' Susan was horrified. Perhaps she'd believed her greater purpose was an understanding Lucas would soon acknowledge. There was no chance of that now. He'd been betrayed more times than he could poke a stick at and further attempts to entice or explain was breath wasted.

'Does it really matter anymore?'

'What are you saying?'

'Win or lose, look what we're fighting over—a wasteland; a graveyard of painful memories and broken dreams.'

'Lucas ...'

'No. We're done.' He left the room, Marcus and his mother nothing more than lithe shadows at his back, vying for supremacy in beliefs each truly believed justified. He knew he'd probably left his mother to her death and reconciled that sooner or later he would have to deal with that reality, but for now Elena and Marianne needed him.

Despite original intentions—the bogus entry and the insurmountable deaths that would occur yet again—Elena had come tonight on account of his request. She would fight and she would shed blood for a cause he had believed was warranted. He had to find her before it was all too late.

They were now amidst another battle to notch on the belt of an endless war. There would be another loved one who would perish under the guise of righteousness and more banging at hell's gate ready to seek it.

The true questions was: when would it ever end?

CHAPTER TWENTY: SNEAK ATTACK

I raced through the warren of abandoned, debris-filled streets, bare feet slapping the ground hard enough to crack asphalt. It only took seconds to reunite with the pack; the wolves dashing past, smoothing their tails across bare flesh and looking to the super city for permission to attack.

Others were quick to join, vampire and vânător alike. There was no hesitation when it came to Lucas. He was loved by everyone and we were more than aware that the window of opportunity was slim. Wasting breath on debating my father's possible strategy for attack was pointless. We were all ready.

I touched those wolves closest to me for reassurance, fur shifting between my fingers like silken threads. And though I could have stood there marvelling at the rightness of their touch, there was work to be done. All it took was one nod in the direction of the city's fallen magical glow and they were off, paws pounding the pavement, nails scraping as they scuttled to find purchase in all the excitement.

I didn't stand idle for long. The vampires closest gave chase and so did I. We moved with purpose. The wind a companion and the earth an accomplice underfoot. Peripherally, I saw that some of our group had jumped, leaping great distances and clearing the city's meagre dwellings and purpose-built security posts to enter the domain of the living and magically defensive. There was no pause, no consideration of consequence, only desire fuelled by years of hate—years of sought retribution and forced suppression.

When the screaming began, I didn't—at first—deign to consider the ramification of our actions. The Protectors had forced our hands and though many innocents would die, I hoped many would be saved. Naivety didn't allow me to dwell on their safety in an outside world filled with a starving populace of blood-drinkers, but I did believe that knowing the truth and offering freedom was a far better deal than enslavement.

Past trends dictated that humans would still try to kill every last one of us. Fear would rule common sense and it was almost certain they would tear the earth apart with bullets and bombs to be free of this reoccurring nightmare, but they still deserved choice. If any of us were to ever overcome the trappings of Lucifer's darkness, then we owed it to ourselves to give choice to everyone robbed of it.

Didn't we?

Didn't I?

There weren't as many people as I thought there'd be loitering on the streets as we entered. I assumed many may have been hiding, closing doors on the violence ensuing to avoid the dawning horror of a brand-new battle always destined to emerge in a war that had never truly ended. I was pleased to see that no one actively sort to disturb that tentative perception of safety. Goals were clear and the Supernaturals had a purpose, each their own agenda to bring about justice in ways they saw fit—as long as they didn't needlessly kill innocents.

My goal was to maintain composure instead of stressing about my brother … and relenting to cravings.

The fresh scent of blood was driving me to distraction. In the past, it had been a temptation I could surpass. Now to smell blood—any blood—was to hunger. My stomach rolled, twisted and begged for reprieve. I didn't just need it, I lusted, craved and ached for it like never before. It was almost difficult to separate coherent thought from the whims of undead desires. I'd never truly understood the inner turmoil messing with sanity. To be a vampire was to constantly fight with your conscience and battle desires so richly ingrained with sin it was impossible to remember humanity.

I was relieved that whatever humans were left had hidden themselves. I wasn't certain that if I crossed one bleeding, helpless and vulnerable that I'd be able to resist.

Another scream snapped me free of those dangerous thoughts. More blood flowed followed by the sound of ripping and tearing. The crackle of magic proved the unearthing of my caution as the unsuspecting in our group stumbled, froze, began to levitate or wound up dead. A fight with The Protectors had been inevitable. Their magic was virtually an unstoppable force, but I'd

292

hoped the element of surprise would give us the upper hand. It was almost as if they had known we were coming.

'Something's not right,' Caleb shouted. He echoed my sentiments as he vaulted old trash cans and street signs, perhaps hoping to outrun the pursuit of wolves determined to take chunks from his rear end. I thought they had bigger fish to fry, but Caleb clearly thought otherwise as he continued to glance over his right shoulder.

As I followed his line of sight, it became glaringly obvious that Caleb wasn't the slightest bit concerned about his ass. In fact, the too-wide eyes and open mouth was a result of surveying the converging barrier once again solidifying around us.

Why would The Protectors re-erect the barrier knowing we were inside with them? Our numbers were strong and we were hungry for their destruction. Surely to trap us all together was suicide?

I stopped. Running towards the fight seemed pointless when it was now all around us. Instead, I began to dwell on unhealthy thoughts, my brain essentially a ticking time bomb, scenarios of all shapes and victories flowing freely within the grey matter. We had assumed that our attack was impromptu—impossible to predict. But more and more Protectors began to appear, filling the windows of apartment buildings, abandoned shop fronts, side alleys and streets. Magic licked at their fingers like the battle-hungry drool of my half-starved vânătors.

I quickly counted over two hundred genetically-modified magical entities dispersed in the near vicinity. My unbeating heart clenched with uncertainty. We were trapped with more Protectors than we'd anticipated and also humans now hiding in the shadows, eager to protect captors they were unaware farmed them for blood.

'This is not good at all.' Caleb was now right beside me, lips pressed together, his words hushed. The worry etched upon his features was merely an echo of the panic that tried to paint a stain across my vision. All I could see was red—not from anger—but the blood that would soon flow freely this night.

'We've walked into a massive trap,' I murmured, entirely unsettled as I looked at our compressed group, eerily quiet and seemingly smaller than when the night had begun. We were hemmed in by our foe, their patient observation and stillness a sure sign of their confidence. As some of our kin had already fallen victim to The Protector's magic—and efficient efforts of modern weaponry wielded by those we sought to free—I questioned the strength I'd believed we had.

'How did they know we were coming?'

I shook my head, vague ideas circling. 'I suspect Susan. I'm guessing the compulsion didn't work.'

'How can you be sure?'

I nudged Caleb to look up at the top of the building beside us. I felt Lucas's presence as surely as the cold pavement touching the soles of my bare feet may have implied seasonal threats. He hung limply in Susan's bloodied arms, his head knocked about as she attempted to place him not-so-carefully into a hunting vehicle. From this angle I didn't know his state, but despite my skewed senses, I believed him to be alive.

'He's sleeping,' Caleb confirmed. 'His heartbeat and breathing are steady.'

'Drugs?'

'I couldn't say for sure.'

'And Susan?'

'She's been attacked. Her back is shredded and her arms and the side of her neck have been bitten.'

'By what? I can't pick up anything other than blood right now.'

I was aware that the pack and the Vampires that had entered with our group were antsy and awaiting orders. Some bounced from foot-to-foot with nervous energy while the Wolves growled and scraped their paws through broken pieces of asphalt to tend their anxiety. The end was near and everyone eager to get a jump-start on its defence. I wondered if elsewhere in the city my father and his group sampled victory or crushing defeat or sat upon the fence of indecision as we did now, surrounded by opposition and uncertainty.

Caleb busied himself sampling the wind and every scent upon it. 'I can't be sure. It's vampire, I think.' He sniffed again, closing his eyes to narrow distraction down to a minimum. 'Actually …' His eyes snapped back open. 'I can be sure!'

'Who is it?'

'You wouldn't believe me even if I told you.'

'Try me.'

I had a second to observe Caleb's face lose the inconsolable fear of defeat. The corners of his supple lips upturned and his eyes sparkled with renewed hope. He now nudged me to look back. The rooftop door flew open behind Susan, admitting a vampire thought to have been missing for nearly ten years.

'Holy shit it's Marcus!'

'And he doesn't look happy.'

'What are you waiting for?' Susan screamed, mouth cupped by bloodied hands. 'Kill them all!' She had only a second to spin around before Marcus was upon her, clawing at every inch of exposed flesh as they tumbled to the ground, hidden from view. The ledge of the rooftop barred their bloodied encounter, though I had little doubt—despite Marcus's somewhat feminine tendencies—he'd no intention of scratching her to death.

Mass panic erupted in the form of battle cries. Wolves howled and barked, the Vampires hissed and leapt for victims in the form of easy targets—humans. Guns exploded and The Protectors began to charge. My present world blurred. Everyone moved faster than my vampiric eyesight could contend with. Magic was thrown around like fireworks in the night sky, claws skittered across the ground and teeth snapped together like thunderous claps of a storm. Bodies were suddenly everywhere—more dead than alive. And blood? That sprayed upon the ground like the eruption of shaken soda cans at a kid's party. It was something I could no longer look away from. It was everywhere, eager to spread its crimson hue like creeping vines choking the life from anyone crossing its path.

'Elena, stay behind me,' Caleb warned. He ducked, slapping a hand against my chest and pushing me roughly away from an incoming bolt of magic.

'Stay behind you?' I hollered back, turning just in time to strike some guy under the chin with my palm and toss him into the next alley. His discarded gun skittered across the ground and came to a stop against a rubbish bin. 'I know you're older than me by about fifty years, but I'm trained for this kind of thing, you know.'

'Lucius said to protect you, so that's what I'm doing. Just for once do you think you could help me out rather than hinder me?'

'Hinder you?' I grabbed Caleb's shoulder and flattened us against the nearest wall. The *Hevannatara* curse careened past us,

295

streaks of blue only inches from our faces. 'When have I ever got you into trouble?'

'I don't have enough fingers to count.'

'You are so full of shit, Caleb.'

He pushed me forward and we both rolled to the ground, coming back to a kneeling position within seconds. Two Protectors emerged from a blown-out window located directly above our position. A smattering of dislodged glass was the only tell-tale sign of the descent from above. We looked up just as they were almost upon us, Caleb leaping to the left and out of harm's way, me bracing for direct impact.

I snarled and jumped to greet one of them, my fangs lengthening in the prospect of a kill. We collided like lightening on an iron roof; our toughened skins—though malleable to each other—were still beyond human touch.

Falling quickly to the ground, the crackle of magic was like static through the tips of my hair. I expected to be caught blinded, frozen in time or bound by levitation, but my instincts served me well. I went for his jugular before we hit solid ground, wounding but not maiming. An opportunity missed? Perhaps I still believed a Protector could atone for past misgivings. I also didn't like the taste of their blood, so ending life for the sake of a small victory seemed pointless.

Caleb had no qualms about serving his version of justice. Blood sprayed in an arc across his cheeks, pink lips now glistening with the life-force of the other Protector. They'd both moved swifter than the wind, but the true predator had been Caleb; the vampire with pink hair, spitting out tainted blood and wiping his face with the back of his hand.

His eyes narrowed on the puncture wound I'd inflicted. The remaining Protector clutched his neck to compact blood loss, eyes wide and screaming for mercy as his mouth gaped open and closed as if trying to suck down air. I had him pinned against the chest with a knee, my taloned fingers ready to strike. Even if I wasn't sure what I was going to do next, Caleb looked as if he wanted to finish what I'd started.

'No, don't kill him,' I said, clutching Caleb's shoulder as he drew closer than necessary.

'They won't show you mercy.'

I nodded. 'I know.'

He shook his head, bewildered, but only for a split second. Confusion passed and his view of common sense suddenly ruled. He pushed my knee aside and ran his knife-like talons over the Protector's bobbing throat desperate for breath as liquid life invaded. Caleb watched me as he did it, a glimmer of predatory satisfaction flashing defiance through his deep, blue eyes. 'A conscience is a nuisance,' he said mildly, a singular talon still embedded in torn flesh and spasming muscle. 'It's a luxury that none of us can afford.'

Though I gaped at him like bloated pond fish, I knew on some level he was right. I had made some very unsavoury decisions in the past not necessarily backed by what he called my *conscience*. But still …

'Don't look at me like that, Elena,' he muttered, avoiding eye contact as he stood, brushing off his pants as he did so. 'A long time ago I might have just picked his pockets or compelled him into emptying his bank accounts, but the war has changed the currency. Either we kill him or he kills us. It's a simple concept; life over death.'

I swallowed the veritable lump in my throat. 'I don't disagree with you on any particular point.' Blood now gurgled within The Protector's windpipe, running down the perforated skin of his neck in haste to escape the flailing body. My hands fluttered somewhat uselessly in pursuit of the morally right thing to do and coming up empty.

'Then why the surprise?'

I finally looked away, dragging my gaze from the oozing warmth of the Protector's impending death to focus on the blue depths of Caleb's seemingly merciless eyes. At least he now surrendered to my distain. 'Should I ever stop being surprised by murder?'

'Murder?' Caleb choked on an outburst of sardonic laughter. 'I've watched you kill a lot of vânători, Elena. Don't be a hypocrite.'

'I never said I didn't …'

'Then what are you accusing me of?'

My shuddering sigh was lost to the battle cries emptying into the streets around us. 'It's not specifically you, Caleb. It's all of us.'

Caleb yanked me back to my feet and then slammed me sideways into an alley wall. At first, I was stunned by the sneak attack until a bolt of deadly magic inched past my left shoulder and exploded into the shell of an old Volkswagen. It erupted into inconsolable flames and I was grateful. He then grabbed my hand and pulled me into the safety of a hidden doorway. The battle on the streets spilled in our direction, but for the moment we were safe, coveting the shadows.

'Please tell me that the Sleeping Beauty routine for the past ten years hasn't converted you into a Born Again?'

'What?'

'Sebastian's angel wings didn't dump feathers into your brain while you were sleeping?'

'What are you on about?'

'It's called survival, Elena.'

'I know what this is, Caleb. I may have been dead for the last ten years, but I haven't forgotten any of the shit I've been through to get to this point.'

His fingers tightened around mine. 'Then don't start to doubt yourself or me now. There is no shame in wanting to live and doing what is necessary to make it happen.' His breath was warm against my cheek, his lips a whisper from my ear.

'It's just getting harder to justify killing. I mean, really, what are we fighting for?'

It was such an inopportune time to be having a crisis of faith. And yet here I was, wishing we could all just shake hands and move on from our past grievances. Sometimes I could be so naive it was scary.

'Well, right now we're fighting to save our own asses.'

'From what?'

'Them!' Caleb scolded. He eyeballed me with a new level of impatience, once again dragging me through shadow and alleyway grit searching for some semblance of safety.

Protectors edged their way towards us, shooting magic at any vânǎtors vying to get a piece of the action. Some of my wolves were frozen or blinded, silver daggers swiftly following the spray of bullets and ending the task of life. I needed to help them.

Caleb wouldn't release me. Instead, he relinquished my hand and wrapped his arms around me, cocooning me in what he thought was steel-gripped protection. I could have assaulted his instep, cracked his ribs with my elbow or broken his nose with a palm thrust, but to injure my friend was a deed I would not partake in.

Lucas was on the rooftop above us. He needed help and honestly, if Caleb's protection ensured I got to him sooner and in one piece, then I could shelve my ego for the time being. Lucas was essentially my only reason at this point for fighting for an existence that wasn't all together worth celebrating.

Defeatist attitude in check but not stowed, I'd always found cause to fight in the past. Now my motivation was driven by Lucas's safety, but the end game—post keeping him safe—wasn't exactly a prize worth winning. I'd done what I could to stop The Protectors, fought the Vânătors to the point where I now ruled them and also had come to understand that the trappings of vampirism could be managed.

The world was a different place now. Synth Corp was gone and food was limited. The skies had been darkened with pollution and humans were a commodity, a seemingly dangerous and self-depreciating species that cared little for consequence. And The Protectors? Where did I even begin to start with the travesties the IMI had been a party to?

Perhaps Araqiel had been right. Humans had been screwing up since Adam and Eve took a bite of the apple. They've always been lured by the darkness. My own father had fallen victim to his grief and damned a whole legion of vampires to an eternity in hell. Now we warred with ourselves and with the very humans we depended upon. What was really the point of it all?

Now it was just me and Lucas in this crazy, mixed up world. Yes, I technically had my father, but I had lived so long without ever truly knowing him that our connection was still tenuous at best. I cared for and respected him, but time had served little purpose in us really getting to know each other. Would we ever understand one another when learning to live in a place so far from normal now negated the past and relinquished our humanity to baser, animal instincts?

'Elena, we have to keep going.' Caleb moved on instinct and not on permission. Spinning from his hold like a ballroom dancer about to take the final dip, he snatched my fingers and slotted them tightly between his own, yanking me further into the depths of the alley.

Why? Was the silent question on my lips. Lucas had and would always be the driving force behind my decisions, but when all choices made in the past had been erroneous, how could I be trusted to do the right thing in the present?

Get your shit together, Elena. This is your life now. Sebastian is gone. You need to deal with it.

Everything feels wrong without him. Everything seems pointless …

Seriously, you're being a whingey dick. The world has moved on and now you should too.

But …

I wish I could say a self-depreciating pep-talk helped, but my mind was still a jungle of uncertainty. It did, however, motivate my legs to move, my knees to bend and my muscles to negotiate the jump several stories above. The very thought of Sebastian's loss was indeed crippling and the unending sense of pointlessness coated the existence of all that still lingered in the present with uncertainty, but I simply needed to get over it! I needed to put one foot in front of the other and hope that it led somewhere good— anywhere bar the grief-stricken portion of self-defeat.

Caleb released my hand as we touched down on the roof above. I'd barely made a sound, but Caleb sprayed concrete, dust and brittle tar up my ankles as he landed beside me. We shared a brief smile, once again united in purpose and the shared memory of us bounding across rooftops in the past.

Smiles abruptly faded. Lucas was awake and was now sandwiched between his mother and Marcus, a hand on each chest keeping distance between them. His safety was a coin toss of chance.

'Step aside, Lucas,' Marcus hissed. 'I need to finish this!'

'Like you thought you finished me in the lab, Vampire?' Susan taunted. 'You should never underestimate our magic!'

'Lucas?' I drew closer, breath hitched and voice uneasy. I wasn't particularly used to or enamoured with the idea of Lucas in deliberate harm's way.

'Stay back, E. I've got this.'

'You're in the middle of two pissed off vampires-ish.'

'I am not a vampire!' Susan shrieked. She levelled her angry gaze upon me, lips curled into a snarl. 'The serum was never meant to make us vampires, it was meant to make us strong and immortal!'

'But you crave blood now too,' I answered slowly. 'That kinda makes you a vampire.'

'Never!' she cried, now wound up tighter than a Hills Hoist clothes line. 'I will never be like you.'

'Mum, it's Elena.'

'I know *who* and *what* she is.'

'I'm sorry, Susan. I'm sorry that I could never be the daughter that you wanted.'

She blinked, stance altering to play defence as she digested my attempted penance with an overly wrought sense of confusion plastered upon her face. Marcus compensated by shifting his feet for attack. 'What are you trying to do?'

I shook my head, moving yet another step closer. 'Nothing, I assure you. All I ever wanted, Susan, was acceptance. I never chose this life. I never wanted to be a vampire. I never wanted to be riddled with vânător blood. I just wanted to know I was safe. I wanted to live with you, George and Lucas in Cairns and just be a teenager.'

'It would have never worked,' she whispered, arms slowly lowering to her sides. She sniffed and wiped a bloodied hand across her forehead, softening her hardened composure. She realised her guard was slipping and abruptly readjusted her feet, pivoting only slightly to face me. 'Our world changed long before you were born, Elena. It was never going to end well for an enemy born into the clan.'

'We didn't have to be enemies, Susan. You were supposed to be my mother and raise me. You're the one who taught me to protect human life, to defend the weak and do what is right despite personal gain.'

'You're right, I did teach you that and I did try to protect you for as long as I could—but in the end—Chester knew about you and knew what you would one day become. I could never have stopped him without being excommunicated from the IMI.'

'And now?'

'And now Chester is dead.'

Lucas crumpled the shirt his mother was wearing between his fingers, pulling her closer to his face. His other hand still pressed Marcus back, but for how long was unknown. 'Then why are we still fighting?' He whispered to her. 'Why don't we end this? Chester is dead, society is crumbling. We *can* co-exist.'

She turned her vacant, carefully controlled expression upon him, leaning forward to kiss the top of his forehead with trembling lips. 'No, we can't, sweetheart.'

'Why can't we?'

'Because you can't save what has already been damned.'

Well wasn't that the truth.

Marcus had reached the end of his tether. A ferocious growl erupted from his puffed-out chest, exploding into an angry snarl. He twisted sideways, knocking Lucas's arm free and manoeuvring fast enough that he blurred further interception. Marcus was soon breathing Susan's air, fingers now wrapped tightly around her jugular. Talons disappeared into the quicksand of her flesh, blood falling like a steady stream down the column of her throat and the swell of her breasts.

Lucas screamed; a sound more haunting than I could amply describe. Tears welled and words were lodged somewhere in the pain seeking to barricade his throat. He was reaching— pleading, but Marcus had already crushed her windpipe.

Susan spent those last few minutes with her eyes transfixed on Lucas. No words would ever again pass her lips, but everything she had ever felt—ever fought for—was written in the depths of the fading light within those orbs. She had loved her son.

The warm blood of my own unexpected tears traced a wet path down my sunken cheeks. I was almost unaware of them, mesmerised and paralysed by the look of utter devastation now written upon Lucas's face. His eyes were red, salty tears filling their rims and erupting, lower lip trembling.

I wanted to reach out. I wanted to touch him, hold him and tell him that everything was going to be okay, but in the end we both knew the truth. There was no such thing as 'okay' anymore.

'What have you done?' Lucas croaked, wiping tears angrily from his cheeks. He shoved Marcus hard. 'That was my mother!'

'She was no mother,' Marcus uttered, reaching out to comfort him.

Appalled, Lucas slapped his hand away, sneering as he scuttled backwards, stopping only when he appeared to impact with something unseen. He looked up, swallowed and then backed away. His arms were defensively wide, head moving from side-to-side as his eyes searched seemingly nothing within the night sky.

'What is it, Lucas?' I asked.

'They're everywhere and I can't protect any of you now, I'm too weak!'

'What is everywhere?'

He shot me a look that spoke volumes. I suspected he considered me mentally defective in that moment. 'Are you kidding me?'

I reached for him, but was stopped by an invisible force. My limbs were rooted in concrete, each heavier and more immobile than the last, my flesh tingling with the touch of magic. I couldn't even warn Caleb and Marcus. My lips were frozen. I could only watch in horror as a strategic attack aided by magic stole from me what little hope I had left.

Lucas attempted a hasty defence, raining blows upon what looked like air, dodging the incoming bolts of streaking light, but finally took a blow to the back of the neck. He sunk to his knees, not nearly fast enough to assemble an offense or resist further attack.

There were apparently just too many to fend off.

I watched in morbid horror as Lucas was assaulted again, eyes shuttered and the ground coming forth to greet him in a very real way. Roofing concrete split his cheek and stole consciousness. All I could do was silently scream and pray that I would regain control over my body again soon.

My heart sunk and hope faded as a silver blade was plunged through the top of Marcus's exposed shoulder blade. Hidden by the *Revatarus* spell, there was no way he could have seen it coming.

He grappled for it, trying in haste to pull the poisonous metal free of his flesh. His cry of pain rang guttural and was laced with surprise. Before he could reconcile the damage and pull the blade free, another followed. The malicious tool spliced his mid-section, opening him from chest to belly button. Things you should never see tried to empty themselves from his insides before any form of self-healing could repair the damage.

He gripped his chest and fell to his knees. He too looked to be on a collision course with broken roof tile and flaking concrete before a fistful of his hair was knotted through fingers of an invisible force. Another blade now glistened against the reflection of the moon, hovering in a lethal promise in front of his throat. I tried to cry out. I tried to do anything other than stand and watch Marcus's impending death, but I was useless under the spell set upon me.

Caleb attempted to dodge any form of movement he heard coming as being able to *see* anything proved futile. He yelled out my name profusely, begging for help, but there was nothing I could do. Protector magic was infallible and the very reason the Vampires had been scared enough to create the Vânătors in defence.

I tried summoning telekinesis, throwing up temporary barriers of protection around Marcus, Caleb and Lucas. But since our assailants were many—their weapons and speed created for our demise and their magic a rather practiced and successful form of deathly permanence—it was only a matter of time.

Marcus's attacker was forced to relinquish his deathly grip, shiny weapon rendered useless as my bubble of power encompassed Marcus completely. He rolled onto his back, breathing hard, face panic-stricken as he clutched his innards, waiting to heal.

Caleb ceased spasmodic movement, aware that he too was now surrounded by safety and could take a second to compose and consider strategy. He inched cautiously to my side, eyes wild and searching, feet moving uncertainly across the rooftop.

Laughter that aimed to mock and unsettle erupted. We could see nothing, but could hear and feel their dominating presence. The streets below quivered with the same sense of unease. Howls, barks, cries of pain and unexpected tortured shouts of terror were verbal echoes of the thoughts of dread on replay inside my head. We had once again underestimated the IMI—underestimated their wrath for blood drinkers.

Agh …

Pain suddenly exploded through my entire right side. To scream would have provided an outlet. To look upon and press shaking hands upon the jagged portion of flesh torn open just below my ribs would have been an act of free will, but I couldn't. Their magic held sway and their weapons crumbled any sense of strength our vampirism had ever implied. I'd stupidly assumed that my lack of mobility—as a result of their magic—would be enough to avoid further backlash. I'd protected my friends and forgotten myself.

'Whatever you're doing to protect the others, I suggest you stop doing it now or we'll kill you too.'

This unexpected voice right before me was unnerving. I would have been startled if I could have moved. I also would have physically revolted given the chance, but with the silver blade still firmly lodged in my side and tickling my kidney, I was in no position to argue.

The stench of their breath and the scrape of fibres from rustled clothing indicated there were more Protectors in the vicinity than there were of us. Isolating senses to differentiate between position, size and ability was ineffectual. I was overwhelmed by the steady stream of my own escaping blood as it dripped upon the rooftop, only muffled by the screams of the injured or dying on the streets below.

'Did you hear me?' The man before me repeated.

Of course I'd heard him. I just couldn't bloody speak! And though my tongue tingled with a vicious rebuttal, my lips resisted. And yet, a mumble of slurred denials somehow managed to escape.

'Don't think us stupid, little girl. We've been studying your kind for centuries. We know what you can and cannot do. We know about your weakness for silver and direct sunlight. We also know about your telekinetic abilities thanks to Susan's reconnaissance.'

I could hardly deny the truth even if I wanted to. My telekinetic abilities were on display and our weakness for silver had already been proven. Now all we needed was to be staked and flambéed at sunrise and their hypothesis would be complete.

'We want you to surrender.'

I toyed with the idea of reanimation, wiggling my fingers and stretching those stubborn lips. A half-snarl may have formed and total movement was a distant promise, but I could feel my tongue again. 'N-never going happen.'

Another blade sought to taunt my unblemished left side, a threatening pledge of all that awaited if I continued to pose an obstacle. Granted I could have spun around when the spell wore off and possibly overthrown my attacker with brute strength, but without eyes on other would-be attackers, it was a mistake to overestimate my reach.

Yes.

I just admitted that.

God help me, I'm becoming … sensible.

Instead, I gathered focus from the pain in my side and channelled it into finally encompassing myself within a telekinetic barrier, ejecting the jutting blade in my side. It was difficult splitting my energies in four different directions, but nothing my pulsing head couldn't handle.

Now free of my silver encumberment, I started to rapidly heal. I just needed time to figure out our next move and how to survive.

A tremor to my left indicated attempts to penetrate the shield. Slicing the finely woven particles of air would prove ineffective for now. But, as another sharp object pressed for entry behind me, I knew I would eventually begin to weaken and thus become a pin cushion if I didn't find a way out of this mess soon.

'Clever trick,' The Protector said. 'But not very smart.'

Marcus climbed unsteadily back to his feet. His eyes fought with invisible soldiers as he tried to dodge fresh, incoming waves of attack. He was safe for the time being, but as he held the healing skin across his abdomen, it was clear he was unsure as to how long. He was very lucky he was a thrall and not a turned vampire, though his odds of escaping this mess were about as slim as mine despite his ability to heal.

'You will all die tonight,' the man said in a patient tone. 'There's no point pretending otherwise, so you might as well get back on the ground.'

Marcus now huddled defensively in front of Caleb and I, pressing closer and urging us back. His eyes moved as if he could see each of our opponents in minute detail, though I knew he couldn't. It was also the first time ever Marcus had stood to defend me. In the past, I'd taunted him by destroying his Barbara Streisand Cd's or taping over Project Runway with MTV. I felt semi-guilty about all that now as he attempted to protect the annoying brat I'd once been.

'Suit yourself, but I will kill, starting with the dark-haired vampire.'

Marcus and I took a second to assess one another from our peripherals. At any other time, it might have been amusing that as the two with dark hair we were wanted for target practice, but since neither of us had any intention of dying tonight, amusement remained vacant.

'My apologies,' the man continued, somewhere in front of us. 'I forgot you cannot see. I was referring to the male vampire. But you will all die. It's only a matter of time. I'm simply starting with the biggest threat first.'

That freaking bastard …

'We won't go down without a fight,' Caleb responded, chin jutting forth to prove the stubborn streak he'd developed during my comatose years. If *my* acid tongue had been completely operational, I would have nailed our assailant with an expletive explaining just how bigger threat I *could* be.

'Well, that's to be expected, though surely you don't think we'll go easy on you after you slipped into our city, into our territory? Look what you did to Susan. She has been a key member of the IMI for over thirty years and you killed her in front of her own son!'

'At least she fought us face-to-face. That's more than I can say for the coward that fights in shadow.' Caleb's chin now projected further than his nose.

'Are you not protecting yourself now, hiding in the shadow of *her* abilities?'

'The fight isn't fair,' I managed to eject before Caleb could answer.

'Life isn't fair, *little girl*.'

'What did you just call me?'

Laughter erupted—not just from the speaker—but others who seemed to have surrounded us on all sides. 'Wars are not won by children or those complaining about fairness. War is won through strategy.'

'Do not speak of what you do not understand!' Marcus sneered. 'I was a Legionnaire in the Roman Guard. I fought in countless battles for the Roman army. Do not tell me what war *is* or *how* it can be won. The IMI knows nothing about honour, integrity and justice. You seek power and death in a world that has seen far too much of it.'

'A pretty speech, vampire. But all we care about is ridding the world of your tainted blood. And, since we do have the upper hand—'

'Tainted blood?' Caleb muttered in disbelief. 'You do realise what's in that serum you all jack yourselves up with, don't you?'

'I'm tired of all the talking.' A long and over-exaggerated sigh signalled the end of the debate. I imagined there had been a dismissive wave of his hand to accompany the vocal outpouring of boredom. 'Continue to attack them until her shields grow weak. She can't protect them forever.'

A million taunting responses leapt to the tip of my tongue, but there were only three words I uttered in order to strengthen my resolve, 'Watch me, Asshole.'

CHAPTER TWENTY-ONE: ENOUGH

'**H**ow long can you protect us?' Caleb asked. He dared not look my way, but instead surveyed the area before us, hoping one of The Protectors would let their guard down and become visible.

I shook my head, not wanting to give any information to the enemy. 'As long as it takes,' I answered.

Marcus seemed to have more faith in my abilities and turned to look at me. He touched a blood-stained hand to the shielded area near my shoulder, a gesture of connection rather than a physical one. 'How long have you been awake?'

It seemed strange to have a Q and A now, but perhaps he figured since we were running on borrowed time, now was the time for a family update. 'Just over a fortnight.'

'I bet Lucius is ecstatic.' There was just a hint of sarcasm in his reply.

'And what about you? Everyone told me you left years ago.'

'Is this relevant?' Caleb pressed. 'I mean seriously,' he said, pointing all around us. 'We have bad guys wanting to play piñata with us.'

'I've been here—stuck in this facility,' Marcus answered, ignoring Caleb's call to the present. 'I was captured, starved and permanently imprisoned. I tried many times to escape, but couldn't.'

I overcame the golf ball lump in my throat only to choke out what must have sounded like a horrendous excuse in the face of Marcus's past and present situation. 'Everyone thought you'd left by choice. If they'd known—known you were abducted, I'm sure they would have come looking for—'

'Save it,' Marcus snapped. 'Circumstances being what they are and freedom seemingly out of reach, the past is irrelevant.'

'Which is completely fuc—'

'Caleb!'

'What? Do you see a way out of this? We can't fight what we can't see, and we can't smell them because of the serum. We are trapped. There's no way to get the upper hand unless we can—'

I reflexively lashed out at both of them. Marcus abhorred the hand that pressed against his chest, Caleb huffed at the interruption as I grabbed at the space near his wrist. In that moment I cared little for words or penance. Lucas was being hauled to his feet, still unconscious, a trickle of blood running down the side of his neck.

'No,' I breathed, shakily raising my hands in some form of surrender. I had to erect another barrier around Lucas, but it was tentative at best with whoever was holding him upright and threatening his life.

'Don't bother trying!' A hidden Protector shouted. 'If you attempt to save this one, I'll slit his throat.' The cut now dangerously close to Lucas's jugular seemed to grow in width and more blood flowed anew. 'Is that really what you want?'

What I want?

'Elena, we can't stay like this,' Marcus whispered. 'Lucas is one of their own and will probably be safe for now. They do—however—want to hurt us. Conserve what energy you have before—'

'I can't think about that.' I wasn't ready to surrender Lucas to their grasp without all the fight left within me completely milked.

'You have to,' he urged. 'Right now, we are three and strong. Soon you will be useless and Caleb and I will likely end up slaughtered.'

'Nice,' Caleb mocked. 'That's real nice.'

'Do not make light of this!' Marcus hissed. 'You don't know what they are capable of!'

'Don't we?' Caleb taunted. A single eyebrow shot heavenward. It was a stare down likely to merge into a full comparison of notes if I didn't heed the warning.

'What do you want me to do?'

'You may not be able to see them, but that shouldn't stop you from being able to move the earth right under their feet.'

'I feel a song coming on,' Caleb muttered. He clicked his fingers to an invisible beat and bobbed his head from side to side. He could never be serious for long.

While Marcus attempted to side-swipe him through the barrier, I focused my attention on the cracked concrete of the rooftop beneath our feet. I'd never attempted such a feat of telekinetic power, but Marcus was right. While the advantage currently swayed in their favour, I could reverse the odds with a bit of concentration.

The ground began to split underfoot like Grandma's pants after several helpings of choc-chip cookie dough ice-cream. Fissures opened as long as my arms, widening with every second that passed. Someone yelled something about an earthquake. The smart ones blamed me, though I noticed their voices drifted as if they moved further away from us.

Lucas was abandoned in pursuit of their own life-saving ventures. His left leg was eagerly swallowed by one of the prevailing cavities, his upper body now perched precariously on the edge. I was encouraged by both Marcus and Caleb to keep at it—an easy task if it weren't for my brother teetering on the edge of ultimate demise.

The roof really began to shake with purpose. Chunks of concrete broke away, falling into the enlarged crevices I'd constructed or catapulting into the street far down below. The fear of Mother Nature's interference subsided quickly and The Protectors researched the options within their arsenal once more. Magic was potent and undeniably strong as it repeatedly tested my defences and those of my companions.

Someone screamed as I dismantled the north-west quadrant of the building, bricks and rubble raining mercilessly upon the street below. I must have caught a Protector in the crossfire, but the shouts of panic faded as quickly as their bout of stupidity. It would only take them seconds to invoke a levitation spell to save them from certain death.

I heard them running in all directions, attacking often and scrambling for the upper hand against our defence. Caleb and Marcus crouched defensively, preparing for an attack should my mind grow weak. Lucas was waking.

He rubbed dirtied fingers across his bleary vision until he was sitting up, surveying the scene in front of him. He immediately edged back from the crack in the rooftop that threatened to swallow him whole. He then investigated the back of his head where he'd been struck. Fresh blood painted a picture across his

311

flesh. He rubbed it between his fingers, disorientated and yet undoubtedly piecing together happenstance.

Our eyes met. He opened his mouth as if to say something, but then stopped. His nostrils flared and his eyes lost focus and closed. Concern warred within me until a small, unexpected smile took up residence upon his lips.

The picture became clear as Marianne abruptly cleared the side of the disintegrating building and landed in a defensive crouch near Lucas. She threw her blonde locks back and roared like a lioness protecting her cubs. Her tonsils vibrated and saliva dripped with hungry intensity from the tips of her fangs. Eyes black as pitch and skin transparent, she amassed thin lines of blue blood starved of life, displayed like delicate spider webs under her flesh. The predator within was unveiled and her talons sort to lash out at anyone posing to encroach on her plans.

In a hailstorm of colour, the rooftop suddenly lit up like a Christmas tree. Magic flew in every direction, weakening me, but ultimately seeking out the unsheltered prey. Marianne managed to dodge almost every attack. She moved with the grace of a gazelle and the speed inherited by the cheetah. She was powered by purpose and love—Lucas her only focus other than surviving long enough to aid escape.

Gashes opened on her exposed arms and face. Blood poured freely from every wound inflicted, but it never slowed her down.

'She's like a woman possessed,' Caleb murmured, watching as she then dove over the mammoth dividing fissure in the centre of the building only to land lithely by Lucas's side.

'She's going to get killed,' Marcus muttered.

'She's doing what I should have been able to do for Sebastian.'

Caleb eyeballed me. I didn't want to meet his empathetic gaze and therefore avoided any emotion I might have found there. He never said anything for which I was grateful. It was hard enough to be confronted with the strength of Marianne's resolve, to know that she would die for my brother, risk her life again and again and I'd never got a chance to do the same for Sebastian.

You can save him ... Araqiel whispered through my mind. *All you have to do is go back to the very beginning.*

But then I'd be robbing Marianne and Lucas of their chance.

Do you think Soul mates are a new concept? Isn't it possible that Lucas and Marianne might find each other again?

But if I go right back to the beginning—before creation, before the fall—there is no Marianne and Lucas. There is no me, no Caleb, no Marcus … no one.

There was nothing but silence within.

'Hey, Blondie,' Lucas said, cupping her chin between his fingers. 'I'm glad you came looking for me.'

'I hate it when you call me that,' she replied, quickly pulling him into her now ravaged arms. 'We have to get out of here. This whole thing was a trap.'

Lucas's smile dimmed. He shoved Marianne hard, rolling them both sideways until he deemed it safe to return to his feet. He urged Marianne to stay behind him, but she was having none of it. 'You stay the hell away from her,' Lucas shouted.

'They must be surrounding them,' Caleb said, pointing out the obvious. 'Use your telekinesis, Lucas!'

When it came to protecting anyone Lucas loved, he'd always attempted to be several steps ahead. Fresh waves of magic already rebounded off the newly formed barrier around himself and Marianne. I was more grateful than ever that our blood exchange as kids had endowed Lucas with prolonged mortality and a large margin of self-defence.

'Can you make our attackers visible?' Marcus shouted. The three of us hadn't done much more than stand there under the protection of my mind and hoped a better plan presented itself.

'They aren't parlour tricks, Marcus. I can't pick up the concrete dust and blow it in their faces hoping it will give us an outline. Our magic doesn't work like that. If they want to be invisible, they will be, whether we can reach out and touch them or not.'

'That doesn't make any sense.'

Lucas was shaking his head, clearly not in the mood to debate logistics with the old vampire. Marianne rolled her eyes and then ducked as a concrete pipe rammed the area near her ribs.

'Options?' Caleb asked.

'Bring the building down on top of them.' Marcus apparently had it all figured out.

'There'll still be more where they came from when we hit the street.'

'One battle at a time,' Marcus argued. I actually agreed. At this point, anything was better than standing around and waiting to die.

'Lucas,' I shouted, 'levitate!'

'Can we levitate?' Caleb quickly acknowledged the look on my face, nodding. 'Right. So, we're in for a rough landing?'

'Do it!' Marcus commanded. 'We can heal from whatever injury is inflicted.'

'Yeah, but while we're healing it means we're not run—'

The rooftop underfoot became as unstable as butter in the microwave. The three of us slipped through the molten portions of concrete, cascading to the floors below. My head was pounding and time was running out. At least Lucas and Marianne appeared safe for now, hovering above the destruction and free of being buried under eight stories of rubble.

Caleb, Marcus and I jumped from crumbling brick to erupting formwork as the building rapidly folded in on itself. For now, we were dexterous enough to avoid any real injury, but it was as short-lived as the ill-conceived idea of outrunning invisible, magical assailants.

'Elena!' Lucas screamed from above. 'They're levitating too. It's not going to work!'

'I don't know what else to do!' It was true. I could barely circumnavigate torpedo photocopiers and busted toilet bowls that fell out of the eight stories crumbling around us.

'We have to find Karina. She and I are the only ...' he stopped, distracted.

We hit the ground, scrambling to steer clear of any residual office equipment or earthworks determined to show us the true death. I kept trying to ensure the three of us were protected with my mind, but I needed to understand what had happened to Lucas and thus my carefully erected barriers did fail.

In the midst of peril, all I could hear was laughter. We were surrounded by the dead—mostly our own—the sounds of battle had been replaced with triumphant arrogance. The Protectors outnumbered and had outplayed us and they totally knew it.

'First rule of Protector training, Lucas: Always watch your back.'

I searched the sky for him and Marianne. Something had clearly occurred and I had no way to fix it. 'Lucas?' I shouted, concern riding me hard. I finally caught sight of him way above. He was facing Marianne, holding her rigid form against him. Was she caught in a trance?

'Magic?' Caleb asked under his breath. He dusted off his knees, but remained as vigilant as the rest of us. I had no answer. I was still trying to figure out what I'd missed.

As Lucas tried to shake life into Marianne, a thin line appeared at the base of her neck, expanding rapidly to reveal sinew and muscle as her jugular collapsed and blood flowed like the Hoover dam down the column of her throat. With another desperate shake, Lucas was unaware that it spelled fatality. Marianne's head slid from her shoulders, tumbling towards the earth and towards us.

I bit back bile as what had once been a beautiful face connected with the pavement to our right and exploded in a puddle of bone, brain matter and blood. The rest was still captive in Lucas's shaking hands. The truth of the situation appeared stripped of any sort of realism as he gaped, horrified that her life had somehow been stolen in the blink of an eye.

My mouth was suddenly dry as I stared at what was left of Marianne on the broken pavement beside me. Surprise, anger and revulsion were present. I was lost for words and the meaning of this senseless situation. Caleb and Marcus were as silent as the dead, both transfixed on the horror and as equally confused as I was.

Lucas then plummeted to the earth. His torturous scream did not sound his impending death, but rather the agony that writhed within. The grief was such that he no longer cared to protect himself and thus, simply gave up …

Inaction didn't suit me and I quickly serviced the debris around us to provide some sort of cushioning to obstruct a fateful landing. 'Lucas, please don't do this. Help me save you.'

'What's the point?' he sobbed.

'Lucas!'

He stopped mid-air, his body virtually folding in half with the abruptness of his exit from gravity's hold. A Protector must have seized him with magic—and although I was grateful he no longer fell to his death—I suspected it didn't matter given his current state of mind.

'Just kill me.' They were the exact words I didn't want to hear and yet completely resonated with. 'Nothing matters anymore.'

'Lucas!'

The *Revatarus* spell was uttered among our would-be attackers. Hope was lost as our invisible assailants finally dissolved the illusion that had kept them hidden from sight. There were so many, most of them crowded around the three of us, weapons in hand and poised for attack. Two flanked Lucas several meters above us; one I assumed was our vocal tormentor. He snatched Lucas up by the scruff of the neck, pressing a silver blade against the column of his throat.

Tears blanketed Lucas's sodden face, eyes empty and devoid of any fight or will to live. I knew those eyes. I knew those eyes very well and absolutely forbade my big brother from having them. I didn't care that our situation seemed hopeless. Lucas simply couldn't give up. Not now.

'Lucas, don't do this,' I pleaded, hiccupping with emotion as my own too-wide eyes began to fill with blood. 'I can't do this without you. I lost Sebastian. I can't lose you too.'

He looked down at me, but there was nothing there. 'Then you know how this feels.'

I kicked a loose brick into the dilapidated remains of the building I'd destroyed. Fear, frustration and helplessness were crippling my usual powers of persuasion.

Caleb reached for me with an urgency I'd never known, wrapping his arms around me so tight it was almost as if he knew what I would try to do next. 'Don't you do this to me! Don't you *dare* do this to me!'

'I'm sorry, E … I just … I can't.'

'You're being weak!' I screamed. 'We don't have time for weakness. We weren't trained to be weak!'

'Make it quick,' Lucas whispered to his captor.

'We were hoping you would join us.'

'I have nothing left to give.'

'Stop talking to him!'

'Elena, Lucas knows what he's doing,' Caleb murmured against my ear. The fact that Caleb squeezed his vice-like arms even tighter around me only served to instil yet more panic. Dread

316

battered the sides of my composure, threatening to burst forth in a fountain of despair.

'It's such a waste of talent,' The Protector continued, his dark, beady eyes surveying his peers and drawing comparisons. 'You have abilities we could learn from.'

'I don't care.'

'Lucas! Please do something to save yourself. This is not what Marianne would want!'

'I'm sorry, E.'

My scream of unending torment echoed across the entire city, filling the streets with the note of horror we'd tried so desperately to avoid. Over all the cries for help, shouts of torment and whimpers of pain, I heard only my voice. The shrill horror penetrated the very essence of the wind and carried it in every direction for all to hear.

As I watched the blade wielded by our greatest enemy slice through flesh and spill my brother's blood and life in every direction, the rest of my heart and soul died. Lucas gasped for air that would never again come, crumpling in defeat. He never fought to survive. He simply gave up.

Droplets of his blood fell, painting my forehead and branding me with the consequences of all our actions. It tickled my flesh with its fading warmth and filled me with an anger so potent it was no surprise that I soon sprouted hair and looked at the world through canine eyes.

I'd fought so long and so hard to triumph over The Protectors, the Vânători and even the demons of death. My reasons for fighting for so long had diminished within the blink of an eye and I suddenly felt the weakness that had overcome Lucas. I wanted to give up, forfeit life or this 'unlife' and be done with this charade that seemed so much harder than death itself.

So much had been lost, but there was one last option and it wasn't in my nature to give up entirely. I was lost in a sea of misery, swimming to find the surface of clarity, but there was also nothing left to fight for on this plane of reality.

So, I did the only thing left I could think of.

I threw my head back and howled for Araqiel.

It was time to change the future and right the wrongs of the past.

CHAPTER TWENTY-TWO: TIMELINE

Over time I'd come to feel comfortable in the darkness, the way it hid the body in shadow, blighted memories of the present and distorted ideals of the future. It was a secret place of denial—a place I could turn my mind vacant and forget the search for the light. And sometimes, I just didn't want to be found. This was one of those times.

I fought to keep my eyes closed. I figured if I hid behind the soft flesh of my lids, I wouldn't have to face reality. Reality was a cruel place full of pain and a truth I wasn't quite ready to endure. But light found a path, creeping under my lashes and delicate fingers pried their way inside and filled my vision with layers of white.

The first thing I noticed were my feet. They were absent of dirt, blood and the downy fur of my vânător half. They were human, covered in strappy, white heels that wrapped around my ankles and half way up my calves. Following that line of vision revealed the pressed hemline of a plain white dress that grazed my knees, scooped in at the hips and tightened around the bodice. With arms bare, fingernails conveniently manicured and hair perfectly coiffured, I might have assumed this a dream.

I knew better.

I was in the waiting room; the white box that keeps you captive until your spirit guide appears and moves you on to Purgatory. How I knew this to be true, I wasn't sure.

Memories—often dangerous to allow to trickle forth—in this instance were welcomed. Perhaps it was returning here that amplified the past and applied the logic hidden in truth. Or perhaps it was the thought of being so close to where Sebastian was that allowed the current pressures in my mind to recede.

Recollection was clear which should have been impossible. Araqiel had said I should never remember even a skerrick of detail from Purgatory, but I now believed when you were in love with the Archangel, anything was possible.

I rubbed my hands up and down the bare flesh of my arms, smiling for what felt like the first time in ages. I then pressed a finger to those upturned lips, recalling my time in Purgatory with Sebastian with a desperate longing to reclaim the past. I still felt his arms around me, his mouth everywhere and his body swimming through my flesh. I had given Sebastian everything—my life and body. I'd briefly touched true happiness and then crash landed with a choice to head back to earth.

I'd wanted to protect Lucas. I'd given up an eternity with Sebastian and traded it for the meagre hope that my presence in Lucas's life may have made a difference. I'd naively believed that I could stop The Protectors, end the war and create some sort of preferential peace. Instead, I'd stepped into a fight that didn't really need me. I'd let Lucas down anyway, wrongly assuming that he'd choose life over love—and yet—I'd done the very same thing.

Now here I was in the waiting room again, undoubtedly dead in the real world.

'You're not dead,' Araqiel mused in that quiet, contemplative tone he often adopted to address me. He stood in the corner of the room that appeared to have no doors.

'Well, I assumed because I'm in the waiting room again ...'

'You're waiting for me,' he answered matter-of-factly. The crisp white suit he always wore practically disappeared into the backdrop. If he blinked, I feared he'd disappear completely.

I picked at the hem of my dress now, head slightly bowed. I knew what I wanted to ask, but almost certainly understood it was off topic and would change absolutely nothing. 'So, if I'm not dead ...'

'You will not be going back to Purgatory.'

'So, there's absolutely no chance that—'

'No.'

I took a minute to fully digest that little nugget of information, knowing that as the last vestige of my waning hope was absorbed, I'd never get a second chance to see Sebastian—to let him know that ...

'He knows you love him.'

I nodded, keeping my eyes averted lest they betray my true feelings. 'About Lucas ...'

'No, Elena.'

'You don't even know what I was going to say!'

'You're going to ask me about his fate.'

'I don't believe in fate,' I mumbled.

Araqiel closed the distance between us and rested heavy hands upon my shoulders, waiting patiently until I looked into his silver-flecked eyes. 'If the word offends you then that is okay, but let's not pretend I don't know what it is you're really asking me.'

I begrudgingly met his gaze. All the doubt, sickness and fear that had roiled around in the pit of my stomach since Lucas's death now flourished in the depths of my blood-stained eyes. It was raw and it was pure. 'I need to know if he's like me, Araqiel. Will he be judged as I was?'

'It is almost certain.'

A breath I hadn't even known I held was expelled in a rush of pure relief. Lucas's death was not an ideal situation, but at least I now knew that with his tainted blood—my blood running through his veins—he was neither a suitable candidate for heaven or hell. He'd find some semblance of peace in Purgatory; maybe find Sebastian and Kayla if she hadn't already been judged and moved on.

Araqiel's fingers curled around my shoulders, stiffening. He was skimming my thoughts, working through my deductions and coming to his own conclusions. I may not have noticed it if it weren't for my vampiric sensibilities and the change in tension I could practically pluck from the air and feed upon.

'What is it?'

'You've decided, haven't you?'

I started to lower my head again, but he caught my chin between his fingers and held fast. There was no avoiding this. 'I'm sorry. I just wanted to make sure he wasn't suffering or that he'd tried to go after Marianne.'

'Hell might not take him now, but you also know the strength and commitment of love. He will eventually find a way to her and if not, strike a deal with one of the Demons for passage.'

My relief ebbed as quickly as it had attempted to restore calm. 'What sort of deal?'

'One that I very much suspect Michael will try and aid him in.' His angelic face remained impassive. How could he be so composed in delivering this timeline of veritable disaster?

I shook my head, freeing myself from Araqiel's pinching grip. 'No. Sebastian would never submit to a rematch with Lucifer simply to allow Marianne and Lucas to be reunited.' I kept shaking my head, the action rooted mostly in the fear that I could be wrong.

'Are you sure?'

'The fate of the entire world balanced on the happiness of my brother and his vampiric lover? There's no way. Sebastian would never—'

'Is this why you called me?' Araqiel interrupted. 'Did you want to talk about the possibilities of the world's demise with Michael and your brother's misery behind the helm?'

'No, I just … I wanted to make sure that while I was making decisions about the past, present and future, Lucas wasn't suffering.'

Araqiel moved away, crossing his arms in front of his chest. He began to pace, slow and considered with every step. 'So, you're telling me you've decided?'

Another one of those shaky breaths filled my lungs with uncertainty. There was no turning back now. 'Yes, I'm going to use the Time Contract.'

Araqiel stopped mid-stride, his entire face lighting up with wonder. The smile that followed dazzled with luminosity, all teeth on display and skin glowing with radiance. A sight to behold? It was both perplexing and frightening to see the very depths of his eyes sparkle with possibilities—unknowns I could never interpret. 'And do you believe this is the right decision?'

My brows began to furrow. 'What? I thought this is what you wanted?'

'Oh, it is, but as a divine entity I'm not supposed to persuade you on any one decision, simply offer you the possibilities and pray that you make good choices …' Those all-knowing, glee-injected orbs now narrowed upon me. His beaming smile lingered, but caution was present. 'Selfish motivations will not ensure true happiness. Remember that.'

'Believe me, where I'm planning on going, I won't have a say anymore.'

'Excellent. I am pleased that you have thought about everything I've said, taking into account Lucifer's mistakes, Michael's fall and the impact it had on everyone.' His smile was growing wider by the second. 'To go right back to the very beginning is to reverse every wrong—every humanised mistake ever to plague the world with sadness, hunger, poverty, violence and war.'

'Araqiel, I promise I have weighed up everything you've ever said to me, but—'

'No, no no!' he said, rushing forward in panic to clamp a hand around my lips. 'You cannot reason your decision out loud, not now that you have finally made it.' He released me slowly, reaching inside the breast pocket of his suit, extracting the Time Contract and the Quill of destiny. 'You must write it down and you must be very specific about what it is that you want to change.'

He gingerly handed me both items, the hum of their power crawling over my skin in the form of static electricity. Every hair stood on its end as that ripple of divine intervention rolled through me. I wasn't sure that Araqiel would understand or be happy with my decision. After all, my choices were generally disasters waiting to happen.

So far, my thoughts and feelings had played far too heavier role in the process. I worried that I'd already tainted outcomes by forcing the IMI's hand, the Vânätors, the Vampires and the human race into a web of deceit and constant discontent. I might not fare any better now. If I went back to the beginning, that would also be my decision, but I'd also be leaving 'fate'—as everyone believed it to be—in the hands of no one I trusted or loved.

Yes. I was going to go back—not to creation—but back to before this mess began. I planned on putting this notion of 'fate' back into the hands of the person who was robbed of it. I was going to give them a second chance at the life they *should* have led.

'Are you ready?' Araqiel asked, his hands practically rubbing together in satisfaction. He clicked his fingers and a table appeared, followed by a chair that he chivalrously held out for me. It was an invitation for me to take my place and change the course of history.

I sat down, affording him a look insisting privacy. I really needed to choose my words carefully as I had but one chance to get this right. Having Araqiel peer over my shoulder as I penned an alternate outcome for life as we knew it spelled certain failure.

Thankfully he seemed to understand and backed away, moving into the corner from where he'd appeared, offering the space I so desperately desired. 'Take your time, Elena,' he murmured. 'You're about to change everything, so it matters not how long the present lingers without you.'

'Just shut up, okay? I need to think.' I pointed an accusatory finger at him. 'And don't go poking around in my head.'

'It is forbidden at this point.'

'Good.'

I placed the Quill of Destiny on the table top and proceeded to carefully unfold the parchment. There was a lot of empty space at the top of the page, assumedly for me to write the changes I was planning on making. At the bottom was the fine print—contractual obligations.

I started to read over it very carefully. It stated that I was the chosen half-blood and that my decree in this instance was final and unchangeable. It also mentioned my past would be wiped along with my memory, but I'd heard that crap before. There was nothing in this world that would ever again allow me to forget Sebastian, Lucas or my father; even the annihilation of my existence. I would hang onto the memories of my past and etch them into the fibres of my heart for all eternity. If I'd done it once, I could do it again. In fact, I'd write it into the agreement if I had to.

'You haven't written anything yet,' Araqiel whispered.

I looked up at him, frowning. 'I'm reading the fine print.'

'It will make no difference if you are summoning a time before creation.'

'Is this you shutting up?'

He blinked, swallowed his answer and went back to his casual pose against the corner wall. He seemed so certain with my choice. It was yet more proof why decisions of this magnitude should not have been left in my hands.

I picked up the quill, fairly quivering with nerves. It took me several efforts to position it for writing. I had to stop myself from drilling a hole in the page with my jerky movements.

I stopped, closed my eyes and took several deep breaths until I felt more human and settled with the choices I was making. I steadied my hand against the page—waited for the quaking to ebb—then meticulously thought through every word before transcribing. I knew Araqiel watched on, his mind undoubtedly whirring with possibilities, but I had to ignore him and any creeping doubts that may have lingered. I'd been thinking about this for a while and now I had my chance to make this right … better.

Words flowed easier than expected. I took myself out of the equation and concentrated on constructing an image begetting violence and self-induced hatred. I smoothed out rough edges and crafted a new world based on the deletion of a specific incident in time. I made sure every detail was covered—no matter how minor. I reassured myself with the quill, double checking and triple checking the adjustments I was making.

When I was done, I placed the quill back on the table. I read over everything again and then folded my hands in my lap. I stared at my handiwork, my mind now blank and my conscience clear. Things were going to change, but it was no longer in my hands. They were free to rest in my lap unhindered—free to accept the choices of others older, wiser and more mature to make them.

'Are you finished?' Araqiel asked quietly.

'I'm waiting for the big bang.'

He smirked. 'You just need to sign it.'

'And then what?'

'And then everything changes.'

'Just like that?'

He nodded. 'Just like that.'

I looked down at my feet, uncertain what to say or do in the face of a situation of this magnitude. 'I don't suppose I can take these shoes with me?'

'Shoes are irrelevant now.'

'I guess so. I'm just nervous.'

'You've made the right decision, Elena.'

'How would you know?' I said, cocking my head to the side, eyeballing him suspiciously.

'It's why I chose you.'

'Blah blah. You needed a half-blood and as far as I know, I'm the only one around.'

'That's true, but I could have left you alone to grow up with The Protectors.'

'That might have been preferable.'

'Perhaps.'

I sighed, lowered my eyes from the too-happy angel and focused back on the Time Contract. This was it—the moment when everything would change. Once I signed my name on that dotted line, the world would be a very different place.

Courage, Elena. I told myself. *Just one last time you need to be brave and then it will all be over.*

Another exhalation of nerves saw my fingers reach for the quill one final time. I clasped it tightly and pressed its inky tip against the parchment ... and signed my name. My stomach dropped and my skin tingled with discomfort. I started to reach for Araqiel, voice caught in my throat as he faded right before me. His confident smile was the last thing I saw as I plummeted.

The chair, the table, the white room were all left behind. Everything disappeared and I fell so fast that the wind stopped trying to keep pace. Darkness shrouded my path and my skin wreathed like it was itching to leave my body. I felt everything slipping into the cradle of midnight, swallowed by the power of my intent and the indeterminable path of the future.

The darkness was all consuming, a blanket so thick that I couldn't breathe. I could no longer think, see or feel. I was nothing. I was no more.

I was ... the past.

CHAPTER TWENTY-THREE: AWAKENING

'**Y**ou do realise that father is going to have my head for encouraging this sort of behaviour, Elena?'

I snorted my disbelief, nervously reaching up to ensure my hair was still in place. The long curtain of silk was pulled tightly against my head, a Roman helmet hiding its length from curious spectators. I still felt uneasy. Despite best attempts to hide my femininity, my skin was too smooth, mouth too delicate and eyes framed by lashes altogether too long and dark to be plausibly masculine.

Lucius flicked the side of the helmet, the ring of metal echoing in my ears. 'You look ridiculous. No one is going to believe for a second that you are a man.'

I fingered the hem of the tunic I'd stolen from my father's belongings and the cloak wrapped tightly across my shoulders. Despite my brother's lack of confidence, I did look like any other Roman soldier; albeit donning a pair of long slender legs that were most definitely belonging to a woman ... or Marcus.

I snickered at the thought and then quickly sobered. 'I don't really have a choice, Lucius. I do not want to get married and breed as the other women do. I don't want to watch idle theatre and pass the time at the bath house all day. I want to be a part of something—anything besides marriage.'

Lucius chuckled, blonde hair bouncing in jest with his movements. 'Elena, you *are* seventeen.'

'So?'

'So, you are getting old. You should have been married with children by now.'

Snorting was turning into a pastime. A dismissive eyeroll quickly followed. 'It's not like you can talk. Here I am pretending to be *you* while *you* sneak off to the city to study philosophy.'

'I do not want to be a soldier and I never asked you to take my place.'

'Make love, not war. Is that it?'

He sighed, reaching out to stroke the side of his horse's mane. It yanked itself free of his touch and the hold of his reins, bending down to delight in the taste of dried grass instead. My horse quickly followed suit, clearly impatient by our lack of movement. 'Look, I don't want to follow in father's footsteps. Don't get me wrong he is a great man; a respected general and a force to be reckoned with among senate members, but I do not see this as the life I wish to lead.'

'Lucius, sometimes I think we may have been switched at birth.'

'You make a terrible man,' my brother answered, a smile returning to his face. 'You argue like one, but you are still far too beautiful.'

'Alas you already make a beautiful woman,' I returned with an evil grin. 'Your long blonde hair, delicate fingers and gentle words … I've always wondered if perhaps mother had not been sly in her youth.'

'Be silenced,' Lucius said, slapping the side of my helmet this time. 'I could still tell father what you are up to, not that anyone is going to believe for a second that you are a Roman soldier. I do not know why you keep trying like this.'

'I have to try.'

'Why is it so important to you?'

I shrugged. 'I do not know. I simply feel like I was born to fight.'

'But you *are* a woman.'

'*Spoken* by the man with tousled locks studying philosophy. Are you sure you and Marcus aren't … Whoa!'

Lucius had leant back and slapped the rear end of my horse. It reared up onto its back legs causing me to pitch forward violently, clutching at the reins tighter and squeezing my thighs together just to stay on board. 'Be gone with you, Sister. And try not to get yourself killed!'

My horse lurched forward, hooves bearing against the ground with abrasive impact. I straightened, eyes squinting as the wind leapt forth to greet me, but I refused to let go. I rode with the gallop, moving my body in time with the horse's movements, utterly determined I would ride into the training camp with my head held high if I couldn't get the mare to steady its eager pace.

I clutched the reins tighter as we both found an even momentum. The mare now surrendered to my commands and eased back, turning the gallop into a trot. I could see again. The wind had ceased its pursuit to rob me of clear sight and my derriere was enamoured by the reprieve. My slender thighs continued to cramp, unable to relinquish my cautious hold completely.

I blinked several times to moisten my eyes. The training camp loomed ahead. Weathered canvas made appearance through the thicket of trees and lower bushes. Flags emblazoned with the Roman insignia decorated the apex of every tent, the sound of persistent grunting and fatigue signalled the mass of men honing their craft.

War or its implementation of strategy was always the agenda. Even when idle—as we currently were—The Roman Empire was never impotent, proving worth through city protection or consistently training should the seasons turn the winds of change and unrest become a reality. I wanted very much to be part of something with greater meaning. I wanted very much to exceed my father's expectations of me as a woman and conquer as any man would do in my stead.

Steeling my self-doubt, I bobbed my head in greeting to a few archers gathering stray arrows lost to the forest. As their eyes drifted over my tunic and finally rested on the smooth legs that clutched my horse between them, I knew my guise would soon be revealed. Lucius had been right. There was no way anyone was going to believe I was a man. Yet, I was possessed to continue in the hopes that I could prove myself to anyone who'd previously doubted me.

A break in the forest opening saw me guide the mare down a dirt path veering into a clearing littered with even more tents. Here there were hundreds of men, each purposed with a different activity but actively working as a well-trained unit. On the fringe were the slaves of the officers, tending to the hastily erected tent structures or preparing lunches over slowly simmering fires. Moving closer, there were those embracing hand-to-hand combat both celebrated by the leering cheers of their comrades or the cries of the fallen. There were more archers here; arrows flew high overhead into targets I imagined buried deep within the forest from which I'd come.

Most paid no heed to my approach, continuing with whatever task they were currently immersed. Those that did look up regarded me with caution; first appraising my uniform before hastily dispatching their suspicion for acceptance. Any eyes that lingered longer than necessary clearly weighed up the discrepancies of my physicality, indicative by furrowed brows. Thankfully, they were often quickly side-tracked by earlier tasks—much to my relief.

I pulled hard on the reins, directing the horse to a stop before dismounting and patting her affectionately on the rump. I straightened my stance, kept my head held high and concentrated particularly hard on trying not to walk like a girl.

'Soldier!' a somewhat vaguely familiar voice came from behind. 'What business do you have here?'

I froze in my tracks, unsure how to proceed. I hadn't thought this far ahead. I hadn't planned on speaking at all. I'd naively thought I could jump into a fight like I'd done last time and stir up the men enough for them to forget I was an oddity; shorter, slender and a hell of a lot prettier than the scar-ravaged faces surrounding me. 'I've come to train,' I finally emitted, voice lowered several octaves.

I sounded like an idiot.

'In what field do you specialise? I do not recognise you.'

I turned slowly, hand reaching into my tunic and under the cloak to reveal a blade of perfectly crafted steel. It had been a present from my father a few years ago. He'd wanted me to gift it to my husband on our wedding day. As far as I was concerned, that was a waste of good weaponry and a clear push towards a life I strongly did not support or intend to fulfil.

'Swords,' I said, casually swinging the blade around before us. It was both a warning to stay back and a show of handling skill. 'I am a proficient fighter.'

I had to stop myself from cringing and showing any signs of outrage as the soldier looked back at me with clear disbelief. No more than fifteen or sixteen years of age, he had short dark hair with piercing emerald eyes and a strong jaw crafted like a sculptor's masterpiece. He also had incredibly distracting lips, so supple and pink he made beautiful seem an inadequate description.

I began slicing the blade through the air to furthermore impress upon him my skill and clear any doubt from my own mind and hopefully his. Yes, I looked like a sparrow in comparison to

330

the flock of men close by, but I figured perception could be altered if the skillset warranted the attention more.

He continued to look upon me with disparaging inadequacy. I silently fumed. Yes, I was a woman or perhaps a feeble man in his eyes, but I was almost certain that I could take him down with simply a flick of my wrist. However, his lingering disbelief made me consider turning heel and running. For one, I found him attractive and familiar in a way that threw me a little off my game. And two, his undisguised judgement made my blood boil. He was younger, probably not as well trained and yet had been permitted to rank because of a high-ranking father or sibling.

And of course, he was a man.

'I must go,' I muttered, pulling my gaze from his.

'Where are you going?' he asked, catching my arm in long, slender fingers that wrapped almost entirely around my bicep. I really needed to eat more meat.

I kept my eyes averted and hastily attempted to yank free of his grasp. Distraction key, I pointed my sword at a ring of men not too far. 'Over there. There's a fight with my name on it.'

'And what would that name be?' my captor persisted, fingers tightening on what he must have thought were chicken arms.

'Lucius,' I said, shaking free. 'Lucius Valerius.'

'The very same name as our general? I do not think so.'

He attempted to apprehend me again, but I sidestepped him, twisting around so that I appeared at his side, my blade now pressed against his throat. I may have been small, but I was fast. 'Lucius *is* my father,' I added, almost choking on the extra low octave I was trying to achieve. I coughed, cleared my throat and tried again. 'I am his son and I've been taught since birth to defend myself so think very clearly about your next move.'

The soldier seemed to relax in my grip, breathing a sigh of relief. 'He speaks of you often, Lucius, though he has also spoken of your disimpassioned view of the Roman army.'

'My father does not know that I am here today and I would like to keep it that way.'

'Why would you keep such a secret?'

'I wish to surprise him with my skill.' I let the soldier go, clutching the sword in my hand and making tracks towards the men up ahead.

'My name is Volusius Marcellus,' he said, falling into step beside me.

'Tiberius's youngest son?' I asked, my surprise enough for me to momentarily forget to disguise my voice. I covered my mistake with another guttural throat clearing and continued on.

'Yes. Have you heard of him?'

'My father speaks of him often.' In fact, my father spoke of him so often lately that thoughts of assassination had entered my weary mind. Apparently, Tiberius's oldest son Septimius was vying for my hand in marriage. I was sure Septimius was a more than suitable match for me, but I held no interest in love and marriage. I wanted only to fight and follow in my father's footsteps. I'd been so determined in this mindset that I had refused to meet with Septimius on any account.

'If you wish to prove your skill to the General today, I could go and tell him to keep an eye on the proceedings?'

I laughed, appreciative of Volusius's enthusiasm, but not nearly as eager to offer myself up to my father's mercy just yet. I was so close to proving my worth, to show that as a woman, I too was capable of great things. 'No, do not do anything. I'm only here to train with the others.'

I could feel his speculative glance grazing every inch of my slender frame yet again. 'Let it be known now that I feel you may be ill-prepared to fight with the men. Even my father does not allow me to entertain notions of hand-to-hand combat and I am clearly twice your size.'

I tried not to bristle. 'I may be small, but I am fast and not without skills.'

'I mean no offence, but the muscle tone in your arms alone suggests you will not be able to hold that sword for long.'

I ignored his warnings and pushed through the group of sweaty men passing as spectators for the current clash. I was instantly swallowed by their height and girth, my determination the only thing guiding me through the crowd.

I breathed a sigh of relief as I finally waded to free air, climbing under the arm of one last soldier and breaking into the circle of combat. Silence sprung up around me as the combatants paused, taking a few seconds to observe my entry. Eyes glided across my body, the lingering silence now evenly matched by the confused stares of everyone present.

I straightened, careful not to puff my heavily bandaged chest too much. 'My turn.'

I could almost hear the blink of confusion as approximately fifty lashes melded together in a squint of incredulity. Mirth twinkled in the depths of every eye upon me, expanding to their lips which then automatically resulted in a fully-fledged grin.

The sudden eruption of laughter was virtually deafening. I could feel my sword lowering with my spirit, the tip grazing against the solidly packed dirt at my feet. My shoulders hunched and my face sagged. Embarrassed didn't quite cover how I felt in that moment.

'Hold on, hold on,' one of the soldiers said, wiping the smile from his face with dirtied fingers. 'You say it's your turn?'

The crowd quietened down waiting for my response. 'Yes.'

'Yes?' The crowd begun to snicker again as the soldier in question came closer, crossing his arms in front of his chest and circling me slowly. 'How old are you, boy?'

'Of age,' I replied, keeping my answers simple.

'Then why do you wear your helmet? Are you hiding something perhaps?'

'Do you wish to fight or not?'

The soldier drew round front again, rapping his knuckles against the top of my helmet. He was elated, enjoying the attention of the crowd and my indignant response as I stood my ground. 'I fear I may kill you, boy.'

'You're right to be afraid,' I answered, raising my sword in warning. 'Your reputation will be shot once I beat you.'

The crowd fell quiet, measuring the seriousness of my claims. Cockiness leeched from the soldier's face and his cheeks flooded with colour. He responded by reaching for the sword sheathed at his side. Fingers gripped the hilt tightly as he released it from its confines, sweeping it back and forth across the empty space before us.

Focus was my companion now. I'd belittled him in front of the crowd and shifting my attention to watching for patterns in his movements was crucial to avoid retribution. The sword was only an extension of his intent. Father had taught me to see everything before it happened, to pay attention to the smaller

333

details and capitalise on the bulkier movements given up by the 'tells' of preparation.

The calf muscle in his right leg swelled as the weight in his foot moved back. I knew in that instant he was going to lunge. The sword play in front of me was showmanship; an act of distraction that now proved my theory as his arm swung backwards and …

I spun to the left, catching my sword on the side of his and deflecting the would-be blow. Surprise rode his pock-marked face while I captured the advantage and attempted a jab of my own.

He tilted his shoulder at the last second, but I still managed to nick the corner of his tunic, loosening thread and drawing a surprised cheer from the spectators.

Grunting in earnest, the soldier started a shuffle, walking us around each other in a tight circle. Again, I watched his feet, glancing back up just as quickly to keep an eye on his face and the twitching biceps in his arms eager for compensation. He took a deep breath, his spine curving backwards as his sword began what seemed like a slow arc around the top of his head.

I ducked as the blade swooped over the top of my helmet. Knowing how heavy these blades could be, I took advantage of the fact it would take him several seconds to counter attack with round two and quickly slashed my blade across the front of his chest and then twisted out of reach. This time I drew blood. Not much, but enough that the soldier, stumbled backwards, lowering his sword in surprise as he touched his chest, rubbing blood between his fingers in disbelief.

To be angry was not a good way to fight. It often clouded judgment and stopped you from noticing subtleties in movement. This soldier was quick to it now that his ego had been wounded. Some lunges were predictable, clunky and easier to deflect—but on the downside—he was also now motivated to win.

Being slight, speed was on my side. As the soldier came at me again and again, I managed to constantly duck and weave his incoming blows. I had yet to be marked which drove the crowd wild with frustration and applause, but I was also growing tired. Volusius had been right about my arms being weak and the blade heavy. In some cases, I barely had the energy to greet metal with metal. And yet, when our swords sparked upon greeting, I was quick to lower and retreat.

'Stay still!' he barked, circling slowly for what felt like the hundredth time.

'Am I wearing you out?' I desperately wanted to wipe at the sweat that marked my brow, but there was no way I was going to give him a reason to attack. I could see he was also waning, but his muscles weren't quivering like mine. It was simply his stamina that was lacking.

His poor wife …

The soldier growled and cussed, words I probably shouldn't have been privy to. His tunic was a plumage of cotton threads and congealing blood. The idea of these camps was to train, learn from each other and perfect certain skills, not kill each other in the process. A flesh wound would be all I'd inflict despite the hunger in the soldier's eyes. He'd need at least a smattering of my blood to restore a skerrick of his tarnished reputation.

'I'm seriously thinking about killing you, boy.'

'You have to at least wound me first,' I taunted, ducking another swing and counteracting with a cross jab that was met with his shiny, unblemished blade.

'There will be trouble for you when I do.'

'*If* you can.'

The crowd had grown rather large now. Officers, slaves and other combatants had strolled in to determine the ruckus. I heeded them no attention. I couldn't afford to lose focus now. I had only a few good lunges left in me before my arm was certain to fall off. I could duck and weave for hours, possibly run circles around the opponent twice my physical size, but alas, I would learn nothing other than the fact I can run away.

The soldier came at me again, predictably shifting back onto his right leg before he started swinging the blade high above his head. I conserved energy by tapping my blade on his right side. He automatically twisted the bulk of his weight away from it, teetering a little dangerously on the unstably planted left leg. While he over-corrected, I circled on the right, moving fast enough that I was behind him before he realised his mistake. I jumped up onto his back, swung my left arm around his neck in a choke hold and quickly pressed the blade against his throat.

The crowd went as still as the soldier, waiting with baited breath for my next move. Blood trickled down the length of the blemished surface, mingling with the dried crust of previous encounters with his flesh. Unless he wanted his jugular exposed, he would have to relent. 'Thank you,' I whispered in his ear.

The soldier twisted in my grip as I lowered the sword and slowly dismounted his back. He appraised me with narrowed eyes, albeit angry ones. 'For what?'

'For not taking it easy on me.'

'And why would I do that?'

I shrugged and re-sheathed what felt like my three-hundred-kilo blade. 'No reason.'

As I turned my back, foolishly believing there was honour to be had in victory among peers, my opponent lunged. With my sword re-sheathed and eyes now mesmerised by Volusius's dawning look of respect, I didn't have time to react. As footsteps thudded against the dirt behind me, I automatically ducked, thinking he would take aim with his own blade. Instead, my rear end met with his foot which was kicked with enough force to send me flying face-first into the crowd.

They parted as I fell, quickly scrabbling backwards to stay clear of the fray. I had but a moment to roll onto my back before he grabbed me by the throat, hauling me quickly back to my feet to face him. 'Never, turn your back on your opponent, boy!' he yelled in my face. 'A Roman soldier makes sure his quarry is dead before retreating. Do you understand?'

I nodded frantically, feeling like a total idiot as I scratched at his hand, trying in vain to invite more oxygen in.

With his free hand, the soldier reached for my helmet, egged on by the taunts of the crowd. I simply couldn't allow my only source of cover from the already excessive judgement of a male orientated grouping to reveal my true identity.

I stopped struggling against the hand on my throat and opted to remain hidden instead, reaching back to keep the helmet safely in place. I would never be accepted here and my father would never forgive my efforts for trying. As it was, he was still angry with me for following him on his last campaign and getting myself into trouble with our enemies.

'So, you do have something to hide?' my captor taunted, trying all the more to relieve me of my mask.

'Stop!' Volusius interceded from the sidelines. 'His father is one of us. He simply wants to make his way among us without recognition for his bloodline.'

The soldier stilled, though the pressure around my throat tightened enough to make me gasp. 'You'd know all about that, wouldn't you little, Volusius?'

Volusius stood tall, determined not to be intimidated by his peers. The crowd—of course—sucked all this in like dried sponges, held completely captivated by one of their own challenging the ranking of an officer's son. 'Yes, I do,' he agreed. 'Which is why you should let him go and admit your defeat. He has learnt his lesson, now you should learn yours.'

I cringed, watching as the soldier's face filled with disdain. There really was nothing worse than being told what to do by a minor, especially one who ranked higher based on blood than actual skill. I could almost empathise with the brute trying to 'out me' and simultaneously strangle me.

'So, who is it that I should be admitting defeat to?'

'What's going on over here?'

Perfect …

I closed my eyes sending up silent prayers to whoever listened for absolution. I had hoped to avoid my father at all costs, knowing with absolute certainty that if this soldier didn't strangle me to death first, then it was almost certain that the leader of this faction of the Roman army would.

'Just settling a dispute, General,' the soldier uttered through clenched teeth.

'Then settle it and let us be done with this.'

I took one last strangled gasp as the soldier ripped the helmet from my head. Waves of dark hair instantly cascaded around my shoulders and down my back. Cries of dismay rang out among the spectators. The feral curse from the soldier's mouth as he dropped me was the last indication that I could no longer hide who and what I was.

'He's a girl!' someone said, shouting out the obvious.

'And she beat Octavius!' another cried as laughter ran riot.

I clambered quickly back to my feet, defiantly brushing the hair out of my eyes and doing my upmost not to burst into tears.

'And she's pretty! I'll take her on next, show you how it's done, Octavius!'

'Silence!' my father bellowed. 'I will hear no more!'

'But, General, we could share …' a more defiant soldier persisted.

'Be quiet!' Volusius said, entering the centre of the ring, drawing his sword and circling me in defence. 'Do you not realise who this is?'

'My future wife!' another shouted, followed by the more aggressive laughter and unashamed cheers of debauchery.

'Don't do it,' I whispered to Volusius, 'please don't tell them who I am.'

'You deserve their respect!'

'I want to earn it.'

'Well you've earned mine.' He inched closer, eyes constantly on the leering crowd. I assessed my father's reaction, his whole demeanour oozing discontent.

'He's ashamed of me,' I mumbled. 'Anything you say now is only going to inflame the situation.'

Volusius shook his head, emerald eyes finally finding mine as he spoke, 'No one could ever be ashamed of you.'

'That's sweet, but—'

'This is Elena Valerius, daughter of our great General Lucius Valerius! Show some respect!' Volusius shouted above the ongoing din of the crowd.

The soldier previously choking me to death dropped to one knee and bowed his head. 'Please forgive me, I did not know …'

'That was kind of the point,' I muttered, glaring at Volusius. It didn't matter now anyway. The cat was out of the proverbial bag and my father was beyond angry. I expected him to launch into a tirade, grab me by the hair and drag me all the way back to his tent for a lecture. Instead, he did something much worse.

He turned his back on me and walked away.

Ordinarily that wouldn't have bothered me so much if we were fighting in the privacy of our villa, but here in front of the men I so desperately sought acceptance and understanding, it left a stain I'd never be able to wipe clean. Never again would any member of the Roman army take me seriously. I would be the tale fathers told their daughters, warning them of the dangers of reaching above their station. I would be the laughing stock of history.

I *was* a laughing stock.

The crowd turned from me as my father had done, dispersing quickly to resume earlier tasks. Even the soldier at my feet made haste, enduring a few jibes as he re-joined the men in another arena. That left Volusius at my side, blade still drawn as if anyone even cared about challenging me now.

I spun on my heels, heading for my horse. I had to get out of here before the mocking stares ate me up and spat me back out again.

'Where are you going?' Volusius challenged as he jogged to catch up. 'You don't have to leave.'

I shot him a sideways look. 'You're not serious? I am nothing but a joke now—an embarrassment to my father's good name!'

'That's not true.'

'Isn't it?' I hissed, pushing past him.

'Of course not.'

I shook my head in disbelief and quickly mounted my horse before I said something I might regret. I gathered the well-worn leather reins in my hands and pulled to the left, twisting the horse back in the direction of the forest.

'Elena wait!' he shouted after me.

'What for?'

'I'll come with you, make sure you get safely back to the city.'

I tried very hard not to turn back around, dismount and rearrange those perfect features. I was angry, ashamed and certainly not in the mood to be reminded of my gender and perceived lack of capabilities. The only thing that stopped me was his youth and blatant lack of understanding. 'No thank you, I can look after myself.'

'*Elena* ...'

'Don't *Elena* me!' I stopped, feeling the words slide across my tongue in a caress I was intimately familiar with. I turned, eyes narrowing on Volusius's face, surprised to see he was equally as vexed as I was by the last exchange.

As I looked deep into those emerald pools, I knew without a doubt that we had uttered similar words to each other before, somehow constantly locked in a battle of wills where neither one of us would relent. Today would be no different. Regardless of the fact that I seemed to be recalling some distant memory, logic dictated that it was a seemingly impossible familiarity.

'You don't know me,' I breathed, still unsettled by our current exchange. 'So do not presume to lecture me.'

Volusius took a few more steps until he was beside my horse. He looked up at me slowly, his eyes surveying me in a completely different light. 'Then why do I get the feeling that I do know you?'

'I don't know.'

'You feel it too, do you not?'

I sniffed, now strangling the reins between slightly shaky fingers. 'I feel nothing but shame and humiliation. Now step aside before you get trampled.' I kicked my horse into movement, delighting in the speed in which my present situation quickly became the past. As we galloped into the forest and were swallowed by the trees, I could finally breathe a momentary sigh of relief. And though I wanted badly to linger in the reprieve, I knew the worst was still to come. Father would eventually return home and when he did, there were bound to be serious consequences.

CHAPTER TWENTY-FOUR: PENANCE

I sat quietly in the courtyard, watching as the sun dived into the depths of the horizon leaving behind the orange haze of its previous existence and the echo of warmth upon my skin. Stars had already begun to make their presence known higher in the night sky. I was mesmerised by their beauty, but not nearly distracted enough to forget why I sat in wait.

Father was coming.

Word had been sent and the horses could already be heard in the distance. Tonight, I would meet my fate and I was to do so with the grace and poise my mother insisted I was bestowed with. I had yet to find it, still tormented by my embarrassment and yet harangued by my anger. Acceptance was such a small thing to ask for, yet I knew I would never have it even though it felt as if I'd been fighting for it my entire life.

Lucius—who sat beside me—rested his hand on my arm. His smile was warm and genuine, but there was concern entrenched in the fine lines around the corners of his eyes. 'It will probably not be as bad as you are thinking,' he said to me.

'Of course it will be.'

'Elena, father loves you very much. Your punishment will probably be minor.'

'In this case, I have to disagree with you. I have a feeling that I am really going to get it this time.'

'You know, it astounds me how often you are in trouble.'

I scoffed. 'Just you wait until he finds out your studying philosophy instead of military strategy at the university.'

His features pinched considerably as he regarded me with a degree of suspicion. 'You are not going to say anything, are you?'

'Of course not. You may be a dumb ass, but I am not going to point that out.'

Lucius jerked beside me, his hand sliding from my arm. 'What did you just call me?'

I blinked, trying to recall the foreign words pouring forth from my mouth. 'I do not know. I apologise, Lucas. I do not know what I was thinking or saying.'

'Lucas? Elena, I have never heard you speak in this manner.'

'Nor I.'

'What overcomes you?'

'It is strange,' I said slowly, 'but I do not feel as though I am myself lately. Just the other day I spoke as if I were possessed.'

Lucius slapped a hand across my mouth and shook his head violently. Blonde hair flirted with his shoulders, blue eyes dancing in warning. 'Do not speak of such things out loud.'

'Did I tell you I met Volusius Marcellus?' I mumbled through his grip.

He lowered his hands. 'You did not.'

'I think I have met him before.'

'But you have not.'

'I am aware, Lucius, but regardless, his face and voice were familiar, his words and persona even more so.'

'Dispel it from your thoughts,' Lucius countered with a flick of his wrist. 'You have more important matters to contend with.'

'Hush now,' mother replied, as she approached us, reaching out and gripping my other hand tightly. 'Your father approaches.'

I could hear the horses more clearly than ever, their hooves pounding against the ground in desperation of a destination. But the approach of impending doom was no longer what concerned me. It was the hand holding mine, so warm and comforting in the past it now felt foreign and unknown. Why did the touch of my own mother feel inexplicably wrong?

'Mother?'

'Come now, be silent.'

I studied her profile with renewed interest, curious by the crook in her nose, the dark hair that vaguely resembled mine and the blue eyes handed down to Lucius. Her skin was as pale as my own, with high cheekbones and thick, full lips she'd had the good grace to pass onto me. I could see her in me and Lucius despite our obvious differences, but it was like we had never met until now. I knew everything about her and yet I felt nothing connecting the two of us as mother and daughter.

'Your father is fair and honourable, but your behaviour is not underserving of punishment,' she said, drawing me back to the present.

'I'm sorry, I was not listening.'

'I said that your behaviour of late justifies punishment.'

'I know,' I mumbled. 'I just wish that I knew what it was so I could prepare my rebuttal.'

Mother glared at me dangerously. 'Do not even think about it, Elena. You will accept your father's will with grace and you will do it without protest.'

'But what if—'

'No more talking.'

I pressed my lips together as the thunderous gallop of several horses plotting course over our cobblestone path drew close. When they'd reached the old wooden door, several servants rushed to greet their master, helping him to dismount and then guide the horses round to the back of the stables.

I turned my head as footsteps proceeded, physically shrinking in my seat as Tiberius, Marcus and Julius entered right behind my father.

Great. I'm going to have an audience.

Mother pulled me to my feet beside her and then tugged on my arm until we'd curtseyed our greeting to the other officers. Lucius politely bowed in greeting, swooped to grab the book he was reading off the arm of the chair and quickly made a retreat before the screaming could begin.

Mother dropped my hand as father approached, embracing him boldly and returning the fevered kiss he bestowed upon her lips. I turned away, catching a quick wink from Julius as his Mediterranean blue eyes met mine across the room. I didn't know what was worse; watching your mother and father express themselves physically or having one of the younger officers openly rub in the discomfort with flirtatious mannerisms.

'Lucius,' mother moaned against his lips, 'I have missed you these last few days.'

'And tonight we shall remember one another—but for now—business my love.'

She bowed her head and took a step back from his embrace. She placed her hand in the small of my back and propelled me forward. 'Greet your father, Elena.'

'Hello, father.'

'My daughter, I am pleased to see that you greet me today in your own clothes as opposed to my ill-fitting tunics.'

The officers coughed to contain their amusement, turning away when they each caught my angry glare and the now determined set of my chin.

'Now you are angry with me,' father murmured, placing a finger under my chin until my eyes met with his. 'Am I supposed to apologise to you now, is that it?'

'No, father,' I murmured warily, looking away again. 'I am … repentant.'

'No, you are placating.'

'Father, please,' I begged.

'Come,' he said, dropping his hand from my chin. 'We shall talk in the Great Hall in private.'

I followed quickly, grateful for small mercies. An audience was the last thing I had wanted and clearly he agreed with the sentiment.

As he closed the double doors behind us, I settled onto the love seat in the centre of the room. Some servants still lingered, lighting the chandeliers for the dawning night and fussing over father with wine and platters of cheese and fruits. Others were busy stringing floral garlands around the cornices and windows in decoration, scrubbing walls clean and repolishing the floor.

I frowned. I had been confined to the house for several days since my return and yet no one had spoken to me about any upcoming celebrations. 'What is this?' I asked, momentarily side-tracked from the true intentions of our conversation.

There was an ominous pause. Assumptions aside, nothing good could come from my father either lost for words or choosing them carefully. The deep breath that ensued the pregnancy of silence confirmed my fears as he uttered, 'This will be your engagement announcement.'

Protestations found my lips all too quickly. 'My what?' I practically shrieked.

'Sit down!' he bellowed.

I immediately planted myself back down, unaware that I'd even risen to my feet in outrage. 'Father, please tell me this isn't true?' I begged, desperation all but dripping from my voice. 'I cannot be married!'

'You have embarrassed me for the last time, Elena.'

'Father, please. I will do anything you ask of me.'

'This is what I ask of you.'

'Anything but marriage!'

Father sighed, slowly lowering himself into the armchair across from me. He waved the servants away still intent on filling him with dairy. 'You leave me no choice. What you did the other day, how that reflects upon me—'

'I'm so sorry. It will never happen again, I promise.'

'Elena, I want you to be happy and safe, can't you see that?'

'Of course, but I could never be happy just being a wife and mother! You raised me to be so much more!'

'And I am extraordinarily proud of you.'

'But—'

He raised a hand to silence me. 'I know what a skilled fighter you have become and I know that no matter what you will always be able to look after yourself and this family if the need arises. But, Elena, you have been born to a time where it is unacceptable for you to pursue anything other than what I can offer you. Is it not enough that I can see your worth and that I know what you are capable of?'

My bottom lip quivered as tears stung the rims of my eyes. 'I am meant for more than marriage and motherhood … I know it.'

'And perhaps one day it will be yours—but for now—you must do as expected. You must make me proud, Elena and fulfil your duty to this family.'

Tears spilled across my cheeks and fell into my lap. Great sobs found their way into my throat and I gasped to hold them back, knowing I would not stop if I released all emotion now. 'Please …'

'Now, as you can imagine your display at the camp the other day has somewhat limited your options.'

'You mean I actually get to choose?' I snivelled, wiping frantically at the tears in frustration.

'Not anymore,' my father said with yet another deep sigh of resignation. 'There are only three who would take you now. One I have ruled out on age alone and the other I believe is simply doing it to win greater favour with me.'

I hiccupped, defeated and suddenly uncaring. What did it matter? I would never be happy marrying a man I didn't love, settling into a life of subservience and frivolous agenda. I wanted excitement, adventure—danger.

My life was officially over.

'Marcus, I believe is—'

'Marcus!' I shrieked, lifting from my chair again. 'Father, you cannot be serious? He is almost forty and I'm fairly certain not attracted to women!'

'Sit down, Elena!'

I dropped back down again, gripping the arm of the loveseat so tightly it was certain to break. 'I'm sorry. I speak out of turn it's just that Marcus—'

'Is unsuitable,' he finished more calmly. 'I am more than aware of Marcus's sexual orientation.

'It's that toga he wears and the hair,' I persisted. 'Does he even realise … wait. How do you know about his preferences?'

My father's face hardened only fractionally, but it was hard not to miss the colour that rose to his cheeks. 'The second suitor,' he said, ignoring my question, 'is Volusius Marcellus, but he is young and too inexperienced to run a successful household yet. I cannot entrust my daughter to his care.'

I made another attempt to wipe away stray tears. 'Volusius wants to marry me?'

'He said that you and he shared a connection.'

I snorted and turned away. 'What a ridiculous thing to say about someone you only just met.'

'He finds you attractive,' my father mused, leaning back in his chair and crossing one leg over the other. He rested his hands on the arm of his chair, studying my reaction with considerable interest.

I felt my face grow hot under my growing discomfort and his lingering scrutiny. 'That's not really the point, is it?'

'Are you not attracted to him?'

I ran a hand through my hair a few times until I had nothing left to do but answer. 'Father,' I began, choosing my words carefully. 'If you are to force me into marriage, is it wrong for me to want what you and mother share?'

'You speak of love. I thought you considered it foolish?'

'I do, but if I am to be with someone until the end of days, surely it should be with someone who I care for in return.'

He nodded his understanding. 'But unfortunately, Elena, you have left me little choice in this regard. I offered you three years to find your own husband and you refused. Now I am forced to take the only avenue left available to me and that is selecting Tiberius's eldest son Septimius Marcellus to be your husband.'

'No!'

'You do not even know him, Elena!'

'Then make it Volusius. Please, at least choose someone I know. I can't marry a stranger!'

Father shook his head, his face falling in sadness. 'I'm sorry, Elena but there is no one left who will have you and I will not see you marry Volusius when he incapable of supporting himself.' He signalled to one of the servants to open the door.

I turned my face from everyone as Tiberius, Marcus and Julius entered the room.

'It has been decided,' Father said grimly. 'Elena will marry Septimius.'

'He will be pleased,' Tiberius said gruffly. 'Forgive me, General, but despite her recent behaviour he has assured me that she is still his chosen bride.'

'What kind of man wants to marry someone they haven't even met?' I chided, a fresh wave of tears overcoming expected etiquette.

The men in the room grew silent, no one quite sure how to answer me.

Julius was the first to say anything, stepping forward until I was forced to look up at him—lest I stare at his crotch. He bent down until he was kneeling in front of me, reaching out and taking one of my shaking hands into his own. 'Everything will be alright, Elena.'

I snatched my hand from his grasp, frowning heavily at his proximity and presumption. 'What would you know of such matters?'

'I too was part of a semi-arranged marriage.'

'You were?'

He nodded, but made no attempt to touch me again. 'We were married last year and at first I was not thrilled by the prospect. Granted, I had always been attracted to her, but I valued what you are clinging so desperately to—freedom to choose. But in time I have come to love and appreciate my wife very much. I would go as far to say that I would do anything for her—even die for her should the situation call for it.'

'Good for you,' I muttered. 'That doesn't change anything for me.'

'*Elena* ...' my father warned.

I rolled my eyes and pushed up from the chair. How could I be seated when hot embers of despair burned deep within my very core? 'It's not the same thing. I appreciate what you are trying to press upon me, but at least you still get to be whom and what you want to be.'

Julius frowned, dark eyebrows slanting across eyes so blue and vibrant I caught myself staring for a little too long before glancing away. 'I fear I do not follow. Septimius is renowned for his good looks and enigmatic persona, his quick wit and bravery. You should be overjoyed ...'

'To be the trophy on an officer's arm? All I'll ever become now is a wife and mother and this is simply not something I can settle for!' I lunged for the door, sick to my stomach to be forced to endure this torturous turn in events.

'Elena, return to your seat, we are not finished!'

'I'm sorry, father, but I cannot do it. I would rather die than marry for the wrong reasons!'

'Elena, this is no longer a matter open for discussion. Please do not force my hand on this.'

'Then do not force mine!'

Regret was instantaneous; a sombre attack of the conscious stilling my moving feet and drawing my hands to my lips in an effort to catch the words and place them back on my insolent tongue. I felt my father's oppression on the back of my neck like chilled breath, iced fingers of silent madness stroking my flesh with mounting ire. I had pushed beyond limitations.

The room was silenced by the thrum of his beating anger. There was nothing to be heard but the brush of his tunic against his legs as he strode quickly and firmly across the room. Collective breaths were held and no one moved, including me.

I swallowed the ensuing panic. My father would not hit me, but I had defied him publicly, dismissed his decision and offended my intendeds' father. I had threatened him with retribution—an unforgiveable act that would be shown no mercy.

His shadow on the floor loomed so close it swallowed me whole. He did not reach out and touch me. He did not strike me and he did not try to sooth the coming blow. He simply delivered his decision with finality that dared not to be challenged.

'Elena you *will* be married within the month,' he whispered against the back of my neck, his breath warm yet chilled by tone. 'You will address your actions this night and you will accept that by tomorrow night you will be engaged.'

I spun on the spot, my face awash with a new kind of grief. 'You will have me engaged to Septimius by tomorrow night?'

'Yes, Elena and that is *final.*'

'Then there's still time,' I muttered under my breath.

'Time for what?'

Time to kill myself. I thought sadly.

Yes, it was dramatic and innately over the top, but for me there were little options left. I couldn't run away. Whether inside these walls or outside, I was still a woman and hence liberated of any real choices. At least in death I believed I could plan for an afterlife of my choosing. At least in death I could escape a loveless marriage and a life of un-fulfilment.

'Elena?'

'Yes, father?' I mustered through gritted teeth, my jaw clenched so hard that the muscles in my cheeks were aching for reprieve.

'I am sorry it has come to this.'

'As am I.'

I turned, gripping the door handle beneath my fingers, wrenching it open and running for the shelter of my room as fast as my legs could carry me. I dashed past my mother's look of outrage, ignoring her cries to stop as I took the stairs two at a time. When I reached the landing, I found solace from the door in front of me, throwing it open and slamming it behind me with gusto.

I wanted to die. I wanted to crawl up in a ball and die. What would be resounding joy for so many women, was literally my end to life's happiness. I was broken, in defiance of my father and feeling so out of place that wretched didn't quite cover it. I was a tumultuous mess of emotions that felt somehow borrowed. Everything about this decision felt forged and considerably wrought in a frustration I couldn't decipher. When had I become so rebellious and defied my father?

'Elena?'

I looked up through a fresh wave of unshed tears. Through blurred vision I saw Lucius propped up on my bed, his face marred with concern. He held a book in one hand which he promptly tossed aside when he took in my dishevelled, self-piteous behaviour.

'It has not been good news, has it?'

The opening of his arms saw me tripping over the rug to reach him. I fell clumsily onto the bed beside him, grappling with the pillows and covers until I was cocooned inside his familiar embrace. I hiccupped, letting the tears spill over with real gusto, ejecting all the pent-up aggression that coursed through my body.

'What happened?' he murmured against my ear, his hand smoothing my back in calming motions.

'It's horrible, Lucas,' I sobbed. 'Father is forcing me to marry Septimius Marcellus within the month.'

'It's all going to be alright, E, you'll see.'

I eased back while he attempted to dab at my tears with the corner of his tunic. My eyes were narrowed and my sobbing had ceased thanks to the unsettling, yet somehow familiar wave of memories flooding through me. 'You just called me *E*. You never call me *E*.'

'And you just called me Lucas again.'

'I did? I am so sorry.'

He shrugged, his nose wrinkling in contemplation. 'I do not think I mind it. Lucas feels … familiar, though I'm not sure why.'

'So does *E*.'

'I wonder why?'

It was my turn to shrug. 'Repressed memories? A past life?'

'Is that what you have come to believe?'

'I believe in nothing anymore.'

'Do you honestly think that father will follow through?'

'Of course he will.'

'What are you going to do?'

It was a good question, one I didn't have a definitive answer for. I had twenty-four hours before I was forever tied to a stranger in a world that somehow did not understand me. Despite how much I loved Lucius, my mother and father, I had to escape this seemingly impossible fate. There was no way I would marry Septimius Marcellus.

There was no way Elena Manory would marry anyone.

Errr … Elena Valerius.

Who the hell is Elena Manory?

CHAPTER TWENTY-FIVE: FLEE

Admittedly death had sounded like a splendid idea. I dreamt of merging clouds edged in silver and spun from silk, the pearlescent gates of heaven gleaming back as welcoming arms embraced me. I'd thought about my troubles rolling away with the echo of my past. I'd thought death would bring me some kind of peace, but I hadn't been able to do it.

I looked at the blade in my hands, its sharp edges pressing against my palm seemingly fearful of drawing first blood. I'd wanted it to slide so easily across my flesh, spill my life and take with it my current plight, but reason was a pressing obligation. However much I had tried to consider an exit, reason stirred my instincts for survival and my urge not to disappoint the ones I loved.

These new feelings inside of me were trying, a pressure on my soul I wasn't quite accustomed to. I had never considered myself weak in the past, but now I found myself looking back on all my decisions and reflecting on the present. How could I have possibly considered suicide? How could I have been so selfish to leave Lucius, father and mother? Yes, my world was darkened by the prospect of marrying a stranger, but surely death was not the answer?

Who are you? I thought to myself, dropping the blade and running my hands up and down my bare arms. *What are these thoughts in your head?*

'Elena? Is that you?'

I closed my eyes and muttered a word I'd never heard of before, but was certain it echoed the correct sentiment. When I opened them again Volusius Marcellus was in front of me, crouching down to meet my eyes with his own magnetic emerald pools of green.

My breath caught. Volusius was so familiar, but in ways I couldn't quite comprehend. I tried to search my memory for his face, but I saw nothing to recall, yet I knew that we had met before, that his eyes had looked into mine and that we had whispered words that made the hair on the back of my neck stand tall and my hands shake with uncertainty.

'It is you,' he said, slowly lowering himself onto the grass beside me.

I shifted, putting some space between us. It was not forgotten what my father had said of his attraction. I was also alone in the forest, miles from the villa and away from the prying eyes of others. 'How did you find me?'

Volusius took longer than necessary to answer. I gazed at his profile, watching his eyes dart backwards and forwards across the ground as if searching for the right words, his brow crumpling marginally in confusion.

'I am not sure,' he finally answered, reaching out to torment a blade of grass between his fingers. 'I heard from my father that your household are looking for you.'

'I have not run away if that is what you are thinking,' I chided, covering the sudden wave of guilt that slithered through me. There was a certain degree of truth to that statement. I hadn't run away. I was merely seeking out space and time to think. It just appeared to be taking much longer than I'd originally intended. Also, my timing hadn't been spectacular. The servants had literally put the last finishing touches on my hair and dress when I'd fled through my balcony door, climbing down the trellis and disappearing into the garden. It had just been too much to see myself dressed and adorned for a life of future disappointment.

'The engagement celebrations are to be held within the hour. I do believe they think you have run away from your obligations.'

'They are forcing me to marry a stranger.'

'My brother is a decent man, Elena.' He took a deep breath and picked another blade of grass. 'He will protect and love you—that much I can say for him.'

'I really do not care anymore. It is clear that my feelings on the subject are moot.'

'Then why are you here?'

'Why are you here?' I argued, watching as that look of confusion crossed his features again.

354

He shrugged. 'I do not know. We arrived at the villa as expected and were shown to our rooms when one of your servants yelled out that you were gone. I wanted to ensure you were all right.'

'Yes, but why are you *here*?'

'I don't understand what you are trying to ask me.'

I gestured wildly to the rocky outcrop in front of me, the grass beneath us and the view before us. 'No one knows that I like to come here—not even Lucius. Of all the places you could have looked for me, why here?'

He shook his head. 'I do not know. I simply had a feeling that you liked to be up high, that ...' his voice faded and he looked away.

'What is it?'

'It is crazy talk for me to pursue this conversation. I apologise.'

'Yes, but now I am curious.'

'And I am clearly a fool.'

'And how am I to judge the truth in that statement if I do not know all the facts?'

'You would like to call me a fool?' he said, looking at me from beneath his long dark lashes.

'I would like to know how you found me and how you know that this is my place of contemplation.'

'Elena, I must not say. My father has spoken to me, asserted that Septimius will have you despite my best efforts.'

'Volusius, I do not understand what that has to do with you finding me here.'

'I have a memory,' he practically shouted, startling me enough that I placed yet more space between us. He snatched a handful of grass between his fingers this time, splitting each blade in half before throwing it away again. 'We know one another, you and I.'

'Alas I remember your judgmental assessment as I rode into camp the other day.'

He shook his head wildly, throwing away all blades of grass and edging closer so that our knees were touching. His look grew ever intense as he said, 'I remember you before this last encounter, Elena.'

'Our fathers are united in battle. It is safe to say we have possibly frolicked as children.'

'No. I am referring to us.'

'Us?' I mimicked, unsure where he was going with this.

'I found you here this day because I remember—I remember lying beside you on a cold steel rooftop overlooking a city I cannot even begin to describe.'

'It was clearly a dream, Volusius. And, there is no *you and I*.' I climbed quickly to my feet, stopped short by his strong grip as he pulled me roughly back to the ground beside him. I had a sheer moment of panic, forgetting every second of training my father instilled under the touch of a clearly troubled young man. I was torn between a strange desire that warmed the pit of my stomach at his nearness and angered by the forceful touch that suppressed my freedom.

'I will fight my brother for you,' he said, pulling my hands against his chest. 'We could be happy.'

I struggled to break free of his grip, his fingers holding onto me so tightly I feared I would bruise. Under his tunic the beat of his heart was frantic, his skin warming the layers and fuelling my fear of this encounter. 'Volusius, let go of me!'

He dropped my hands instantly, his face cracking with sorrow as he edged away. 'Forgive me. I did not ... I—'

I jumped back to my feet, stumbling slightly as I rubbed my bruising hands together. I edged closer to the path in which I'd come, ensuring my break for freedom was in sight should the need arise. I also sought enough space to fight him should the situation gather further momentum.

'Please, do not leave just yet.'

'You leave me no choice, Volusius. Your behaviour is unbecoming.'

'I am struggling to understand what is happening between us.'

I shook my head and took a calming breath as those emerald eyes stared back at me, pleading. 'How old are you?'

He seemed momentarily baffled by the question, but nevertheless quickly answered. 'I am fifteen years.'

'Volusius, I am seventeen. You are far too young for me. You must understand that I cannot consider you—'

'Based solely on my age?'

'Of course not,' I said calmly.

'Are you not attracted to me?'

'I am not immune to your charm that is true, but …'

He stood slowly, watching me with caution as if the slightest of movements may have cause to scare me away. It was an accurate assumption as his body unfurled unhurried and purposefully until he reached full height, at least a head taller than I was.

I backed into the tree behind me, assured by the support of its gnarled and solid trunk. I also reassessed my exit strategy, double-checking the path ahead remained unobstructed. But Volusius now stood before me, full of confidence and assertive in stance. If I needed to run, it would not be without consequences first.

'That is close enough.'

'Perhaps I can change our father's minds,' he whispered to no one in particular. His mind appeared lost to the unfocused thoughts he murmured aloud. He rested a hand on the trunk behind me, boxing me in from the left and only ensuring my flight or fight response elevated. 'I may be able to convince them of our pairing.'

My only option was to square up and look upon him boldly and without demure, feminine intent. I needed to stand my ground and project the confidence of my will. Although his eyes were captivating and worryingly filled with underminable conviction of the past, present and perhaps future, I was not prepared to try to interpret what his eyes now begged. 'You are just a boy, Volusius. I cannot be with a boy.'

'You said my looks did please you.'

'I cannot deny your presence warms me, Volusius, but I will not be swayed. I do not wish to be with anyone. I do not want to be married and I do not want to be cornered by my intended's younger sibling.'

Volusius reeled as if stung by my words, but was ever determined to voice his reasoning. 'But I have seen us together, Elena. When I touch you—'

'I will break your fingers.'

His hands balled into fists at his side and he took several deep, calming breaths. Good. He needed them. His manner was unbecoming and frankly, unwanted.

357

'I came here to get away from what my father has forced upon me,' I continued, voice rising, but not quite shrill. 'Now you are trying to compel me with your desires and I will neither allow it nor listen anymore.'

In that moment I wanted to shove him over the precipice, force my legs into action and run as far away as possible, but it was starting to become clear that running only created a different set of problems. Wherever I went, whatever I did, I would always be forced into a situation that did not become my ideals. I was never going to be happy while I approached every obstacle as a death sentence.

'Elena, I—'

'Stop,' I said, my voice lowering several octaves. 'Enough of this. I have much to think about and I wish to be alone now.'

'Is there nothing I can say?'

I shook my head, urging understanding and compassion to burn just a little bit brighter inside of me. 'I am running from my responsibilities and you are running to them in an effort to please your father. Leave me be so I may surrender to my fate.'

'You will marry Septimius?'

'You say he will love and protect me?'

Volusius swallowed the lump in his throat and turned away. 'My brother is many things, most I cannot explain, but I do know that he is honourable.'

I nodded, feeling the full weight of responsibility weigh upon my shoulders. 'Then it is time for me to make my own father happy.' I turned, stopping only when the brush of Volusius's hand against mine drew my attention back to the emerald depths of his eyes.

'He will make you happy.'

'I cannot rely on that.'

'Then rely on my words,' he said gently as he laced his fingers through mine. 'I may be young, but I have seen things lately that have reshaped my current reality. I know that Septimius will draw eager breath from your lips and laughter from your soul. I know that when times grow dark again, he will be there to protect and cherish you.'

'Yet you plot against your brother,' I murmured, my eyes drawn to the warm fingers wound tightly around my own. Seconds before I would have tended thoughts about his demise, now I concentrated on the energy pulsing between us, curious by the unfurling warmth inside.

'Septimius will have you within the hour.'

'Of this you are so certain.'

Why does my voice sound so coarse?

Volusius started to smile, lips curling at the edges to reveal prefect white teeth. 'Septimius exudes a certain charm.'

'It matters not. This is still an arrangement not backed by my support.'

He took another step closer and my spine bowed against the rough tree bark, our fingers still linked tightly together. Thoughts ran riot through my head about pulling free, but something kept us tightly bound. Every fibre in my being recognised him, remembered the feel of his hand in mine, yet common sense and my warring soul told me this was not right—that his touch was not meant for me.

'Volusius let me go …'

'Is that what you really want?' His other hand caressed the side of my arm until all our fingers were linked and tucked snugly behind my back. Pinned, Volusius leant his body against mine, his eyes focused entirely on my lips. 'One hour and you will belong to another,' he whispered, his breath warm and sweet against my lips.

'I belong to no one.'

'Then for this last moment we are to be free, let me release you.'

'Release me?' I murmured, intrigued by the sentiment. 'Do you truly believe you are the one to do it?'

He grimaced and the whisper of his smile disappeared into the line of his creasing forehead. His hold loosened as the weight of his uncertainty eased from the warmth of our pressed figures. 'I want to be.'

'I want things too,' I said gently, leaning forward to catch his fallen eyes with my own. In that moment I saw everything; his mounting sorrow and my own fears reflected back at me. His emotions were unveiled in the most raw and potent state, a press upon my chest that would not cease as truth conjured dreams or perhaps realities of the past. I no longer knew what was real or a dream within my own mind. What I knew for certain was that this strange meeting of either chance or destiny was a marked moment

I would always ponder, but would have to disregard now due to the events about to unfold.

'But we cannot have what we want,' he stated simply.

'It would seem that way.'

Finally locked in some semblance of unexplainable understanding, we stared at each other for the longest time in silence. Our heads only turned as peace was disrupted by the beating of fast-approaching hooves against dirt and debris.

'Your father ...'

'He will not be pleased.'

A smile started to weave its magic upon his face again. 'Why? Because we are locked together so intimately?'

'No,' I chided, earlier restlessness creeping in as we hurriedly disentangled ourselves and placed acceptable distance between us. 'He will be furious that I left the villa in the first place.'

'He will not be pleased to see me here ...'

'Then perhaps you should slip away into the shadows before we are discovered.'

'Alas, you will undoubtedly spread rumour of my cowardice.'

'Should it be your desire, you could speak of the loose morals of the Valerius girl who sneaks younger men into the forest.'

'I would not.' He was genuinely aghast by the suggestion which only served to make me snicker.

'Then I too shall keep your secret.'

Volusius rewarded me with a winning smile, his green eyes once again restored with sparkling mirth. 'I would like to wish you well, but I fear—'

'I understand, Volusius. You do not need to speak the words aloud.'

'So, this is goodbye?'

I shook my head as my father's voice rang loud and clear above the dulcet sounds of the forest. I cringed. My name was suddenly a fierce bellow that sent birds scattering in all directions— a tormentor of peace to be sure. 'No,' I whispered, eyes scouting the trees for my father's unwanted appearance. 'We are to be family.'

'I have not forgotten,' he said, face falling.

'Neither have I.'

I hurriedly waved Volusius away as the sound of my father's sandals crunched against gravel and dried brush below us. He'd found my pathway to the precipice and was almost upon us. Panic thundered through my veins as Volusius offered one last lingering look before he disappeared into the shadows of the rocky outcrop, undoubtedly descending the opposite side of the precipice in haste. I hoped his footing was sure and decisive in its placement on such treacherous ground.

'Elena!'

'I am here, father,' I shouted towards the path, aware it was far better to answer than continue to ignore his pleas. In the clearing below, two horses with soldiers sitting astride their backs sat in wait. I could now see my father, approaching alone and grappling at tree roots to pull himself onto the shelf in which I'd believed was previously unknown to him.

'Elena,' he said, voice gruff. 'What are you doing out here?'

'Thinking.'

'Thinking?' He echoed my answer with a breath of trialled patience that was quickly expelled in a powerful whoosh of mounting anger. He heaved himself over the last boulder and started up the path towards me, beyond irritated. His eyes were wild with fury, his hair slightly dishevelled and his dress toga now dirtied by underbrush and grass stains.

'You draw my temper far too frequently, Elena. You are to meet Septimius within the hour and yet you flee?'

I folded my hands in front of me and curled my shoulders in submission, eyes downcast, all manner of defiance lost. 'This is a big decision, father.'

'A decision I removed from your hands last night if you recall.' He brushed his hair into shape and straightened his cloak. Perhaps annoyed that I kept my eyes firmly on the ground at our feet, he pinched my chin between his fingers and raised my gaze to meet his angry one.

'I remember,' I answered demurely, not at all tempted to challenge his ire further. I adopted honesty instead. 'I have been considering how to accept your decision.'

Lucius huffed, anger turning into annoyance. 'The day grows long, Elena. You will return to the villa *now*.'

'Do you trust him, father?'

361

Lucius appeared taken aback by the question, his hand dropping from my chin. He busied himself with the fixture of his dishevelled clothes instead. 'I do not understand.'

'Will he treat me well?'

Lucius stopped fussing and eyed me speculatively. After several tense heartbeats of time, his rugged features softened and he drew me into a rather comforting embrace. He had not held me like this in quite some time. My constant disobedience had driven a wedge between our once air-tight relationship. I missed the acceptance and comfort of his touch, a sense that no harm could befall me with him in my corner. 'Daughter, he is the best possible choice for one so spirited.'

My nose wrinkled. 'Now it is I who does not understand.'

'Come. We have wasted much time out here,' he said, squeezing my shoulder reassuringly. 'You will see soon enough that Septimius is an excellent choice.'

'What if I hate him?' I pressed, accepting his help as we began our descent down the uneven path. I suspected that he hung onto me more to keep sure-footed as opposed to offering me the comfort I so desperately needed right now.

'You will not. Septimius has a certain appeal.'

'But if I do, if I despise him with every inch of my being, what then?'

Lucius threw his head back and laughed. 'Then I shall just have to release you.'

'Release me?' I'd heard this sentiment thrown around a lot today and I was beginning to think that no one really understood what that meant.

'Yes.'

'Father, yet again I am at a loss …'

'Your loss will soon be your gain. Do not fret, Elena. I promise this day will not end in tears.'

I was speechless—lost for words—an oddity to be sure. Contemplating what my father proposed should I openly reject Septimius left me robbed of ideas. How on earth could my father be so assured of my future happiness?

All I knew with any degree of certainty was that I'd made the conscious decision to invest in the choices of my own making. Marriage may have been an inevitability I could not escape, but my own desires were not something to be ignored either. Married or not, I would stay true to the spirit that swam within me.

Septimus was in for a crazy ride.

I almost felt sorry for him … almost.

CHAPTER TWENTY-SIX: ENGAGEMENT

For the first time since returning to the villa with father, the flurry of activity in the upstairs passages had desisted. All attention had been diverted downstairs where finishing touches in the great hall were being addressed. Guests had started to arrive and I could already hear my mother usher them towards the courtyard with an enthusiasm that made my stomach clench painfully.

I checked that the coast was clear one final time and slipped from my bedroom and hurried along the passage. I tread with caution, tiptoeing so that the sound of my feet connecting with the terracotta was muted.

I was nearer to my goal, stealthily slipping past the opening of my father's bedroom as I headed for the end of the passage. I took periodic gulps of breath, filled with nerves as I hoped not to encounter a single soul during my mission to uncover my fate.

A wooden door loomed—my destination and by happenstance—the room of my intended. The open grate that was inset high into the solid oak practically beckoned a quick peek via curious eyes. I should have shown some semblance of caution and definitely avoided spying on the man that I would soon be married, but circumstances called for this rash behaviour. I needed to see for myself who I was contractually obliged to spend the rest of my life with.

Another pull of unsteady breath filled my lungs with a fevered flood of uncertainty. And yet, I pressed up higher onto my toes, fingers gripping the edge of the rusting grate to peek within. And though I'd had numerous opportunities to meet with Septimius in the past, none had been on my terms. Curiosity now powered my limbs as I pressed taller upon the balls of my feet, scanning the room for Volusius's brother.

I visually sketched a room devoid of any personal detail. A simple fur warmed the cool tiles underfoot and a plush bed lay in the centre of the cavernous space, currently decorated with tunics and an array of cloaks in varying colours. The walls were absent of the hand-painted murals that adorned my own family's rooms and the balcony without of any form of privacy dressings. But even identifying the unadorned guest quarters, there was no mistaking a man's presence in the room.

I gasped and drew back from the door before I was spotted. Septimius had been lounging in the bathtub adjacent to the door. Thankfully his back had been turned and it was unlikely he'd discovered the depth of my espionage, but it was possible he'd heard my intake of breath.

The prospect of being seen was almost too much to bear and thus, I covered my traitorous mouth in shame and ducked down for a proportionate amount of time, listening for a response.

What are you doing?

Shaking my head to silence inner dialogue, I crept back towards the door, pressing my ear against the timber, straining to hear the sounds of splashing water or encroaching footsteps beyond. All was silent.

I glanced over my shoulder, studying the empty passage for what felt like the umpteenth time and slowly rose back up onto my toes. I approached the opening slowly, once again bracing my palms against the door and fingering the edge of the grate for stability. I was both astonished by my boldness and complete lack of regard for protocol.

My almost too-wide eyes were automatically drawn to the bathtub; Septimius was still immersed within the warm water, his form perfectly still. Long dark hair spilled over the edge like a veil of silk, his muscled arms braced on the rim. He looked perfectly relaxed, perfectly at ease with the impending night's events.

I clenched my teeth, unreasonably annoyed by the calm he exuded. How could anyone be so casual about being tied to a stranger? Marriage was only the beginning. What was I supposed to do on my wedding night, drop my clothes and give my flesh to a man who had … who had …

Septimius stirred, leaning forward until he was sitting. Water poured down the smooth surface of his back, the ends of his hair now damp as they clung to the moist flesh of his shoulders. The muscles in his arms tensed as he braced himself against the rim and pushed himself upright.

I covered gaping lips to prevent sound from escaping as I watched him stand. I followed the trail of water with ever-widening eyes as it traced the curve of his back and fell all the way to the dip in his spine. From there it collected between his legs and ran freely back towards the water below.

I couldn't look away. My eager eyes traced every inch of his rear profile, observing every curve and tanned exposure of flesh I could endure. Breath was hard to come by as I quarrelled with my own ideals, reasoning my original intent for spying on this man. Morality was just a word without meaning as I drunk in the sight before me. To desire someone I had never met was irrational.

To even have lukewarm sensations for this stranger who planned to shackle and breed with me was an outrage. Yet why did a very small part of me ache for some distant affection that echoed within the depths of my mind and soul?

I needed to be slapped—hard.

Why was I even having such thoughts?

What did I think spying on him would change?

Septimius turned, reaching for a drying cloth. He promptly began to wipe all moisture from his arms and chest. Muscles I wasn't even sure existed flexed and tensed as he moved with purpose across his upper torso. I flushed, trying to remember how to breathe as he moved lower, simultaneously stepping out of the bath and flashing me sights I had no business admiring.

'Elena?'

I ducked, whirring around guiltily to greet Marcus who stood watching me with raised brows. I had no intention of admitting to my subversive behaviour or drawing attention to it. The only semblance of dignity I could take from my actions was to walk away with my head held high and pretend that I had not just been scrutinising my intended while he bathed.

'Yes?' I croaked, annoyed by the frog in my throat. I stubbornly raised my chin and tried to ignore the warm flush that hastily gathered momentum across my cheeks.

Marcus moved closer, knowing eyes assessing the great flourish of humiliation setting up camp within the capillaries beneath my flesh. Conclusions drawn, he then glanced at Septimius's door that was thankfully, still closed. 'Your father asked me to fetch you.'

I peered nervously at the light that streamed into the passage from his partially opened door at the opposite end. Father only ever called me to his chambers when I was in serious trouble. 'Am I in troub—'

'Not yet. Unless …'

'Unless what?'

'You would give him cause to believe otherwise?'

I sighed, going for nonchalance even though my own flesh betrayed my guilt. 'All is well, Marcus, let us go.'

'What was it that you were looking at, I wonder?'

He knew. He was simply attempting to torture me. 'Nothing.'

'Nothing?'

My lack of response and jockeying from foot-to-foot with nervous energy spoke volumes. As he moved forward to study the innards of the room beyond for himself, I offered a pleading look, placing a finger against my lips in an effort to get him to keep his voice lowered. 'Please …'

He pushed me aside, but kept a firm grip on my upper arm as he pressed his face against the grate. Any further protesting would only serve to make our presence known to Septimius and my father if he were in fact waiting for me in his chambers. 'I see,' Marcus murmured.

'Enjoying the show?' I taunted, finally exhausting all efforts of diverting my earlier actions. He already knew exactly what I'd been up to and I was mortified and yet positively curious about what could possibly be left to sponge down.

'I do believe you are missing the finale.'

'Where?' I pushed him hastily aside and took up prime position in front of the grate again. It wasn't long before the skin of Marcus's smooth cheeks were pressed against my own as he vied for his own positioning, our eyes fixed upon Septimius's buttocks as the toga he'd chosen slid into place, covering the last vestiges of his naked form.

I sighed and moved away from the grate, Marcus a little slower in averting his gaze. I found myself smiling at his antics, shaking my head hypocritically as his eyes finally found mine. He wouldn't want to give me a hard time about this—not now.

'What?' he said, straightening and brushing a hand through his long, dark hair.

'You are an imposter.'

'I beg your pardon?'

'You cannot really have wanted to marry me.'

'Of course not,' he scoffed. 'I find you—'

'Do not finish that sentence if it is to be unpleasant.'

'I was merely doing my duty. Your father is a very well-respected man. I did not want him to lose standing among the men simply because you could not fulfil your obligation.'

'And you would have given up the affections of men,' I said, pointing at Septimius's door, 'for the sake of my father's reputation?'

Marcus cleared his throat and looked upon me with a hardened gaze. 'So, it is *you* who puts this idea in your father's mind?'

Good manners and etiquette forced me to shelve the eye roll that had attempted to surface. I straightened my own toga instead, busying my fingers with the various folds of the linen. 'My father is neither blind nor stupid.'

Marcus was silent as he continued to glare at me, temper rising. His knuckles cracked and face darkened with the tightness of thinned lips and a clenched jaw. 'I have never liked you, Elena. You are far too young for me, careless, disobedient and speak the language of the ill-informed and uneducated.'

'Remiss in my education I am not, and though I echo your dislike, I do understand.'

'Understand what?' he seethed, teeth gritted.

'That you are trapped by societal expectations. My choices are limited and yours are judged by the very sex you desire to please.'

'Enough,' Marcus rasped, tossing his hair over his shoulders as he began to stride with purpose in the opposite direction. 'Your father waits.'

I huffed, quickly darting in front of Marcus before he proceeded down the staircase. Clearly we weren't heading to my father's chambers—a good sign. I took the steps two at a time to put distance between us. How my father could have ever considered a union between us I had no idea.

'Elena!'

Great.

'Yes, mother,' I said, skidding to a halt by the fountain that marked the entrance to the courtyard. Diplomats were already gathered holding goblets of wine and picked from platters of cheese and fruit. Most were distracted by conversation. Others watched my rather unladylike entrance with curious detachment.

'Straighten your toga and fix your hair, we have guests,' mother reprimanded.

'Of course.'

'Lucius?'

My father and brother turned at the sound of their name being called. Both wandered over to our location, practiced smiles plastered across their faces. 'Elena, I am surprised by your early entry. I was just about to send Lucius up to retrieve you,' my father said, wrapping an arm around my shoulders. 'I am pleased.'

'Marcus said you wanted to see me.'

'Marcus?' my father echoed with confusion. 'I asked no such thing.'

I shot Marcus a sly look as he skittered past to join a group of soldiers drinking merrily by the garden's edge. Their raucous laughter and eagerness to accept Marcus into their fold eased the apprehension that had ridden his shoulders since our disagreement. Apparently, I hadn't been the only one curious about Septimius's assets.

'Should Elena and I usher everyone into the great hall now, father?' Lucius asked, eyeballing me curiously. He had a rather annoying way of being able to read me. And, while my cheeks still blushed with shame, I found it particularly unnerving.

'Of course,' father said, propelling me forward. He was far too eager for this union and it worried me. But then again, what should I have expected after my years of obstinacy? He was undoubtedly pleased to be passing me over to someone else.

'What is going on?' Lucius asked as he pulled me away from the prying ears and eyes of our parents. 'I thought you might have run away while you still had the chance.'

Tempting though the thought may have still been I said, 'What would be the point? Father would just hunt me down and drag me back here.'

'I expected you to at least put up another fight. Have you had a change of heart?'

I cleared my throat, attempting a final time to restore normality to my still wavering voice. 'No change of heart,' I said a little too quickly. 'I want to be a soldier, nothing changes that.'

'But?'

'But nothing. I merely owe it to mother and father to at least meet this Septimius. If I hate him, then father said he will release me.'

'And what do you suppose that entails?'

'I do not know,' I said, frustrated and more than a little uneasy, 'but what other choice do I have?'

'You could marry Marcus.'

My sudden eruption of laughter forced all eyes upon me and brought the entire room to silence. 'My apologies,' I said, bowing my head to the startled guests. 'If you will follow Lucius and I into the great hall we can begin.'

I avoided the curious gaze of all who passed as they swept into the hall to partake in the festivities of what I knew to be a very long night ahead. I was about to be paraded like prized cattle and sold off to the highest bidder. It really didn't matter that the highest bidder looked utterly delectable without clothes on. He was still trying to milk me of my dreams and shackle me to the barn!

At least I wouldn't have to marry Marcus.

I'd barely scooped up a goblet of wine, emptied the contents and started on another when an older senate member by the name of Antonius reached for me. His frail fingers grazed my naked shoulder to draw my attention from the numbing wonder of the alcoholic beverages I now intentionally guzzled.

'Elena, my dear,' he said, not bothering to wait for my response, 'You have grown much since I saw you last. It is good to see you again and under such wonderful circumstances.'

If you say so ...

I hiccupped and dutifully bowed my head in greeting. 'Thank you, senator. Thank you for taking the time to attend our home this evening.'

Lucius wrapped an arm around my waist and pressed his lips close to my ear. 'Try not to grit your teeth when you say that,' he whispered. 'You need to at least pretend this marriage makes you happy.'

'When it does not hurt to say it out loud, then it shall not be a problem.'

Antonius carried on regardless of our whispered conversation. 'We were so happy to hear your father announce your engagement and to no less than Septimius Marcellus, a most suitable catch, I would think.'

'I would not know,' I answered truthfully, forcing a smile. Truthfully, I had never paid attention to any young suitors in the past, especially Septimius.

Antonius frowned, but carried on regardless. 'We all thought given your extended reluctance to marriage that you would remain husbandless.'

'That was the plan.'

'Thus, I have heard rumours of your attempts to infiltrate the army.' He started to chuckle, apparently highly amused by my ambitions. 'Very comical, yet highly unlikely.'

'Yes, I'm sure to some it is,' I muttered, fighting the urge to headbutt the supercilious grin from the old has-been's face. Instead, I rolled my shoulder to loosen his unwanted tether to my skin.

'Does the idea of this marriage not excite you?' an eavesdropping wife interjected as she waddled past, scooping up a handful of cheese in her wake. 'You are to be the bride to one of Rome's most coveted soldiers.'

'Am I not lucky, then?' I muttered sardonically, grabbing yet another goblet of wine from a passing tray and throwing back the contents to hasten the numbing process.

'Dear heavens,' she said, clutching her ample bosom in shock. 'You scorn the very sanctity of this union!'

I shrugged, certain no answer without mocking agenda was going to pass my lips.

'Elena,' Lucius chided, 'for father's sake, at least edit your answers.'

Outraged, I elbowed Lucius in the ribs as he apologised on my behalf to the meddling, corpulent wife. It was probably for the best that I kept my tongue in check, instead indicating to the servants that I needed yet another refill. My throat already felt hot and my stomach warm. There was a pleasant buzz on the tip of my tongue that I hoped would continue to spread to conscious thought.

'Elena, there you are!' another wife cried.

Well-wishers seemed to keep popping out of nowhere, biding their time and then pouncing on a break in the conversation. Some merely patted me affectionately as they passed while others toasted me in encouragement. I kept drinking, the action hindering composure.

A blonde with bouncing curls and ivory skin rapidly approached my swaying form. She was familiar, but I couldn't remember why and it was rude to ask. Therefore, it was almost certain that in this inebriated state, I would.

Lucius suddenly grew uncomfortable, itchy in his regimented posture. My interest was ignited as he cleared his throat, shifted from foot-to-foot and then allowed his openly subversive gaze to linger upon every portion of her exposed flesh. When I eyed him speculatively, he quickly looked away, embarrassed.

'Elena!' the blonde pressed, pushing her way through Antonius and the busty wife who still looked as though I'd admitted the world was round. 'Do you remember me?'

Should I?

'Her name is Mariana,' Lucius whispered. 'Be nice.'

'Mariana,' I echoed, bowing my head in false recognition. 'It is nice to see you again.' I leaned closer to Lucius and said as quietly as possible, 'And just how is it that you know her?'

'Long story.'

'I can make time.'

'You have your secrets and I have mine.'

'Congratulations,' Marianna murmured, her smile fading as her gaze finally met with my brother. 'You must be so happy.'

'Must I?'

Marianna's crumpled brow spoke volumes.

'Elena has a rather tragic sense of humour,' Lucius enlightened her, all the while glaring at me.

'How do you know my brother?'

'Oh, um ... well ...'

'Senator!' Lucius practically shouted, 'I'm very curious as to how the last senate meeting ended. My father said there was a dividing vote regarding the—'

Marianna didn't let the obvious interruption slow her down too much. 'Well, truthfully, Lucius and I re-connected at the bath house a few months previous. He was kind enough to escort me home in my husband's absence. You understand how dangerous it can be in the city for a woman alone?' Her words dripped with innocence, but the all too familiar glances between her and a determinedly distracted Lucius were open to much interpretation.

'Re-connected?'

'We met a few years previous. My husband Decimus was invited to the villa one evening for a meal. You and Lucius were immersed in studies—perhaps the reasoning behind your cloudy memory of our first encounter. So, to accept kindness from your brother most recently, rounds off our familiarity.'

'Of course,' I countered, scrutinizing her from head to toe. 'I suspect your husband would like to thank Lucius in person for protecting you from would-be attackers. Where is he this night?'

'Decimus?'

'Naturally.'

'He is still with the soldiers left at camp.' Marianna's features crowded together with a hint of justifiable fear. 'I came alone.'

'Then perhaps Lucius can escort you this evening too, protecting your virtue once again.' I saluted the idea with a long pull on my wine. When I realised there were only a few mouthfuls left, I shrugged and swallowed them down hastily.

Lucius disbanded the menial conversation with the senator all together. He started to laugh nervously, clutching me tightly by the arm as he pulled me away from the group. 'Forgive us, we have so many people to meet and greet tonight that we must take our leave.'

'But, Lucius,' I said, all innocence. 'This conversation was just growing interesting.'

'And dangerous,' he mouthed against my ear.

'You have some serious explaining to do.'

'Not tonight.'

I was pouting and knew it, but seemed unable to control lips that suddenly felt numb and overinflated. 'You are no fun.'

'And you are drunk.'

'I sure hope so.'

'Elena?'

What now? I thought, spinning slowly on the spot with Lucius's assistance. This was the problem with house festivities.

You couldn't get away from the guests until they left the premises—even the ones you sort of liked.

'I came to congratulate you.'

I studied the blurry outline of Volusius's form, swaying only fractionally as I accepted his hand and the lips he placed gently against the flesh of my knuckles. 'Are you certain that may be your motive?' I pressed, breaking into a fit of giggles as I thought back to our earlier encounter in the woods. 'Weren't you trying only an hour ago to convince me *not* to marry your brother?'

'Elena!' Lucius hissed as he clamped a warning hand around my slender wrist. 'You are drawing unnecessary attention to yourself.'

'Is that not the whole point of this ridiculous gathering?'

'What is wrong with her?' Volusius asked, features rearranging to reflect his concern.

'She has had too much wine,' a new voice countered.

Oh goody. More people.

I rolled my head upon my shoulders until I smiled up at the emerald green eyes of Tiberius, my father-in-law to be. It felt as if he towered above me. 'You are wrong.'

'Am I now?' he said patiently, gripping the arm Lucius wasn't already trying to keep me propped up with. 'And just how do you think I am wrong?'

'I am still awake.'

'Yes ...'

'Therefore, not nearly as inebriated as I had hoped.'

'Would it really be so bad to be tied to my son?'

I took a minute to really focus on Volusius standing in front of me and the question his father posed. 'No,' I finally answered, satisfied by the justification forming in my mind. 'Volusius is handsome and given his presence at the camp the other day most capable of wielding a sword.' I tapped my chin thoughtfully. 'I suppose it would depend on the binding. Are we talking shackles or rope? Never mind, let us make it rope so I can still escape.'

'Elena ...' my brother groaned, slapping a hand to his face in shame. He excused us from several nosey onlookers, guiding us all to a quiet corner of the room.

'Is there something Lucius or I should know given your request for Elena's hand?' Tiberius focused the question entirely to his son. He looked rather annoyed. 'Have you sullied her?'

'Of course not,' Volusius answered, panic present in the waiver of his voice. 'I approached Elena at the camp and made remarks on her beauty and suggested intent to future rendezvous before I realised who she was and the intent of her fate.'

I blew a raspberry to clearly establish my objection of that claim.

Tiberius was silent for several minutes, his posture tense as he digested Volusius's explanation. He looked as though he had more to add though I suspected he would tuck it away for later investigation when there weren't swarms of gossiping wives or senate members trawling for information on the general's daughter.

'Elena,' he finally spoke, voice calm, 'I was referring to my other son, Septimius—your intended.'

'Oh ... *him.*'

'Yes.' He chanced a quick look between Volusius and I. 'Is there anything you need to tell me?'

'I have run out of wine.'

'Elena ...' my brother pleaded, 'Please come back to yourself ...'

'But my goblet is empty,' I whined.

'You must sober,' Tiberius agreed as he helped Lucius escort me to an armchair. They helped me to sit, Lucius kneeling on one side of me and Tiberius towering over me on the other. I wasn't sure I liked him looking down on me, but what other choices did I have, the room was spinning!

'I understand that this is hard for you, but Septimius is a fine man with many qualities a wife would be thrilled to attain. It is time you grew up and threw away your fanciful ideas. Your father and I expect more from a woman of your age and standing.'

'He is hard,' I agreed, already picturing all of that lean muscle flexing simultaneously in the bath water. 'And full of fine qualities, I am certain.'

'What is she talking about?'

'I will fetch her some water,' Volusius added helpfully, taking the time to give me a righteous frown as he backed away from the armchair.

'But I didn't see anything,' I hastily added, simultaneously realising no one had actually mentioned *bath* water. I was my own worst enemy.

'What?'

'What?' I echoed to no one in particular.

'Is she delirious?' Tiberius asked my brother.

Lucius shook his head, colour painting his cheeks as he continued to look between me and Marianna cautiously. He clearly had other things on his mind besides my declining behaviour.

I hiccupped and leaned towards my future father-in-law, drawing a blurry gaze level with his. I was losing control fast. 'What does Septimius gain from this marriage besides my father's good graces?'

He was frustratingly calm and quiet again before he smiled patiently. 'Why do you not ask him for yourself?'

I slapped my hands against my knees, resolute. 'Fine. Then where is he?'

Tiberius touched gentle fingers to my chin and turned my head to the right. He stopped, waited until the crowd of people making their way to the food table cleared a path. I followed feet at first, eyes blurring in and out of vision as I forced myself to look up. Brightly coloured hems of cloaks and togas crossed my path shadowed by glittering jewellery, muscled arms—and finally—a looming figure across the terracotta.

'Here is your water,' Volusius said, reappearing in front of me.

I pushed him slowly to the side, ignorant of his disgruntled protests or attempts to refocus my inattention. I was now mesmerised by the flowing cloak of his brother; vibrant in colour and richness of fabric, it hung like a second skin. The well-defined and sun-kissed arms that clasped his hips expectantly, now dropped to his sides as our combined energies collided. I covered the full length of him, marvelling at the soft silkiness of his dark hair as it brushed his shoulders and the way his lips seemed to smile even on an expressionless face. And finally, I settled on his eyes; a turbulent mix of grey and emerald green, emotive in so many ways I couldn't explain.

My lips parted, but breath remained absent.

I tried to speak, but words were incoherent.

I tried to move, but my legs continued to fail me.

Expectation and reality are rarely the same thing, tonight proving no different. Though sometimes reality far outweighs our expectations and has an uncanny ability to set our souls on fire, surprising us in the most unexpected of circumstances.

I'd never been more surprised in my life.

Reality suddenly exceeded all expectations, now, then and undoubtedly, tomorrow.

CHAPTER TWENTY-SEVEN: RUSH

My head was spinning or perhaps the world was off-kilter. Everything around me was filled with moving colour and a turbulent rush of emotions and memories that my addled state seemed potentially incapable of handling. I was bombarded with image after image; faces, names, places I'd never heard of and people I'd never met. Their identities swirled inside of me, filling every crevice of darkness and lighting up the world anew, pouring a familiar knowledge of the past within.

Transient faces moved before me, superimposing themselves over various guests in the room and even my own family—apparitions of memories seemingly past. I gripped my brother's hand for support, but his own features were distorted. They twisted unnaturally and played havoc with my sanity and all that I knew to be real. Was I screaming? The fear of the unknown echoed through my head, tormenting me with the promise of understanding and yet showing me …

Lucas …

Realisation of Lucius's true origins snapped the apparition of the past and the physical being of the present back together, unifying them. Unfocused eyes now narrowed and saw my brother clearly for the first time ever. He was exactly the same and yet somehow different—a complete and utter paradox.

Volusius crowded in, kneeling beside his father, the two of them patting my inflamed cheeks and talking to me in a muted and foreign language. I tried to understand, unsure why their tongues would speak such nonsense. Their faces were now as equally tampered with as Lucius's had been.

I studied Volusius's expressive face; the flush in his cheeks, the intense concern he held within his emerald eyes and the shadowy figure of the past tampering with his features. As he moved, it moved, sometimes smiling at me with lips not entirely foreign to my touch.

I brushed my fingers against their softness, knowing that I had tasted those lips and surrendered any form of conscious thought to their exploration. I had run my fingers through the short, dark thicket of hair and pressed myself against the rock-hard planes of his chest to feel his comforting embrace. He had been there for me during times of doubt, but he had also damaged me in ways I couldn't quite describe.

He had changed me …

He had loved me …

William …

The apparition snapped into place and I was left looking at Volusius or William; a much younger and inexperienced version. To his left Tiberius also gained clarity as his true self engaged. He was slightly older here, touched by mortality and the pressing concerns of Rome's interests and the happiness of his sons. I remembered his tears and unending loyalty to those he served and loved.

I was remembering more than I had ever lived.

I was remembering more than I cared to understand.

Now—studying my past and my present combined—I was confused by the raw emotions that swam through me and the unending persistence of remembrance. I closed my eyes to the unnatural sensations. Focusing, I could hear the raucous laughter of the guests and their endless chatter. Despite looking for solidarity, the rolling imagery kept pouring in a tidal wave of constructive thought. I could now see everything with a clarity that made my stomach leap into my mouth and my heart out of my chest.

Werewolves, angels, demons—and of course—vampires now took precedent in my thoughts. Blood was a permanent fixture and pain and suffering seemed a foregone conclusion. Violence had reigned supreme and yet through everything … there'd always been *him*. William may have led me astray on more than one occasion and he may have lied, may have tried to change what fate intended, but somehow—even now in the distant past—I had found what every stirring recollection had been searching for. I had found the one person no one could keep me from.

Sebastian …

My eyes snapped open as truth and destiny had finally made a mark upon my soul. I could no longer say that fate was bullshit and unending love a myth. I was disproving my earlier reproach on the subject, falling victim to the catastrophic, wonderful embodiment of love's embrace—true providence with just a hint of faith.

I was back and my eyes were now open as wide as they would go. I was renewed—restored. I was impossibly blessed with every memory I should have forgotten or never known and filled with the sweetest expectations of a peaceful future, knowing what I had overcome in the past.

'Elena? Do you hear me?'

The bilious fog of oblivion cleared as reality rushed back to greet me like an old friend. An hour ago, I'd wallowed in self-pity; a character flaw I was going to amend immediately now that I was one with my soul again. I had been over-indulged and underexposed in this life. I was pleased that I could finally understand it, but things were going to change. Elena Manory was back and the incarnate I embodied was about to cop a harsh beating from the woman I knew I had truly become.

'Elena?' Lucas slapped my face to gather my attentions.

'Ow! What the hell, Lucas!'

'Elena?' he said, looking at me with a baffled expression on his face.

'Hey, don't look at me like that, dumbass. You should know by now that slapping me in the face is not going to gain you any favour.' I playfully slapped him back and then laughed as the total surrender to shock mixed heavily with his already confused features. 'On the upside, I am so happy to see you.' In contrast, I now threw my arms around his neck and squeezed him tight, winking at William and Tiberius who also regarded me with total and utter bewilderment.

'I know you're confused right now and that's okay. I promise you'll get used to me if you don't soon remember who you really are.'

'Elena … I'

'Ooh, another thing,' I said, cutting Lucas off. 'Don't *ever* quit on me again, okay? I am sooo not a fan of you dying in front of me, hence the rewind to *Gladiators are us* timeline. Otherwise, I am going to have to ban you from sharp instruments permanently.'

I slapped a hand against my thigh. 'Well, would you listen to me? I'm totally grilling you in Latin right now, how cool is that? Hey, do I know French too?'

'What?' Lucas managed to emit.

'Never mind. I'm digressing because I can't believe it worked. That stupid angel was right about the Time Contract. Who would have thought?'

'Is she well?' William whispered to his father. 'She speaks strangely.'

I focused my attention back on William, cupping his face between my hands before he could pull away. Unfortunately, I wasn't as strong as I used to be so he ended up yanking his head free. I didn't mind his obvious reluctance or my apparent weakness. At least we were all clearly human—a massive plus given our past tendencies towards blood and a heavy-handed approach. 'William, I'm just dandy. You don't have to worry about me anymore, okay? I know you've always thought you were protecting me, but everything is going to be fine now even if you have no idea what I'm talking about.'

His blank look spurred me on.

'But I promise you this—despite our tumultuous past— I'm always going to have a special spot for you right here.' I touched my heart for emphasis. 'But now that our long and seemingly angst-ridden story is finally over, there's a special girl in this world here somewhere. Her name is *Karina* or most likely something of a similar nature. When you find her, you will know what I'm talking about, okay?'

'Who is William?'

I laughed, leant forward and kissed him on the cheek before inclination had him running in the opposite direction. '*You* … in about 650 years' time.'

'And you,' I said, focusing back on Lucas, 'I would never encourage this normally, but I think you should know that your little secret with blonde hair and sapphire eyes is going to make you very happy. I may want to slam that bitch in the face sometimes, but I know that she loves you with every fibre of her being and I owe her for that.'

'Elena, I believe the wine may have—'

'It's not the wine. Things have changed, Lucas. I know you'll see it eventually, when you're ready to remember—if you can remember.'

'Who are you?' he said, shaking his head in disbelief, his mouth gaping like a gold fish. 'You are not the E in which I am related.'

I smiled knowingly at the slip of inference. 'Oh, I'm still me, just um … the kick ass version that's totally going to rock this millennia.'

That earned me a small, albeit frustratingly perplexed smile.

I glanced down, nose wrinkling and disdain present as I picked at the threads of the toga I wore. 'Ugh, what am I wearing? A bed sheet? Butterfly effect or not, I'm totally going to invent jeans and a bra. I mean really, how did women get through the dark ages? I look like *Casper!*'

'Let me fetch her father,' Tiberius murmured. 'I fear she may be ill.'

I stilled him with a firm hand upon his shoulder. 'No, I'm fine … honestly. In fact, I'm better than fine. My brother is alive, my mum and dad are happy and in love and I have all of you here with me. If this turns out to all just be a dream, then I don't want to wake up.'

'It's not a dream, *Elena.*'

I froze, trapped within a moment of ecstasy so pure all I could do was shudder with delight as the sound of his deep melodic voice reverberated through every fibre of my being, filling my heart with a thousand choruses of pure unadulterated joy. I was afraid to answer, terrified to look upon him only to learn that my choices had altered his presence here too.

But I had come too far, suffered greatly and lost everything. In this pivotal moment in time and history, I would never again act the coward and shy away from my truest feelings. I would look upon him now with the eagerness of a child on Christmas morning, knowing that even if it couldn't last, I would do everything within my power and knowledge to save us.

Slowly, my eyes crept heavenward, tracing the length of his body from foot to head, stopping only when our eyes finally met. A ghost of a smile waited for me, reluctant and filled with caution should I not return the favour. His eyes were hesitant, his heart undoubtedly pounding as he reached for me; an invitation to accept the bitingly real present.

'Septimius,' Tiberius declared, shaking my hand free of his shoulder and stumbling back to his feet, 'I fear your intended may not be up to introductions this evening.'

'No, I'm good,' I hastily added, eagerly sliding my hand into Sebastian's warm one. I fought the urge to close my eyes and marvel at the touch of his flesh against mine. A million emotions tore through me. Most centred on the desperate loneliness I'd felt since leaving him in Purgatory and the cutting pain of knowing his death may have been permanent and resurrection a distant hope. I'd thought we'd never see each other again. I'd thought that my heart would never have a chance to heal.

I had been wrong.

Sebastian pulled me slowly to my feet, his eyes drinking in the sight like a man who had not seen water in a very long time and thirsted for just one drop. Holding me at arm's length, I could feel him trembling, the thought of any space between us increasing the arid taste of desperation. He closed the distance between us quickly, eyes always roaming, searching for validation in this seemingly impossible truth that we were once again reunited. Never again would either of us thirst.

I was finally home.

'What have you done?' he murmured against my knuckles as he laid a gentle kiss upon my flesh.

'Just the usual—kick ass, save the world, turn back time.'

'And you remember?'

'Everything … now.'

'Well, what a happy pairing this appears to be!' my father bellowed as he drew closer. He clapped a hand on Sebastian's shoulder and patted the side of my cheek affectionately as he observed our eager expressions—and of course—the bewildered ones of William, Lucas and his long-standing friend, Tiberius. 'Am I to be missing anything?'

'No, dad,' I chuckled, eyes never straying from Sebastian's. 'I guess it just took a while for me to come around to everyone's way of thinking. Thanks for never giving up on me.'

'Dad?' he mimicked. 'What is this *dad*?'

'May I be permitted some time alone with my intended, Lucius?' Sebastian politely asked.

'I thought they had never met before this night,' William muttered.

'Of course,' Lucius said after a few blinks of indecision. 'Do not go too far, we have guests.'

Sebastian bowed respectfully, wasting no time as he tugged on my hand insistently, leading us from the great hall with haste. Inquisitive gazes locked upon us like heat-seeking missiles, predominately from my shell-shocked friends and brother. Lucius appeared secretly pleased with his match-making skills, not at all concerned his daughter now took the stairs two at a time, desperate to slam the door on her old life and sink into the arms of this new one.

When we reached the passage of the second story, I took direction and yanked Sebastian towards my bedroom. I was breathless with excitement and laughing by the time the door slammed home behind us. He now cupped my face between gentle hands, eyes flashing the mysterious silver of his angelic origins.

'So, it's true,' he whispered, pulling me in close enough that I could taste his warm breath on my tongue. 'You do remember.'

'It was your eyes,' I breathed, wrapping my arms around his waist. 'You'd think it would have been your butt since I was spying on you while you were bathing earlier, but there you go. Some things are more memorable than others, I guess.'

He laughed, the sound bubbling in his throat and finally escaping his upturned lips. 'It shouldn't be possible.'

'I promised you in Purgatory that I would never forget you, Sebastian—that I would never forget *us* again. I meant what I said.'

'I am pleased to hear that.'

'Ooh, which reminds me, I have the rest of that promise to fulfil.'

'And that would be?'

'This ...'

I closed the measurable distance still between us and pressed my lips against his. Clichéd though it was, birds sang, chorus lines rejoiced and the whole world got a little bit brighter within the circumference of his touch. I kissed that arch angel like he'd never been kissed before, filling it with every ounce of love and desire I could muster until finally we were both staggering backwards searching for breath.

Sebastian braced the wall for support, the grin on his face unmistakable. I too mirrored the sentiment, edging my way closer to the bed and beckoning him to me.

'What are you doing?' he asked, eyebrow piqued in curiosity now.

'I'm not a fan of the toga.' I released the brooch on my left shoulder and let the first layer of the garment dropped to the floor.

'Elena, of all the times …'

'Sebastian, I'm not wasting another minute. We've been given a second chance and you've been gone for far too long.' I released a secondary section of my attire, amazed and honestly dismayed that when it to fell to the floor there were still linen cloths wrapped to hide my modesty. The art of seduction in ancient Rome was turning out to be a bitch!

'Elena …'

'Don't *Elena* me,' I mocked, slowly unravelling the last of my modesty. 'The Sebastian I know and love would be all over this by now.'

'But we have so much to say to one another,' he murmured, though I'd noticed he'd already begun unhooking his own cloak and toga much to my amusement. They fell to the floor in a coloured bundle of silken thread.

I barely noticed.

'We can talk later,' I whispered, my breath mostly expunged by the rippled muscles, lean abdomen and naked flesh standing in front of me.

'Your father is going to wonder what is keeping us.'

I blew a raspberry and then grabbed him by the wrist and pulled him closer. He tripped over the edge of his disrobed tunic and fell onto the bed laughing. 'Elena, I am quite sure this is a very bad idea right now. We've only just been reunited and I'm sure you have questions. For one, whether or not Lucas will regain his memories of your past—and of course—the Time Contract and the ramifications of your choices.'

'Well, I do have one question,' I said, boldly climbing onto the bed and straddling him with intent. His eyes fluttered closed and I watched his throat bob up and down as he swallowed a groan that still managed to betray his body's somewhat controlled response to my positioning.

'And what would that be?' he croaked, resting his palms against my hips in an effort to desist my rather slow and insistent gyration.

'Are you sure you want to marry me? I mean really, I am a complete pain in the ass and there is an excellent chance that I will try to dominate you every chance I get.'

'Baby Vamp, I don't doubt that for a minute.'

'Negotiations then?'

'How about hypotheticals?'

'Okay, you want to play that game? It's been a while, but I'm game if you are.'

'It has and I am,' he murmured, his lips now catching my collar bone and working their way down, stimulated only by my hitched breath and shameless whimpers of encouragement. 'Ladies first.'

I cleared my throat to gain some semblance of clarity. I wanted my intentions to be perfectly clear. I didn't want this opportunity screwed up by careless disregard for the past, forgotten memories of the sacrifices we had endured or expectation that the gift we had been given was everlasting. 'Well, let's just say that there's this girl and she's really freaking stubborn.'

'I thought we were playing hypotheticals?'

I slapped him playfully. 'Shut up, Sebastian and listen, okay?'

'Then please … continue.'

'Okay, so this stubborn girl has done a bit of recent time travel and despite appearances she has been changed.'

'In what way?'

'Are you ready for this?'

'I'm listening …'

'She doesn't want to fight anymore.'

There was silence and no movement for several seconds before Sebastian's muffled laughter shook my bed frame and sent positive little vibrations rolling through me.

'What's so funny?'

'Your father will be pleased.'

I sighed, contemplating recent behaviour in my hijacked form. 'I know. Let's just say I was young and stupid. I was driving him crazy yesterday at the thought of marrying you. FYI, Septimius is a stupid name. Anyway … then *bam*! All my memories flood back and I realise I just want some peace and quiet for a while.'

Sebastian was still laughing when he asked me, 'And how does this affect our marriage to come?'

'Said domineering attitude starts with you.'

'I don't understand.'

'No more playing soldier, okay? I don't have my kick-ass skills anymore and I can't save you from everyone.'

He sobered, pitching forward to rest on his arms and stare at me squarely with shining silver eyes. 'Elena, I am the arch angel, Michael.'

'I know who you are, Sebastian, but I'm just going to be selfish for a while and ask that we leave saving the world to someone else for a change. It took over two thousand years to find each other the first time. Now that we're back here rocking out the human thing for a while, let's just enjoy.'

'That was not a hypothetical request, was it?'

I shook my head, leaning down until our foreheads touched and our lips were aligned. 'No, it wasn't.'

'Then I have a hypothetical request of my own.'

I took a deep breath, trepidation creeping forth. 'What is it?'

He rolled us on the mattress until I was positioned underneath him, his eyes intense, but his crooked smile giving way to his more playful nature. 'I want to be on top.'

'Hypothetically I'm going to say yes, but if you don't get this show on the road soon, we are going to play swapsies.'

'No, Elena. I want to be on top on our wedding night.'

'Now … then … whatever.'

He kissed my lips gently and then pulled away. 'I think you're missing my point.'

I stared at him blankly for half a second before realisation dawned. 'Oh, no no no no no, virgin boy. Don't you dare play coy now that you've completely riled me up.'

'Elena, you said yourself that we waited two thousand years before, what's another month now?'

I didn't want to, but I could hear the whine in my voice as I said, 'But what about Purgatory?'

'It was a mingling of spirits,' he said as he slid away from me. He scooped down and collected my garments, handing them to me one-by-one. 'Our physical bodies did not exist in that plane—so truthfully—we have never committed ourselves so wholly.'

'So, I just took all this crap off for nothing?' I said, waving my medieval clothes in his face. 'I hope you realise how difficult it is to put them all back on again.'

His chest rumbled with laughter. 'I'll help you.'

'You're a bloody tease,' I muttered, standing up and turning around as ordered. He started to wind the linen slowly around my breasts and lower extremities, stopping occasionally to kiss me slowly and thoroughly. He really wasn't helping.

'I want to do this right,' he said as he slid the under tunic over my head.

'See, that's the problem with falling in love with a bloody angel—too many morals!'

'And you're going to have to *hypothetically* work on your language.'

'Yeah well, hypothetical this,' I teased, collapsing into a fit of laughter as I flashed him a view of my erect middle finger. 'I can't believe I had an opening to use that line on you twice in a lifetime!'

'That's what happens when you turn back time,' he said, sharing in my levity. He pulled his own clothes back on quickly while I clipped on the brooch and made some finishing touches to my rather tousled appearance.

'About that, do you think I made the right choice?'

'You made the only choice you could.'

'You don't think Araqiel is going to be pissed at me for not using the Time Contract and Quill of Destiny to take you all the way back before creation?'

'Of course not. It was beyond your understanding.'

'Are you mad?'

'No!' he said, immediately closing the distance between us again. 'From the minute I first saw you, I never wanted for anything else. Elena, I will choose you time and time again no matter how far back we go.'

'But will I choose you?'

He held his hands out and gestured to room around us. 'The track record is holding up so far and now you remember everything. Things will be different now, Elena. You won't ever have to go back again.'

'Promise?'

He kissed my forehead, nose and finally closed in on my lips, taking them with the full force of his passion until my palms splayed against his chest for release. 'I promise that no matter which obstacles may try to block our future path that we will overcome them together and that I will never—until the end of time—stop loving you.'

'Okay, Romeo, save it for the vows.'

He kissed me again, his curved lips mirroring my own smile. 'We should be getting back.'

I patted his chest and moved from his embrace. 'You're right. On the upside, we're about to make my parents and your father blissfully happy.'

'And what is the downside?'

I hesitated, squeezing his fingers tightly between mine as he walked us slowly from the bedroom and into the upstairs passage. 'Do I really have to call you Septimius?'

'You really don't like the name?'

'You sound like that weirdo from *Harry Potter* that wears all the black.'

'Elena, you're going to have to be careful about mentioning idioms from the future.'

'Worried I'll scare the natives?'

He tucked a lock of dark hair behind his ear and shot me a sly grin. 'They're already measuring you for a strait jacket.'

'If they knew what one was.'

We allowed ourselves a brief chuckle as we descended the staircase. 'So then, if you don't like Septimius, what would you like to call me?'

I cackled, shaking my head. 'You know, you really shouldn't leave yourself wide open like that.'

His expression turned wry. 'I'm going to have my hands full with you, aren't I?'

'Hey, I think you just wrote my vows for me.'

Once we'd descended the stairs, we slowed our pace to a crawl until we stood outside of the great hall, taking one last moment of serenity for ourselves.

'Are you ready?' He asked, curling his warm fingers tighter with mine, his eyes now a slithering mass of storm cloud grey and emerald green. He was perfect—everything I had ever wanted or ever imagined, everything I was ever going to need.

I nodded, summoning a new kind of courage—the courage to move forward. For once I didn't have to look over my shoulder. I could simply exist, laugh, learn and enjoy. There was nothing holding me back now. I was ready for this future.

'Okay … Bring it!'

EPILOGUE

Wind whipped through the trees, teasing the branches into movement, delighting much of the foliage into release. So far, the weather had held up grandly, despite the incessant breeze and ominous clouds lurking in the distance.

Araqiel looked up, eyes searching the heavens for a sign of things to come. 'You know, this was not how I planned things,' he murmured, picking a stray leaf from the tips of his wings and discarding it with haste.

'Araqiel,' Nakir answered patiently, a hand now resting on his shoulder. 'Did you really expect that she would choose to go back to a time before the fall?'

Araqiel shrugged free of his brother's grip. 'I expected her to make the right choice for everyone.'

'And what if she has? Elena and Michael are happy—just as they have always been in the past and the Vampires are no more as a consequence of her actions.'

Araqiel adjusted his footing on the branch of the tree in which he hid, spreading a clump of foliage in front of him to the side and looking down upon the flurry of action below. Garments of silk and brightly coloured linens swarmed the well-worn earth. Red, greens and gold adorned most of the guests, fingers and wrists marked with gems and wreaths of precious metals. Most of the men wore togas with brightly coloured cloaks. The women donned fine tunics or more elegant forms of the toga should finances permit.

'Their personal happiness is of little consequence to me, Nakir.'

'How can you say that after all that Michael has done for us in the past?'

'Michael is an archangel. It was what he was made to be. Spending his days placating humans is not the measure of his

393

worth. He should be in heaven, ruling with our father as he once did.'

'Ahh,' Nakir remarked, folding his arms in front of his chest, his wings stretching slightly to keep his balance on the tree limb, 'so it is not their happiness that disturbs you, but their continuation of it?'

'Not exactly. With all her rough edges I can understand why he chose Elena, but I cannot understand why she did not choose eternal bliss and why he would choose this place.'

'Michael knows what he wants and *she* doesn't understand. How was Elena supposed to know that by unravelling the fall that the separation of good and evil may never have partaken? She could only choose what she knows—what she thought she could control.'

'It was a decision made by youth. I had thought she was ready. I had thought she understood what it was that I asked of her …'

'Araqiel, you cannot be dismayed by her decision to choose love. This is what we fight for, remember?'

'We would not have had to fight any longer if we had digressed.'

Nakir smiled patiently. 'I gather you are not a fan of ancient Rome?'

'It matters not where I am,' he said, staring off into the distance. 'All hope is lost now. Elena was the last half-blood among us. Heaven only knows how long I must wait before I find another candidate eligible to use the Time Contract.'

'Does it really matter, Araqiel?' Nakir said, gesturing to the smiling and laughing crowd below. 'Look around you. This is bliss. The love and happiness we fight for is being celebrated as we speak. Take stock in this and applaud your efforts. If nothing else—dear brother—you have brought Michael and Elena together yet again and had a hand in vanquishing vampirism.'

Araqiel did indeed study the happy couples below. Smiles were pasted on every face and laughter was shared freely among them. Through the throng of pressing well-wishers, Araqiel could finally see Elena and Michael, the two of them braced in certainty, arms holding each other with the promise of forever.

The vows had been exchanged not long before, tying them once again in the ongoing saga of their unified souls. All was seemingly going well in this version of happily ever after, but the storm clouds in the distance made Araqiel feel uneasy. Elena's recovered memory had been unexpected, just like her choices. Araqiel knew better than to pin the hopes of the future on the present, especially given Lucifer's unchanging nature.

'I fear I cannot applaud that which might not have been truly altered,' Araqiel answered carefully. 'This wedding may be part of the ongoing miracle of blossoming love that so many of our angelic brethren seek to behold, but I cannot shake the feeling of uneasiness settling upon my wings.'

'You speak of the winds of change,' Nakir murmured, turning his face to the oncoming breeze. He closed his eyes, turning his head slightly to the side as if listening for instruction.

'Something is not right. You must be able to feel it too.'

'I feel something,' Nakir admitted. 'I am unable to distinguish whether it is good or bad.'

'It cannot be good, brother. The Time Contract has been used, but due to its execution Lucifer was denied Michael yet again.'

'Michael did suffer in Purgatory,' Nakir reasoned, opening his eyes slowly and focusing them back on Araqiel. 'I watched over him as Samael and Mammon relentlessly pursued him. Lucifer may not have had his hands directly on him, but his need for revenge would tirelessly push his minions to resolve his frustrations.'

'The restrictions of Purgatory meant that he could not unleash Lucifer or that he ultimately could not be maimed by the Demons.'

'That did not mean they could not make his life a misery.'

Araqiel turned from his brother's probing stare. 'Nevertheless, things have changed.'

'Yes, obviously. We are back in ancient Rome again thanks to the Time Contract.'

'No. You are missing the point entirely. The power of the Time Contract is absolute. Elena should not have gained her memories of the past. For all intents and purposes, she was born to this life—and as such—should not remember a time that has technically been wiped from existence.'

'We remember and Michael remembers.'

'Naturally, but we are other. It is necessary that we keep track of time in all its forms.'

'Brother, what are you saying?'

'I'm saying there must be a reason Elena can remember that which she should not.'

'You do not believe it is her love for Michael? They are soul mates, Araqiel. Never before has heaven bound someone so heavily to an earthbound charge.'

Araqiel shook his head. 'I cannot be certain enough to correct your insight, but I do believe there are other forces at work.'

Nakir turned his face to the wind again. 'Perhaps you are right.'

'I fear it.'

'What are you going to do?'

'What can I do? As I said, Elena was the last half-blood with the power to use the Time Contract. If nefarious intentions are afoot, she can no longer reverse the damages possibly inflicted. In this life she is merely human, despite her recollections.'

'She does not need to change time again,' Nakir said, a small smile pinching his lips. 'As you said yourself—she remembers.'

'And?'

'So now she has the power of foresight. No matter what the foreseeable future may bring, she knows what has occurred. Between Elena and Michael, I feel confident that they can lead anyone on a righteous path.'

'So, it is agreed that something is amiss. Should we warn the others?'

'No. The winds of change will bring news soon enough. For now, we must let fate rest in the hands of those we have learned to trust.'

'And what of you?'

'I must head back to Purgatory. I have left Munkar by himself for far too long. Heaven only knows what Samael and Mammon have tried to pull over him in my absence.' Nakir pointed a finger directly at Araqiel's chest. 'You must also lay low this time. Your plan didn't exactly unfold as you had hoped, but life has still found a balance.'

'For how long?' Araqiel protested. 'The Demons know that Michael, Sebastian and Septimius are one-in-the-same now!

They will come for him soon and once again disturb the balance you speak of.'

'Michael knows this better than anyone, but we must have faith that there is reason as to why they have not yet come for him. It has been a month since the transition. You cannot hide in trees and continue to watch Michael and Elena from a distance. You cannot aid in their protection again. You are interfering. These are our rules which you know only too well.'

'I know the rules …'

'Then you understand why you must let Michael and Elena be. If anything changes, we will know of it soon enough. Michael is more than capable—'

'I know what Michael is capable of. It is not him that I worry about.'

'Then what?'

Araqiel took a deep, unnecessary breath, turning his face to the wind filled with the moisture of a coming storm. Uncharacteristically shivering, dread dared to touch the tips of his rustling feathers. 'I fear the unknown.'

'There is nothing to be done about that.'

Araqiel was at a loss, his body usually void of emotion suddenly swamped by a terrifying abyss of trepidation. 'Isn't there?'

*   *   *

Julius studied the crimson life force that coated his fingers and palms. Like paint, it clung to his skin, staining and ever present, determined to etch new colourful layers on other areas of relatively clean, exposed flesh.

He rubbed his hands together, feeling the stickiness slide across his skin, repulsed by the squelching noises made as he squeezed them into fists. Blood oozed through the cracks of his knuckles, relentless in its pursuit, reminding him of whom it had belonged. His wife still lay upon their bed, eyes wide, expression vacant. Her mounded stomach had sunk to some degree, but the proof of her pregnancy lay sheltered within her rigid embrace.

Julius ached to look away, but his gaze was locked on all that had been lost within the last hour. He should have been at a wedding. He should have been clutching his wife's hand, smiling down at her as they shared in Elena and Septimius's happiness. Yet here he was, hunched over their marital bed, hands writhing in blood still trickling from his wife's lifeless form.

Julius had once protested their marriage—but over time—grew to love her deeply. His heart now ached for that loss; her unmoving form and empty eyes now void of any warmth or instruction on moving forward. It was not just her departure from this life that kept him immobile. It was the tiny bundle in her arms—quiet, still … dead.

Dead.

The word clung to his tongue and a bad taste that would not cease. Childbirth was risky and often aided with help, but there had been no time. The baby came with little warning and thus Julius had attempted to deliver the child himself.

How hard can it be? He'd thought to himself.

How hard indeed.

Head slumped; his forehead made contact with his wife's ankle. It was still warm, but experience told him not for long. Death was a state he'd become accustomed to as a Legionnaire. The vacant stares and rigid flesh of strangers and enemies held no meaning in comparison to this senseless death. Blood that had stained his hands then had been earned through battle—justified by the war cries of his General. Now there was no one around. No enemies, no war, no justification for an innocent's death. Childbirth had robbed his wife of life—and with it—stolen his first-born son to deepen the already gaping hole in his heart.

What was left to celebrate? What life was there worth to live with a dead wife and child lying under his touch? How could he go on knowing he had failed to be the husband she needed and the father his son would never know?

Julius fingered the blade in the sheath by his side. Death had once been a concept reserved only for his enemies. Now he considered its simplistic ending held merit. He'd always imagined dying in battle, his flesh rushed upon by the blade of a worthy opponent, never being the bearer of his own sin.

Counter reasons emptied through his mind, each trying to lay a path of logic. He searched for reason where there was none and hope among the darkened confines of his heart. He was ready to retire. He didn't want to mourn. He didn't want to think about his loss and the prospect of moving forward. He didn't want to think about anything anymore.

He wanted it all to end.

Pungent wisps of sulphur tickled the edges of his nostrils. At first, he ignored the putrid smell until breathing became tainted and its origins more than a passing concern. Forcing his weary head to lift, he slowly opened his eyes to investigate the source. He shut them almost immediately, consumed by unexpected fear and justified by the unholy images abound.

He massaged his closed lids, feeling the warm stickiness of his own blood oozing from the corners of his eyes. Every inch of him ached, suddenly overwhelmed by a scorching heat that preyed upon sanity.

Do not look. He commanded of himself. *You are sick with grief!*

Ignoring his own advice, he tentatively peeked beneath sodden lashes. At first, there was nothing but red; perhaps his own blood blurred vision and had blinded the truth. As focus was applied and imagery more certain, it was impossible to ignore the bile that rose within the column of his throat.

His whole body now convulsed in revulsion. Naked flesh filled his vision with unspeakable clarity. Bodies both whole and mutilated were strung like washing in the breeze upon every wall of the cavernous space he had somehow appeared. As far as the eye could see, human beings were collated and stitched together. They wreathed as if still alive, reaching with disfigured limbs and screaming silently, eyes wide, tongues removed, lips sewn shut.

Julius skidded backwards, shrieking when a member of the disembowelled grabbed a thatch of the long dark curls he'd carefully quaffed over the years and pulled. As the tuft ripped free of his scalp, Julius cupped the gaping wound and sought to find space beyond the reach of this nightmare.

Flames erupted, drawing a wide circle around his position. Still cradling his head-wound, he watched the fire rise to impossible heights, pressing heat against his sullied flesh and burning the tapestry of victims present. Moans exploded from every piece of writhing flesh nearby. The tortured mass moved with purpose, parts reaching for mercy while soulless eyes begged for release.

As the flames ebbed, so did the cacophony of noise. The recently charcoaled figures were now a gruesome picture of blood-slicked skin that was once again stretched, torn and sewn back together in preparation for another flaying.

'Well, hello there,' a calm voice said from behind.

Julius turned quickly, hoping to find sanity within these mysterious walls of a dream he'd somehow fallen victim. Black, highly-polished leather strangely enveloped the place where a man's toes would be. These devices covered all areas of the foot and were seemingly decorated by slender cords pulled tightly across the top and tied together. Julius supposed these cords held these strange sandals in place as he walked.

Trailing upwards, the legs of the man before him were loosely wrapped with foreign, lightweight grey material cinched at the waist and further adorned with a leather fixing and silver brooch. Above that, an impossibly well-stitched version of a long-sleeved tunic; red and fastened by minute, rounded toggles down the centre.

Strange garments …

'Are you mute?'

Julius swallowed the lump wedged within his throat, eyes growing unfeasibly large as what appeared to be a set of large white wings spread like the rays of the sun from behind the man's back. If that wasn't peculiar enough, his hair was as white as the snow and his eyes as red as the blood that covered the walls of this insidious place.

'What a waste,' the man continued, crossing his arms over his chest. Spider-like veins crept along the length of his flexing muscles. 'I thought I was onto another winner with you, but I suppose I'll just have to string you up like all the others.'

'W-what is this?' Julius stammered, somewhat annoyed by his show of fear and yet unable to control it.

'You're in Hell. Where did you think you were? Not a dream, surely?'

'H-how …?'

The man rolled his eyes and then pointed straight at Julius's chest. 'Did you think that playing with knives wouldn't have repercussions?'

Julius could now see the blade protruding from his chest, the wound haemorrhaging blood, but pain absent. He remembered driving its wicked edge deep within his flesh, waiting for the agony of his wife and child's death to pass. 'I'm dead?'

'Bravo,' the man muttered, clapping his hands in wry amusement.

Shock starting to weave its spell upon him, Julius tried to focus on the winged creature before him. 'Who are you?'

The man looked horrified as he now placed his hands on his hips. 'You know, this is always so embarrassing when people forget who I am. I only led the rebellion against Heaven and became the ruler of Hell!' His eyes flashed crimson—a warning.

'Lucifer?'

'Bingo.'

'I do not understand ...' Julius's vision blurred momentarily as he once again allowed himself to spectate upon the deluge of horror surrounding him. Surely this was an outrageous dream—a vision he'd conjured in his moments of grief? 'W-why ...'

'You all ask the same stupid, mundane questions,' Lucifer commented. 'Isn't it obvious why you're here? You're either a massive prick or a suicide. What do you think?'

Julius's breath hitched as he found his voice and steeled his nerves. 'How do I leave this place?'

Lucifer's lips twitched, a smile slowly forming across his supple mouth. 'That's more like it. I was beginning to think torturing you would be the only form of entertainment I'd see today. What is it that you want?'

'I want my wife and child back.'

'Let's pick something realistic, shall we? They are probably frolicking on the fluffy edges of the clouds right about now.'

'Then I want to die.'

'*Beep*. Wrong answer. You're already dead.'

'Then what else is there?' Julius whispered, his whole body sagging from the insufferable heat that constantly licked his sweaty, blood-slicked flesh. His knees buckled, but he refused to fall under the weight of a heavy heart battered again and again with unending waves of inconsolable grief.

'You *could* work for me.'

Julius did not answer, merely stared back with empty eyes extinguished of hope and any lust for life.

Lucifer clicked his tongue and immediately gestured to the cavern walls once again alight with torturous flames charring mangled flesh. 'You could join the canvas if you prefer? I see a piece up there that's missing a few parts.'

Julius's eyes followed the madness. This time he was unsuccessful in his attempts to avoid physical revulsion, spilling bile and excess stomach contents past his lips and all over his legs. He wiped his mouth with the back of his hand as the flames died once more and the bodies became intertwined corpses.

'Hmm, I can see you're not very excited by the prospect.' Lucifer sighed dramatically. 'Such a shame ...'

'What would you have me do?' Julius answered carefully.

'Oh, just the usual. Drink the blood of the innocent, rape and pillage—nothing too excessive.'

'I cannot do this ...'

'Aww come on, it'll be fun. I'll give you super-strength, speed and immortality. You'll have forever to find another wife— and if you don't—you can always *make* a few like-minded individuals along the way.' Lucifer began to pace, his demonic gaze always set upon his prize. 'Of course, I'm going to tweak things a little this time. No blood transmission will be necessary. I'll make it a simple bite to turn vampiric and a scratch to make a ghoul. I haven't done that before!' He clapped his hands together in excitement. 'It's been a while since we had an epidemic.' He was mostly talking to himself now.

'I do not understand—'

'You will. Do we have a deal?'

'No, I cannot possibly—'

Lucifer snapped his fingers and Julius's body was ripped apart by unseen forces. Drawn and quartered, he amazingly stayed conscious to witness every, single second of torment. Pain perpetrated every fibre, blinding and tearing jagged breath as blood sprayed in every direction. 'Shall I continue?'

'Wait,' Julius gasped. 'Please.'

'Do you want to know what comes next or are you willing to sign my contract?'

'Please ...'

'No need to beg,' Lucifer mocked. 'I'm sure it hurts, but I have a solution. All I ask is that you feed your urges and return back to earth unhindered by your conscience.' He dove into his pocket and pulled out a piece of parchment. 'But first you must sign this.'

Julius continued to pant, his breath shallow, the pain unbearable.

'Here, allow me.' Lucifer plucked one of Julius's dismembered fingers from the air. He plunged the tip into an eviscerated arm socket, inking the digit with blood before pressing it against the bottom of the parchment. 'See now, that wasn't so hard, was it?' He discarded the finger and then proceeded to step on it. 'Now for the fine print.'

Julius cared little for response or details. He was enraptured by the boughs of his own pain, praying only for an end to this madness.

'I now own your soul. Sorry about that, but compensation must be made since I couldn't collect Lucius's soul after he made this same stupid mistake.' The devil's contemplative gaze laid to rest upon what was left of Julius. He stepped around the various puddles of blood, scratching his chin as if deep in thought. 'You won't be able die—at least not unless I permit it—and you will need to feed regularly. Hmm, let's make it daily this time, enough to reign havoc upon those around you. The choice is yours whether you turn them or kill them.'

A guttural moan from Julius spurred him on. 'And one other thing, the man you call Septimius ... I want him dead. If you kill the girl too, I'll give you a pat on the head. I want the two of them back in Purgatory and as close to my control as possible. Any questions?'

Lucifer had stopped tip-toeing around the blood and was now tapping his foot, impatient. His agitation grew like a dark cloud before a storm, but then he seemed to realise he'd forgotten the missing piece of a puzzle. He paused, chuckled maniacally before he snapped his fingers again. Like the rewind button had been pressed, Julius was suddenly rearranged to good health.

'Okay, now that's sorted ... bugger off!'

Good health was a sketchy explanation. Julius may have been glued back together, but he was not the same man he'd been in life. Ebony talons now sprouted from the tips of his nails, weaponised with sharp intent. His once bronzed flesh now lay waste to alabaster skin, translucent and streaked with the same spidery veins that marked the winged angel of the underworld. His gums throbbed as his canines ruptured and doubled in size, his vision sharpening beyond perfection. He was a monster. 'I will not do it. I will not kill innocent people.'

Lucifer shrugged, his wings fanning around them both in a beautifully horrifying warning. 'Don't be so naive. You're going to have to eat sometime.'

'I will not feast on the innocent or stain the earth red with the blood of this hell!'

'Famous last words,' Lucifer hissed. He clicked his fingers a final time and Julius vanished, his carnivorous body tossed back to reality with the force of evil fuelling his ascent.

'He's not like the last one,' Samael said, ambling slowly from the dark to Lucifer's side. 'Lucius sought righteous justice and willingly accepted his fate.'

Lucifer nodded in agreement. 'Ahh, but this one is an asshole and a coward-to-boot. He hides behind his grief and justifies his decisions by calling it revenge. Just you wait, Samael. Things are going to be different this time.'

'What about Michael and the girl?'

A storm cloud from earth rumbled ominously from above and they both looked up. Rain pursued its thunderous wake, breaking upon the arid ground and trickling through to the bodies that wreathed around Hell's Gates. The past had been altered by man using the Time Contract and Quill of Destiny, but the truest of elements now ushered a new beginning.

'Let's just say that I have a feeling we'll be seeing the two of them soon enough.'

'You have a plan, Lucifer?'

Lucifer winked, his mischievous red eyes filled with mirth and a promise not yet fully realised. 'Don't I always?'

www.ingramcontent.com/pod-product-compliance
Lightning Source LLC
Chambersburg PA
CBHW071146020726

47502CB00002B/292